LIVING INSIDE
RAINDROPS

LUKE BUTLER

The Book Guild Ltd

First published in Great Britain in 2020 by
The Book Guild Ltd
9 Priory Business Park
Wistow Road, Kibworth
Leicestershire, LE8 0RX
Freephone: 0800 999 2982
www.bookguild.co.uk
Email: info@bookguild.co.uk
Twitter: @bookguild

Typeset in 10.5pt Adobe Caslon Pro

Printed and bound by CPI Group (UK) Ltd, Croydon, CR0 4YY

ISBN 978 1913208 677

British Library Cataloguing in Publication Data.
A catalogue record for this book is available from the British Library.

To my dad, John
(1950–2005)

These characters would not have
breathed without you,
nor would I

Seeing a dead body, it changes a man. Especially if that man was only really a boy at the time. Seeing two, well… what difference did that make? It was who they were when they were alive, that's the difference. One German, two British; that made three.

He could trace each line of their bodies. They didn't look the same, they never did, not like they were when living. Their bodies melted together to become one; coiled spines like two white snakes.

But it wasn't what Jimmy had seen which had got him *here*. At least, that wasn't assumed at the time, that wasn't the *usual* things people thought about.

When your biggest fear as a child is losing those you love, what then? Can you risk giving yourself over entirely to another, knowing that one day, it's a dead certainty you will lose them too? What was the point in it all? In life? In war? He hadn't known the difference.

Jimmy was too young to be a soldier, several years too damn young. But that's only if you measure life by the number of years it has been lived in.

PART ONE

1917

I felt a cleaving in my mind
As if my brain had split;
I tried to match it, seam by seam,
But could not make them fit.

EMILY DICKINSON: THE LOST THOUGHT

CHAPTER ONE

FULL CIRCLE

WEDNESDAY 13ᵀᴴ JUNE 1917

THE POINT OF THE black bomb scythed the station roof. Concrete folded like liquid waves. Lead and blood and flesh in all directions. Trunks and limbs of skin like wax dummies laid.

Jimmy ran in motions so slow, like a giant net had been cast over him. Inaudible begs from Wilfred died on silenced ears. He fell to the platform, losing his cap. He crawled through dust and grey clouds of smut and smog and smoke which he now inhabited. Coughing, spluttering, he disappeared like a soldier seen amongst the mist for the last time in no man's land.

Masses scurried over one another like louse. Some were

upturned in shock; others, unrecognisable doll parts. He crawled and crawled, clasping his hand around the ankle of a man rocking back and forth. His bare torso spotted like a red and black leopard, surrounded by the fabric of old clothes.

Silence.

Plane engines.

Animal screams.

The train was hit this time. The carriage wood splintered like bone. Glass blasted into atoms. Pillars toppled. The world crumpled inwards. No memory of a life outside the blast radius, only purgatory within.

More engines. Passing planes.

Jimmy unclasped his hands. His face was speckled with blood and ash, inanimate and human.

He crawled to the lip of the platform edge. The track below was hollow. Up against the wall, empty eyes stared back. There were flaps of lung where skin should be, brains where skulls should. Their left index fingers sparkled from a myriad of diamonds.

Jimmy didn't respond. He was nowhere. Carted away from London, four tons heavier; he was living inside the raindrop.

As the foetid smell seeped through his nostrils, his thoughts – if you could call them that – were terminated, replaced by an orchestra of creaking doors, metal trays, the rattling of utensils. Unfamiliar voices surfaced under the strange white honeycomb.

"Can you tell me your name, sonny?" a man with an imperial moustache echoed down his well.

Jimmy was numb. He could barely lift his head. "Jimmy... Jimmy John Ford," he whispered back from the darkness, a stranger to his own words.

"Can you hear me?" came the voice again.

"Jimmy John Ford," he repeated, his voice languid and meek.

"Let the young lad rest, Betsy. He'll come around soon enough."

"Shall I restrain him, Doc?" There was silence whilst the doctor was thinking.

"Yes, restrain him."

Jimmy's arms mechanically formed a cross against his chest. His legs stretched out and forced together.

"Remove his uniform too, we don't want his first thought to be embarrassment when he wakes."

"I'm awake!" Jimmy blubbered from the bottom of his well.

"Christ, they make them young, these soldiers."

"Shell shock again, Doc?" cooed the gentle, feminine voice.

"We won't know until he wakes." The doctor fiddled with the curls of his moustache. "I'll send Doctor Turner in. He knows more on these matters."

"Right you are, boss."

"Offer him something when he is lucid, Betsy, it'll help with the nausea. This man has seen hell over at Liverpool Street Station. Probably a damn sight more if he had made it to the front."

"What time the Norfolk and Naspburys arriving, boss?"

"Ah, don't remind me. Six, I believe. This relief is only

short-lived. We'll end up back with the worst cases."

"What to do about the overcrowding?"

"Right, well, leave the lad in here, Betsy."

"This is the children's ward, boss."

"So it is. Who is he bunking with?"

"Oren."

"Very well. Brief Oren."

"Brief Oren?"

"Tell… Oren, not too many questions when our soldier wakes. He knows how it feels when you first come around."

"Good day, boss." The squeaking of shoe soles.

"Oh, and Betsy, don't call me boss."

"Sorry, Doctor Campbell, sir."

Doctor Campbell nodded. "Frederick will do."

The sound of footsteps receded. The muffled voices dispersed.

Jimmy could see himself as if from another camera angle, out of body. Clothes began to slip from him, a mannequin being undressed in a store window. His sooty khaki uniform was replaced by soft cotton pyjamas, white.

After the transformation, there was a groan, a heavy door sealed like the entrance of a great vault. Then, reticence. Not harrowing, nor deathly, more the sensation one could expect from the womb, the ebb and flow of amniotic bliss.

Jimmy's eyes tore open. His pupils expanded like blue ink droplets, sockets diluting memory and comprehension. He felt the damp white sheet below his cheek. It didn't taste like his usual pleasurable dribble. It tasted tannic, like the remnants of metal rain. Jimmy attempted to place himself.

Everything in the room was clinically white, too bright for his new eyes. He felt as though he'd been asleep but couldn't recall his dreams. Blurred, watery vision; fuzzy, helpless. He was weak and thirsty, as if his lips hadn't tasted water in weeks. *I've lost time again*, he thought. He attempted to move his arms to wipe his wet cheek. They sprang back to position, bound by threads of white rope.

"H-h-hel-help," he garbled. His voice sore; his throat husky. The creaking door jarred open and in flew a lady clothed in a wire black dress and white apron.

"I gotcha, wee one. Don't panic." Her face was distorted. On the back of her head rested a blurred white cap.

"Grace?" stuttered Jimmy, trying to rotate her upside-down face.

"It's Betsy, dear. Settle down now. Hush those lips. You've had an episode, but you're all right now. You're with us."

Jimmy peered down over the white cotton pyjamas. "W-w-where am I?"

"Hush now, dear, let's get this off. Only a precaution so you didn't hurt yourself. We suspect you've had a fit. Doctor Turner will be here in a moment to assess you."

"D-D-Doctor… B-but—"

"Rest now, you must be exhausted."

"W-w-where am I?" said Jimmy again, mesmerised by the nurse's busy hands. He felt the pinch as the head of the needle was detached from his thigh.

"We've got you, you're all right."

Jimmy let the darkness take him once more.

He saw her mouth first, always her mouth. It parted and popped in a rose-coloured pear drop. He watched her tongue as she licked the dusting of sugar, coating her fleshy pink lips. Her rounded cheeks and nose, that generous sprinkle of freckles. Then her eyes, the flecks of green and brown that glowed like lanterns.

"Grace," he whispered sweetly.

He combed through the short ringlets of remaining hair, sweat coating his palms.

"Who is Grace?" came the interruption. Jimmy realised he had been talking as he slept. He blinked his eyes open and closed like a broken zoetrope. As his vision cleared, he saw a boy in matching pyjamas crossed-legged on the iron bed opposite. The boy had grey rings around his eyes and teeth like tombstones. He crunched down as brown crumbs tumbled from the biscuit and landed on the white bedsheet.

"Feel incredibly tired after mine, I do," came the young common slur. "D'you remember a thing after you've had yours?" Jimmy slowly shuffled his body and leant back, panting against the wall. He felt an ache in his wrists and rolled back the white cotton cuffs. Deep, brown lines ran like muddy trenches. "I'm Oren," said the boy between bites. Every time he spoke, the ridge on his rounded forehead lifted his two bleached brows.

"J-Jimmy."

The bulbous head of the boy bowed satisfyingly. "Here, take one of these. Doctor Turner says that sugar helps after an episode." The brown Creola biscuit landed on Jimmy's lap. He took it between his shaking fingers, witnessing the dirt and grime beneath his nails. He lifted it to his nose; his dad on Christmas Day. He began to sob.

"Don't worry, Jim, this isn't the mad ward," said Oren, trying to reassure his new roommate. "Though it's all one, really!"

Jimmy's sobs turned into wailing. His body rattled the bed rails. Oren dropped his biscuits and leapt across the gap between their beds. Jimmy wheezed as if he'd surfaced from the sea. "Gaaaaarrrrrr, geeeeeerrrrr," he choked, his airways slender and swollen.

"It's all right, soldier, you're safe now," said Oren, patting him sweetly. Jimmy's cheeks inflated as he blew through the handkerchief that Oren had bestowed.

"W-Wilfred... where's Wilfred?"

Oren folded his bottom lip. "I know how that feels," he reassured, bald head reflecting the sun pouring in from the barred window. Oren wasn't entirely bald, he had hair, it was just so light that it blended with his globular skull.

"Who is Wilfred? Your... comrade?" Jimmy moved a stray brown curl from his eye and shook his head. Without warning, his body contorted forwards as bright yellow bile rocketed across the floor. "I'll get the doctor," called back a fleeing Oren.

The act had given Jimmy some temporary relief from his physical pain. His head had felt like a tightly wound vice. Temples, two pulsing walnuts ready to spurt from their shells.

"Wilfred," he whispered, rocking with arms tightly drawn around his knees. His friend would have to wait.

The door squealed and in marched a man with a small brown beard and wireframe glasses.

"'An occasional, sudden, excessive, rapid and local discharge of grey matter…'" Jimmy spluttered and gazed up at the man from bloodshot eyes. "John Hughlings Jackson, father of neurology." Jimmy listlessly offered a hand.

"Oh, not me." The stranger smirked. "The quote!" Every face of the man was magnanimous. He strolled over to the chair where a soldier's jacket lay neatly folded. His glassy eyes felt for the stitching. "Ah-hah, Private Jimmy Ford. It's a pleasure to meet your acquaintance," he said, loquacious and hirsute. The doctor cupped his thin lips to one side of his hairy face. "Call me Ishmael." He winked. "Hold his hair back now, Oren, we don't want the private puking on those curly browns, do we?" Oren giggled, revealing himself from behind the doctor.

Jimmy's hair was almost shaved short on the sides, but it was obvious that the top would grow out that way.

"Betsy, dearest!" shouted the doctor, his eyes squinting from the weight of his tremendous grin. "We have a caretaker's dinner!" In came the nurse with all the necessary mopping tools. "Right you are, Doctor Turner, sir." She busied herself with the yellow floor. The doctor possessed an energy, an electricity that howled and enticed.

"You're in shock, Private. Perfectly natural. This biliousness will pass." Jimmy tilted his pasty face towards him. "Doctor Andrew Turner's the name." He leant in and Jimmy offered back his arm. The doctor shook it and wiped his hand down his trouser leg. "Don't worry, this dormitory is only temporary. It's the children's ward. Hence, Oren here. I'm afraid we have a rather busy schedule today, so you may have to suffer your surroundings for the time being.

Now then, I believe you've had a seizure. I believe that you have epilepsy. It's rather severe, and common. Oren here has it too. In fact, a lot of our cases do here at the asylum. Unless, of course, they have typhoid. Epidemic's back. Bad timing, I'm afraid. Betsy will sort you out with inoculation soon enough."

"A-asylum?"

"Ah, she speaks. Great to hear a soldier speak. It's the quiet ones you got to watch." Doctor Turner tapped his nose. Hair sprouted from his nostrils; hair sprouted from every orifice.

Jimmy gazed for answers in his large, brown eyes. Behind the magnified glass, his pupils were colossal and kooky, which only seemed to multiply his mad energy. "Asylum. Quite right," said Doctor Turner. "Take no notice of it. Putrid word. Terrifying. Think of it as a hospital. All manner of folk here; policemen, postmen, army officers, tradesman, teachers, school masters, pilots—"

"Patients?"

"People," corrected the doctor. "All of us here are people, Private." His sausage fingers toyed with his Adamic beard. He let Jimmy absorb the words a while. "Now, I'll tell you how it is around here. We are understaffed and overcrowded. A hundred of us are out fighting besides the likes of you," poked the doctor proudly.

"I wasn't fighting," said Jimmy.

"Right. I heard. Gothas nearly got you. Dropped their bombs on a school in Poplar too." Doctor Turner shook his head violently and tutted as if closing a lid on the thought. "You're a lucky one, Private, when they found you, you were

13

having what we describe as a grand mal, and I presume that wasn't your first?"

"Lucky? They're dead!" muttered Jimmy in anguish. He saw their diamonds glinting from behind the sheets of bark which had encased their skin. His anger retreated; fear took hold, shaking him by his trembling hand.

"Now, who is your next of kin, Private? We can telephone, inform them—"

"I'm no soldier," snapped Jimmy.

"Right, your uniform. Well, we tend to only allow officers to wear uniform here, you will have to get used to that, I'm afraid, white cotton helps—"

"I'm a soldier's son," Jimmy whispered to himself, muddled by where those words had come from.

"First off the factory floor with that haircut, our very own Whitman in the making. Well, you're quite safe here."

"Why does everyone keep saying that? I don't want to fit right in, I want to go… back." Jimmy hesitated.

"I'm afraid that just isn't possible, Prince Myshkin… your condition."

Jimmy looked up, curious at the man who couldn't have known his passion for books.

"Found *The Idiot* in your inside pocket, laddie. What a completely beautiful human being." Jimmy's doleful eyes peered up at the strange, hairy man. "Prince Myshkin, not Dostoevsky… I do believe that was his intention for him, was it not?" Everything to Jimmy felt dead, even with the doctor's terrific vigour. Even his passions. "You know…" went on Turner, unremittingly, "…when Dostoevsky arrived in Geneva to write that book, he had his first fits.

And what fits they were! Apparently, the finale was written in personal inspiration, at the cost of two epileptic fits, one after the other!"

Jimmy searched the room for something that could swallow him whole. He couldn't find it. "He… had…?"

"Epilepsy. That's right. Happens to the best of you." Doctor Turner smiled.

"We're in Brentwood, I presumed you'd come from the barracks—"

"Brentwood?" Jimmy's eyes flickered with the life of a dying star.

"Yes. It's to the east," said the quizzical doctor. "Where are you from?"

"Brentwood!" Jimmy grappled, attempting to stand. "I must… get… home."

The doctor caught him just in time. "Too soon, laddie," he said, beckoning him back on the bed.

The buxom nurse passed Jimmy an enamel cup and opened her palm to reveal two white pills. Jimmy contorted. "W-what are these?"

Doctor Turner sat beside him on the bed. "Sorry if this isn't too comfortable. It's straw, you see. The rest of the mattresses here have been kitted with hair, but, well, we find that straw can alleviate symptoms of…" Jimmy didn't care, and the doctor knew it. He was still studying the pills in his hand.

"I don't want these—"

"Potassium bromide," interjected the hairy doctor. "Don't worry, it's only a small dose: six grams. We use it here as an adjunct to phenobarbital. It's an anti-convulsant,

15

Jim. Can't do you harm!" Jimmy looked back into the doctor's bulging brown eyes. He put one on his tongue, looked around the room and swallowed. "You have high levels of chloride, you see," added Doctor Turner. "Chloride increases your neural activity and leads to your seizure. The bromide will compete with the chloride for its turn with your brain."

Whilst the doctor was talking, Jimmy had swallowed the second pill. He felt as though they'd met before. He trusted him. He had to. Jimmy drank his body weight in water. The water even tasted dead. Betsy took the empty cup and left the room.

"We'll get some colour back in there," said the doctor. "And life back in there." He tapped his forehead. "Shame, you would have made a good soldier. *Ha!* Jimmy... Ford Madox... *Good Soldier*!" Jimmy was oblivious. "No one?" Doctor Turner hunted the room for recognition. "What's wrong with you young'uns, none of you read?"

"I do," corrected Jimmy. "I was studying an English scholarship."

"Enviable accomplishment!" The proud doctor smirked. "Nobody should ever stop reading, not even for a war!" He paused. "Or watching. You like the movies, Jim?" Jimmy nodded. "Let me guess, Chaplin?"

"The best!" Jimmy wiped his face with the remaining corner of the handkerchief.

"Found the ticket you'd been using as a bookmark..." Jimmy managed a feeble smile. "Sorry, Jim, it's procedure with all new admissions." Jimmy's face sunk back to neutral. The idea that he was considered an admission was hard-hitting. "Well, plenty of time for talk," said Doctor Turner. "Have you got that next of kin we should contact to let know you're here with us? Your mother… sweetheart?"

Jimmy shook his head mournfully. Doctor Turner sure was serving him a concoction of medicine. "Grace," he said. "She's… she was, my—"

"It's OK," reassured the doctor.

Jimmy lifted his small dirt-covered hands to his face and inspected them again, remembering everywhere he had been.

"Brentwood, huh," said Doctor Turner. "Well, to think of that. You'll have plenty of visitors. You've gone full circle, Madox!" You could tell he was a thinking man, for his forehead was seared with lines. "Well… when you're quite ready. I have a few questions concerning your condition to help us find the best cure… remedy," he corrected. Jimmy pursed his lips. "Not now. Now you rest. This will be conducted somewhere privately. Has Oren shared his biscuits?" Doctor Turner spotted one on Jimmy's lap. "Very good. Eat that, for now. Supper time won't be far off. All our people have it in the dining hall. You'll hear the bells." The doctor scuffed the curls on Jimmy's crown and took a wide, animated step towards the door. Doctor Turner's arms were long for his slight stature, almost silverback-like; he certainly had the hair to boot. "Oren!" called Turner. The small, golden boy followed him out. "We don't lock the doors on this ward, Madox. Get some rest and then come find me." The heavy white door clanked shut.

Alone at last, Jimmy flopped his head down onto the mattress. His mind came howling. He didn't know which way his thoughts were leading him, a wild horse pulling an unmastered cart. His body and brain were exhausted beyond command. Exhausted by the day, by what he had seen, by those he had lost. Yet, there was a piece of him, the part that longed for Grace, the part that needed to survive, if only for her. But he couldn't bear it; she couldn't see him like this, here. His mind was a contradiction of thought.

He crooked his neck, watching the sun flicking its last torrid discs. He flew above himself and across the blue skyline. He calculated the time it would take him, the distance he would need to travel. He was above her house now. He flittered down through her bedroom window.

He imagined her sweet breath as it lingered like pear drops on her pillow. He wondered if she was there, where he imagined her. He closed his eyes and moved his tongue to the roof of his mouth and felt hers, warm and smooth. How he longed to kiss her again, taste the perspiration of her skin as he moved his mouth from her soft brown mole to the tepid parts of her, behind her ears and down her neck. Her slight hairs standing to attention and causing his own skin to pimple. With adolescent glee, how his hands would wander over new territories. Their voyage around her untouched, wanting body, within the silk crevasses and over the curved, womanly mounds that had formed in recent months. How his body did ache, how his body did yearn and tremble.

"Grace," he moaned.

Jimmy awakened to find himself in a pool of sweat. It was dark; the bed beside him was neatly turned. No sign of Oren. His heart was swinging like a pendulum. He drew the deepest breath to calm himself.

He watched the diaphanous shadows dance in the dim light beneath the slit of the door. He drew back his eyelids, tight and resolute. He wasn't ready. By conforming to those scratching along the corridor walls, he was accepting it. Accepting the madness.

But it was no use; what did he expect? He was left with a deep guilt, a sickening, sinking, stench of death. He looked above and saw their bodies again, two coiled spines amongst the strange white domes.

Jimmy heaved his body to standing; he needed another view. Anything. He ambled around the small, empty room, moonlight casting cerulean light across the bars of the window.

Wilfred! his mind spat venomously. Where the hell was his best friend?

Survival. His body knew that much. That small something inside of him which kept his blood pumping and the occasional crackling synapse. Survival. If only to know what had become of Wilfred.

Jimmy attempted it again; he flew through the bars, now using the stars like a gymnast pulling on silver rings. He recalculated. His friend lived near the barracks, only a mile or so from his own home. He dropped down over his house and imagined him there, chubby and cosy and sleeping soundly, choking on his snores. He felt temporary relief, contentment that his friend had made it home safe. He would sooner be here, with everything that had happened to him, with all that he had lost, in this asylum, providing his best friend was safe.

Jimmy turned and noted how neatly his uniform was

folded on the chair. He rifled through its pockets to try and find his watch. No luck. What was the use for time now? Time wouldn't heal his wounds. But the watch itself meant more to him. He must find it. He dug deeper into his pockets, finding the book Doctor Turner had mentioned earlier. This was no place for books. No place for escape – not within the walls, at least. He pulled out the photo of his mother and remembered the moment he had placed it there. Yesterday. By God, it was only yesterday! She smiled; supple skin, snow-white. A dimple adorned her cheeks. *If only she knew*, he thought, *her only son confined to an asylum.* He tucked the photograph in his waistband and lifted his hand to massage the side of his pulsating temples. As he pulled away, he spotted the short, shaven hairs which lay against his ash-covered fingers. There was no mirror in the room, there wasn't much of anything in the room. He combed his fingers through the top of his hair again, expecting them to tangle and catch in his brown ruffles. *Why?* he sneered. *Why did I do it? Why was I stupid enough to think it would work? Now they are gone, and I am here.* He gazed back up at the hexagonal arched domes. He felt suffocated, like he was imprisoned in one of the pores inside the honeycomb. He was exhausted and battered by life. Powerless, like he was owned by this place: the clanking door, the white walls, the hollow ceiling. Like he would never be in charge of anything again.

I must get out of here, he thought. *I need her to know. Something like this can't happen and Grace not know. I'll escape. We'll get Wilfred and together, the three of us will make it to the front. This time, together. But first I'll go… home.*

"Home," he repeated aloud. The word couldn't have tasted less homely if it tried. It's only a home if there are people living between its walls.

He paraded towards the lead-laced window, biting down on the Creola biscuit. As he approached, he saw small pockets of life, the other boxed dorms of the asylum. From each room, the dying flicker of light practised its last waltz.

The others, the patients, standing there, motionless, like ethereal spirits behind suffocated glass.

Jimmy didn't dare look. He craved distraction. He peered down over a scant cemetery.

Jimmy's heart jumped; he recognised it immediately. He saw the rounded shade of Wilfred scraping his stick along the tops of the graves. He saw the incandescent stones from that very night, the knowing statue of the Virgin Mary and the white Japanese blossom, now overflowing with buds, in full bloom.

"*Full circle*," echoed the doctor's words. Brentwood. He was back in *Brentwood*. Back at the asylum. After everything he'd been through, after all his efforts, of escape, to become someone, somebody. To make a name for himself, or rather, write it, etch it in thick, black ink across the pages of the world. He was nobody once more. A fraud with nobody left; nowhere to go but a madhouse a mere mile from his home.

1914

"A wise man marvels at the commonplace"

CONFUCIUS

CHAPTER TWO

GEORGE FORD

THE FORD & COX tailor shop was located on Wilson's corner at the top of the high street. George Ford and Alfred Cox had been friends since their school days. Well, George's school days; he was once Alfred's pupil and he gave the poor man hell. The shop was the centre of their universe and in some respects, Jimmy felt at home there because he knew his father felt the same way. It wasn't the shop itself that was at the centre of Jimmy's life; it was George.

The door dinged as Jimmy shuffled in.

"Over here, my boy," George called from behind mountains of coloured fabric. Jimmy was amazed that he always knew when it was him coming. George remained hidden in the maze of clutter and tools. Jimmy sniffed and engulfed the distinctive haze of dust and cloth.

"You're like a bull in a china shop, you are," said the familiar, creaking voice. Out from behind stacked brown boxes emerged Alfred, his tiny head made smaller by his encroaching mossy, white beard. Alfred had a huge conk that looked like a kosher slab of meat which hung from a butcher's window. Either side of his nose, his eyes were two small, dark pins like the buttons on a teddy bear. His face was almost entirely symmetrical so that every corner of it was cosy and welcoming.

"Alfred!" Jimmy ran over, arms stretched.

"Easy now..." gasped Alfred, standing hunched over on one crutch.

"What happened?"

"Oh, caught it in a drain picking up dresses last week," slurred the crusted Scottish tongue of the elderly man. "Had

26

to drive home with just my crutch pushing the peddles. But hush now, I don't want sympathy."

"It's always the women that cause you the most pain," said invisible George.

"But that was your good leg, Uncle Alfred."

"Jimmy... I only have one leg." His grandad grin drew Jimmy closer. "Anyway, it won't be bad for long... I've had worse."

Jimmy inquisitively lifted up some of the fabric Alfred was working on. "Why do you need ladies' dresses, Uncle Alfred?"

"Parachutes."

"Parachutes?"

"Yes, we've heard the Germans have started to use them when they throw themselves out their planes. We figure that it's only a matter of time until our boys will need them... right, George?!"

"Yes, sir, a great giant Jack, falling to safety from the stars."

"I read an article stating they weren't too keen on the idea, said the pilots would jump out at the first sniff of danger, dampens the spirit," said Alfred with a whisky slur. "Well, you know how stubborn your father is, so here we are, making them anyway..." He rolled his buttoned eyes like one half of an elderly couple.

"Didn't you hear about the chap jumping off Tower Bridge, Alfred? Worked a charm. The army would be stupid not to take them up."

"You mean down?" joked Alfred.

"What happens to the plane if the pilot jumps out?"

said a curious Jimmy.

"It crashes," said George. "But it's better than the pilot crashing down with it, right, Jimbo? It's someone's life, not some hunk of metal."

"Expensive metal though, eh, those planes?" Alfred winked at Jimmy.

"Well, we like to do our part," said George.

George finally emerged. He dunked and devoured a Creola biscuit and gulped down his last sup of tea. He stood tall and thin on his long feet. Funny, really, Jimmy was short for his age, a parting gift from his mother.

George glanced at his inside wrist; you could tell he was an ex-military man. His gold-plated watch was held in place by a brown leather band. He was smartly dressed from head to toe, as all good tailors should. He wore a high-necked iron-grey sack coat, double-breasted with its front lapels curving away at the bottom. His lapels imitated the curve of his moustache which wreathed his friendly face and complimented his dimples when he smiled so frequently. The curls of his moustache pointed forward, so you always knew which way he was heading. Jimmy liked a kiss on the forehead from his dad, because he liked how the bristles felt. His hair was as black as boot polish and slicked back with a glug of petroleum jelly pomade. He combed either side to form a regimentally straight whitewall down the left of his scalp. A sallow green waistcoat rested high on his chest with eccentric slashes, subtle of wheat. Eccentric because he was so. Wheat because he no longer ate meat.

George was born into the austerity and refined sensibilities of Victorianism. None of it stuck, except for his stride. He always walked with palpable purpose and ingenuity. Jimmy was born a happy Edwardian, unaware of how things were before, and it suited George just fine to keep it that way.

George paid himself around twenty-five shillings a week as a tailor and did not wish to be a mercantile man, and he may well have been. George was certainly an educated man, destined for great things. But that was before the tragedy of twelve years past. It also depends if you measure greatness in wealth. George certainly did not.

Twenty-five shillings a week. A simple living if he had six mouths to feed, but George had only two and this meant the pair could live comfortably. The rent at 10 Myrtle Road was ten shillings a week; convenient, really. A very good price, all luxuries considered.

"I can't imagine Morris Angel stitching together a parachute, can you, George?" said Alfred, pulling at the seam through a squinted monocle.

"He is earning his keep in other ways, Alf, entertaining Jimbo and I."

"Oh, aye, and how often do you get to see his costumes?"

"Not much nowadays, Alf. London is at war, if you hadn't noticed. No place for a boy. Besides, the Palace here serves us just fine, right, Chaplin?" George reached out and drummed Jimmy's cap. He ushered the boy to take a seat and proceeded to wheel him around the shop like an invalid. "Well?" he hollered.

"*The New Profession*," Jimmy mustered between giggles.

"Correct!" said George, coming to a halt.

"You've lost me," said Alfred.

"Remember the scene when Chaplin slips on the eggs whilst trying to control his wheelchair?" Alfred stared glumly at the boy.

It had become quite the tradition amongst the Ford's that whenever the master of cinema was mentioned, a scene from one of his productions was played out with immediate effect, so that the other had to guess its origin.

"Yes, well. The old man doesn't get out as much these days," mocked George.

"Aye. And when were you last in London George?"

"*Sleeping Beauty* was our last, Pa."

"Hmm… so it was, Jimbo. The cast sang 'It's a Long Way to Tipperary'. Oh, and George Graves sang a song for you, Alfred… 'Sister Susie's Sewing Shirts for the Soldiers'!"

Alfred rolled his eyes again towards Jimmy. "Aye. London has changed. Full of foreigners nowadays," commented Alfred. "Especially down Charlottenstrasse."

"Not anymore, Alf. The Huns have been sent back to fight and the frogs… well, they're defending their pond."

"It's not just them. I hear all sorts, Russians… Poles, all talking under their big noses."

"Ah, sorry, you mean *friendly aliens*," George uttered sarcastically. "You can talk, Alfredo. You have a nose larger and more crooked than the lot of them."

"Yes, but I have all flaps of skin intact, thank you, George." Jimmy chuckled.

"Good for you, Alf. At least you're safely back in Brentwood now and not down Ally Pally! Next, you'll be saying you've spotted these 'aliens' talking to pigeons and erecting transmission on the roof of the Ritz!"

"Whose side you on, George, you Hun-coddler, you!"

"There are no sides, Alf… only war."

"I beg to differ. Sainsbury changed his German sausage to luncheon sausage, and you know Hanz's Barbers on Weald Road is now The British Barbers of Brentwood, don't you? They wouldn't change names if we were all on the same side now, George, would they?"

"Blimey, Alf, you'll be kicking dachshunds and burning books next!"

"Wouldn't read the German ones, anyway," said Alfred in no uncertain terms.

"Ah, so you're worried about losing your job to someone whose name you can't pronounce… is that it? Old man, you need to get with the times. Watch out, Alf, there'll be girls driving motorcars next…" Alfred chuckled.

"I'm modern, George. I once stitched a German gymnast his uniform. Muscly little fella. Married an English rose. Wouldn't want to meet him in close combat, mind… I wonder which side he's on."

"He probably didn't have a choice, Alf. Deported home, I expect. Or wound up in one of those internment camps."

"Yes. Well. He is German." George tutted.

"Yes, and he is human. We can't help where we are born, Alf. Some of these Germans have been on British soil since they were younger than Jimbo here. British-born wives with British-born children."

"Quite," admitted Alfred pensively. He didn't mind accepting defeat to George; he was a good man.

"Come on, old man, you've been on your bum long enough." George stood lanky over Alfred's shoulder. "Make us a cuppa, will you?" He slammed his ceramic white mug into Alfred's palm. "My throats as dry as St James' lake."

Jimmy gurgled. "A dry lake, Dad?"

"Drained it, haven't they Jimbo. Stop the zeps seeing it."

"And why would they want to bomb a lake, George?" asked Alfred sardonically.

"It's not the lake they'll bomb, Alf. It stops them navigating their way towards our king at Buckingham Palace!"

"The Kaiser won't target the palace, George, not with his family there."

"They're Germans remember Alfred." George winked, turning tables.

"How are the Germans related to us, Dad?"

"Alfred?" George called upon the old, wise man as he lumbered to his feet.

"He was the grandson of our Queen Victoria and Prince Albert, I'm afraid, Jimbo."

George replaced Alfred's position under the sewing machine. Alfred took the posture of a weathered pirate. He sure moved slow with his legs the way they were. He toddled his way towards the back room.

"Check these out, Jimbo!" said George, hoisting up some naval blue cloth. "Twenty-four of these go to the Royal Navy volunteer reserves in charge of shooting down all those zeps should they pay us a visit. Be proud to wear a uniform like that, wouldn't you, dear boy?"

"Aye, that you would," piped Alfred, still slowly shuffling out of the room. "And I hear women fly those zeps!" Jimmy fondled with the cloth draped over the corner table. There were little tags at the hem of each one: YMCA huts, VADs, Liverpool Street and Waterloo Station buffet attendants. Uniforms for all manners of proclamations.

"What's WPS?" said Jimmy, tugging at a long, blue, serge skirt and matching felt hat.

"You ever considered munitions work, George?" said Alfred.

"Christ, you still here, old man?" contested George, crooking his long neck.

"My dad, the munitions worker," chuckled Jimmy. "He couldn't handle the urine!"

"It's not urine, Jimmy," said a confounded Alfred. "It's the TNT… the toxins that make you jaundice."

"He's very aware of that, Alfred, thank you," defended George. "I don't fancy blowing up too much either." George filled his lungs. "You shouldn't smoke in here. It's a munitions factory!" The three of them laughed as Alfred disappeared down the scullery step.

"Is the coast clear?" whispered George. Jimmy gave a reassuring nod. By now he was accustomed to his father's pranks. "Grab us some of those black drawing pins, will you, lad?" Jimmy sprang across the room. "And some glue…" he called back after him. Jimmy was prepared for whatever George had up his sleeve. "That should do it, lad. I am going down there to distract the old fool. You smother this, first over the scullery door handle, must be on the inside, real thick, you got that?" Jimmy nodded, already exploding with giggles. It was like George was back at school and Jimmy here was his new accomplice. "Shhh," George demanded, placing a finger over his thin lips. "You mustn't, or he will sniff us out instantly, the bloodhound!" Jimmy calmed. "OK, then, you place these…" George passed back the box of pins, "…around the seat. Not too many or he will spot them, just enough to give him a nice kick, eh, Jimbo? OK, here goes… Oh, Alfred, darling?" Jimmy sniggered. He composed himself and followed his father into the backroom. "Alfred, tell young Jimmy here about the story of Hubert de Burgh. He's learning it at school, you see, so don't leave anything out."

"Wow, are you, Jim? I wish we did local history at school," said Alfred excitedly. Jimmy smirked from behind his father, just an arm's reach away from the door handle. "Well, what have you learnt so far, Jim?" enquired Alfred.

"Hm, not much," said Jimmy distantly. "Maybe start from the beginning and I can… sort of, fill in the blanks?!" George crossed his arms as he leant against the counter, blocking some of Alfred's view.

"Well, where to begin…" Alfred smirked delightedly. You could tell the poor fellow was in his element.

Alfred proceeded to regale Jimmy with the illustrious life of the first Earl of Kent, making sure to leave absolutely no stone unturned. Meanwhile, behind his back, Jimmy had managed to get the cap off the glue and began to furtively feel the cold, sticky liquid ooze out onto his palm. He felt the handle to ensure it was well and truly covered.

"So, denying court, Hubert then scrambled through the chapel doors… right here in Brentwood High Street!" Alfred pointed out with one hand whilst still balancing between his wooden leg, his crutch and stirring the tea. "In the chapel, he could claim forty days of blissful sanctuary… but instead… three hundred soldiers arrived shortly after to march him down to Tower Hill in the dead of night, to lose his head!"

"His head?" little Jimmy gasped.

"Well, not sure that part is entirely true, actually, I think I added that in for effect. But he was here in Brentwood, and so were the soldiers."

"That's truly fascinating, Alfred. Got any more?" quizzed George.

"More? Why, yes, but they won't help with Jimmy's schoolwork?!"

"Ah, forget the schoolwork," George fanned his hand.

"Right, well, there was the fire across the road there, at Wilson's Department Store. That was, my, five years ago, nearly to the day. But you probably remember that, Jim. You would have been, what, seven?"

"He was," George pitched in. "I remember the store windows shattered and the big clock face nearly crushing you!"

"How could I forget?!" Jimmy cackled.

"Come on, Alf, you must have more stories for the boy. You're like a hobbling history book."

"Let's see… much older then. There was Thomasine Tyler, the Bell pub landlady. She used that same chapel as Huburt once. I don't recall the year… but one night, she headed thirty militant women inside. They were all armed, you know?! Pitchforks, bills, spits, bows, hatchets… sharp stones… the lot."

"Why were they armed, Uncle Alfred?"

"Didn't want their chapel left to ruins."

"Was anyone hurt?" asked Jimmy, now sincerely absorbed. He had finished applying the glue and was in the process of concealing the evidence in his back pocket.

"Why, yes! Poor Richard Brook, the church squire. He was tossed out; beaten and bloody he was. A dozen or so constables battled to get the women out. Something like seventeen escaped unpunished."

"My, my," George pondered, coiling round towards his son. "Well, isn't that a tall tale, Jimbo?" Jimmy winked, giving George the signal that the trap had been set. "Now let us carry those teas for you, Alf," said George, beckoning.

Jimmy grabbed two ceramic handles and ran hastily into the shop to place the pins. Out George followed with the remaining mug, pulling the door to as if by accident.

"Ah damn, sorry, Alfred. I've closed the door and now I have my hands full." Jimmy burst into laughter in his quiet corner over by the chair.

"Don't be silly, George, I'm no invalid. I can manage a door."

"If you insist," George sang, all legs, skipping his way across the room with tea spilling everywhere.

"God damn!" yelled the usually tranquil voice. George and Jimmy erupted in laughter. They could hear Alfred shuffling the other side of the door between wooden crutch and wooden leg.

"Now you've gone and got me all stuck in here!" Jimmy was upturned on his back. "My hands' bloody stuck, damn it... jeez!"

With the tea down, George crept silently back to the

door. He ushered Jimmy to be quiet and return to his position away from the bogus chair. With a single thrust, George yanked the door open and towards him came Alfred and both bits of timber.

The pair laid out on the floor, Alfred like the miniature cake topper rested above. From a distance, Jimmy stored this moment in his core memory. The pair of them, two adults, laughing with wet eyes on the floor of their grown-up shop.

George helped Alfred over to his seat and placed his tea down on the desk in front of him. Down Alfred went with his face still flustered from smiling and back up he came with a contorted expression of sheer pain.

"You bloody…" he erupted. His face was redder than the shepherds sun. "Bastards," he hollered between grinding teeth.

At that moment, there was a ding of the bell and in swayed an attractive middle-aged woman in a red velveteen dress. She was pulling behind her a small wooden cart. *She looks like a modern magazine wife*, Jimmy thought. Her flesh was like silk. Her hair, fire-roasted chestnuts padded in a radium bun. A radiant version of his own mother. A radiant version of Lily Elsie!

"Well, hello, Vinolia!" cooed a smiling George as he walked over to assist.

"I'm sorry?!" said the lady with the porcelain face.

"Your… skin… it's like the advert."

"Beauty on duty has a duty to beauty," recited Jimmy. The lady gave a tremulous smile, revealing the quirky gap between her two front teeth.

"I've come to give you some damaged fabrics."

"Damaged?" piped up Alfred, trying to compose himself for business.

"Well, yes, combat clothing, worn by the soldiers."

"What condition are they in, ma'am?" asked George, gesturing towards her cart.

"It varies really. But most aren't too bad. Otherwise I would have taken them to the depot you see."

"Well, aren't you a clever little thing, Mrs…?"

"Miss Miller… Poppy." George smiled at the comprehension of her title.

Although the top of her went straight down, her hips gently rolled around the creases of her skirt hem. She was a woman, all right. He envisioned her as naked as a pearl. George peered under the sheet. He had been cast.

"Can they be mended?" her voice chimed sweetly.

"Sure, we'll mend them for you. We'll even send them back too."

"We will?" Alfred chirped. "You can't make a silk purse out of a sow's ear, George. Best get the carbolic soap over them then—"

"Ah, Alfredo, stop being Rumanian," said George over his shoulder.

"I'm sorry, Rumanian?" asked Poppy.

"Yes, Rumanian officers, they wear makeup, you see. Eyeshadow. Powdered and painted. Like a… well, lady!"

Miss Miller giggled timidly. She covered the break in her whites with two luscious red lips. George didn't want her to. It must have been something that had bothered her all her life, but to him it was what made her so unique and delectable. He was enamoured by it, the single only thing he knew of her so far. "Jimbo, help this young lady. Take all the uniforms from the cart and pile them down there, would you?" George's pupils were never taken away from Poppy's lightly freckled face and forget-me-not, amber-tinted eyes. Jimmy looked up, confused, studying the rules of his father's staring contest. The guidelines may as well have been blotted in white ink.

"Why, thank you," Miss Miller said, eyes transfixed between George and the floor in her bashfulness.

"This is my son... Birdman. Well... Jimbo... Jimmy... he has no mother..." George placed his hands on his forehead coyly. "I mean, I have no... wife... I'm George."

"I see..." Miss Miller blushed. "Nice to meet you... *Birdman?*"

Jimmy capped his hat. "One day I want to be a pilot, ma'am."

"I see..."

"Oh, and this is A-A-Alfred. He cleans up round here!"

Miss Miller laughed. "Well, it's sure lovely to meet you all." Poppy double took a glance and loosened her shoulders. "Jimmy. Do you attend South Weald Council School on Junction Road?"

"Yes, ma'am."

"Yes, he sure does, Poppy," George overlapped excitedly.

"I thought I spotted you there at my induction. I'm starting term there on Monday! You can't miss those curls, can you?"

Jimmy blushed.

"Filling in for Montrose?" said George.

"Why, yes. How did you...?"

"He is off fighting at the front. He was a terrific teacher to Jimbo… is, was… but I am sure that you—"

"It's quite all right," Poppy reassured. "I'm quite nervous, in all honesty."

"Before he left, he ensured Jimmy here got on a scholarship for English. He should be out by Christmas, so you won't have to put up with him for long…"

Poppy's cheeks flushed red. "I'm sure if my class are at all like Jimmy here, I have nothing to fear… see you Monday, Jim. And thank you… George." Just like that, she was top of the food chain.

Poppy smiled and left the shop with an empty ding and a jazz, her dress bouncing, spread tightly behind her lovely poached cheeks. The pause between thanking him and his name was enough for George to be caught on her line, her lovely hip swaying and derriere dancing line.

"Not quite *pure new wool* now, is it?" Alfred spat, holding up some of the ripped fabrics, his rear still in pain, tea dripping from his downy white beard.

"We may be able to give them to the Labour Corps we've been reading about, right, Dad?"

George sat on the corner of the table, gawking vacantly out of the shop front. "Right, Jimbo!" he finally said, distracted as if on the cusp of a clever idea.

"Labour Corps! Ha, some of these poor boys have been torn apart by trench mortars!" Alfred looked up, realising in his haste that a child was still present.

"I wonder how a woman like that gets hold of cloth like this?!" George pondered, still transfixed on the glass world outside.

Jimmy looked up towards the back of his father's head. "Dad, I'm going to make Wilfred a soldier doll… like Ghosty… except he will look like… Harry."

"Very good, *Birdman*," replied George vacantly.

"I might not have it in time for embarkation next week, but—"

"Excuse me, boys," said George, standing to attention. "Must dash!" Out George went with a ding. Alfred and Jimmy barely caught a glimpse of his silvery grey flecks.

"Well, I think that's a swell idea, Jim," said Alfred. "But what exactly will you do with the doll once it's made? Seems a little voodoo, if you ask me."

"Wilfred and I will race them!"

"Race them?"

"Yes, down the river. We often use tin soldiers. You assign ten men each to a raft or a half-cut Canthrox tin; the person with the most men once they've passed the steam mill is the winner! They get one hell of a ride, I can tell you!"

"Well, I say—"

"These dolls will be just fine too. Ghosty versus Harry, we'll strap them to rafts, release them down the river and the first to leave Brentwood shall be declared victorious!"

"I see," said Alfred. "And why is leaving Brentwood considered victorious?"

Jimmy shrugged. He did not wish to offend the old man. As endearing as Alfred was, he was too prescribed for Jimmy. His persistent need to have everything practical and ordered didn't sit right with him. Likewise, the Fords' spontaneity and seemingly chaotic nature probably didn't rest well with the old man either.

"Huh," he simply said. "So, that's what kids get up to nowadays?!"

As Alfred bumbled on about homing some Belgian refugees, Jimmy walked over to the window and gazed out. His dad was across the street, helping load Poppy's cart with rare fruit from the stall. Through the Georgian panes, he could see them laughing and gesturing. A silent romantic movie playing out as Jimmy had been witness to countless times on the big screen, except this movie's cells had been painted in the most beautiful of colours.

CHAPTER THREE

WILFRED NEEDHAM

THIS SMALL, INSIGNIFICANT BROOK in Brentwood could not be compared to the great rivers of the world, but to see it as insignificant would be a huge oversight. For this river serves a waterhole for thirsty badgers, ferrets and ginger-faced foxes. It nourishes the shoots and stems of overhanging willow leaves. It moistens the backs of restful toads who ribbit under secret sunsets whilst farmers filter its supply and funnel it over their prospering wheat fields to provide food for grumbling soldiers overseas. It's an underwater haven for pike, carp and roach. It's a battleground for grass snakes and hedgehogs who shuffle their tummies through the tickling grass to silence ribbiting toads. Life that lived and croaked from one throat that died and digested in another.

In the spring when the waters run lazily, fisherman wade on its shallow banks where the wildflowers and grasses flourish. They throw out their fly casts and roll up their coveralls to dip their patient toes amongst the glistening round pebbles. More than ample for the children who hurtle themselves over it on tyres and rope swings tied from the neck of some great tree, burning palms fearful at the prospect of ever letting go. Yes, it's more than ample for the needs of children at play.

Ever since Jimmy could remember, Wilfred Needham had been his best friend. Not only had they shared a desk at school since the age of four, they had spent most of their child years exploring. The river ran between their houses, which was why the railway viaduct made the perfect meeting ground. The wooden structure was bounteous in its purpose; built from solid timber trestle, it lay dormant within a dense coppice of woodland between the golden wheat fields from which their homes nestled. Built around 1845 to transport passengers and freight between the coast and the city, this two-track bridge crossed the brook at the adjacent steam mill, and it was this great wheel of water that Jimmy heard when first entering the woodland. He inhaled the scent of yesterday's rain and the dampened woodchip of the morning.

Although the agreed meeting hour was the same every Sunday, it was Jimmy who always arrived there first. From the bend in narrow banks of the river, between the gaps in the overhanging creepers, the silent viaduct revealed itself.

The entrance to their den was where the trestle banked the earth on Wilfred's side of the water. It had to be that side, otherwise Wilfred would never cross the viaduct, not on his own. Khaki-coloured curtains, made to measure at George's tailor shop, hung from the suspended boxed section of the bridge. It was this small alcove which served as a solid grounding for their base. Jimmy knew immediately that Wilfred wasn't there, because the curtains were drawn. He was forever lecturing his friend about leaving them open for the world to discover their treasure.

Clambering up the slats, he drew back the green drapes. Hanging from one of the horizontal trestles, spinning inside his tunic, was Jimmy's soldier doll, Ghosty. Jimmy's heart tumbled in his chest at the unsightly posture of the doll and his ill-fated end. He had forgotten placing him in such a position before he closed the den last weekend. His father had hand-stitched the uniform in the colours of his country. He had even sewed a rifle patch and a pair of shoulder straps, held in place with shiny brass buttons. The left arm presented some stitched scars: three wound stripes. Aside from the carefully crafted uniform, the facial features of the soldier were somewhat inimitable. The texture of the skin was so white it was almost transparent, and the eyes and brows were distinctively darkened beyond comfortable viewing. These distinguishing qualities had earnt the soldier the unfortunate nickname, Ghosty. Poor Ghosty was surrounded by broken, limbless doll parts, a playful representation of other, more permanently wounded men.

Once his heart had made its recovery, Jimmy unhung the soldier doll and piled up the limbs.

In the corner of the den, the children were using an upturned log as a kind of table. On it rested a photo of Jimmy's parents. The first thing he did once the curtains were closed was study it. He often wondered what lives they had led outside the constraints of that picture frame. His mother's smile; supple skin, snow-white. A dimple adorned her cheeks, appearing as if on cue at one of father's awful jokes! But Jimmy never even got to tug at her skirt.

He looked and studied her hair, inventing the smell of smoke from the inglenook fire entangled within those auburn curls. In his mind, like the photo before him, she would always be sewing on that parlour room couch, her flaxen fringe bouncing gleefully across her brow.

It was strange how a photo can capture a moment and cheat the perception of death. His mother was certainly no longer there, yet it was the same couch, it was the weight of her body causing the hollows that appeared so clearly in the photograph. Jimmy didn't remember her, but studying the photograph so often made him feel like he knew her. She had died during childbirth at home, in the parlour room, on that very couch!

"Where are you?" he whispered into her bright, enigmatic eyes. Jimmy often sat in the very position of where she would have been that day, twelve years previously, her belly swelling with his own body forming inside her. He always disappointingly felt nothing when he sat there. His imagination was vivid all right, but not brilliant enough to believe in things that just weren't there anymore.

Although he and his mother's paths only crossed once in that shared, single traumatic moment, Jimmy felt her love for him daily. He would often hear her voice in answer to the questions he found easy to ask but impossible to answer for himself.

"Why do I have to be born young and grow old?"

"Why can't movies be shot in colour like real life?"

"What is a zeppelin made of?"

"Why can't children fly planes?"

"When do I learn to breathe underwater?"

"Why did we used to be monkeys and why aren't we still so?"

"Do babies even know that they are alive?"

"What does it feel like on your last day being a child?"

"Why doesn't the sky ever run out of rain?"

To him, she possessed the knowledge of a blustery leaf, scudding across the country's expanse on an autumn breeze, seeing everything all in one go. She didn't always answer him, but he found comfort in her at least, listening.

Jimmy looked across the photograph to his dad and lifted it closer. Since his distressing entrance and her departure of this world, instead of resenting the child who killed his wife, George had collected the love he had for her and gave it in bucketloads back to Jimmy. For twelve years now, George had played both parts; that was a big a role as any man could muster.

"Don't leave me," Jimmy whispered. "Never… leave me." Satisfied he received an answer, he got straight to business.

In the adjacent corner of the den lay a mess tin filled with all sorts of farewell artefacts. Whether it was the precipice either side of the viaduct that enticed soldiers to throw their unwanted baggage from the train windows overhead or the same space which created a vacuum of wind grasping it involuntarily from their hands, neither of the boys knew. Nevertheless, it was a wonderful spot for a hermit collector.

The soldiers had always fascinated Jimmy. The way they looked, the way the acted, the pulse of war they paraded through their boot soles. Jimmy shuffled his body into a seated position beside the tin and swiped at the untamed curls from his young, freckled forehead. He inspected each artefact like an antique buyer: watches, buttons, tobacco cases, putties, rank insignias, wound stripes, name badges, cap badges. About the only item they hadn't collected from the river was a medal. Although the other articles were shrouded in mystery, nobody seemed to be throwing those out in a hurry.

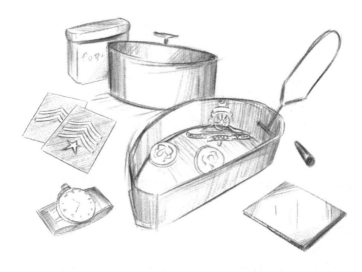

But Jimmy's favourite finding wasn't related to the war at all. Rather, a large sulphide, a clear glass marble sphere with the small statuette of a white wolf inside. As Jimmy twirled it between his fingers, the kaolin clay shimmered silver, refracting the light seeping through the wood of the viaduct. Jimmy was confused whether the item was cherished by a child or discarded by its owner due to a curse. Either way, it held a mysticism worth holding on for. He slipped the marble into his pocket. He would make it famous amongst the pupils at South Weald Council School, he would ensure it was forever known throughout the playground and around the gullies, simply as Buck.

Once he could be sure Buck was safe and secure in his trouser pocket, he picked up the *Captain Magazine Volume XXV* and laid on his back; the dappled sunlight casting coloured prisms across the open slats above. He knew that Wilfred wouldn't be long now.

Ever since Jimmy could remember, he had wanted to be a writer. And like all good writers, he knew that he needed his own adventures to write about. His pa once said, "With your mind, Jimbo, you could catch a yawn by reading it from a character in a book." Jimmy always slept with a book beneath his pillow at night in hope that the stories would soak through his skull.

"I would have the authors take refuge in my room if I

could!" he once babbled to his father. Jimmy wanted to read everything. He wanted to absorb and be everything. Not in the nerdy sense. He just knew that without knowledge, he may as well have been born something else.

Jimmy was astute for his age, in English literature, at least. Before he was summoned to the front to serve his country, his teacher, Mr Montrose, had put him forward for a scholarship at the affluent Brentwood School. Good old Montrose had refused to board the ship until the papers were signed. Jimmy was due to start at Christmas. By then, the war would be over, and Montrose could marvel at the makings of the poor middle-class boy.

Aimlessly flicking through the first few pages of the magazine, he came across a photograph of his favourite aircraft, the Be2c. Jimmy could not fathom a greater sensation than viewing the Earth from such angles. He looked at the great sun through the gaps in the wood. If the pages of a book were the masterpiece, the plane was like the pen which could carry him there.

Folding back the pages, he observed the same model of the Be2c he had hanging from the main trestle which separated the den from the railway track. He had helped his father, George, build it with balsa wood, shavings and…

"Glue! Pass us the glue, Jimbo!" said George. This was before Jimmy was wise enough to his father's tricks. The glue wasn't accessible; of course, the glue was itself glued to the garage tabletop and Jimmy went the colour of grapes trying to prize it off.

Last month they had painted on the targets and added a machine gun beneath the arc. One day, Jimmy would like to add a real shooting mechanism to the model, but more eagerly than that, Jimmy would adore to fly. For a romantic, there was no greater dream than the aptitude to fly. Free as a bird. Not that he wasn't free already.

"There's no chains holding *your* wings down, Jimmy," said his father, lifting the model of the plane skywards upon completion. "Today we built it, tomorrow you will fly it!" Jimmy was mesmerised; by the plane, by the prospect of one day truly becoming someone that his father was proud of.

Half the reason Jimmy wanted to be a pilot was how much Dad commended his boys. Jimmy knew George was already proud of him, of his writing, but to wear the clothes of his country, well, one could only imagine the adulation.

But Jimmy had seven full years before he could fight.

"It may as well have been seven hundred," he would say. Everyone in Brentwood knew that the war would be all over by Christmas.

The model of the Be2c began to slowly manoeuvre around the ceiling; a train was coming. Jimmy knew the drill. Keep all limbs inside the den, otherwise smack: adios, good riddance, sayonara. A kid could lose his head that way.

The rails directly above him began to hum, then clatter. The model of the Be2c oscillated in wide orbits.

"Here it comes." He saw the pony truck first, then the undercarriage, piston rods, driving wheels, crossheads and firebox. The whole den rattled with life, clanging items in the mess tin against one another in fury as the train rumbled overhead. This was a long one, no doubt pulling the empty rusted containers back from the city to be reloaded with war ammo at the barracks beside the sea.

Once it had passed, Jimmy popped his head through the slats and watched as it disappeared around the bend. But something was different; the humming didn't seem to subside. Jimmy felt the beam closest to him. There was another train coming; this time, the coastal line, this one was heading for the city. Before he could spot it, he heard the snapping of twigs; it was Wilfred.

Good old clumsy, lumbering Wilfred. He could identify the hunched porpoise shadow of his dear best friend from anywhere. Wilfred's head was low, keeping command over his flat feet. Jimmy shuffled his body subtly over so that his head sat in the centre of the sleepers between the reverse track. From where Wilfred waddled, it couldn't have been better timed. Black, viscous steam rose from behind the wall of green trees. Then emerged the head of the black, shiny monster, this time pulling passenger carts. The noise came as futile as a horn.

Wilfred finally raised an eyebrow and shouted with all his efforts.

"Train!" he warned. Jimmy remained steady, head facing obliviously in the opposite direction. "Jimmy… get down…

t-train!" Wilfred's throat wobbled and his vocal cords went with it. He attempted to run, to warn his friend before he was decapitated in front of his very eyes.

Too late. Wilfred threw his porky fingers over his face; he didn't dare look. The treetops soughed as the heavy load thundered past. Standing just short of the bridge, Wilfred was hit across the narrow shoulders by something round. He squealed and cried, not allowing his hands to drop from around his swollen lids.

The chugging subsided. Wilfred waited, frozen to where his ankles rested beside the bank. He whimpered amongst the serenity of the woodland.

"All right, Wilf?" finally came the cheeky voice.

"No. Away. Go away," he pleaded.

"Wilf... it's me." Wilfred squealed. Jimmy raised a hand and ushered Wilfred's arm down to reveal his snout, the enflamed cheeks of a teething baby.

"Bastard," he sneered between plump lips, eyes squinting in the midday sun.

"Bastard yourself." Both boys laughed.

It's funny, the pair could have inhabited a disparate species of human altogether. Though similar in height, Jimmy was like a Neanderthal from the Engis Cave with his frizzy locks and wide, periwinkle blue eyes. He could have been born outside. But aside from their physical variances, Wilfred possessed a simplicity of mind from which Jimmy could not succumb. Jimmy could not be the piggy, nor in the middle. He simply loved living life and Wilfred gained great pleasure from observing Jimmy live it.

"Want to know how I did it?" asked Jimmy.

"Nope."

"Ah, come on, Wilf, it was genius."

"It was stupid."

"It had you fooled for a second."

"Only because of what you threw at me!" Wilfred searched the floor for the object which so closely at the time resembled the head of his best friend.

"Throw? I didn't throw anything… it must have come from…"

"The train!" both boys cooed. Jimmy joined him in the search. He pointed a little downstream to a white ball, drifting languidly along the surface current.

"There, quick! Before it reaches the mill!" Jimmy raced back up the viaduct and along to where the pillars dropped down towards the river. He slid the vertical struts of timber like a fireman's pole, spread his legs out wide and clamped his knees tightly around the lowest trestle. Suspending his body upside down, his brown ringlets covered his face.

"What is it?" demanded Wilfred the moment Jimmy had the white ball in his grasp. "What is it, Jim?" he called again eagerly from the bank. Jimmy laid the damp white paper on the trestle and gently unfolded it. "Jim?"

"It's a letter, Wilf!"

"What's it say?"

"Hold on, would you?"

"Hurry!"

"Oh, I'm sorry, Wilf. Why don't you have a go at reading it?"

"You know, that isn't funny," whimpered Wilfred.

Jimmy was sure enough of himself to laugh at a joke at his expense. Wilfred on the other hand, was not.

"Meet me at the top," demanded Jimmy.

"But what if there is another train?" Wilfred gulped. Jimmy didn't oblige him with a response. He was stubborn. Wilfred knew that if he wanted to know what was in the content of the letter, he would have to climb up on the viaduct and hear it first-hand.

By the time Wilfred dangled his wide legs off the edge of the slats, Jimmy had successfully prised open the letter. Sodden and creased, he held the edges like the gentle, suckered hands of a starfish. He noticed that further down the page, there was thick, black brushstrokes. He would have to wait to find out why the letter had been purposefully discarded.

"Dearest Katherine."

"Who's Katherine?" said Wilfred. Jimmy turned to face his friend. A look was all it took. He cleared his throat.

"Dearest Katherine. Miss Letchfield... *Mrs* Thompson! I start this letter to you but fifteen minutes from departing your company. I am heading west towards our nation's capital, a married man. Every soldier in my battalion shares my good fortune by now and a tot of rum has past my lips twice already. I am grateful beyond the words in this letter for being able to spend this last week of summer with you beside the seaside. How fortunate for Shoeburyness barracks to be my embarkation point before fate takes me over to France. A husband and a father in one week. I don't quite know if any man has had the luck of I since Sunday last. You must keep writing; I want updates daily on the size and weight of your sweet belly as it swells these next nine months.

I write to you now as I approach that ghastly place where your poor brother John remains. I remember how much he ~~meant~~ means to you when we were just three innocent broods playing on your dad's farm. I know you fear for me, my dearest small wife, fear for me, like you ~~feared~~ fear for dear John. But I am in the hands of the lord now and he wouldn't bestow such beautiful news upon us if he had other intentions.

It cannot be easy for him, an Officer as he ~~was~~ is, surrounded by the ghosts of all those ~~madmen~~ …"

Jimmy stopped. He looked at Wilfred.

"I wonder what he means, Wilf, all those madmen? He's crossed it out too?!"

"Who cares… finish it. I want to know about the baby."

"Wilf. The baby has only just been conceived. It takes nine months!"

"It does?"

"Unless she's a guinea pig!" Wilfred spluttered and Jimmy got a good glimpse at those crooked teeth.

"How does the bum stretch enough for the baby to come out? Always wondered that." Jimmy broke into hysterics. Wilfred started to blush. "Oh, no… no, wait, I forget… it comes out the belly button!"

Jimmy bent double. "Ah, Wilfred." Wilfred frowned, attempting to read the situation, with his wide lips creased, they finally gave way to laughter. In all the excitement, Jimmy dropped the soldier's letter.

"No," he yelped. "Please…" He attempted to snatch it back from the air but missed and watched it float down, off the bridge, towards its watery fate. He jumped to his feet and ran to the other end of the viaduct. Even Jimmy wasn't fast enough. He watched as the letter drifted along effortlessly, dipping and diving through the gaps of the wooden struts. He knew the mill would swallow its ink and the soldier's story would be erased from existence. There was no guarantee where a road would take you, but all rivers flowed towards the sea. Jimmy wanted to see where it would wind up. Would it ever leave Brentwood? Would its author ever write another? Regardless, it was the only copy of that exact story.

"We have to find it, Wilf."

"What? It's gone, Jim. We will never get it back."

"Not the letter. The place. The officer!"

"Eh?"

"You heard him. He said that John was surrounded by madmen and he was approaching that ghastly place!"

"We don't even have his proper name."

"Sure we do. It's John… Officer John Letchfield." Jimmy was already on the other side of the viaduct. Below, the light shingles glistened in the autumn sun and a hint of rosemary permeated from the moist, violet bushes that lined the bank. Dandelion seeds drifted across the surface of the water and settled safely on the other side. "Have you ever left Brentwood, Wilf?"

His cautious friend shook his head. "You know I haven't, Jim."

"Well… don't you think it's time we did?"

"I'm not so sure, Jim—"

"Look, Wilf, 'nothing happens until something moves'."

"What's that supposed to mean?"

"It means, we need to see what is beyond the viaduct!"

The railway lines had always paid homage to their youth. Nets of light slanted their way through the line of poplar trees and bounced their last rays off the steel tracks.

"Race you to that post," said Jimmy. Wilfred didn't even attempt it. Poor, wheezing Wilfred, with his asthma and extra layer of puppy fat. God wasn't going to give him the pleasure so easily. Instead, Jimmy hurled himself up on to Wilfred's back.

"Christ," he said, caving under the weight of his small, wiry friend. Both children fell amongst the ballast.

"Well…" Jimmy said, dusting off his sooty trousers like a chimney boy. He rolled the grey cotton over one knee. "That sings a little… stings," he corrected. The blood oozed like an innocent millpond, speckled with bits of purple rubble. It was the proud graze only a fearless child would receive. The blood trickled over the cap of his knee and coagulated.

"Ouch," said Wilfred, admiring the ocean blue eyes of his brave friend.

Jimmy stood and began balancing on one of the tracks. "Not long now, Wilf."

"Yeah? How do you know?"

"I just know."

His chubby friend bent forward on to his knees and exerted every effort to stand. "What makes you so keen to leave Brentwood anyway, Jim?" asked Wilfred, picking bits of purple ballast from his dimpled hands.

"You know we won't actually be leaving Brentwood now, don't you, Wilf?! The place we're going is only up here." Wilfred let out a sigh of relief. "Besides, in Brentwood, I know everyone, Wilf, and everyone knows me."

"So? You go somewhere else and you will still be you."

"I want to be me, Wilf. Just, another kind of me, you know?"

"What kind?"

"The kind where I at least get asked where I want to go and what I want to be. Here I'm just Jimmy Ford, son to George Ford, the tailor. Destined to take over the business. Destined to stay." Jimmy stretched his arms wide like the wings of a biplane. He began a purring sound with his lips.

"You can be a writer anywhere, Jim."

"I know, but if I'm stuck here, what am I going to write about? Dad's shop, Alfred's leg, school?"

"You could write about the letter we found?"

"That's not my story, Wilf, I need my own." Stones clattered either side of the tracks as Wilfred tossed some ballast from between his sweaty fingers.

"And John, what do you suppose his story is?"

"That's what I intend to find out. An officer—"

"Like my dad," said Wilfred proudly.

"Exactly, but back here… surrounded by madmen? I'm sure he has a story! And when we find him, we can ask, hear it straight."

There was a long pause.

"What are you running from, Jim? You've done nothing wrong?"

"I'm not running from anything, Wilf," chuckled Jimmy. "Can't you see? I'm running towards something." His patient friend waited. "Look, I don't expect you to know. *I don't know.* But if I never leave Brentwood, I never will!"

"You know, Jim, the war won't last long enough."

Jimmy dropped his arms back by his sides and ceased the engine purrs he made with his lips. Wilfred had just coshed his dreams. "I can still be a pilot, Wilf."

"Sure, sure." Wilfred wiped at the beads of sweat which trickled through his ginger strands, strands that glistened like fermenting carrots. Wilfred's hair was closely cropped, shaved on the sides, fitting for the son of a military man. Jimmy watched as the sweat rolled over his bulging forehead, down his pulsating temples and into his eyes. Jimmy studied his friend; his head sure was big and round, but then it gave way to his more pointed features: his nose, his chin. The lower half of his face looked as though it had been sucked in by the nozzle of a vacuum cleaner. Jimmy chuckled.

"Why don't you just leave then, Jim?" interrupted Wilfred, agitated by the heat.

"You know I couldn't do that, Wilf." Jimmy reached over and helped himself to a clump of Wilfred's cheek. "I couldn't leave you here, could I? Not alone, in charge of our treasure!"

Wilfred batted his friend away. "And George, you couldn't—"

"Yes. I know, Wilf. It's just a dream, all right. I'm allowed that, aren't I?" Wilfred hoisted himself on to the other track. Jimmy knew what he was doing. He was trying to beat him. But Jimmy always kept his balance the furthest; he simply had to. He couldn't let Wilfred win.

A few paces later and Wilfred was back trudging through the ballast. He squinted his eyes, watching the shade stretch long out behind his friend.

"Your shadow looks like Pippa!" Jimmy pushed out his long, feral tongue and began to pant, mimicking the actions of Wilfred's old tatty dog. "'Cording to Pa, you'd get fleas and lice in seconds in those trenches." Wilfred gestured towards Jimmy's wild locks.

Jimmy saluted. "The hair of the head will be kept short… Ha, at least your Pa doesn't have to worry about that… he's bald as a badger's backside!"

"'N' the chin 'n' under lip will be shaved." Wilfred mirrored the salute, arm jiggling like whale blubber.

"…But not the upper lip," both boys declared in unison.

"That makes your Pa fine for service too then," Wilfred said, his eyebrows raised towards his high and tight tapered hair. "Hey, why doesn't George join up… he's not ill or unfit?"

Silence.

"He's eligible, he can volunteer." Jimmy hesitated. "If he did go, though, then, then I wouldn't have any family left, would I?" It was all too true. Some things just are. "That's why, you see, Wilf. Why I could never—"

"You have Alfred?!" interrupted Wilfred.

"He's not family, Wilf, he's Pa's partner… friend."

"But you call him uncle?!"

"I've always called him uncle." Jimmy shrugged. "He's always been there, I guess."

"You mean he's not really your uncle?"

"No, Dad hasn't got any brothers or sisters… our family is… small."

"Hmm," Wilfred pondered. "I wonder what happened to his prop?"

"Alfred's leg? Lost it when he was little… hepatitis."

"Hepatitis?"

"I mean… meningitis."

"Meningitis?"

"I don't know." Jimmy shrugged.

"His wooden leg is kind of stylish, though?"

"I guess," said Jimmy solemnly, eyes dull, unsure of anything.

"You think that's why he doesn't fight in the war?"

"Probably," contemplated Jimmy. "I still would. If I was born earlier, I would fight in the war. No matter what!" He thought for a moment. "That is… if Pa did."

"Yeah. It's not fair," said Wilfred. "Billy gets to fight beside *my* dad."

"What about Harry? He doesn't embark until next week, does he?"

Wilfred nodded; his chin jostled. "Billy should be back on leave tomorrow, then Harry will be embarking with him next week, together."

"And your Pa?"

"Maubeuge."

"More-bouche?" laughed Jimmy. "Oooo," he squealed, feet sliding off his rail.

"Yes, I did it," said Wilfred. "I stayed up longer."

"No fair, Wilf, I had lightning crotch!" Wilfred didn't dare ask. "You never got lightning crotch, Wilf?"

"What is that?"

"Lightning crotch," repeated Jimmy. "Shooting pain right up your bum! It's painful, but only lasts a second or so."

Wilfred laughed. "Can't say I have, Jim."

"And the flu, I love it when I get the flu."

"You're nuts, Jim."

"When you're laid up in bed, it's cold outside... but you're completely snug. You sweat and your body aches so much that you get the giggles. Covered with covers, so tight that you can't move, even if you wanted to! It gives you a reason to just lay there. Just... be."

"There's something seriously wrong with you, Jimmy Ford!"

"Perhaps I belong with John!"

"Dead?" said Wilfred.

"Nooooo. The letter said he was surrounded by madmen, Wilf, keep up."

Intelligence aside, Jimmy sure had a skewed view of the world. He was a ubiquitous dreamer, emotionally guided. The heart was always victorious over the brain. He had un-rational, seemingly disjointed and spontaneous thoughts, often understanding them but lacking the words for expression.

The boys were approaching a bend in the track.

"Did he really lose his leg to meningitis?"

"Alfred? I told you, Wilf, I think so." Jimmy's tail

turned bushy. "Hey, would you rather have a wooden arm or a wooden leg?"

Wilfred thought for a moment. He was used to Jimmy fleeting between matters, especially matters of importance. "Arm," said Wilfred.

"Leg!" Jimmy added as if he held the correct answer. "Then I could still fly planes… and write!"

"I don't know, Jim. Cycling would be tough, and Block Home Save All?!"

"Yes. I guess it would. But we won't be children forever, Wilf." Wilfred gawked, a little perplexed. Jimmy pointed up. "When I'm older, Wilf, I'm going to be a fighter pilot. I'll shoot all their zeppelins out our skies."

"But I thought you want to be a writer."

"Can't I do both?" Jimmy laughed.

"What is it?"

"Well… I can write about flying planes, but I can't exactly fly whilst writing."

"You can stop those zeppelins throwing down those poisonous sweets, though."

"I'm not sure the Germans really do that, Wilf."

Wilfred shook off the whole thing. Jimmy looked back up at the sky. Low, wispy clouds began to form. "When we have time, Pa and I want to make it so the machine gun on my Be2c can fire through the arc… when he has time," he corrected.

"How do the pilot's bullets not hit the propeller blade?" asked Wilfred.

"Maybe the blade is too fast?"

"Faster than a bullet?"

"Possibly?!"

"But surely with thousands of bullets fired, at least one of them would hit the blades?!"

"Ah, I don't know, Wilf. All I know is that Garros probably had some part in it—"

"Who?"

"Roland Garros… he's French! He was involved in the first ever air battle. Flew his plane directly into a German zep, killed the pilots… and himself!"

"Never?" Jimmy nodded as if the whole thing was a matter of fact. "Well, when I'm older, Jim, I want to join me brothers in France and kill the Jerrys at close range."

Wilfred was top of their class when it came to rifle practice. Those never-flailing feline eyes of his. Perhaps he would have made a good soldier, agreed Jimmy. Better to have a purpose than none at all.

"How you going to shoot any Huns with one arm?" Jimmy giggled.

"How am I going to run at them with one leg?"

"How you going to run away, more like?!" Jimmy play-punched his friend in the arm and the flab jiggled.

"Isn't it a shame?"

"What?"

"That the war won't last long enough." And just like that, like all children's thought dreams; their futures were settled.

"Come on, Wilf, we need to make it to John before it gets dark." Wilfred followed Jimmy's gaze up towards the clouds.

"Jim… where do you suppose this madman of yours is?"

"You know what, Wilf? I don't suppose it's him that's mad!"

"Why?"

"Well, he's an officer, isn't he? Like your dad!" Wilfred smiled proudly.

"How much further?" The rattle of rails interrupted the boys. Wilfred looked fearfully across the tracks to his leader.

"Relax, Wilf. It's just a train." Jimmy pulled out two shillings from his pocket. "I have an idea!" He placed the half crowns on the track nearest to them.

The boys took a step back and waited as the chugging got louder. Wilfred stood, as curious as a cat. The train emerged, thundering towards battle. Jimmy remained steady, dangerously close to the passing carriages. His curls whooshed over his face and eyes. Wilfred jumped back with fear and checked his close crop.

After what seemed like minutes of constant roaring, the end of the train turned the bend and out of sight.

"The iron horse with steam for plasma," said Jimmy. Wilfred was still aligning his hair as if that was his greatest worry. "It will continue its journey under bridges and through darkened tunnels to haunt London, then, who knows what those brass eyes will see?!" Jimmy had a voice he adopted when he prattled as such; it was how he imagined Chaplin would sound if he had a voice. A deep, blue-blooded-type gentry fellow. Jimmy leapt back on the track and picked up both shillings. He laughed uncontrollably and placed them one at a time onto Wilfred's palm. "Meet Frederick, Earnest and Albert," he bellowed, reciting one of his father's bad jokes.

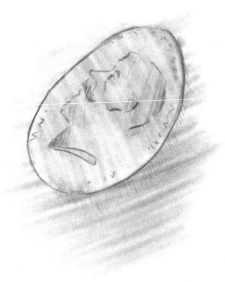

Wilfred observed the curiously flattened coins. "It's warm," he stated, a little too obviously.

"Here, you take one… and I'll keep this." Jimmy ensured that he took the least artistic of the two coins.

"For keeps?" said Wilfred.

"For keeps!"

The boys balanced on either side of the tracks, the sun spurting down like the pink juice of a grapefruit.

"What do you think is up here then, Jim?"

"I told you Wilf, I have an idea—"

"You do?" Jimmy didn't oblige and Wilfred didn't question him. They couldn't have possibly known what lay at the end of this golden path. This nothing place, where everything happened.

"D'you think German kids are doing what we are?" asked Wilfred.

"Doing what?"

"I don't know… playing and exploring and stuff?!" Jimmy looked up at the clouds and across the red sky, eastwards.

"You mean… being kids? Yes, yes I do!"

CHAPTER FOUR

OFFICER LETCHFIELD

THE SUN HID ITS extraneous face behind the imposing towers as the last flicker of light glinted above the toothed gables and through the harsh mullion windows. Copper clouds sprouted from the tops of the red and brown brick.

Jimmy didn't have much of a plan when he and his friend came to an abrupt stop. But he had been right about what he was looking for.

The pair stood frivolous beneath the dark gothic gates, Wilfred's body panting beside him after the climb up the hill from the tracks. Jimmy fingered the jagged, rusting letters that stood in the centre of the gate: 'Warley Lunatic Asylum!' Underneath in macabre markings was the date: '1853'.

The structure of the building was Ruskinian gothic of the sharpest order. Octagonal towers grew monolithic against the rusty sky.

The boys, perilous beside the gate house; a small glow flickered from inside. They were more than 150 metres away from the building, yet its existence swallowed them whole. It was like everything had grown overnight. In the centre of the main entrance, an impending clock face, branching east and west were long, cloistered corridors, like the tendrilled arms of a rotted tree. Connected either side were symmetrical pointed edifices with a hundred small, lead-laced windows, stained glass of soft blue and gentle violet; the manic and the morose. The windows had uninterrupted views over the countryside, free access to air and sun. From where the boys stood, they felt neither.

Wilfred wanted to be back at home, where people breathed and spoke in verse. His barrelled chest felt tight and his weary heart began to plan its escape. *Surely people*

aren't in there?! He imagined that looming there in the dark lay prickly monsters with one eye and spiked centipedes with hundreds.

"Well?" Jimmy said concertedly.

"Well, what?"

"What we waiting for? How do we get in?"

"Get… in?" Wilfred's voice shivered. "We've done it now, Jim, we left Brentwood."

"Hardly, Wilf, we're in Warley, it's basically the same town! Besides… you were hit on the head by a letter written by a soldier who mentioned John… tell me that isn't fate?!" Ignoring his friend's hesitance, Jimmy hovered his arms out like aeroplane wings and began that chugging sound as he glided down the hill. "Let's try this way, shall we?" Reluctantly, Wilfred hauled his large rear behind him.

The asylum was parallel alongside the boys, eyes burning. The thin, iron poles on the serrated fence were the only strips of black obstructing their view. Abruptly, the fence chased inwards, and the paving turned to woods.

"This looks good," Jimmy called back from an opening in the shadowy bush.

"Define good!" yelped Wilfred.

"Let's see where this path goes." Jimmy didn't want to be antagonising, but he knew Wilfred needed pushing if he wanted to live at all. Wilfred begun humming 'Keep the Home Fires Burning', his only defence in staying sane.

The distant call of a church bell chimed three times. Jimmy enjoyed the sound of them. "Someone must be getting married," he said.

"Or, someone has died," gulped Wilfred.

"Someone important, perhaps?"

Imminent fear crept over Wilfred. His bobbly bits quivered as he begrudgingly followed his captain into darkness.

The first clearing led to some empty pig sheds, a vacant chicken coop, an abandoned cow shack, a barn and a gardener's house. A frail man with wizened cheeks and white pyjamas raked the soil. At first, Jimmy thought they had taken a wrong turn and wound up on a film set. It had all its props; its own moon. Fog drew in like it was coughed out from some great machine. The boys gently turned down on the soft, foliage floor and knelt tacitly in the shrubbery. The figure was emaciated and alone, his eyes turned inside out between grey craters. It appeared that he wasn't focused on any task at all, plonked there by a higher being; a child on detention, looking inwards, distracting himself from undeserved punishment.

Soothing music played from an open window: *A London Symphony* by Ralph Vaughan Williams. The night approached as softly as that sweet melody. Overhead, he didn't know it, but the stars of Pleiades began to natter.

"This happens around the corner from my house every day and I'm missing it!" whispered Jimmy. Although, missing what, he wasn't entirely sure. "We must return one evening and explore the inside."

"In... side?" stuttered Wilfred, panting as he folded his wide legs up like a deckchair.

The asylum was a whole new world, a microcosm of life hidden from society as they knew it.

"This man must have been here every day, turning that

soil continuously since he was my age," said Jimmy. Wilfred didn't answer. "The dancer in his rags of white, swaying by moonlight!" There was a pause as Jimmy took everything in. What Jimmy couldn't see was that the man had no eyelids. He had used scissors to remove them after the voices told him to *keep them peeled at all times.*

"Stephen?" came a soft, feminine, Yorkshire accent. Jimmy glanced up towards a glowing door behind the agricultural ghost. The outline provided by the backlight made Stephen look even more dishevelled. "Stephen? It's Betsy, dear," came the voice again as a buxom figure emerged clothed in a wire black dress and bonnet. "Ah, there you are. It's teatime, Stephen, did you not hear the bells?" said the nurse. Stephen raked, shook and raked some more, his gaunt jaw pointing towards his soil. The buxom nurse approached him slowly, edging around his harrowing frame and to the front of his vision. "You poor man, you must be freezing out here! Where is your coat? Come with me, Stephen." She had to tiptoe to place her arm around the fabric which hung from his skeletal blades. Betsy beckoned him in towards the welcoming warmth. He was still clutching that damn rake. "That's it, this way, let's get you back inside." Stephen shambled alongside his carer, eyes still fixed low towards his precious earth. The rake slowly fell to the ground and just like that, the pair were gone.

Jimmy turned and realised he was alone. Wilfred was far along the trail, skull reflecting in the moonlight like a line of carrots in a field.

"Wilf, you missed it!" he shouted in whisper.

"Pssst, over here, Jim. I've found some graves!" Wilfred

summoned him. Suddenly, Jimmy didn't feel like playing along. He trampled slowly along the sheltered track. What did all this mean?

As he approached the second clearing, Jimmy got a good view of the rest of the asylum. The scale of the place was overwhelming. The main block gave way to a washroom and mortuary; a village within a village. The boys were on the fringe, toeing between the two.

Arranged in two uniformed rows were headstones of all shapes and sizes. Stone crosses, arches, flats, peaks, heads with shoulders, heads with extra shoulders. Some graves were standing proud and tall; others had given up, even in death. They were sinking, illegible, into the churned earth, praying never to have been known by name. Luckily for them, this was a desolate church where nobody sane ever congregated.

A slight glow from the nearby chapel illuminated a small proportion of the graves. A snowy stone fountain with a statue of the Virgin Mary stared down at them. Behind the statue was a towering oak tree. It was so great; its hundred years shadowed the small cemetery of young graves. It must have been old enough to witness the entire history of the place. It would have seen the asylum built up, brick by brick. It would have been witness to the mad masses in white, mumbling past in answer to voices they heard during recreational activities. It would have seen the holes being dug in the ground and the new occupants move in. Then, without remorse, it would have fed on the remains and made itself all the stronger and wiser for it. For death escapes madness.

Jimmy thought of his family headstones at Woodman's cemetery, all stuck in the same soil, having never left the town of Brentwood. *Lucky, none of those were mad*, he thought.

The wind cracked, and out from its darkness, a single white Japanese blossom blew its last bleached leaves.

Jimmy studied some of the graves, its occupants all so young. As darkness fell, he read the remainder with his fingers, most of the epitaphs now illegible. Feeling thwarted, he turned amidst the frozen fog which had encircled them. Jimmy looked up, eyes drawn towards a stone being harassed from the blustery twigs of a nearby bush. He peeled back the gnarled boughs:

In memory of John Walden
Of Downham
Who for 31 years was employed as
Labourer on the asylum farm
Died July 1 1899
Aged 77 years

He escaped the bush and admired the feat of engineering John Walden had helped create. St Raphael's chapel sure was a masterpiece. Another magnificent structure comprised of red and black bricks. The conformity, this time, was broken by the existence of holy white stonework which softened its presence and put Jimmy at peace.

St Raphael was the patron saint of the blind, of happy meetings, of nurses, physicians, travellers and the mentally ill. At this moment, Jimmy and Wilfred were certainly the travellers, but what could they ever know about the mentally ill?

John was seventy-seven. Jimmy felt some relief, but he couldn't be sure why he was basing the fulfilment of life only on the number of years. Besides, it was the wrong John. He felt hopeful that the John he wanted was still out there somewhere. He looked back at the asylum building. *Or rather, in there*, he thought.

Jimmy caught a sudden glint of candlelight emerge at one of the windows. He squinted to make out the figure of a small boy in white. Slowly the boy raised his hand to the glass. Before Jimmy could comprehend it, footsteps echoed from a nearby pavement. The boys took one terrified look at each other and darted into the tangled roots of a giant maple tree.

"This ain't the same way we come," said a hoarse Wilfred.

"I know, but it is a way, isn't it?! Why would we want to go back the same way?"

Wilfred shrugged and dragged his feet forwards. The path was narrowing now, and the trees barricaded the boys from any conceivable exit.

"Jim, do you think Harry will get one of those?" Jimmy's skin prickled.

"One of those what?"

"Graves."

"Don't be silly, Wilf, Harry won't need one of those... somewhere to hang his medals, maybe?!"

"I'm not so sure. Everyone says he's too... unpredictable."

"Unpredictable?" Jimmy questioned. "Well, better for your brother to be unpredictable than boring!"

"Yeah, but boring don't get you killed, does it?" Jimmy, sensing Wilfred's blue mood, broke out into song.

"There's a silver lining,

Through the dark clouds shining,

Turn the dark cloud outside in

'Til the boys come home."

Wilfred chuckled at Jimmy's exaggerated, operatic interpretation. He wrestled his slender friend to the ground behind the wall of flora.

"Well," laughed Wilfred, pinning Jimmy down. "We won't ever know what happened to John now!"

The voices got louder. Jimmy hastily cupped his hands over Wilfred's plump lips.

Doctor Frederick Campbell was dressed head to toe in a wire corduroy suit and hobnailed boots, and he always welcomed the fresh air. He hadn't noticed the rustling from behind the bushes because far more important things occupied his mind.

Campbell had been an alienist at the asylum for fourteen years. In that time, he had treated all sorts of patients. Those with depression, anxiety, delusions, suicidal inclinations, dementia praecox. Those with venereal disease, degenerative disorders like alcoholism, syphilis, tuberculosis. He was responsible for suggesting the addition of verandas to the asylum wards, for Pete's sake. Quite literally, for sake of Peter Lynch, one of his more severe tuberculosis patients. He had used phenobarbitone in hope to cure epilepsy, he'd injected malaria to alleviate paretic dementia and general paralysis of the insane. He had cured those deteriorating, those wanton, those desperate. Those malingering, who simply didn't want to be. Worst of all, those he couldn't cure. And he had seen more of every case since the war.

It was always Campbell's bad fortune to need a pipe break when the new night orderly, Francis Nesbit, started his shift. *I mean, why did Nesbit need a cigarette before his shift had even started?* Regardless of reasons, Campbell's heart sank every time he noticed Nesbit spotting him stepping down the conservatory step and out onto the manicured lawn.

Campbell believed that Nesbit was better suited to a mortuary assistant than a ward orderly. And he would have been lucky to have been that. All he did was lift. What would be the difference?!

Nesbit was a thirty-year-old soldier, if you could call him that. He had hubris and insolence, not too cleverly cloaked as humility. He was shot in the knee during the opening seconds of war. His haughtiness would make you think he was officer of his platoon or brave Private John Parrs at Mons. Besides, he was too short to be an officer. *On average, privates were four inches shorter than their commanding men. Smaller coffin, too.* Campbell let the idea wallow a while as he adjusted his small, rounded specs.

"I tell you, the first dead soldier I saw. The photo is still being developed on me brain," Nesbit rattled on, gesturing with one finger and tapping the side of his temple. Campbell silently sneered at the thin, wet strands of black hair Nesbit had tangling like pond weed across his forehead. Everything about Nesbit angered him, especially the aggravating tendency he had of chewing his tobacco between cigarette puffs.

"It's not the dead that's bothering him," said Campbell, wringing the moisture from his silver, Shakespearean beard. "Officer Letchfield is suffering from neurasthenia… Shell shock… from a shell that didn't go off."

"A dud?" Nesbit spiffed. "Bad blood, that's all it is!"

"It's nothing to do with moral deficit, eugenics, poor breeding Nesbit!"

"If you ask me, he's one of the lucky ones."

I wasn't asking you! Campbell thought bitterly. "Why? Because he's still alive? That's what got him in here in the first place. Pallid skin; purple shadows under the eyes; unsteady hands; shaking, trembling teeth; constant ducking to avoid shells. I would say the man is far from well, wouldn't you?"

"Well, he can't exactly arrive dead now, can he? The guv wouldn't have it!"

"That may be. But part of him still died that day."

"Part of him? Ha, he's bloody mute, Frederick!"

"He won't always be," said Campbell, benign but firm.

"How do you know?"

"He has night terrors. He's quite vocal about those… and the church bells. We need to postpone those damn bells!"

"Ha, yeah. Letchy loses his mind when they ring! At least it brings life into the bugger. Better than him giving you the thousand-yard stare! Better for him that he wasn't court marshalled!" grunted Nesbit.

"Officer Letchfield's battle nightmares have got worse." Campbell nodded for the only time. "His neurosis, he's devoted so much vigour to repress those damn memories. I don't blame him…" he mumbled to himself. "After what he's seen. He needs to take time to slowly remember. Don't allow the thoughts to fulminate, gain power. Don't linger, nor analyse, but simply take it at face value. A few times a week at first, but gradually they need to be talked about and discussed like anything else. Watering it down to the value of any other memory. These are things that have happened, they can't be buried!" The two men pulled from their smokes. Nesbit, still smiling smugly, couldn't even attempt to join the conversation. He tucked one side of the loose, wet hair behind his protruding helix. "Abnormal behaviour to a quite normal situation is perfectly normal," Campbell concluded. "If a man feels nothing, that's when one should worry."

"Eh?!"

"Put it this way, Nesbit. To be committed to an asylum, one must act… abnormal. But only abnormal in proportion to the degree of one's usual, normal self."

"Huh?!" Nesbit bleated like a foghorn.

"A boy at my school. He had a terrible time keeping up. Unsociable chap, Raymond. Didn't interact with anyone, wouldn't even look you in the eyes. But he was always like that. Ha, only now I realise poor old Raymond probably had some form of auto-schizophrenic syndrome. Mind, he was frightfully bright considering. The only reason they kept him on." Frederick got lost away somewhere in his memories. "Anyway, they would sooner send him here if he suddenly started to speak and lark around, you understand?"

"Not really. Surely him speaking and acting up was a good thing?"

"Yes. But it was abnormal for him to… suddenly do so." The two men exchanged glances as if they dwelled different planets. "OK, bad example," Campbell continued. "What would you suppose the normal thing was for Officer Letchfield to do in his… situation?"

Nesbit shrugged, mopping back the last of his shiny hair. "Laugh it off. Count his lucky stars. Get… pissed."

"Get drunk? Why? Because he survived?" Campbell lost his train of thought to enmity. His face curdled like cream. "Men are falling all around him, every single day, Nesbit. Men his age… boys! He's ordering them to the slaughterhouse. Have you seen the casualty lists already? Children of seventeen, parts of them are left in the dirt and all their mother receives is a bloody t-t-telegram," Campbell blew. Nesbit looked bewildered at this rebuke. Campbell's face turned red in the acknowledgement of his own stutter, his smoking hand visibly shaking.

"That aside," Nesbit went on unremittingly, "why would he suddenly crack at an unexploded shell and not the death of a comrade? Nothing significant actually happened to him the moment he turned lunatic!"

Campbell despised that word. "And lunatic he is. Detain the mentally ill. Churchill's orders, sir, not mine. He feels that the sources from which madness is fed should be cut off and sealed up before another year has passed! He's lucky he didn't catch VD… Letchfield, that is."

Nesbit spiffed again. "General paralysis of the insane… that's what most of them have got in here! Letchfield's fate is better than that."

"Put it this way," Campbell seethed, ignoring Nesbit's opinionated lark. "The event itself is insignificant." He paused for a moment. "Well, not entirely insignificant."

"Yeah, too trivial, see—"

"No. Events may only be individually trivial. Add them all together and there is nothing ordinary about them. It's the gradual and consistent pressure and stress of inordinate responsibility. The command and fear over his men and their lives, governed over a prolonged period of time. That caused young Letchfield to lose his voice, not an unexploding shell." Nesbit looked as vacant as a koala bear chewing on eucalyptus. "Don't you see? Imagine a loaded gun. Every experience Letchfield endured during his time in France. Every time he sent a soldier into no man's land, another on night watch, every limb or life that didn't return. Damn it, even every shell that did explode. All those experiences are the bullets." Campbell paused to twirl his white moustache, somewhere between imperial and gunslinger. "Those bullets, his experiences, go into the barrel of the gun. Once the gun is full, all that's left to do is…"

"…pull the trigger," both men chimed in unison. The only common sentiment between them.

"Right. So, the unexploded shell was the final straw, after months of filling his gun with bullets, it was the trigger which caused Letchfield to… well, wind up here."

"Huh, I see," Nesbit said dumbly.

Campbell drew a long drag of nicotine. "Broken contact with real life," he mumbled inaudibly. "We must re-establish the vital connection by means of work cure. Or, was it rest cure?" His shaking hands acted nervously around his thin lips. "All right, Nesbit… let me ask you this," he said, determined to go undetected. "Do the insane dream sanely?"

"Not by the noises… no!"

"The noises are a rational reaction to atrocities they have witnessed, Nesbit. A sane reaction to an insane… situation!"

"Eh?"

"Never mind, Nesbit," he said, finally spent. "Officer Letchfield will talk. He just needs something important to say!" He pulled from his pipe and exhaled. "These men are the first men. We must learn from them." The billowing smoke uncoiled like dispersing question marks. Everything had been answered, or so he thought.

"'Ere. What's the deal with that Ellis fella?"

"What do you mean? He's a pilot."

"Yeah. And 'e's the first. Why do you think we've never

had one of those through here before?"

"What, in the past month? Well, they break down far less frequently and far less severely."

"Why?"

"Not as helpless, I suppose. Especially when you compare all those poor fellows floating there in their observation balloons."

"Ah, yeah, we've had lots of those!"

"Exactly. Utterly powerless, sitting there like ducks. When they breakdown, it's again, due to prolonged strain, their inability to impact the circumstance they find themselves in. It's not down to sudden shock. Not by a long stretch."

"OK, why are there more women here then?"

"Simple. More confined lives, on average, that is. Less... practise, dealing with stress. So, when they do—"

"They lose their mind!"

"Well... not to say they aren't under extreme stress, not knowing if their husbands and sons will return home. Waiting for that telegram to arrive—"

"Take it you heard about Nurse Harrison last night?"

"Indeed," replied Campbell glumly after his interruption.

"Escaped *again*, didn't she?"

"Yes, well... she isn't very well either. And she didn't *escape*, Nesbit. She had every intention of coming back."

"Intention?" Nesbit snorted. "She's bloody barmy, that one. Ears like elephants."

You can talk, thought Campbell. In Nesbit's excitement, his ears now married the pink flesh of his face.

"Dressing up in all that gear. Whose was it this time?"

"You know perfectly well it was Betsy's…" Campbell had to bite his tongue. "Regardless of what she may or may not have done. This war has nearly damn paralysed this hospital. That makes the count one hundred and three!"

"Dead?"

"No, staff lost, in general, overseas or… otherwise. They will be taking the damn furniture next!"

"Well, the number of patients we're losing each month, we can probably afford to lose a few more…" Nesbit stopped in his tracks, sensing Campbell's indignation at what he was about to say.

Campbell was exhausted with the conversation, exhausted with Nesbit and exhausted with the day. He snubbed his calabash and toyed with the corners of his moustache again. He had heard enough.

"Oi, what your thoughts on that new Turner fella?"

"Doctor Turner? The epileptic doctor?"

"I hear he gets a little sentimental, philosophical like—"

"Yes, well. I'm sure there is a time and a place for such measures. Not everyone drinks from the same cup."

"His cup is overflowing, if you asked me, boss! The sooner this war ends, Frederick. The sooner we can get this place back to… normal. Eh… get it, Campbell… normal?!" He chuckled at his own humour, unaware of Campbell's irresponsiveness. Campbell hated it when Nesbit called him *boss*.

Jimmy removed his hand from Wilfred's plump lips. His palm had been licked sodden.

"Calm down," he whispered, attempting to stop Wilfred's barrel belly from wriggling. There was a snap of twigs and the woods rustled.

"Who's there?" called out Campbell, glad for the interruption.

"It's all right, boss. I got this." Nesbit began creeping forwards, dragging behind his wounded leg; a bony alley cat after a scrap, one scruffy paw at a time. He approached the edge of the woodland. There was a swoosh and the retreating pitter-patter of crunching, stumbling feet. "Whoever it was, they gone now, boss!" Nesbit turned to face Campbell, who looked bemused from the edge of the paving.

"A patient?" Campbell questioned, rubbing a smear from his specs onto his jacket. The two men gazed as a small, round ball rolled from beneath the weeping ash and rested on the damp lawn. Nesbit grabbed it and raised it up in the air. It gleamed, doused in the pastel light of the crescent. If it could, it would have howled.

"Well, what we got here?" Nesbit enquired.

"A marble?" Campbell called out through squinted eyes.

"A white wolf."

The boys wriggled free from the brambles and back onto the wide roads. Jimmy ran with the burden of a new moon upon his shoulders.

"Buck!" He yelped, patting his empty pockets. "My marble, Wilf, we have to go back!" Jimmy looked at his friend who was bent double, fear pulsating from his eyes. Not a chance. Buck belonged to them now.

To think of it, a letter had been hurled from a moving

train; a letter written by an unknown soldier which contained the whereabouts of one Officer Letchfield, a stranger to Jimmy. Nevertheless, he had found him here, the man he was looking for. The man he really knew nothing more about, only that he was here and that he wouldn't be able to share his story after all. But it wasn't the man which troubled Jimmy. It was where the man was.

1917

CHAPTER FIVE

DOCTOR CAMPBELL

THE ROOM WAS AS luxurious as any he had seen. It had floor-to-ceiling windows with grape draped curtains, arched brass lamps and an open hearth, with w-atercolour paintings adorning its merlot walls. A stuffy haze hung in the air over the giant, broad oak desk.

"Oh, what a joy it was being young..." said hairy Doctor Turner as he felt the presence of someone else join him in the room. "When you noticed the soft light pouring in from the window or how carpet felt against the palm of your hands or the true colour of a book cover. There is simply no time to take all those things in now. I have time, we all do, externally. But somehow your mind is filled with so many other things that it just isn't possible to hold them there in that moment." Doctor Turner looked like a humorous dwarf behind the desk; but then, it wasn't his desk. As Jimmy drew closer, a plaque on the front informed him that it in fact belonged to a Doctor Campbell. Doctor Turner didn't have his own desk, let alone his own room. Turner wouldn't have it any other way; he was amongst his *people*, not above them.

Jimmy hadn't had the pleasure of meeting Doctor Campbell as yet, but from what he had heard, his reputation had certainly preceded him.

"Isn't it funny?" said Doctor Turner, still unable to look up from his book. "Your greatest life achievement or your longest time could have been spent in one room. Then that room is transformed or destroyed, perhaps the entire building is, and then you look upon the air where you would have once sat or celebrated and try to imagine all the things that happened there, all those accomplishments and merit, but you can't, because it's gone…" He clicked his fingers. "Time! And you're gone with it—"

"I—"

"We had a pilot here once, you know?" said the doctor, looking across at the boy as he took the chair opposite him. "Ellis, his name was. Doctor Campbell treated him."

"And where is he now?" The hairy doctor pointed upwards. Jimmy couldn't be sure if he meant he was in heaven or he had regrown his wings. He didn't dare ask.

The doctor placed his hairy hands gently upon his lap from behind the desk. "Doctor Campbell won't be long!"

Jimmy gave a feeble smile. He distracted himself, rummaging through the pages of the book he held. "Whitman, he describes the moon as…"

"'Swollen, as if with tears'." Doctor Turner smiled.

"Yes!" Jimmy looked up from the page. "You know, I once thought the moon contained seawater, and that it was inhabited by sea creatures, and that one day, the moon would explode, and all the sea creatures, they would tumble to Earth!"

"You are one curious creature, Jim."

"I mean, I was twelve at the time."

"One should never lose that childhood perspective. It's what keeps the magic behind things."

"Why is the title called that?" asked Jimmy. "'Out of the Cradle Endlessly Rocking'?"

"Well, the cradle, symbolises birth..."

"But birth isn't really... featured?!"

"Birth, death, rebirth, birth over death—"

"What do you mean by death?" The doctor looked curiously upon the boy.

"Death... well, it's a prerequisite. Death must come for rebirth to begin. As Anatole France says: 'For what we leave behind us is a part of ourselves; we must die to one life before we can enter into another'." Jimmy nodded. He couldn't be sure if it was the doctor who was wise or if he simply channelled wisdom through those he admired. "A little like you, really." The doctor chuckled. Jimmy looked perplexed. "Relax. I don't mean that you died. I just mean that you came back, reinvented; a soldier one moment—"

"A patient the next," said Jimmy.

"Yes, well... so some believe... then there is reincarnation—"

"What's that?"

"Well... it means the body, upon death, takes a new physical form in their... next life."

"Like a butterfly?"

"Not quite," said the doctor. "To transform you must first decay. If you opened the chrysalis partway through, you would find neither a caterpillar nor a butterfly."

"Then... what would you find inside the cocoon?"

"Well... goo!"

"Goo?" The doctor nodded. Jimmy spread the brown curls from his brows.

"What's wrong, Jim?" asked the doctor.

"I feel like I've gone from a butterfly... into a caterpillar." The doctor pressed his brass frames back against the ridge of his nose.

"I wouldn't exactly say fighting in a war was spreading your wings, Jim. What do you suppose happens to that caterpillar of yours when it's back inside its cocoon?"

Jimmy peered over the desk. "He will turn to goo!"

They both laughed.

"Of course he will," said Doctor Turner. "But then he will grow wings again, and one day... fly." Jimmy looked down at his fingers, toying with the pages of his book.

"Did Whitman believe?" he said.

"He certainly believed in rebirth, at least. After all: 'And as to you life, I reckon you are the leaving of many deaths, No doubt I have myself died ten thousand times before'." The doctor looked proudly upon the young man. He felt stimulated by his conversation. Jimmy was becoming one of his favourite people in the asylum to converse with, other staff included. Most of his other patients spoke merely in monosyllables.

"I liked this bit, hold on..." The Doctor gave a

tremendously joyous smile as Jimmy searched the precious page for the right words. "Here… 'I wait and I wait till you blow my mate to me'."

"Ah, yes. Why that part, Jim?"

"Well… he sounds stubborn, patient. Like he knows she will come back providing he just… waits."

"Ding, ding, ding," said the wild doctor, as though he were running a stand at the funfair. "Patience is a virtue, dear boy! There isn't a soul in this establishment who hears it." Jimmy smiled at the mad doctor. "Grace?" said the doctor.

"Grace!" Jimmy nodded, sunken-eyed. "You know, I resented her for keeping me in Brentwood. Before I left, we had a fight. I thought by leaving, I was being true to myself, true to my purpose, but I was being selfish, only thinking of myself, my silly, stupid idea of myself… I left her, I left her and now…" He shrugged. "Now, I'll never get to tell her!"

"You will."

"From here?" The doctor nodded as if here were as good a place as any.

"Why does the boy call the bird his brother?" said Jimmy, changing the subject.

"He understands him… understands what he is going through."

The room turned silent. Jimmy peered down at his lap and became teary-eyed.

"What is it, Jimmy?"

His fingers fidgeted. "I never got to say that I loved them," he muttered. The doctor stood and walked round, placing his hairy hand on the boy's shoulder.

"We quite often don't say what we mean to one another.

It's the type of love you don't have to, Jim… they knew!"

"And Wilfred? He will never know."

"You don't know that, Jim. Wilfred may still turn up."

"Turn up. Where, here? Like me?"

The doctor didn't respond. He let Jimmy wallow a while.

"Who am I supposed to be?" asked Jimmy.

"You are supposed to be you, Jimmy."

"Yes, but what if I don't know how to be me? If I never got to know who *me* is? I mean, what are we all doing here?"

The doctor looked at him in wonderment. He knew he didn't mean *here* at the asylum.

"One day, Jimmy. That knowledge will creep up before you even realise that you have it in you. Then, before you know it, you will be *you* and your purpose will become clear."

"Is that how it happened to you? Becoming a doctor?"

Turner nodded. "But what we do as a profession doesn't always define us or who we truly are."

The scene was disturbed as the large door squealed open. Jimmy wiped his face.

"Doctor Campbell!" greeted Turner with genuine surprise.

"Doctor," tipped Campbell, a little less zealous.

"Well, I'll leave you to it, shall I?"

"Please…" said Campbell sternly, ushering Turner out the door. On his departure, Doctor Turner gave Jimmy an affirming nod. Jimmy noted how the doctors' faces adorned matching specs. Their beards were similar too, in the way they pointed. Although very different in colour: Turner's a peanut brown, Campbell's a cashew white. Other than that, there was absolutely no physical similarities between them.

Doctor Campbell was a serious man. Tall on his toes, he wore a wire corduroy suit and hobnailed shoes which clunked loudly against the wooden floors of the asylum each time his heel flopped down from such a height. He had a white to yellow imperial moustache and a personality to boot.

"Now, do you understand why you're here, Jimmy?" he said clinically, through thin lips. He tossed his file and took position on his throne.

Jimmy looked around the room for the first time since he'd been seated. Doctor Campbell now seemed like a giant behind the broad oak desk; the thin, gawked silhouette of Dracula. Jimmy idly twiddled his fingers in his lap, vulnerable and small.

"Because of my epilepsy?" he whispered meekly. That morning Jimmy had filled out a questionnaire declaring if anyone in his family was mad.

"Yes, very good. But do you know the reason why you are seeing me today and not Doctor Turner?"

"The dreams—"

"Exactly. As Freud says, all dreams are wish fulfilment. These recurring dreams you've been having—"

"I wouldn't exactly say they are dreams." The doctor frowned his dark, sharp eyebrows. He gestured for the boy to continue. "Well, don't you need to be asleep to dream?" He leant in and nodded; the ridge of his glasses clattered against the sharpness of his pointed nose. "Well, I'm not sure I am really asleep… or if I am actually… awake."

"Perfectly natural."

"It is?"

"Hallucinating in the half-waken state is perfectly common in…" he looked Jimmy up and down, "…*children.*" The doctor sounded like he was reading from a textbook. "They aren't psychotic hallucinations; they occur between being asleep and awakening… hypnagogia!"

"Hypna…?"

"…gogia! Mary Shelley said she wrote *Frankenstein* from one. A waking dream. Doctor Turner said you like reading?!" Jimmy nodded. "You know, Frankenstein isn't really the name of the monster?"

"It isn't?"

Campbell shook his head. "That was the name of his inventor. Always a common misconception! Now then, Jimmy, what are they saying to you in these *dreams* of yours?"

He shrugged, peered down skittishly and inspected his nails. "D-didn't Andrew… Doctor Turner tell you?"

"He did, but I would prefer to hear it from you!"

Jimmy pressed his knuckles together. "I cannot return to them. Circumstances have… changed… and I must… I must listen."

"I see…" said the doctor. "Sorry about your predicament, kiddo." He turned the corners of his lips sympathetically. "I hear that next week is the big day?" Jimmy nodded, his head still tilted down. "Funerals aren't fun, I'm afraid, but they are part of healing. Doctor Turner tells me you are brave enough to say a few words to honour them both."

"I've tried," he blubbered.

"Well, after our session, get yourself down to the library. I'm sure Doctor Turner will provide his right brain a while!"

Jimmy wiped his cheeks. "I tell you what. If you are still having the same old dream… this time next week, after… after their funeral," he hesitated, "then come back up and see me and we shall combat this together."

"I'm not sure I want them to go."

The doctor frowned, removing his hand. "Don't they disturb you… cause you great harm, distress, disconsolance?"

"Yes. But I am scared. Scared I won't remember. If they go, I've lost them… I'll have, nothing, nobody!"

"I see…"

"I would like to lose the other nightmare, though!"

"There's another?"

Jimmy nodded. He knew what was coming next.

"Please…" said Campbell. "Proceed…"

Jimmy shook his head violently. "I can't… No, n-n-no way!" His mind bulged as his memories threatened to surface.

"Try Jimmy… please." Outside, the sound of blades cutting grass. Stephen must be up. He imagined his eyelids, or lack of. He heard the snipping of the blades and his lids fall like feathers into a bloody mass on the floor. Jimmy got himself in a state, trying to shrug everything away but unable to in the presence of this new stranger. He squirmed in his chair, *Jimmy John Ford, Jimmy John Ford.*

"I d-d-don't want to d-do this anymore!"

"Do what, Jim?" said Campbell calmly.

"T-t-this… I… d-d-don't feel well."

"Jimmy?"

There was a pause.

"Y-yes?"

"You're all right."

"I-I-I know."

"Jimmy?"

"Yes?"

"You're all right."

"I-I know." He flicked his watery eyes to meet the doctor's gaze.

"Jimmy?"

The boy nodded. "Well, it is everything that happened that day. Exactly how it did," he said matter-of-factly.

"Exactly how it did?" said the doubtful doctor.

"The train journey…" He paused. "Wilfred and I in uniform. The drunken captain, the sleeping private, the navy officer, the man wearing the red cross, the couple who'd just stepped out of the cinema, the poem…" he said as if he'd rehearsed a thousand times. Doctor Campbell didn't push him. He waited patiently, his long fingers clasped, X-ray eyes looking through him, analysing the meaning of everything.

"Then the planes… the roar of them over our heads and all the passengers leaning out to look for them in the sky… sometimes I try and trick it, I try and run into the next carriage and give myself up. But they aren't there. They are strangers, passengers I don't know. And I retreat to my compartment, waiting for the inevitable to happen… but in a way, I'm happy with that, I'm happy that I don't find them—"

"Because it means they weren't really there," said the doctor. Jimmy nodded. "Is that when you wake up?" Jimmy shook his head, raising his terrified eyes towards Campbell.

"I can't seem to take any other path. I h-h-hear the h-hatch on the p-plane." Jimmy's body trembled in his chair. "Obviously, I-I couldn't really h-hear that s-s-sound in real life but that's the s-s-scariest s-sound because I know what is c-c-coming n-ne-next. I hear the b-b-bombs f-f-falling through the air. Although, now I know that they are bombs and they take their d-d-damn time about it too! Then nothing... I can't remember, I'm... I'm s-s-sorry!" Jimmy opened his hands like a fan and slapped them over his eyes before drawing his fingers to a close. The doctor had reopened the file and was busy making notes throughout the reconstruction, specifically taking consideration to those words which caused the stammer; those fearful phrases, those imminent fears.

With the war had come new illnesses, new learnings. Campbell had the additional responsibility of determining which soldiers were fit to return to duty. Was he qualified? He certainly thought not. He didn't know which was more exhausting: the patient meetings or the paperwork. He had treated mute privates and stammering officers; mute officers! The first worldly encounter of mass slaughter brought him war neurosis beyond his understanding. He had taught himself new techniques to attempt resolution. Hydrotherapy, talking, dream analysis. He had more patients die on him this year than any other in the history of the asylum. He was determined not to lose any more lives. After all, shouldn't that be any leading doctor's priority?

Jimmy was certainly a unique case. A soldier admitted for epilepsy who, from Campbell's recent observations and understanding of neurosis, seemed to be suffering from something resembling shell shock.

"Huh!" he confirmed aloud, not meaning to let his analysis slip.

Jimmy widened his fingers, so he could just about see the doctor. "Why do you want to cure the soldiers?" asked Jimmy, as if reading Campbell's mind.

"Why?" He had never been asked such a question. Not even by himself.

"Yes. You cure them but then you send them back there, and… well, then they die anyway!"

The doctor paused for a moment. "We don't cure all for the slaughter, you know?! Some get general discharge, so they leave here and go back and contribute in other ways. Mostly to the war effort, in an administration capacity and what have you. They still wish to serve their country. We don't take that away from them."

"But some are cured so that they *can* go back and fight?"

"Sure!" There was a long silence. "It's my… it's our duty, Jimmy."

"Does that make it right?"

"No. It doesn't make it right. But we are only human. Only animals. Animals kill their young if it is for a greater cause."

"Is that what *they* did?"

The doctor reached over to the distressed boy. "Jimmy." He sniffed and squinted his eyes in attempt to hold back the tears. He half-nodded. "You are so very brave. You are nearly there. If you can just finish. Just keep going—"

"I can't!" he screamed. "I won't!" He rocked. "I don't remember!"

"Jimmy," said the doctor in a low, soft whisper. "It's OK, you are OK. I am here, I will be here with you… for this final bit… take me there, Jimmy." He slowly lowered his hands. Campbell could see that his mouth was upturned like a thin crescent moon. Jimmy shook his head.

The doctor didn't push; he had been here before. He clicked the top of his ballpoint pen, and as the nib retreated, he stood tall on his toes.

"I need you to lay on this sofa for me, Jim," he said, patting the rim of a beaten oxblood Chesterfield. The sofa married his bloodshot eyes from many consecutive sleepless nights.

"I-I... I don't think I want to—"

"You don't have to, Jimmy. But, if we don't try, these nightmares, they won't go."

"What are you going to do to me?" he said, beginning to bite his nails.

"I want to try a technique called hypnosis. It won't cause you any harm... physically. I promise you that. It will allow you to rest for a while."

"Rest?"

"Yes. In hypnagogia... between the place of sleeping and awakening."

"No!" Jimmy shook. "I d-d-don't like that p-p-place!"

"You don't like it when you have to face it alone. This time, this time I will be there with you. We'll be strong this time... together!"

Jimmy sat still a while. The sound of the mower outside had ceased and the room carried an air of tranquillity. Birds chirping in the summer sun, the sun splicing tangerine shards in pretty patterns across the floor.

"For Grace," he muttered beneath his breath.

Jimmy stood; he stayed bolt upright for a while. Doctor

Campbell tipped his head for reassurance, his moustache twitched. Jimmy scuttled over towards the sofa. He wiped a flat palm across the fabric, checking for tricks. He sat. His toes, even when tipped, were unable to touch the floor.

"Place your legs up, Jim, make yourself comfortable." The doctor firmly tapped the cracked leather cushions. Jimmy looked at his shoes. "Don't worry about those." He swiped the air. Jimmy felt paranoid, like a fly was watching him from every conceivable angle of the room. He lay down anxiously, flat. "OK, good." Doctor Campbell opened out his jacket and produced a golden pocket watch. "I want you to watch the clock, Jim, very carefully." Doctor Campbell was very aware how easy it would be to put Jimmy under. He knew that he wouldn't even make it to the room at the bottom of the softly carpeted stairway.

He rocked the clock face side to side as he described the deep descent; step by step, number by number. "Eight, another step down... deeper and deeper... Seven, your eyelids are feeling heavy... Six..." Jimmy's pupils darted in time with the pendulum motion. "That's it, let your eyelids close of their own accord. "Five..." Jimmy's eyes now hidden behind his own soft blinds. "Four..." Complete darkness. "Three, that's it, you can see the doorway, just a few steps away now... Two." His lids shifted sideward in REM. "One!" As the doctor suspected, he didn't need to describe what was behind the door; that was all down to Jimmy now.

"Platform nine," he muttered languidly. "I'm waiting. Waiting until they go, so they won't catch me."

"Who, Jimmy, who is going to catch you?"

"They can't see my uniform!" Jimmy's cheeks turned moist; tears were seeping out of his closed lids. "They are holding hands," he smiled. Doctor Campbell took his seat. By the time he looked back at the boy, his face was strained, distressed. He squealed ever so softly. "Don't!" he warned. "Don't get off!" His head was tilting to the side as if looking through the carriage window. "They're coming, they're here, they're knocking." His head ruffled against the leather sofa.

"Who's there? Who's coming?" asked the doctor.

Jimmy's voice transformed. "Spooking, maiming, bleeding... NO!" he yelled, tears tumbling. "Don't go out there, they're coming!"

"Who, Jimmy, who?"

"The Germans, the Gothas, the grizzly bears!" He was shouting now, terrified. "I hear them, they're coming. Don't go out there! Come back, come back!"

"What's happening now, Jimmy?"

"*Whiiiizzzz. Bang. Boooom!*" he yelled from the depths of his throat. "*Whiiiizzzz. Bang. Boooom! Whiiiizzzz. Bang. Boooom!*"

"What is happening now, Jimmy? What can you see?" said Campbell.

"Don't get off! Don't get off!" Jimmy's body started convulsing violently. "They're coming, they're coming! *Whiiiizzzz. Bang. Boooom! Whiiiizzzz. Bang. Boooom! Whiiiizzzz. Bang. Boooom!*" He stiffened, trapped inside his nostrils was the scent of smog. Two coiled spines flashed in front of his eyes, two marred bodies with white snaked spines. Diamonds. The glint of shimmering diamonds. Wilfred's face covered in blood and ash. A surge of energy gurned in the cracks of his cheeks. Again, he heard the hatch opening, the whiz as the bomb tumbled out. "*Whiiiizzzz. Bang. Boooom! Whiiiizzzz. Bang. Boooom! Whiiiizzzz. Bang. Boooom!*" Again, he tasted the blast.

Jimmy's body rolled off the sofa and onto the heavy floor. His lips ceased but his body kept rocking. Blue veins pulsated down his neck; red blood trickled from his torn tongue. The doctor charged across the room, swept a cushion from the sofa and placed it under Jimmy's restless skull. He grabbed several more and attempted to hem him in. He turned him on his side. Foam, bile, blood. Silence.

1914

CHAPTER SIX

GRACE BERGMAN

G EORGE FORD HAD ALWAYS possessed a certain quality which allowed him to speak profoundly, without the intent of overwhelming even a child. He wasn't eloquent, or even silver-tongued, but his words carried subtle messages of kindness and warmth, and never offence. George was solicitous, and yearned for life, for both himself and for Jimmy. Life, and a pace of life he achieved with little thought. One which was ladled in a haze of contentment; a contentment without effort. In all his militance, he also had morals, proving that a fine balance could be struck between the two.

So, when Jimmy had finished regaling his story, he simply said, "Asylums are special places you go to get a plaster on your brain. You see, Jimmy, the mind is a complicated machine and sometimes, some people become ill, not physically ill, but mentally so. Life gets too much. Some poor folk are born like it. And soldiers, well, they're not exempt. They get ill too, not wounded on the outside but mentally scarred on the inside from the terrors they have seen. That's war, you see, kiddo; it frightens the bejesus out of some people, and they need places like that up there to get themselves better." He had then gone on to ward Jimmy away from repeating such encounters, to which Jimmy himself had agreed before the words had passed George's lips. And that was it. Nothing more needed saying on the matter.

Monday morning, Jimmy heard the school bell ring out as he climbed the hill at the bottom of Junction Road. He was late because George had accompanied him for half the journey to purchase a profusion of flowers from the little station florist. Jimmy was his delivery boy and he wasn't hiding his embarrassment well.

Amongst this prize-worthy bunch were carnations: white for luck and deep red for affection. White anemones, snowdrops, red poppies, berries and scented bouvardia. At centre-stage, standing tall and proud, was a single lavender rose; love at first sight. The little tag dangled and danced with the morning breeze. It read:

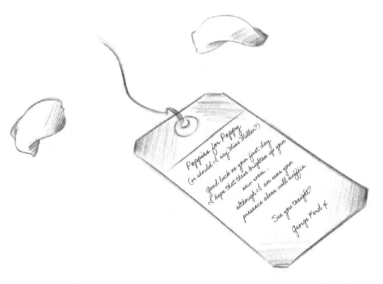

Poppies for Poppy.
(or should I say Miss Miller?)
Good luck on your first-day.
I hope that these brighten up your
new room...
although I am sure your
presence alone will suffice.

See you tonight?

George Ford x

Miss Miller had already written her name on the blackboard as Jimmy entered the raucous room. He placed the flowers down at her desk, his red face matching the colour of those poppy heads. Accompanied by a roar of laughter and points from his classroom friends, he marched, head low like an ashamed soldier. Except, this soldier was not wearing uniform; no one at the school had to.

Himself and Wilfred shared a double desk with a planked seat in the last row. During the warmer months, Jimmy preferred being at the back of the tiered classroom with over fifty schoolboy haircuts in front of him. His back was supported by the wall and it was easy to nod off if obliged. It was also his favourite spot in the cinema, but not because he wanted to sleep there. On days like today, though, with the early-morning walk of shame and the temperature dropping, he wished, unlike most soldiers, that he could have been a little closer to the front and to the fire.

With chalk in hand, Miss Miller smiled over towards her flowers. Her straight, white teeth, with that forbidden gap, accentuated her prettiness. She could breathe in the dreamy, fragrant smell of flora from where she stood. Poppy wanted to stop time completely and take them all in, sight and smell. She hoped to nurture them with pride and arrange them within a prime position in her home. If these flowers were any reflection of who *she* was, then George would be a very lucky man indeed.

"Nice one, Jim. You took the tension off my trousers!" thanked a blushing Wilfred, showing off his humiliating crotch rip as Jimmy approached the desk.

"Anytime, Wilf."

"Good morning, class," bleated Poppy.

"Good morning, Miss Miller," the boys all sang back in chorus.

"That's… right… I *am* Miss Miller, your new… teacher." Poppy, with her hair tied like a walnut whip, was aware that she was stumbling, posing in front of the blackboard which had her own name etched on it. "So… I know you have had a disjointed week back. Mr Montrose… he is fighting for us… over there."

"I heard he killed seven men on his first day, Miss," Paul called proudly from the middle row.

"I heard fifteen," said Louis.

"Apparently, he's at the front now, so the war won't be on much longer, Miss. You don't have to worry about that," yelled Willie, the smallest and squeakiest of the class.

Poppy smiled sweetly at her newly devoted clan. "Well, I am sure Mr Montrose will do us all proud and be back

before you know it… But for today, we have geography."
The class let out a unified sigh.

It was apparent before long that Miss Miller was a
different kind of teacher. A good one. For a start *she doesn't
have that white foam in the corner of her mouth when she
speaks*, thought Jimmy. Miss Miller had gone to the effort of
crafting a sketch of a world map which was now pinned to
the wall, nestled between a print of the vast British Empire
and a photograph of King George V. Each pupil, one by
one, had to select a named country from the box and pin
it to the correct place within the outlined parameters. The
next task was to select a correlating piece of card which
listed the country's capital city. The game would go on until
the entire world was laid out in front of them.

Jimmy observed from the back row as Miss Miller
called out each boy in turn and dedicated equal time and
effort to them respectively. Poppy took down their name
and if they struggled with the assignment, provided them
with stereotypical clues or word associations. Some of
which were surprisingly comical and witty. She was far
from the shy girl he had witnessed at the shop. *Maybe it
was the flowers*, he thought.

After their turn was up, each boy dawdled for a moment
just to spend a little more time next to that iron stove with
its embers. Or was it to be closer to her and that dancing
dress? No music was playing, yet she always appeared to be
swaying.

Wilfred stooped over their desk and used his arms to
push himself up. He plodded his way through the sea of
heads towards the front. You can tell a lot by someone's

walk. Some people look like they are floating on a breeze, others like the breeze could blow them away. Wilfred neither floated gingerly, nor could he be pushed. He must have come into being that way, the calf of a cow slipping out the dark and into existence. He must have landed on those thick legs and trudged off in the first direction he fancied. The fact that Wilfred was so barrelled in the belly only exacerbated his narrow shoulders; he barely had them. *He could have been born in a tin*, thought Jimmy.

Miss Miller let no one feel silly, even when Wilfred held up Russia, the biggest nation of all, and tried to squeeze it, between porky fingers, into the Antarctic. He then drew the piece of card displaying Paris as its capital city. *Perhaps leaving school this year isn't such a good idea.*

Finally, it was Jimmy's turn. Up he stood to the toots and whistles from the rowdy bunch. They certainly hadn't forgotten his earlier gesture. Poppy looked concerned and was about to intervene. But then, he did the unexpected. Planting down one knee, he said "'I'm not afraid, I should fold my arms and admire you. I'm speaking very seriously'…" Jimmy let a smile crack through and Poppy's face relaxed. Silence filled the room. "'What I wish to say to you, is that I find I'm in love with you'."

The barking grew and subsided into applause. Miss Miller, grinning, ushered him to stand. "Portrait of a Lady," he obliged.

Jimmy knew enough by now that if you let anything get to you in front of this herd, you would be the lonely sheep at the back, getting your legs nipped by hungry, wild wolves.

"No looking, Jim," Miss Miller reminded him as he

closed his eyes and reached into the box. "I don't trust you, Jimmy Ford," she added vivaciously, placing her soft, perfumed hands across his closed lids. For a moment, time stopped.

Jimmy recognised the shape the instant his eyes were open: *Germany!* In quick succession, the nation was placed, and the capital city of Berlin found. The pack booed and hissed. The game wasn't the same after that. With every nation pulled, the class would cheer or curse depending if the country was allied or an enemy. It was an education and a hoot, nonetheless.

There were three assigned monitors in Jimmy's class, on account of their good-natured souls, as Montrose put it. Simon was ink monitor. Every Friday he filled up the inkwells with a prodigious tub of black liquid. Joseph was blackboard monitor, so when required he would scrub off the day's knowledge with a rub of hairs from the large duster head. Jimmy was assigned the proud bell-ringer.

Every playtime, lunchtime or home time, Jimmy would walk into each classroom and tug at the string which operated the handbell. His face was getting famous amongst the girls' classes because he was always the bearer of good news, their saviour from the spinsters, an early release to head home and exert themselves on their chores. Some even worked the land; he had seen them in farming attire as they left the school gates.

Jimmy would always tarry a moment longer than necessary before tugging at that first cord. For just that instant, the corridors were completely his. He felt powerful as he patrolled them like a night watchman. Today, it was the smell of mutton stew and Atora suet pudding which crept into his nostrils from the nearby scullery. *Wilfred would be pleased*; he could have Jimmy's mutton. Jimmy had lost his taste for meat since George rationed it at home and more importantly, he knew that Wilfred would be grumpy if he didn't eat.

Jimmy peered through the nearest door into the girls' classroom. *Such curious creatures*, he thought. He inspected the rows of delicate white faces, some peppered with freckles, others sporting buns with big bowed ribbons. Many of the girls wore pinafores of white cotton. His eyes stopped. Her stare was hooked on his. It was as though she was looking right through the surface of him, digging deeper than soil, scratching at his soul. He had seen her many times before, but today she was the prettiest of all. On one side of her delicate face, her auburn hair draped down her shoulder. On the other, it was tucked behind her ear.

Their moment was cut short as Jimmy saw the duster head fly in her direction. He gasped and stepped out of sight.

"Daydreaming again, Grace?" rumbled the spinster's voice. Every teacher had their own armoury. For Miss Dakers it was the duster; a chalk-filled wooden grenade which exploded and covered you in surprised terror. In many ways, it was worse than a real grenade, as you never got a five-second warning. Miss Finnemore had a cane, beat thrice across the sensitive palm. It hurt like hell to hold a pen after that one. Mr Montrose never did. "Lose temper and you lose power," he would whisper in a controlled manner. Respect reaped far more rewards than fear and that respect was earnt. Not everyone saw it that way, just those who knew something more than everybody else.

Jimmy peered back around the door into Grace's blushing face, her cheeks lightly powdered in chalk. She gave a slight sideward smile as she dabbed at the settled snow. *Boy, she is pretty.* She had an inimitability which made her so. A cherub's face, plumped cheeks and lips, and eyes like crocodiles. She wore a modest bow in her wavy, auburn hair, she didn't need it any larger.

"She's perfect!" whispered Jimmy.

The stillness of tongues was building. The girls knew Jimmy was outside and when Jimmy was outside, they knew that meant lunchtime – freedom. Jimmy ruffled his brown hair away from his eyes and reached in to tug the bell. The sound was immediately replaced with the shrill of an air raid horn. Grace giggled at the irony and for that moment, Jimmy joined her.

The air raid shelter was fringed either side with slatted benches. Boys one side, girls the other; two hundred and fifty of them in all. The spinsters scattered themselves around the exits to ensure that no child escaped. One may hope to have the world outside to themselves for a moment.

"Think of the endless possibilities if every street, shop, stall, pool and cinema was vacant?" Jimmy told Wilfred. The tin roof pattered with rain and this made Wilfred's muggy face perspire. Jimmy loved wet weather; it meant most people stayed inside and he could have the land for himself like an avaricious king.

The entire right row was holding out in front of them

this month's copy of *The Boy's Own Paper*. There were images of brave British Tommys posing with one leg on a parapet and rifle in hand. Their daring dogs at their feet, each collar adorned with medals. The dogs were barking into the faces of cowardly German officers. The Germans wore dark black and were sometimes just silhouettes with no visible facial features at all. The enemy; nothing human about that.

Some of the boys were giggling in groups at the jokes and poems. Others sat silently with their tongues flopping to one side, attempting to conquer crosswords with words like 'Ferdinand', 'Wilhelm', 'Churchill' and 'Lenin'. There were puzzles and trench mazes you had to escape with your pencil after a German invasion. One group of boys sat on the floor cross-legged around a board game, 'Kill Kiel'. The purpose was to sink German submarines with sea mines before they intercepted supplies heading for British land.

Jimmy and Wilfred were squeezed in the middle of the mob, taking it in turns to play trench football. The aim of the game was simple, but the game itself was very tricky. At least Wilfred thought so. You had a small, steel ball which was placed in the bottom corner of the wooden casing. The player had to hoist the board upwards to release the ball into the trench maze. From there, one would have to navigate around the entire German opposition, avoiding the dummy holes in the grid. Falling down a hole before reaching the Kaiser would mean instant loss. A child would have to balance the board just enough to avoid dropping below, steering themselves around the likes of Von Kluck, Von Hindenberg and Count Zeppelin. Routing the ball successfully into the Kaiser's mouth meant a goal was scored.

So far Jimmy was winning two games to nil. On Jimmy's turn, Wilfred would watch him intently to see if he could learn the skill and technique from the master. When it was Wilfred's go, Jimmy looked around the shelter and observed the delicate faces of the girls as they read their own papers. Unlike the boys, these were filled with images and advice on knitting, needlework and culinary tips.

One girl caught Jimmy's eye; it was Grace.

Grace's green eyes flicked up towards Jimmy and back down at her magazine. Her cheeks topped up red like a wine glass; cheeks like speckled poached pears. Was she flush because she was caught by Jimmy looking at him or because she caught Jimmy glancing back at her? Neither child could tell, but in the dank shelter, both felt the spark.

"Got the Kaiser!" Wilfred hurled with excitement.

"2-1," Jimmy muttered, eyes fixed on Grace. It was as though he was trying to connect the freckles that had been delicately sprinkled over her face to make a pretty picture. Not that he needed to; the picture as it was would do him just fine.

"Your turn, Jim," Wilfred interrupted, shoving the board clumsily into his ribs.

"You get another go if you score a goal, remember, Wilf?"

"Well, I wouldn't know… that was my first."

Jimmy observed as Grace's fingers toyed with her plaited hair. It seemed funny to Jimmy; her face was youthful, yet her mannerisms ran far beyond her years. She was peering at the page describing gastronomic tips, but the language may as well have been in Latin: 'Win the War Recipes'. She wasn't seeing words at all.

Jimmy bit his lip and felt the bones in his body grow. "Waste not, want not." He smiled cheekily as he cosied the space around her. You could tell that he was excited, like a dog with the longest tail. The two girls sat either side of Grace giggled and dispersed like the gossiping tide. "I'm Jim," he finally offered like he had never questioned anything in his life. "Jimmy Ford,"

"Grace, Grace Bergman." The girl beamed with a sense of timidity.

"Nasty weapon, that duster," Jimmy dived right in, looking directly into the girl's eyes. He noticed that one of them was emerald green, the other brown like an almond; complete heterochromia. Grace stroked the side of her blushing cheeks to check for chalk. From beyond the powder emerged a soft, brown mole.

"You mind if I…" He gestured at the bench beside her. She nodded, peering up at the confident boy with his untamed curls.

There were two hollow knocks against the heavy oak door.

"You mind if I…" George said presumptuously as he entered her empty classroom. You couldn't tell that he was excited, more composed, like a dog with a docked tail.

"Where shall it be for tonight…?"

Miss Miller turned. George paused, speechless for a moment, enamoured by her delicate beauty. "Buying a lady some flowers immediately denotes dinner, does it?"

"I-I… er…"

"Well, it does," she added playfully. "That was very sweet of you, George."

He took a deep breath in. "I heard the raid as I was coming down the hill. I expected you to be in the shelter… spinsters by invite only, is it?"

"George!" She chuckled. "No. It was my discretion. Too much to plan for this afternoon… I'm not so good at teaching carpentry."

"There won't be this afternoon if a bomb drops."

"And why aren't you in the shelter then, George?"

George lifted some wood, chisels and saws from the front trays and began to help distribute them on to the desks. "Can't worry about such things, can you? Otherwise you'll spend your whole life worrying… me, I want to be living!"

"I feel like I've known you a thousand years, George." He smirked through his response.

"My Jimbo still seated here?"

Poppy nodded. George took some chalk from the board and, under Miss Miller's watchful gaze, proceeded to smother it under the desk where his son would soon sit.

"You can't do that, George—"

"Miss Miller, please… minor details, my love. Jimbo will know I've been here… it's a sort of endearing family tradition."

"George!"

"Why, back in my school years a teacher would get a bird in his drawer… that was a surprise to Alfred, I tell you!"

Poppy raised her delicate eyebrows in amazement. "Alfred, from your shop?"

George nodded. "Can't you tell he was a teacher?"

Poppy's dimples showed. "Yes… but yours, George?!"

"Once, we snuck a friend from a different school into class, he was none the wiser for two days!" George returned from his childish, crouched position, still brimming with nostalgia. "Time?"

"12:15."

George tutted. "…to collect you, Miss Miller!"

Poppy blushed. "6pm."

"From here?"

"No, George, I need to freshen up."

"You look ravishing."

"George…" she said, partly amused.

"So, 4:15 at the gate," he instructed. "Don't be late, Miss Miller, places close early these days!" He placed the chalk into her palm, rolled her fingers over and dropped a kiss onto her knuckle. Just like that, he was gone. They had said everything worth saying.

Miss Miller hurled the duster towards the closed door and chortled like a schoolgirl.

"We have a new teacher… Miss Miller…" Jimmy smirked childishly as he took his seat. "Can't ever imagine her throwing a duster." Jimmy didn't really have a plan as such; his heart had led him over here and your heart was the only thing to follow, George had always told him. "My Pa, he likes her. Made me bring in flowers for him this morning—"

"What about your ma?" Grace asked innocently.

"Well… she, sort of… died," said Jimmy. "It's OK,

though," he added quickly to avoid the sympathy. "I was too little. Why do women… girls, love them so much?"

"Your dad?"

"Ha! No… flowers."

"Oh, sorry." She retreated in embarrassment at the sentiment. "It's the memory of why they were bought in the first place, I suppose."

Jimmy wanted her to speak forever. He noticed the tip of her nose twitched every time she did so. She had the most perfect turned-up nose.

"But then they just curl up, their colour fades and they just…" Jimmy gestured with a limp hand.

"Why, yes, but it's like anything, I guess. When they're alive, they're… beautiful."

"Flowers?" Jimmy questioned wittingly. Grace became a shrinking violet. "Do you ration much?"

"Sorry?" she replied in a daze. Jimmy placed his finger on the magazine pages.

"I-I… er…"

"We've started to. Pa says they need as much meat as they can get, the soldiers."

"Yes. Well, we haven't really, not yet. We do bits in other ways, I mean. Knitting socks, mufflers, balaclavas, that kind of thing. We also grow vegetables and fruit, the vacant land beside the school. And my sis, she works as a clerical worker…" Jimmy nodded for her to continue. Her voice was smoother than the lady running the switchboard. Jimmy read from her lips, nestled between those cushioned cheeks. It was like every word she said lingered and Jimmy lingered with it until it finally fell and that sweet nectar seeped out of her. "And... I-I-I'm in the girl guides. We package up clothing from Fords & Cox and send them—"

"Well I never," Jimmy interrupted.

"What?"

"That's Pa and Alfred's shop. He's my uncle. Well, I call him that..."

"I see."

"They've started making parachutes, so you'll be getting your hands on them soon enough," Jimmy added as if undertaking himself a grubby deal. Although it had only been a month, the pair knew little of life *before the war*.

"I've carried stretchers and learnt first aid. Not had to use those skills yet, though, thank God."

"Do you believe?"

"In war?"

"In God."

"Oh... well, yes, of course, we're Jewish, you see... we believe in the shawl's afterlife."

"Even during war?"

"Especially!"

Jimmy hadn't spoken to a Jewish girl before. Whatever it meant, he liked how it felt.

"Pa says the only fondness he feels for religion is the pilgrimage. Pa says that the person... people behind writing the Bible must have one hell of an imagination... and had years and years to do it in!" Jimmy blushed a little, noticing Grace's lack of reply. "S-sorry, I didn't mean to offend." She raised her hand; no offence caused. "But if there was a God, would there be a war on at all?" Grace folded back her book. She was beyond pretending to read. "Pa doubts that there is. He says that mules probably think God is a mule."

"I don't understand," Grace said, trying her damnedest to.

"Well, you see, if there are so many gods with so many different rules, how are we meant to keep up and know how to act?"

"We don't believe in a number of gods. We just believe in one," Grace said, proudly reciting her learnings.

"Yes, but then all other religions claim that they have their own gods, so there ends up being rather a lot of them... all with different orders."

"Hmm... I never thought of it that way."

"Plus, would God then be on the side of us Tommys or the Bosch?"

"Both, I guess."

"But how can he be on both?" Jimmy chuckled, remembering the argument George and Alfred had at the shop.

"Hmm... You're clever, Jim, I thought you just rang the bell." She winked.

"I like that job," Jimmy said honestly. "It gets me out of class, and it seems everyone is always happy to see me."

"Yes, I suppose they are... you mean dinner." Grace winked again. *I must stop winking*, she thought. "I've worked on the allotments too, you know?" she mentioned proudly, a second chance to repair earlier nerves. "I haven't helped out in the munitions yet. Ma says I'm too young to be a canary!"

Jimmy nodded. He didn't want her to change from exactly the girl she was now. "Pa wants me in the scouts. I can camp and cook beans anytime, though."

"I think they may do a little more than cook beans.

There's a boy down my street, he acts as a messenger during the raids and he collects eggs for wounded soldiers!"

"Eggs?" Jimmy questioned.

"Yep. And in our first aid class last week they acted as our patients!"

That clever pervert, he thought. Jimmy would lay still and get his temperature checked anytime she wanted.

"Pa has some come up the shop on occasion to cart away the khaki... maybe that's where he got the idea for me to enlist?" Grace nodded along. "There's an aircraft factory in Hammersmith making biplanes. I want to fly, you see, and that would be a good start. Pa says he doesn't want me going into the city, though... I feel older than twelve most days, don't you?"

Grace gave a nod as if she knew exactly what he meant. "You're brave, wanting to be a pilot," she said. "Don't you read the casualty lists?"

"Not much." Jimmy shrugged. "Pa says it's only the names of dead officers. He always says, what about the other men who are dying for our country every day? Officers' coffins are screwed down too, you know? Not nailed like soldiers' ones." Grace pondered in exquisite wonder. "Besides, I won't be a war pilot when this all ends. I could enrol younger, but not for a few years yet and by then... it will all be over."

"You mean by the time you've grown out a moustache?"

Both children giggled at the thought.

They had wandered in and out of each other's minds unannounced. Grace had gained no end of confidence since Jimmy had sat beside her. She felt more her peculiar self than she had ever done before, her shrinking violet had been watered and was budding.

Jimmy studied the lines of her face. He looked hard, so he knew he could never forget it. "Would you like to fly with me?" he said boldly.

"Jimmy Ford. The day you become a pilot, I'll be your first… observer… observer, that's right, isn't it?" Jimmy's spine tingled. She knew his name… his full name! And she knew what an observer was! What a team they would be. Jimmy turned fanciful, the fragrance from Grace's almond hair filling his cockpit as it danced with the wind at 10,000 feet. "Is each plane different?" Grace asked. "To fly, I mean."

"Yes, I guess they are. I haven't actually—"

Paul, a cocky boy in Jimmy's class, stood up on his bench opposite them both and began to chant in that unmethodical way children sing:

"A silly German sausage
Dreamt Napoleon he'd be,
Then he went and broke his promise,
It was made in Germany…"

His screeching voice teared through the shelter and teared apart Jimmy's daydreams.

"Paul's balls haven't dropped," he said freely. Grace erupted in cheery laughter. She was prettier than any flower when she smiled. Jimmy wondered if that conversation could have gone any better. He pondered whether there was a Grace and Jimmy somewhere else in this world, having a conversation which was going nowhere near as well. With that breezy thought, the pair and the rest of the children joined in the song:

> "...He shook hands with Britannia
> And eternal peace he swore,
> Naughty boy, he talked of peace
> While he prepared for war.
> He stirred up little Serbia
> To serve his dirty tricks
> But naughty nights at Liege
> Quite upset this Dirty Dick.
> His luggage labelled 'England'
> And his programme nicely set,
> He shouted, 'First stop Paris,'
> But he hasn't got there yet."

Jimmy wasn't thinking of the words, rather just going through the motions. He looked towards Grace and singled out her soft, sweet voice. He was lost in those crocodile eyes of hers, lit like beautiful green lanterns. He could live inside them. Except if he did, he would only ever see her face from her reflection in the mirror.

The spinsters joined in the parade and the whole shelter shook with patriotism:

> "...For Belgium put the kibosh on the Kaiser;
> Europe took the stick and made him sore;
> On his throne it hurts to sit,
> And when John Bull starts to hit,
> He will never sit upon it anymore."

George heard the choir as he clambered his way back up the high street towards his shop. He would have been happy making this same trip many times or more. He turned and looked back down over the town from the top of its highest crest. He breathed out a long-contented sigh and thought of his comrades back in the Boar. The clang of bells rang out and the boy scouts sounded their bugles, highlighting the *all-clear* following the raid.

There are so many ways something can be beautiful. It was as though he hadn't seen life in such colour before. He thought of Poppy and how he wanted to climb under the floorboards with her and stay there a thousand years until their bones were dusted off by archaeologists.

Long-limbed George took a detour towards the music hall. He planned to collect two tickets for the evening's performance of singers, comedians and conjurors. A fundraising event. All for a good cause. It was sure to be a flag day of some kind.

Suspended against the brick of the music hall hung a beige poster adorning the face of Field Marshal Lord Kitchener, his right hand raised and his finger pointing beyond the frame. In chalky red letters read the words: 'BRITONS, JOIN YOUR COUNTRY'S ARMY. GOD SAVE THE KING'.

"Me?" laughed George, pointing to himself. "No, sir," he barked. If tonight he was pulled back up on the stage to enlist, with Poppy by his side… could he say yes? Surely, he couldn't consider it?! Not even with the incentive of a kiss from a pretty drafting lass.

George skipped along as though he had no more

questions about his life or any other. Poppy had left her mark on his brain like glinting myriads of diamonds. He would wait until he was forced to die. He had her to think of now, and he had his boy. For this was surely the centre of his universe now.

CHAPTER SEVEN

PEAR DROPS

A s the bell to the entrance chimed, a sweet waft pervaded the air. Jimmy held the door open like a true gentleman and lead them through the haze of sugar which hung like a cloud. As they meandered, colour exploded from the glass jars which lined the oak Dickensian shelves. Mrs Walker – whose name was ironic given that she spent her entire life static – stood tapping her long, bony fingers against the rubber mat, tormenting the three small children. A white witch against a kaleidoscope of colour. The brass scales glinted in the falling sun which cast golden squares across her sharp, serrated nose. Her hair was black, thin and scraggly. She was just missing the broom.

Mrs Walker didn't speak, she simply frowned and tutted her disappointment at the time it took children to choose their sweets. When it came, and when the children drummed up the courage to ask, she grunted orders at poor Mr Walker, a dumpy man with a dimply face and grey moustache. Mr Walker spent *his* entire life running behind the counter and hoisting his stout body up the ladder, sweating to reach the requested jars. Mrs Walker never took her eyes from the terrified children. She simply stood open-handed, awaiting the jar to be placed there by Mr Walker. When it had, she would turn its lid without even a glimpse in its direction. Then, she would grunt at the children to repeat the quantity and begin pouring the contents onto the brass scales. When the dial was satisfactory and not a quarter ounce over, she would place her flat, bony hand out and cough until the exact money was passed. Only then would she tip the scale's contents into the brown paper bag and order Mr Walker to roll and seal its top. In case they hesitated, Mrs Walker would point with one scrawny finger in the direction of the door. It was time for the children to leave.

Mrs Walker's face curdled when she saw Jimmy, almost to the point that she was disgusted by the smell of him. Brave and boisterous children were the smelliest of all.

"I told you they would have pear drops!" said Jimmy, placing his hands down on the counter. Mrs Walker sneered. "See… right up there, top shelf, far right!" Mr Walker sighed, wiping his soaked brow with a dirtied white handkerchief.

"Four ounces, please," said Grace innocently. Mrs Walker stared at the girl like she was looking through her flesh. She quivered; Jimmy intervened.

"That's all!" he said boldly. Mrs Walker turned her attention to the feral boy, her look showing she despised his very existence. She reluctantly obliged, grunting her order at poor Mr Walker. He caught his rasping breath and with his portly legs, ascended the ladder. Mr Walker was not built for the job, or, at least, the shop wasn't built to accommodate his short limbs. Once at the top of the ladder, it took his full effort to reach the jar; all the while Mrs Walker didn't take an eye off the children. Once weighed and bagged, the jar was replaced; Mr Walker had returned to his former position on firm ground and that's when Jimmy put in his request.

"Actually…" He lingered. Mrs Walker scorned. "I think *I* would like some sweets. Another four ounces of pear drops, please!"

Mr Walker groaned. He looked for confirmation in his wife's narrow, black eyes. She snorted her long, sharp nose and back up the ladder he went. Grace watched Jimmy with a knowing smile. Mrs Walker caught this moment, so Grace bit down on her bottom lip and quickly dispersed her grin. Once the sweets were weighed and the jar back in its position, Jimmy proceeded to spend his life savings, one small order at a time. It was executed perfectly. He ordered sherbet lemons from the top left shelf, aniseed twists from the middle right, Fruit Pastilles and gums from the bottom, Liquorice Allsorts, cough candy, rhubarb and custard from the top, candy floss, marshmallows, wine gums… and that was just the sweets. Poor Mr Walker almost had a coronary. His sweat could have filled one of those jars – two of those jars!

"That will be all." Jimmy smirked at Mrs Walker. "Although… perhaps…" Mr Walker clutched at the large mass of fat around his chest. Mrs Walker expressed sheer antipathy. *You just dare,* said her face. Jimmy drew a breath. "No, actually… that's it." Mr Walker gasped with relief. "Oh, but what are these?" mocked Jimmy. "I'll take one Dairy Milk, one Fry's and one… sumptuous *Turkish* delight, please… oh, and one Bournville…"

Mrs Walker's flattened palm formed a stop sign until she had finished counting the coins with the other. Jimmy had purposefully passed over the shortest change he had in exchange for more sweets than he could carry, let alone eat. The old witch lowered, flipped out her palm again and coughed. Jimmy was perfectly aware he was six and three short.

"I guess… get rid of the pear drops?" he said, attempting to contain his amusement.

Mr Walker fell to the floor and the witch outstretched her finger in the direction of the door.

Both children erupted in giggles the moment they met with the fresh air.

"She should be tied to a chair and lowered into a lake," said Jimmy.

"I thought she was going to boil her cauldron and eat you!"

"It doesn't make sense. Why would she work in a sweetshop if she hates children so much?"

"That's what I mean, the witch from Hansel and Gretel lived in a gingerbread house!" said Grace, almost skipping along beside him.

The pair travelled across the cobbles, through the chapel ruins and sat on a bench outside the Palace cinema.

"This spot is perfect," said Jimmy, gesturing for Grace to take a seat beside his chalky trousers. She lifted her white underdress and obliged. She rustled with her brown bag and popped a pink pear drop into her mouth. Jimmy watched her plump lips like he was envious of the sugary sweet and the journey it would take.

"It is perfect, isn't it?" She smiled sweetly. "In fact, I couldn't think of a more perfectly placed bench."

Jimmy and her locked eyes and giggled.

"It has it all," he said. "Truly... I mean, the cinema there, a slice of history here..." He gestured towards the chapel ruins. "Over there... the library."

"The library?"

"Between that and the cinema... the two most important parts of town."

"Jimmy Ford, I never know when you're being serious."

"Well, I am," he said, adopting his aristocratic voice. "I read rather a lot, I'll have you know!" Grace giggled. Jimmy dropped the act. "Mr Montrose, before he left for the front, he arranged for me to take an English scholarship at the Brentwood School over there."

"He did?"

Jimmy nodded proudly.

"Well…" Grace dropped her head.

"What is it?" said Jimmy, leaning inwards.

"At least it's close…"

"Sure, it's close. Everything in this town is close."

"I'm happy for you, Jim," said Grace, her soft, freckly face giving more away than her words.

"It's just a start," he said. "But it's a very reputable

school and once I've got my scholarship, well, it could be the beginning of me."

"Of your writing career?"

"Yes… and leaving here."

"Brentwood? But, Jimmy, I don't want you to leave, not yet, promise me. Promise me you won't leave without me!"

"I won't leave this town without you, Grace, I promise!"

Grace took her eyes in his. She was satisfied. "Now…" she said. "What on Earth are you going to do with all those sweets?"

"You can have them."

"Me? No, no…" she said, waving her hands, the outline of her arms and their fair hairs flickering in the last of the day's rays. "I only like pear drops!"

"Then… I guess I won't have any teeth left when you see me at school on Monday!" Grace chuckled; her soft sweet mole fell between her dimple as she did so. "What do *you* want to do, after school, I mean?"

Grace shrugged. "Well, I told you about my sister. She's a clerical worker. She's in the city, works the typewriter and everything. And she runs the switchboard!"

"Is that—"

"What I want to do? No! I think I want to be a nurse. Help… people."

"I can see that," said Jimmy, smiling.

"You can?"

"A Vera Brittain or Edith Cavell… certainly!"

Grace blushed. "My idols," she said.

"Or…"

"What is it?"

"No. It's nothing."

"Jimmy Ford, I demand that you tell me."

Jimmy didn't need much convincing. "Wilfred and I, last week, we crossed the viaduct and explored the asylum, up there on Warley Hill."

"You… you went… *there*?" Grace was astonished; her voice almost quivered.

"You know it?"

She nodded.

"We had to hide in the bushes, and there was this doctor, two of them, in fact. They were talking about a patient there. An officer who had lost his voice. He was suffering from… ah, what do they call it…? Shell shock!"

"Oh my, I'm not sure I could stomach that, Jim. I want to treat wounds, you can see."

"Pa says that's not always the case during war!" Grace nodded sensitively. "You know, I lost my marble there—"

"I bet you did!" laughed Grace.

"I'm serious! Buck… he was a wolf, beautiful, he was."

"Tell me more about it, Jim."

"Well, he was a sulphide, silver—"

"No, Jim, not your marble, the asylum!"

"Oh, right… well, not much more to tell, really. First there was a man in white rags in the garden, he was raking, a lot! Then he was sort of collected, taken back inside by a nurse. Then there were the graves—"

"Graves?"

"Yes."

"Patients?"

"I'm not so sure, they seemed to be staff, mainly; laundresses and labourers who built the place. I'm not sure where the patients were… the ones who die there." The pair sat pensively a moment. "Although, Officer Letchfield, he wasn't one of them. He was alive in the end after all. Wilfred and I, we found a letter, you see, that's why we were there, why I was there in the first place. We collect things, things that are thrown from the train window… over the viaduct."

"You collect things?"

"Buttons and cap badges mainly, rank insignias…"

"From the soldiers?"

"Passengers. We find all sorts in that brook. And then one day last week, there it came: the unfinished letter, written by a soldier on his way to war."

"Who was it written to?"

"His wife, Katherine. They have a baby on its way." Jimmy smiled, remembering his friend's interest in the unborn child. "In the letter, he wrote about Officer Letchfield. He was her brother, I think… is her brother. He mentioned he was surrounded by madmen, and, well…"

"So you read this letter and thought it would be a good idea to investigate?" Jimmy shrugged. "Fascinating," smiled Grace.

"But he's got shell shock. I guess he is no use to anybody now."

"I wonder…" said Grace.

"Yes," said Jimmy. "I wonder that too." She frowned. "If he will ever return. If his mind will ever come back to the body it's in."

Grace fell into the boy's blue eyes. "The unknown soldier."

"But you know his name?!"

"Not Officer Letchfield. The writer, of the letter. He never finished it, so we will never know who he was." The two of them sat silently a while, watching the wide oak doors of the Palace cinema open and close, squealing as punters passed through. "Oh, but I am sure you will make a fine nurse," he said. Grace turned and faced him. "You never know, you might end up healing one of my wounds."

"Jimmy, and where would that wound be?"

The feral boy gestured to the inside of his thigh. Grace laughed, shoving him. "Oh, I almost forgot," he said. "There was a boy too... at one of the windows... a boy, in white!"

"A boy? Oh, Jimmy, no! No more." She fanned away the thought.

He laughed, catching her eyes in his. "Here," he said, rummaging through the brown paper bags and removing a green Fruit Pastel from one.

"I said I don't like—"

"Hold on..." He pulled a soft brown Allsort from another. He put one of each over his eyes.

"Jimmy Ford... are you trying to impersonate me? Because I don't think that is very funny!"

He quickly lowered the sweets from his vision so that he could read her real eyes. Grace tilted her head back, her mouth widened with laughter.

"Hold on... hold on..." he said, willing her to stop.

"What is it now?"

"I think I had it the wrong way around. Your right eye

is brown!" Grace slapped his arm and the pair studied one another.

"You know. I think from now on, this should be forever known as *our bench*?"

"*Our bench*." Jimmy smiled.

"From now on. When we meet, it will always be here!"

"Is that an order?"

"Yes, Jimmy Ford… that's an order!" The ticket collector poked his head through the double doors. Satisfied everybody had made their way inside, he closed the doors with an almighty squeal.

"You forgot one of the best places in the town," said Grace.

"I did?"

"The Cavern!"

"That's the toy shop next to Pa's—"

"The best!" said Grace. "Want to go?" The pair of them got up and marched, birds from the tree-lined street chirping under the dying light.

George watched intently as her red lips lingered long over the wine glass. He inspected the pillarbox-red lipstick mark she left behind as the glass was placed down on the white linen tablecloth. Poppy flicked her long black lashes, her amber eyes dancing in the candlelight.

The restaurant had all the grandeur of Victorianism. The black-and-white tiles, the glinting arched iron gate, the three-armed chandeliers with brass beige shades, hanging long and low from the ceiling.

"You know, if he had have read a different book at a

different time, he would have been someone else entirely. And I believe that. Jimbo is smart, he will go places, places beyond here, beyond Brentwood!"

"All thanks to you, George." Poppy's burnt chestnut hair fell across her bare silk shoulders.

"Pfft! I don't think so. The boy wants to learn, he wants to absorb. I wasn't like that. Perhaps later in life, perhaps now, but Jimmy is a kid… he's a good kid!"

"He had you," smiled Poppy, that gap glinting between her pearly whites. "Of course he will turn out good."

George smiled and leant in to take her hand. The waiter appeared as if from thin air.

"Ah."

"I'll have the minced chuck steak and lamb's kidneys please."

"Very good, ma'am, and sir?"

"What is that with?"

"Fried in beef dripping and presented with mash potato, carrots and greens, sir."

"Make that two. And another bottle of this," said George, tapping the Weltevrede 1912 Cabernet Sauvignon.

"Very good, sir." The waiter hoisted his hand behind his back and walked away.

"George, I don't usually… this isn't like me, just don't want to give you the wrong impression of me… my partner, Paul, he, he died a few months ago… and…" George was taken aback by the news, but it wasn't a surprise. There must have been some explanation why the lady was not married, and there it was! Poppy drooped, folded and forlorn against the white tablecloth.

George swallowed and leant forward.

"Miss Miller. The night is young, and you are beautiful. We are simply two people eating, conversing and off to listen to some delightful little music."

Poppy dropped her bare white shoulders. "It's all very kind of you, George. I haven't had, haven't felt like this for a while—"

"Well, dear, you say as much or as little as you want to."

She lifted the glass back up to her lips. He watched her every move.

"You know, this is the first meat I've had since the war broke?!" Poppy's head tilted, and her thin triangle eyebrow raised. "There I was thinking I may turn vegetarian!" Poppy leant in over the dancing flame. George's moustache curled up as he smiled. "Donald McGill, he even has a vegetarian cycling club... perhaps I should go the whole hog... or whatever term vegetarians would use."

"How curious, George."

"Yes, well, our boys need all the help they can get over there, don't they?" George reached in, and lifted and tilted the bottle so its contents spread evenly between both glasses. The dark red oozed and a few stray droplets splashed onto the rim. "So, tell me, Miss Miller—"

"Please, it's Poppy." They both smiled, dimples everywhere.

George rubbed his hands against one another. "Poppy, what was it you wanted to do, before the war, I mean, before you got wrangled in to be a teacher."

"Oh, I wasn't wrangled..." George slanted his chin dubiously. "Well... actually..." There it was again, that famous smile. "I wanted to be a veterinary nurse! And when the war first broke. I wanted to join the Army Veterinary Corps, but, well… I was born a woman, wasn't I?"

"Perhaps a woman's touch is the only remedy," he said.

"Yes, well, the horses and mules need all the help they can get out there. I went to sign up, you know…" George leant forward. "If you can treat injured mutts, you can treat wounded soldiers. The drafting officer! That's what he said, not a nice man, really—"

"Said it through red crossed eyes, I bet… but dogs don't bite back, do they?" George reached over and dropped his hand gently on her wrist. "You're not cut out for the scars left on human flesh," he whispered.

"No. Here I am, middle-aged, too fragile to fight, too reliant to run!" George leant back to give her some space. "He… Paul, he fought; he died. The first few days, it was. I don't like talking about it all that much, but since the socks…" George frowned. "The queen appealed for 300,000 socks," she explained. "After the telegram, I got to knitting." Her sadness broke with a smile. "I would have knitted them all had I not forced myself back outside. All I can do now is donate what remains to the army horse fund!"

Jimmy bucked the nag he held and did the best impression he could. He blew out his lips, he neighed, he tossed the soft horse back into its box.

The toy shop was certainly true to its name. It was a cavern, a cubbyhole crammed with boats and rocking horses, wooden trains, fluffy teddies and lifelike dolls made by none other than Sylvia Pankhurst. Drums and balls and safari animals. There were grooved spinning tops with three feet of string and black tin dachshunds riding on small wooden carts. There were Fischer Georg touring cars, complete with tin driver and thaumatropes showing illustrations of whales passing under ships. There were carved horses and goats, camels and ostriches, with leather details, string tails and glass eyes.

Her almond hair had a nice wave to it. Jimmy noticed this as he watched her waltz between the windows of the doll's house. From one side, her green eye would spot him looking at her. From the other, her brown eye would cast a path through one of the windows or open doorways.

"Fascinating, aren't they?" she said.

"I can't say I have ever had the pleasure of playing with one."

"No… you're a boy. I suppose you wouldn't."

"I can see the appeal, though."

"You can?"

"I mean, all the small rooms and furniture, all the corners you can get lost in…"

Grace smiled. "There is just so much detail. So much going on. Look how the table is laid… it's all so intricate, so…"

"Ornate."

Grace looked at Jimmy with both eyes. "This has been a nice date," she said. Jimmy's heart caught the lift into his throat. She tapped her white fingers along the roof of the small house, toying her fingertips between the miniature tiles. "Hey," she said, her eyes settling on the small figure of a boy with bushy brown hair. Grace picked up the small doll from the garden scene and inspected it. "This could be you, Jimmy!" She looked from the doll to the boy in front of her and back to the doll again, pulling it closer to her lips and tapping it against them, watching Jimmy as she did so. He didn't know where to look, but he couldn't take his eyes away. Grace pulled the doll down and inspected it again. She drew it closer. She kissed it. With her other hand she leant down and lifted the tin aeroplane. Removing the pilot, she replaced it with the small doll she held. Jimmy smiled as he watched her fly it around the shop, making cute chugging sounds as she went.

Grace placed the boy back inside the miniature house, propping it in one of the small bathrooms. Jimmy squatted down, leaning inside the room, he watched the face of the small doll in the reflection of the bathroom mirror.

George checked his moustache in the brass-trimmed glass and twirled the corners. It twitched as he did so. *Time to get moving, time to get back to her.* He lost himself in his infinite reflection, taking note of how endless the blackness in his pupils were. He smiled and sighed. It had been one of the finest nights of his life. His stomach hurt from all the laughter and his eyes were moist with tears of joy.

The desserts had already been placed. Poppy's white dress, like the porcelain, spangled in the firelight. As she saw him approaching, she tucked her black hair behind one of her ears and went back to swirling the wine around her glass. There was a delay as the liquid left a trail of dark red in its path.

"This!" she said, her dimples already sharing their

delight. "This is…" chocolate cloying around the roof of her mouth.

"I know—"

"Here, try both together, the apricots and the chocolate…" Poppy placed a hand under the spoon in case she got clumsy. She began guiding it towards George's mouth. A slip of the hand last second and she coated his moustache with the brown, gooey liquid. Poppy leant back and forced her hands over her mouth. "I know I'm laughing, but I am sorry!"

He wiped his moustache onto the back of his hand and licked off the chocolate. "Waste not, want not…" He laughed.

"Oh George… I haven't laughed as much in my whole life. Tonight, has been nothing short of—"

"Perfect," he said, fixing his eyes on hers. "Well, Poppy…" He poured the last droplets of wine into their glasses and raised his. She followed. "During these unsettling times, we have to keep one thing in perspective and that's time itself. You know, in the lavatory, I got thinking, how short but how infinite it all is!" Poppy raised an eyebrow and attempted to conceal her humour. "Let's not waste a moment of it. Every second that passes is behind us. I know there are boys out there suffering unthinkable, heinous suffering. I know your Paul, I know he didn't die in vain!" Poppy bit her lip, trying not to allow herself to choke. "I know death… I know life… and if we let it slip away… *this* slip away and say that when we stop suffering, in the future we will be this and that. No, not then… now, let's be all those things now!" George banged his fists against the table and had to settle his excitement.

His excitement then turned to bewilderment. "Where was I going…?" Poppy swirled the wine in front of him and they both chortled. "The truth is," he said, gathering his thoughts. "I know there is so much suffering out there," he pointed. "But deep down, we are lucky to be alive in this age, in this time, just think about all we have, these moments. Poppy!" he said, leaning forwards and taking her hand in his. "There has never been a war like this one. Not one that affects our entire country. I'm not saying that the town will be ravaged – not physically, I mean. But this war, it will weave itself into society, into the fabric of our flesh!" Poppy's mouth fell open and she squeezed her hand tighter in his. "Now… I don't think I can become who I want to be without you Poppy!" Poppy's forehead furrowed as she reached forward and took his other hand. "I understood what living really meant once and I lost that. And tonight, I thank you because you have sparked something in me again that has been dormant for twelve years! Nothing is more important to me than my boy…" George's eyes watered over; Poppy's had already beat him. "But he's growing so fast. It won't be long until it's just me in that house…" She turned her lip in sympathy. He threw his serviette at her. "I may not believe in some higher being, but I believe the day you walked into my life… quite literally, my shop! That day was the beginning of something!" Poppy's white teeth shamelessly posed. "Look, rain cannot dampen how I am feeling right now, Poppy." He patted his chest with both hands.

"Oh, George," she sighed. "I feel like I've known you all my life…" She moved her cutlery to either side of the chocolate-smeared plate. "Oh, but I have said that twice already." His cheeks puffed up over his slit eyes as he grinned. "Thank you... George. Not just for the meal, although I am sure it fetches a week's wages!" He shrugged indifferently. "And not just the flowers, the words. But tonight... you... you listened to me. I feel as though I haven't been listened to for a long, long time and well..." she overflowed with emotion, "I felt like myself more tonight than I have ever before in my entire life!" He tilted his glass back towards hers. She was very welcome. "George, I do want to do my bit, I do want to be that veterinary nurse that scared girl was afraid of becoming. I know now that I can do it, because... because I have you."

George wiped the red wine from his moustache. "Together," he whispered. "If we go, if we are summoned, we go together!"

"Together," Poppy whispered back, eyes swallowing every inch.

Once the bill was settled, George shepherded Poppy outside.

And outside the heavens opened. Fat droplets of rain splattered on the roofs of the town and rivers ran between the cobblestones.

"Someone heard your speech, George!" mocked Poppy. Within seconds the pair of them were soaked through. George's black hair split across his forehead, Poppy's curling around her lobes and across her bare chest like swirls of ebony. He pulled her close, removed his coat and spread it above them both like a hammock. They skipped across the wet stones and below the ochre pillars of the Palace cinema.

Rain poured from outside their dimly lit shelter, buckets fell from the guttering, creating harmonies with the surface water. The pair of them laughed and laughed. As George pulled away his jacket, Poppy went on to her tiptoes and fell into his chest. He caught her in his arms, studied her amber eyes. She investigated his, diving into those blue pools. They undressed her. Poppy wrapped one of her arms around his shoulder, placing one hand belonging to the other arm onto the nape of his neck. He felt her warm flesh on his; their breath danced in the cool air. In, she pulled him in closer, her eyes engulfing his. Poppy stopped. Time stopped. She closed her lids and clasped her hands around his cheeks and the corners of his moustache. Poppy opened her luscious red lips ever so slightly and drew his closer. Her wet mouth met with his. She opened her lips ever so slightly more and ushered his tongue into her warm, soft mouth. He closed his eyes. He tasted her. She tasted of chocolate, of apricots, red wine and rain. George placed his hands around the small of her back; he felt her tremble, from her body up through to her hungry lips. He lowered his arms to her hips and rested them on the curves. Poppy hoisted her legs up and into his wanting hands, resting her knees around his waist. Palms open, George moved them around to her cushioned cheeks, tight and wet against her white dress. George leant her gently back against the stone pillar. She was panting; the vein in his temple pulsated. Poppy pulled his face back away from hers and opened her eyes again to check it was still him. She took him back in, their noses exhaling against each other's cheeks. His tongue clashed with her white teeth and he felt for that beautiful space in between. She pulled his face back again.

"George, oh, George," she begged.

"Poppy," he pleaded back, breathless.

"George… I love you, George."

"I love you… Miss Miller." Her mouth curled into a smile around his. Her fingers spread like a comb under his hair. She felt around his scalp; it sent tingles through the notches of his spine. "Oh, I love you, Poppy. I've loved you from the moment I met you!"

Once the rain had subsided, the pair linked arms and stepped out onto the empty cobbled street, their diaphanous shadows swimming under the moonlight. They passed through the chapel ruins, the cavern, library and sweetshop. They passed by the bench in its perfect position.

1917

CHAPTER EIGHT

NURSE HARRISON

JIMMY TOUCHED HIS FACE; it felt swollen and sticky where his tears had dried. It took him a while to adjust to normal rhythms. Normal, if there were such a thing. He was in the unfurnished dorm; another fit. His mouth tasted metallic. He wiped it with the back of his hand and was greeted by a dark congealment of blood and a bitter sting on his lips. At least this time, Doctor Campbell had been witness to it. Memory of the session came flooding back to him. The hypnotic watch, the oxblood sofa, the doctor's relentless questions; the train, the smog, the diamonds. He wondered what Campbell's analysis would be. By accepting the therapy, he was accepting the madness, but by rejecting it, would he surely not go mad anyway? He had not known the dealings of such a punishing hand. These past few weeks, Jimmy had seen things. Unimaginable, disturbing things. In his room, in the honeycomb, in conversation. He was going mad. He knew it; he feared it. But by fearing it, perhaps there was still hope. For people that feared madness would fight to their death before it took them.

He knew he wouldn't have survived without their help, without Betsy and Doctor Turner. He had confided in the hairy doctor, expressed all he had seen to him. Perhaps it was bereavement, exhaustion, but the hallucinations, they couldn't be taken lightly, not in a place like this; not in an asylum!

He often woke up in fits of confusion and sweat, seeing the living and dead and the questionable, muddling between the three: Grace wounded and covered in blood; Wilfred, half-burnt; half-alive, Wilfred.

"Oh, Wilfred," he whimpered. What had become of his dear best friend? Was he back home in his kitchen, surrounded by ghosts? Had he been noticed and hugged by his mother? Had she realised how close her own son too had been to death? Jimmy wanted to know so much, but he was trapped, destitute.

Jimmy knew that he could not escape and survive out there on his own. Not yet. And why would he escape? For whom? For Grace? He was a madman; she was a nurse. She could have handled physical wounds… but not this.

Jimmy folded his arms behind his head and peered up at the ceiling, at those deep domes. Before the thought could clamp his mind, there was an abrupt clang as the door swung open.

"They have the same at Colney Hatch."

"What?"

"Those… hollows. Are you rested?"

"I… I…"

"Are you ready for your tour now?"

"Tour?" Jimmy turned his head and caught sight of her white deaconess's cap, white blouse and apron. Her hair, coarse and blonde, was tucked behind satellite ears.

"Why, yes," interrupted the nurse. "Every able-bodied patient at the asylum receives a tour!" She giggled and hushed her ventriloquist mouth with a bony white hand. "What are they fixing inside of you?" The nurse's head tilted low.

Jimmy couldn't read her, something he always prided himself on. She was different to the other nurses he had met so far. "Epilepsy… they think."

"Why, that's just splendid! You'll be right as rain in no time."

Jimmy folded his arms across his knees. There was a strange, awkward air in the room. "I hope so," said Jimmy, fearing the silence. "Then I can leave, and—"

"Leave?" said the nurse abruptly, her neck crooked to one side. "Why on Earth would you want to leave?"

"To go back and—"

"Home?"

"No, not—"

"This is your home."

"This is a hospital… where is Doctor Turner?" he asked, attempting to peer round the door she was blocking.

"In a word, the hospital aims at making the institution really and truly an asylum, a place of refuge and retreat from pain and trouble and sorrow; a hospital *and* a home," recited the nurse, as if greeting Jimmy at the entrance of some great museum.

Oren slipped through the gap in the doorway and sat down on his bed opposite. Jimmy searched his pale young face for answers. He was genuinely gladdened to see the boy with the globular skull again. But Oren seemed undeterred by the peculiarity of the nurse; excited, even.

"Now. Enough of that. Let's start *your* tour, shall we?"

"Oh, boy, Nurse Harrison, can I come?" requested Oren, already back standing. Jimmy frowned.

"Why, patient Oren, you know full well that you've already had *your* tour," said Nurse Harrison.

"Yes, ma'am, b-but that was a while—"

"Thirteenth of August, 1914, Patient 130814."

"Thirteenth! That's my birthday," said Jimmy.

"Patient Jimmy?"

"Yes?"

"What shall it be?"

"What?"

"It's *your* tour. What shall it be?" The calmness of her voice was unsettling.

"Oh, I don't mind," he said.

"Very well, patient Oren, you shall have your second tour, but no disruptions!" Oren skipped out of the white room. "The tour starts at the entrance. As all good tours do," said the nurse. "It's a bit of a walk, so stay close, everyone." Her face faded into the darkness. Jimmy ambled slowly after them. *She even walks like a machine; Tik-Tok from Ozma of Oz!*

The open passageways were hives of activity. If one looked beyond the red brick, they could admire the uninterrupted vastness of the joyous British countryside. Jimmy wasn't one to admire the view at this present moment. There were mumbling men scratching their arms incessantly. One slid his worn cotton shoulder along the wall. He was dressed in the same white nightclothes, yet daylight still prospered through the slits either side of the colonnade.

Skeletons, wide, sunken-eyed, these *people* were looking in every direction but not at anything in particular. Hunched nurses bustled with metal trays from one room to another. Doors opening in silence, doors slamming behind screams.

Jimmy wanted to turn back and close the door to his dorm, but he didn't want to lose Oren or the nurse. The pair of them had appeared in his room like calm, complacent apparitions in comparison to the chaos which ensued these corridors. Claustrophobic corridors which were more like human intestines with occasional bullet holes. Holes that the light from the outside world used to cast gusty shadows.

A tattered, wire-haired lady with a giant wall clock approached Jimmy. Rags hung from her skeleton. She could barely lift such an instrument, hands fixed on 11:40. "You got the time?" she bellowed, falling into hysterical laughter.

A baled man rocked his skull back and forth against the wall, an unkempt lady seated on an iron bench. She lifted her arm violently upwards before dropping it back into her lap. Seconds later she repeated the motion as if she had a pressing answer in response to a teacher's question in class. Oren and the nurse passed her by without so much as a glance. Jimmy braved a side peep; her expression was completely muted. Jimmy watched her as he walked on through the winding walkway. She was like a sunken antique ship, rusting there against that wall.

Jimmy skipped to catch up. "Oren?"

"That's Martha," he whispered. "She's catatonic."

"Cata…?"

"…tonic. She repeats that movement her entire life. Arm up, arm down. Either that or it's stuck at full mast!"

"How does she sleep?" asked Jimmy.

Oren shrugged.

"And the lady with the time piece?"

"Ethel. Borrowed it from the dinner hall when they renovated. Carries it everywhere she goes. Even to the butchers up town where Martin speaks to the sausages."

"Town?"

"We're allowed out occasionally, Jim."

Jimmy let out a sure sigh of relief. "We are?" he whispered. "They are?"

"Of course, Jim!" His mind began wandering; if he didn't need to attempt escape and they would simply let him out the front gate, he could carry on with his life. His life, whatever that had become.

"Do keep up, you two," beckoned the nurse. "Jimmy, these passageways are the longest of any hospital in Europe." Jimmy liked facts, just not when he felt his life was in peril.

Jimmy had a profound number of questions by the time he stood outside. He wanted every patient's story in the order of when they were contained. The breeze soothed and toyed with the leaves as if today was a perfectly normal day. Birds wound down their final tunes and the croaking of frogs took over the march. Shadows crept and lengthened over the gables as dusk engulfed the asylum. From here, the mood almost felt tranquil. It reminded Jimmy of all those long wild days playing outside. Although, things had changed. *This is no longer a game*, he thought. But he must treat it like one. To survive. *How did the grass still smell freshly cut? It's still me here. I'm still Jimmy Ford!*

How did the same sun shine on *his* house? In *his* garden, how can that same sun caress flower heads and the backs of bees and soldiers' flesh? That same sun beat down on the bombs which fell on the station, on this very hospital, through the mullion windows of the wards. He closed his eyes to the sun. It had always been incredibly faithful at being unfaithful.

He felt deathly insignificant below the impending clock tower as he squinted across the common towards the distant gates. He saw the shadows of he and Wilfred there, two autumns past. Their naïve shadows danced 150 metres away, debating how they would get in. Now, he could only consider the opportunity of escape. Where was his young friend now? Back home, with the mother who had forgotten him? He thought of his own silent cottage less than a mile away. He thought of the wooden viaduct just over the ridge and down the hill towards the track. His balsa model of the Be2c in continuous orbit under the wooden bridge, suspended there, oscillating in stupendous isolation. Jimmy felt numb, his mood dominated by the doldrums. He forced a recollection in the hope of sparking some tears: the last person to close that front door, the way his dad would dangle the key inside.

"Right, is everyone ready?" said the excited nurse. She looked around, tucking her blonde locks behind her large, asteroid-like ears. The boys stood silent. "Excellent. Welcome, everybody." Jimmy looked at the huge expanse of space between the two of them. "This is the Brentwood Hall Estate. The land here was selected in 1847. It is eighty-six acres in all. Chosen from twelve other sites and bought from Mr William Kavanagh for £8,000 in 1849!"

Oren lifted his arm. It reminded Jimmy of the poor catatonic he saw earlier and he forced a smile. He couldn't comprehend how surreal everything was.

"Yes, patient Oren."

"Why this site?"

"Why, the water supply, of course," said the nurse triumphantly. The whole thing felt rehearsed. A wonderfully weird circus act. "Advertisement was published for plans. Third place received £50, second place, £100." Oren's circular jaw dropped. The nurse's voice got higher in pitch. "And the winners: Kendal & Pope of Brunswick Square."

"Yay!" cheered Oren. Jimmy looked at the side of Oren's bulbous head and wondered what kind of thoughts it was filled with.

"The foundation stone was laid by the chairman of the committee of visitors on 2nd October 1851. Mr Moul of the White Hart Inn kindly provided the breakfast for the occasion." Jimmy had been there only a week or so ago with his dad. A week ago, when he'd had his first taste of beer. How far away everything was now. How far away his own dad felt. "The original plans were fit for three hundred patients," continued the nurse. Oren lifted his arm. "Yes, patient Oren?"

"How many of us now?" he asked, panning his eyes to comprise the newest recruit. Jimmy felt uncomfortable to be included.

"Almost two thousand!" said the nurse. "No asylum should exceed eight hundred beds!" She cleared her throat to remove the politics. "This main block behind you, to quote the architect, 'is mediaeval of the Tudor period, substantial, cheerful and English in character'."

Jimmy couldn't imagine anything less cheerful than how he felt right now.

"In the building behind me is the nurse's quarter. These…" The nurse gestured with outstretched arms. "These, behind *you*, are the galleries, as we call them here. On my left, you have the female ward. Some, like mine, have all the amenities of a country home. Not too many patients in mine. But some wards have up to 243. We have our kitchen and own dining hall!" The nurse became lost in thought.

"Why does she stay with the patients?" whispered Jimmy. "I thought the nurses stay over there?!"

Before Oren could answer… "On the right, the males, adults only nowadays, lucky for you! And, over the back there under the chapel was where you two just were. At least you have God watching over you both."

"Quite literally!" Jimmy looked across to Oren to guess whether he possessed a religious bone in his body.

"Not all the rooms are dorms either, some are single occupancy, some even have fireplaces. Not suitable for you epileptics, though, I wouldn't have thought." The label hit hard. "You reach each gallery via the covered walkways, many of which, as the ones we walked through, are open air. You have two toilets within each gallery and a porcelain bath!" The nurse was enthralled by such luxury. "And outside round here there is a wash house and a brewery, which we will come to later." As the boys followed the nurse around the side of the asylum, Jimmy recognised where he was that fateful night. "Quicksand," interrupted the nurse. "Quicksand caused a great deal of complications during construction. Swedish *dantzic* wood, wrought-iron-tipped, had to be piled below the water tower and chapel. The poor labourers worked day and night, one team bailing, whilst the others laid down the foundations brick by brick... Patient Jimmy, is this boring you?"

"N-no, ma'am."

"What are you looking for? You strange boy."

"My marble," Jimmy muttered, half in surrealist jest. Jimmy and Oren followed the nurse into an outhouse.

"This is where the laundry workers stay." The room was small and musky. A few distressed faces looked up from the food they were eating, their plates resting on ironing boards.

"Why are they eating here?" asked Oren.

"They have no place else to go. We are over capacity!"

"So where do they sleep?"

"They sleep in the iron building." The nurse ushered the boys back outside under the falling light. "This," she said, pushing open a side door, "this is the needle room. It used to be the old kitchen but now we have one on every block... to cook our own meals."

The nurse side-stepped and opened a second door. "This is the general bathroom… it used to be the needle room."

"Why did they make a needle room out of the kitchen and then a bathroom out of a needle room?" asked Jimmy.

"And here…" The nurse ignored Jimmy, pressing out onto the manicured lawn. "These corrugated iron huts used to form four temporary wards. These are now the Home Farm workshops, the only place in the asylum with electric light!"

"Sometimes you can't see patients from halfway across the room!" whispered Oren.

Beside the workshops was an entrance back into the main building. The door was heavy, black and splintered. Like all the doors and many of the windows, it was shaped like a coffin. It may as well have had a cenotaph in the centre, but there was no honour here. The nurse looked at it a while and evaded it. She continued around the back.

"What's in there?" murmured Jimmy.

"I wouldn't go down there if I were you," said Oren. "That's the suicidal ward." Festoons of cobwebs occupied the corners of the door. Nobody leaves. *Jimmy John Ford*, he repeated. He stayed staring at the foreboding black coffin. Goosebumps crept over his skin like ants. He imagined undressing the door with his eyes and all manner of supernatural beings screaming and shuffling towards him from the darkness.

"You know, some of the groundwork wasn't laid so that patients, when they arrived in 1853, had work to do. It was thought they would make useful employees," said the nurse as Jimmy slowed.

"Who else works here? Besides the doctors and nurses," he asked, attempting to busy his mind.

"How long have you got?" Jimmy looked at Oren.

"Well," said the nurse, preparing her fingers for the list. "There's a medical superintendent, a medical assistant, a Chaplin – although he doesn't take residency here. There's the steward, the clerk, the matron, sub-matron, head assistant, attendants, the engineer and his boy, the carpenter, gate porter, house porter, stoker, ploughman, cook, housemaid, kitchen maids, laundry maids, the bailiff, the baker... oh, and the shoe mender."

"And the candlestick maker... where is he?"

The nurse looked baffled.

"This place is a fortress," muttered Jimmy, looking at its full scale.

"A fortress is somewhere you can't get in," corrected the nurse. Jimmy gulped. Although he begged to differ, he wasn't going to question it.

"Welcome to the day room. This is my favourite room," said the nurse as the high double doors parted into a light open hall. The room was scattered with chairs and separate side tables which didn't appear to be beside anything. "It's our recreation room. This is where you can come to... sit."

"Sit?" asked Jimmy.

"Or stand."

"Stand?"

"This is where we have our Christmas ball," she added proudly. "We have dances here. Music, entertainment, ventriloquists!" Jimmy looked around the room at the subdued patients milling between tables. "We had a fete here once. Eight hundred of us. Celebrated the coronation of our Majesty the King!"

"Hello." A small girl approached Jimmy. She barely looked eight years old. He was sad to see her here.

"Hello, I'm Jimmy."

"Hello, I'm Jimmy," she said.

"Ha, you, you can't be Jimmy too," he played.

"Ha, you can't be Jimmy too."

"That's Lolola," whispered Oren. "Her real name is Lola, but we call her that because she repeats everything you say."

"Everything?" asked Jimmy.

"Everything?" said the girl. Oren shrugged his shoulders.

"Moving on," said the nurse sternly. She wasn't one to have her tour hijacked, especially not in her favourite room.

"In continuation on the theme of recreation…" She pushed open another door at the dark end of a narrowing corridor. The dying light from the outside world poured back in. The lawns this side were again lush green and opulent. The smell of freshly cut grass. "Hmm… Stephen must have done his job today."

"Psst…" whispered Oren. "Stephen, he tends to the gardens here. He was a gardener in his past life."

"Past life. Sounds as though he still is?" said Jimmy.

"Well, I've seen him and all he really does is stand in one place all day raking!"

Jimmy glowered at the familiarity of it all. "You've already told me, Oren!"

Oren went on. "He accused the radio of hypnotism."

"You said."

"I did? Did I tell you he cut his own eyelids off?" Jimmy gave a grimacing nod.

"Here we have the skittle shed: cricket equipment, quoits, bowls, billiards…" Jimmy was preoccupied, attempting to remove Stephen's eyelids from his own mind's eye. "As you can see, we are surrounded by so much green and it's all ours. Isn't it all so cheerful?" The nurse's constant mood changes startled Jimmy.

The three roamed over towards the oak tree towering over the chapel graves.

"I've been here before," he muttered to Oren.

"Here?"

"Yes, my friend, Wilfred. Wilfred and I snuck in here one autumn, a few years back. It was at night. We wanted to…" Jimmy hesitated. He looked over at Nurse Harrison, who was circling the great tree.

"You did?"

Jimmy nodded. He spotted the dormitory window. "You must have been in your room that night, Oren." His mind jumped. "You must have been *that* boy. The boy I saw at the window that night!"

"Our window," he corrected, unfazed.

"Yes! How do you do it?"

"Do what?"

"How could you stand it all this time?" Oren shrugged again. "How old are you, Oren?"

"Twelve… yes, twelve, I think…"

"So you were ten when you arrived here?"

"I guess I don't know much different now."

"Any."

"What?

"You don't know *any* different.

"Yes, any. Didn't you hear Doctor Turner, Jim? He will find us a cure!"

"There is no cure for epilepsy, Oren."

"My sister built this," interrupted the nurse, stroking the side of the oak tree.

"Your sister? Built. The tree?" The nurse tickled her fingers between the engraved bark: MH heart HM.

"Why, yes, of course. She was a patient here. I told you, they left a lot of the construction of the asylum to the patients, it kept them out of trouble!" The nurse was absorbed with the tree. Her breathing quickened. "She loved her Henny dearly."

"Henny?" he whispered to Oren.

"Don't ask. Some doctor she fell in love with… Henry Maudsley. I think she read about him in some hospital records."

"This way, children…" The nurse skipped through another door. Jimmy had so many questions. He took an observation circle. He'd well and truly lost his bearings.

The nurse swung open another large, creaking door.

"This is the… brewery!"

Jimmy was last to enter the enormous, clammy room.

"Why are there tables with heaped cloths?" He didn't receive an answer. "And what's that smell? Are they… are they bodies?" Jimmy grimaced. "This is no brewery, it's a mortuary!" His skin broke out in pimples. "Are we supposed to see this?"

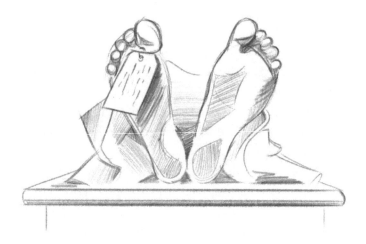

"It used to be a brewery," whispered Oren. "All the information she reads is from the report."

The nurse went on unremittingly. "We used to have so much fun here until Timmy fell into the copper. Made a right old fuss. Lockjaw... died!"

Jimmy grabbed at Oren, he was sweating. "Why are there so many bodies?"

"L-l-lots died this year" stuttered Oren. "Syphilis, usually... and then there's the general paralytics... plus the typhoid that's going around..." Jimmy let go of the boy and held his breath, fearing transmission.

"Before that, we had beers every mealtime. Gin and water, or lemonade... my favourite. Every patient got an allowance," continued the nurse, having a conversation all of her own.

"The doctors think that's what she's got!" said Oren.

"What?"

"Syphilis! According to Doctor Campbell, it mushes the mind. Makes her calm as a lamb one moment and—"

"As crazy as a fox the next," finished Jimmy. "I bloody knew it!" he said, clasping his hand over his mouth. "She was a patient!"

"Nurse Harrison? She still is…"

"What? She's in a nurse's uniform? You're calling her nurse?!"

"I know, they've given up trying to convince her. They just let her pretend. We all just call her Nurse Harrison."

"Pretend? You knew all this time? When she said that she only had a few patients in her home, I presumed that she was an attendant. Well, not presumed, she's bloody dressed like one!"

"Well, she's not causing any harm to anyone," shrugged Oren again, just as strange as the situation.

Jimmy couldn't quite comprehend it all. It was easier for him to think of her as an actress, a method actress in costume, a devoted practitioner of the *Stanislavsky System*. It was no use, his temples sweated. "It can't be, I can't be here. What about her sister? She said that her sister was the patient?"

"Who helped build the asylum. I know. She's never had a sister. Plus, the asylum was built years ago. It's all in the report, I'm telling you!"

"And Timmy?"

"No idea. Apparently, a patient did die of lockjaw, but this was over twenty years before Jack the Ripper. She's just got a wild imagination, that's all. Doctor Turner said you shouldn't let the truth get in the way of a good story!"

"Wasn't that Mark Twain?"

"No. It was Doctor Turner," said a bewildered Oren.

Jimmy observed as she waltzed between the dead corpses. "Christ knows what she really sees," said Jimmy. The nurse pranced around the tables, stroking the cloaked heads like admiring pretty flowers in a field.

"Dinner time, children," said the nurse, even before the echo of bells rang out.

1914

CHAPTER NINE

POPPY FORD

THE CHURCH BELLS HAD long ceased but Jimmy still felt an echo in his brain. Phosphorous bulbs flashed as the photographer pulled the dusty sheet from over his head and smiled at the congregation of the gaily dressed. Jimmy watched as Harry held the soldier doll close to his cheek for one more flash.

"Resemblance is uncanny," said Alfred. "You did a fine job, Jimmy!"

"Certainly did." Harry held the doll out to face him. "Certainly did." Although the complexion wasn't far from reality, there was something ethereal about the doll. Perhaps it was the way its eyes rolled to the back of its head when it succumbed the occasional tilt. Or perhaps it was the way they fell back again, looking through to the soul of any man which stood under their gaze.

"Can't I take him with me, Jim?" pleaded Harry, posing the doll beside his cheek. "Just think what two Harry Needhams would do to the Bosch!"

"I made him for Wilfred. We're going to race them." His plump friend nodded.

"Race me?" said Harry. Harry dressed Jimmy down. "You haven't a chance!"

"Not me, Ghosty! We're taking them both to the stream and letting them go, see who makes it past the steam mill."

"Pfft," said Harry. "No contest." He lifted the doll. "Isn't that right, Harry?"

"You're right," said Jimmy. "No contest, Ghosty will win!" The congregation laughed.

"We were up late painting the hair on last night, ain't that right, Jimmy?" said Alfred.

The curly-haired boy nodded. "Took us a while to get the colour right. Ginger was a mixture of burnt sienna with a little cadmium yellow!" Again, the procession laughed. Harry pulled Jimmy in and knuckled his head.

"You cheeky blighter, Jimmy Ford."

"You were lucky, Harry," said Alfred. "If your embarkation hadn't of been rescheduled, you wouldn't have seen him, and you would have missed the wedding."

"And what a fine occasion too," said Harry honestly. Releasing Jimmy, he raised his glass of beer and toasted the new couple.

The photographer ushered George and Poppy towards the stained-glass window. Frost coated the lawn behind.

Heads of snowdrops and Japanese quince hung almost blue with the December dew.

"Oh, George, I didn't know it would mean—"

"Just keep smiling, dear," George mumbled beneath his teeth. "It's no certainty, hearsay is all." Poppy turned and lifted her white veil to read his eyes. He was taken aback. She had revealed herself to him from beneath the white bird cage; she had unfastened the latch and set herself free.

"But what if it turns true?"

"Well, then it's compulsory, I'll have no choice. I'll have to fight!"

"All because we married?"

"Worth every sinew," smiled George; he leant in for a kiss and the bulbs flashed. "Just hearsay. It will take years to approve. Gentry in higher places. Let's just enjoy the moment, shall we?" Poppy let a gentle sigh pass her mouth and nodded. Her red lips unfurled, displaying those pearly white teeth. She trusted him. She trusted every damn bone in his body.

"Isn't she a painting?" whispered Grace to Jimmy, who stood amongst the congregation. Jimmy nodded in agreement. "I hope I look as beautiful on my wedding day!" She looked to him and blushed, blotches of pink invading her neck like wild roses.

"Like a dove," he said.

Grace smiled. "Yes, quite. Like a dove!"

Two months. It had been over two months since their day at the bench. Two months and his dad was married. Two months and poor Grace hadn't even been asked to be his sweetheart. But things weren't so simple. He wanted to; by God, he wanted to. But he was about to start his scholarship; his mind was occupied with becoming somebody, with leaving Brentwood. Jimmy had made a pact; he would wait to ask her, wait until leaving no longer occupied his mind or staying no longer occupied hers. He convinced himself that if he loved her, truly loved Grace, he wouldn't make such cruel declarations.

"You know, it's not just about Poppy," he said.

Grace turned to face him. "What isn't?"

"Far from it. Dad is happy now, he has her, and that makes it easier."

"Makes what easier, Jim?"

"To leave."

She studied his eyes. "Jimmy Ford, you aren't leaving."

"Is that so?" He smiled.

"I simply won't allow it. Not without me!"

The conversation had surfaced numerous times the past two months. Grace still had a few terms left of school and would begin her nurse's training at the end of the next summer. That suited Jimmy just fine as his studies would surely run the same. Though, when they spoke of such things, Grace had failed to convince Jimmy that it was what she really wanted. He couldn't imagine her lasting any distance from the home and family she so fondly loved. She seemed more of the indoors type. When he mentioned seeing the site of the first motion picture at the factory gates in Paris and tracking down the Lumiere brothers; when he discussed walking amongst the scholars of Père Lachaise, along the Parisian boulevards and over the snow-capped bridges he so often fantasised about, she would plead to tell her more but he failed to imagine her linking his arm, white flakes falling against ghostly cheeks.

Grace's eyes followed his as they lingered on his new family. "Are you happy, Jim?"

"Of course. I am happy *for* him."

"That's not what I asked." Jimmy's eyes streaked with a coolness which mirrored the frost on the windows. "Are you not happy that Poppy is now—"

"What?"

"Well, your…"

"Mum?"

Grace gave a hesitant nod.

"I haven't thought about it," he snapped, capricious and overwhelmed by the turn in conversation. "It just makes it easier now, doesn't it?"

"Easier?"

"To leave. Now that Dad is happy, now that he has someone—"

"Go where, Jimmy, where is there to go? To Paris? Then what?" Jimmy shook his wild locks. It wasn't worth it, not here. "Oh, Jim, can we not talk about this today? Can we go one day together when you're just here, not plotting to get away from me?" The roses on Grace's neck spread, then wilted and away she fled.

"Grace… I—"

"Here he is, the rascal," said George, pulling his son over to the corner, where he and Poppy stood poised for the camera. "Where did she go?" he said, bewildered. "We wanted one with the pair of you."

"She'll be back soon," said Jimmy hesitantly.

"Well, when duty calls…" said George, looking at Poppy.

She nudged him playfully. "You said it would take years, George."

"What would?" asked Jimmy.

"It's nothing," said George. "For the war to finish, that's all."

"But you said it would be over by Christmas, Dad, does that mean I might still grow old enough to fly?"

"Blimey, Birdman, not *that* long!" He scuffed his son's hair and drew the pair tight to him. "Let's have another shall we? Whilst we wait for Grace. Yes, please, operator!" he ordered. The photographer obliged.

Jimmy welcomed the fresh, salty breeze that swirled outside the church. He breathed in a cupful and looked down the cobbled steps to where the land gave way and waves folded against the shingle. *Leigh-on-Sea sure is a pretty little place*, he thought. Painted in the finest of pastels; an old fishing village with wharfs and taverns and hillside chapels perched like parrots on the shoulders of pirate's graves. The town intimately shared its rations of water and cream with the neighbouring shores of Kent. When the tide was out, you could spot the silvery medley of worming creeks. Sea smoke brought over the fragrance of seaweed and kelp. When the tide arrived, the smell of salt spray prevailed. As it so happened, today the tide was retreating with the day and Jimmy inhaled the best of both.

"You know H. G. Wells has been spotted round these parts?" said Alfred, joining Jimmy amongst the gravestones. "He wrote…"

"*The War in the Air*, I know."

"Ah, I was going to go with, what-do-they-call-it?"

"*The War of the Worlds*?"

Alfred nodded.

"I know!" smiled Jimmy. He stared out over the expanse of water.

"If the wind turns the wrong way, you can hear gunfire from over there?" said Alfred.

"I guess it isn't as far away as we think."

"Aye." Alfred's mossy white beard was lifted from his chin and sailed on the breeze. "Hubert de Burgh built that castle Jim!" Alfred branched an arm westward along the cliff. "Well, it's hardly a castle now, left to ruins after falling out of favour with King Henry... How did you get on with that one?"

"Huh?"

"Your school project?"

"Oh, hmm, splendid, thanks," Jimmy's smile unfolded into a giggle. The old man went on.

"King Henry's daughter; Princess Beatrice and Ralph de Binley. They were in love. Attempted to elope to France from that dock down there, much to the king's distain." Jimmy's eyes followed Alfred's down the wiggly cobbled steps to the sand. "They were challenged when attempting to board the vessel which would take them there. Well, whoever challenged them soon died." Jimmy stared at the wizened cheeks of the wise man. "Apparently, he was accidently wounded from his own knife...so they say!"

"What happened to them?" said Jimmy.

"Well..." The old man looked up in thought and tamed

his wild blowing beard. "Beatrice was arrested and sent back to London but Ralph, he was held captive in Hadleigh Castle there…when it was a castle, like. Sentenced to death he was. But he was pardoned on the condition that Princess Beatrice married John of Brittany."

"And did she?"

"Aye. Ralph too had to leave the country of course. And poor Beatrice stood and wept on the steps down there by the wharf until her lover's ship disappeared."

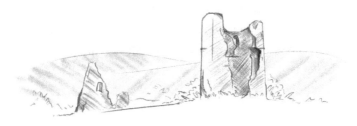

Jimmy's eyes panned down. There she was. He departed immediately, clambering down the cobbled steps towards her.

"Nice talking to you laddie," said Alfred swiping the air and making his way back inside the church.

"Sorry Uncle Alfred," shouted Jimmy. "Something I've got to do…"

Down by the wharf, boats muttered, masts rattled and whistled with the western wind. The breeze whipped her strands of auburn hair like it was composing to the sea.

"It's almost limitless, isn't it?" said Jimmy as he approached the side of Grace, shells crunching under foot. The tide ebbed away, and the wading birds arrived, sifting for clams and cockles left helplessly and abandoned in the mud. "It doesn't feel as suffocating, looking out over water." He observed her wet eyes. "Not like in Brentwood. There's just, well... land!" Grace remained focused on the waves. "I loved my dad bringing me here," said Jimmy. "We often came down for birthdays. We would play on the cliffs over there. Me and my friends, we would all hide amongst the hedges and he would come and find us. Then he would take us for sugary doughnuts down by the pier. Wilfred, he ate fourteen all to himself!" Jimmy chuckled but Grace didn't give him the satisfaction. She didn't look in his direction, in the direction of the cliffs, nor the pier. She simply stared out as the waves weakened. "Then the boating lake. We raced the boats we built on that lake!" said Jimmy.

He watched through tender eyes as sailors docked at the wharf. Fishermen disembarked and hung their nets to dry over the railings of the sea wall.

"What's the catch of the day, boys?" he chimed. Grace turned and mustered a weak smile. He cupped his hands. "Whitebait? Oysters? Mussels? Shrimp? Scallops? Seabass? Jellied eels? Winkles... Whelks?" No response. The sailors started sweeping away the stench of the sea.

"That's it, you let me guess!" he shouted on silent shoulders. Grace giggled. The crew from the fish-smack scampered up the steps of the pub. "Have one on me, boys!" he shouted.

Grace laughed again and turned to face him. "I'll go with you, Jimmy!" she said.

"To the pub?"

She shook her head and her face turned solemn. "If

that's what it takes. I'll come to Paris with you."

"Grace… n—"

"Paris. Or anywhere. I don't care. I just don't want to be left behind."

"Grace… no. It's me. I'm sorry. I say things, stupid things. I don't know what I want really."

"I do," she said, looking deep into his blue, watery eyes.

"I do too." The pair of them leant closer and their lips touched for the first time. Her long hair entangled them both and for a moment, they were inside a nutshell; an impenetrable, warm, passionate nutshell. He retreated his head and saw her eyes were closed; her lips still poised. He leant forward again and rested his mouth against hers a while. His heart was racing, yet he didn't feel embarrassed. It felt right; he felt safe. Her lips parted ever so slightly, and the tip of her tongue twirled around his. They turned clumsy and their teeth clattered together. They laughed and retreated.

"Does this mean…?" said Grace. Jimmy nodded. He had a sweetheart. Jimmy Ford had his sweetheart.

They found a bench and practised their method again and again until they were scholars. A cluster of little skiffs bobbed and swelled with the breath of the sleepy, diminishing tide. The Old Town lights flickered in cosy clusters at the foot of the cliff.

"Sure is pretty!" said Jimmy finally. Grace smiled and the pair sat silently a while, glancing over the retreating tide as it licked and soothed the cracked, grey tar, blanketing the slopes like washed-up whale skin. As the sea pulsed, the waves receded further, leaving patches of creamy foam behind. "Say," said Jimmy, "the moon could have been born in a place like this!"

"Born?" said Grace.

"Yes. Everyone knows the sun is foreign, but don't you feel that the moon was born in Britain?"

"Now you come to mention it…" obliged Grace with a tender grin.

Jimmy adopted the voice of the first radio broadcast. "The moon, born in the Old Town to a young mother. And here we have it, the golden plaque…" Jimmy gestured to the railings behind where the sailors had stood. "Leigh-on-Sea, birthplace of the incandescent moon, four billion BC."

"It's official then." Grace chuckled.

Five rings of the wharf echoed across the flats.

"Last orders at the bar!" Jimmy stood and intertwined Grace's arm in his. Seagulls squawked and clumsily tussled with the balmy wind. They left behind their concoction of mud worms and the remnants of scattered chips. "Tourist visiting hours are over," Jimmy hollered. The pair began their ascent up the cobbled steps underneath flickering lanterns, winding towards the church that Miss Miller had today become Poppy Ford.

From the solitude of the cemetery, lamenting nightingales
sang sweetly, reciting the last of the day's poems to the tide.

CHAPTER TEN

SILENT NIGHT

F ROST KIDNAPPED THE TOWN. The bare boughs of trees spread like bronchioles, the tired, broken lungs of Earth.

Christmas was fast approaching, but festivities were the last words on the nation's tongue. The war should have been over by now; that's what they all believed. Jimmy was secretly glad that it was still raging. Not because the loss of life – far from it. The war kept his dreams alive. One day he would become a pilot and fly for his country. One day he could tell his story, the story of all the men.

Yes, frost had kidnapped Brentwood, the day Ghosty's arms were strapped by his side with twine. The rope was twisted tightly across the doll's chest to keep him firmly on his woven raft.

Jimmy and Wilfred occupied the bank by the wooden viaduct, beside the bubbling creek where they had spent their long summer days collecting treasure. But today, the wind cut like razors. Leaves had de-coloured, curled and shattered in the teeth of winter's bite. Scant branches of trees traced the riverbank and the heads of rocks were shimmering with rime. The willow had wept its tears back into the stream. For all around it was death.

Today it was a torrent; a menace. Not like the languid stream it was in the autumn. There was a rattle as a train passed overhead. The boys stood and watched to see if anything was hurled from the passenger windows. Almost all of the compartments were sealed tight. Today was no day for fresh air.

The chipped flecks of the Harry doll stared back up from the restrained bed of broken twigs. Jimmy had completed the doll at the shop just in time for embarkation, and Wilfred found great solace in having him as a replacement for his brother overseas. Side by side the soldier dolls lay.

"What are the rules again?" requested Wilfred for the second time.

"There aren't any. We can just follow the soldiers downstream on their rafts and see how far they go… see where they end up."

"Oh, OK," settled Wilfred, glad to remove Jimmy's competitiveness from the equation. "You think Harry's strapped in tight enough?" The smirking doll's eyes glazed back helplessly.

"That should do it." Jimmy gave the rope a gentle tug. Beads of snow flurried in front of their faces as if it was never content on landing.

The boys clambered down the bank and perched on flat terrain where the eddies mused the clay edge. Jimmy crouched and tossed a stick onto the liquid to test the speed of the surge. The water was near zero and his fingertips reddened. The stick flounced away as if its legs had been taken from under it.

"We will have to run fast; the current is quick!" Wilfred pined.

"OK, don't let go until were ready to run." Jimmy adjusted Ghosty's raft so that it was aligned with the direction of the flow. "Gaud blimey, that's cold," he said nodding towards his numbing hand. Wilfred bowed down beside him and mirrored his movements. He was whimpering; the water was biting at his sausage fingers. "Come on, Wilf, I'm going to lose my hand here!" It took Wilfred three attempts. Both dolls took first position.

"Here goes…"

"Here goes…" Harry Needham whispered to himself as he submerged his waist below the icy water. Cheers bellowed from his chums occupying the snowy banks of the River Douve. He wasn't sure if that was a new sun suspended above him or a hungover moon who had been up all night and forgot to retire in slumber.

"Come on Needham, a bet is a bet," Private Pepper yelled between curved palms, amongst the rowdy crowd. Harry knew he had lost the damn bet, but he would have done it anyway. *Audacious* was his middle name, double-barrelled with *foolish*. Even foolish boys felt the cold.

Messines had halted several months prior, but the battalion was awaiting their next instructions patiently. Patience led to boredom, practical jokes, dares and reckless antics. Only moments before, Harry had wagered Pepper that Taffy IV was a black Canadian bear who had won the 1914 star for serving in France. Taffy was, in fact, as Pepper advised: a goat. Winnie was the name of the bear who now took residence at London Zoo; his paws hadn't even touched French soil.

Harry didn't mind. A good story was worth the forfeiture. Besides, a bear was far better built for combat over a goat. At least everybody agreed on that.

Harry was stripped of his dignity in nothing but his underwear. He was foolish enough to leave his uniform folded on the bank and caught glimpses of Rice and Reynolds toying with his possessions behind the brambles. He didn't care; that was a problem for future Harry to concern himself with. Present Harry had more than enough to worry about. Avoiding hyperthermia for one, crossing the river without being swept downstream for another. The swirl was ferocious. The pebbles below his feet were crowned in slippery moss. His body quivered and quaked.

"Just a few steps, Harry, that'll do you," yelled Private Smith. "That's far enough, right, Pep?"

"Sod off, Smith. I'm Harry Needham. I'm getting right the way across this cesspool. A bet is a bet."

"You heard the man," chuckled Private Pepper. "The kid's got to learn, Smith."

"He sure 'as," added Jefferies, shaking his head side to side as if spotting himself a lunatic.

"But shells fall in the river all the time, Pepper," whispered Smith.

Pepper shrugged. "I know they do. He can collect us some supper, then, can't he? I haven't tasted fish since we started this bloody mess!"

Rice and Reynolds were now back with the privates, clutching the rudiments of Harry's creased uniform.

"Suit yourself, Harry," said Pepper. He then muffled privately to the other men, "You're a braver man than I."

"Can't leave Messines without a dip in the Douve," Harry insisted cheerfully. "Ain't that right, Pepper?" He winked, psyching himself up. "One... Two..."

"Three," called Jimmy. Both boys let go of their rafts and observed as the two dolls bobbled downstream. They scrambled to their feet. "Quick, Wilf! The currents taking them..." Jimmy was first to the top of the bank. He offered out his muddy hand and pulled his plump friend up. "This way..." he ordered. Jimmy sprinted across the crunchy white grass in parallel with the stream. He got a good distance ahead of the vessels and scaled down the rocks to witness the two dolls bend with the river and descend into sight. Wilfred joined him moments later.

"Ha, ha." He plashed. "Here. They. Come." Ghosty was in prime position, nodding along the surface rush with a grin. Effortlessly, strapped on his sturdy buoy, he followed the liquid road of glinted shingle. "No fair, Ghosty," Wilfred yelped. "Come on, Harry, get a move on."

As if on command, the Harry doll emerged from the rivers crook, his face equally pleased with his achievement. His pontoon parted the water and fabricated a trail of white foam. "It's not a race, Wilf," reassured Jimmy. "I'm just curious."

"It is a race," baited Wilfred.

"Game on." He tugged down at his friend's coat cord and gained a head start. The pair began ascending the glacial stone back onto the path. "Go, go, Ghosty," applauded Jimmy in competitive glee. The boys scrambled further along, moving away from the river due to the overgrown foliage. They ducked and dived, over logs and through curtains of frozen ivy vines. The soundtrack of children's laughter warmed the cold air.

They chopped their way through icy creepers and rolled down the crag, coming to a halt back beside the rivulet.

"Dam!" Jimmy observed.

"Damn what?" asked a querulous Wilfred.

"No, there…" Jimmy pointed along the torrent to a cluster of boulders and branches. "Bloody beavers. They have no chance." Even children knew that there weren't any beavers in Britain, especially in Brentwood, but Jimmy preferred the tales.

"Wait, look!" called Wilfred in astonishment. The first barge appeared from between the valley of jagged brushwood. The occupant was pale and distinct. It was Ghosty all right. He was his usual smug self and was navigating down the face of the mini waterfall without exertion. The edge of the raft where his feet were lay submerged for a second or less at the foot of the fall. It thrust back to the surface, stabilised, facing forward and resolute. Ghosty continued his journey past the boys. He had defied them.

"Harry!" Wilfred howled. The second raft was approaching the top of the chute. Water cascaded down from its summit as the white particles boiled like a cauldron of arctic lava. The raft faltered and toppled onto its side.

"No, no," cried Wilfred.

"Hold tight, Harry," whispered Jimmy. The bottom of the barge was facing the boys. It leapt down the flume askew. On collision with the plunge pool, the Harry doll got stuck in eternal orbit. The raft rotated round and round under the weight of the waterfall.

"He can swim, can't he?" an anxious Smith called amidst the procession of privates who scuttled along the snowy bank.

"I didn't stop to ask him," defended Pepper, rather breathless. "He came up with the forfeit, so I assumed he could."

Harry was nowhere in sight. He had slipped on the rocks after a few steps and began drifting underwater, seawards. Snow sprayed in every direction under foot as the uniformed men scoured the river for any sign of their fallen comrade.

"Damn it, Harry," muttered Pepper. "Why did you have to bet me?" Pepper knew he was victorious even before the confront was concluded. "I shouldn't have let him do it!" he bumbled. "The loss alone would have crippled him. Now it's on me!"

"Harry!" hollered Smith.

"Yes, it's Harry," joined in Jeffries. Five metres or so in the icy heart of the river was Harry's blue face, barely above surface level.

"Oh, Harry," uttered Pepper, eyes fixated on his friend's purple lips. Harry turned his head harrowingly slow towards his helpless companions. He was in trouble.

"Do something," broke in Smith.

"Anything," spluttered Wilfred.

"OK, grab some stones," proposed Jimmy. The pair pulled up handfuls from the river's edge and proceeded to hurl them in the direction of the Harry doll who was still wrapped inside a helical corkscrew below the gushing surge.

Wilfred went for a scattergun approach, casting hundreds of the small pebbles into the air. None hit their mark. Jimmy aimed one at a time, slow and precise. He missed the first few but adjusted his aim accordingly with the size and weight of his ammo. One by one, closer and closer they came to their target, splashing either side of the revolving barge, until…

"Direct hit," screamed an excited Wilfred. The raft

barrel rolled. "Yes!" Wilfred jumped in jubilation as if it was his bullet. "Hey, he's upside down again!" Closer the boat sailed towards them.

"We won't reach it." Both boys looked at each other woefully. The water was too cold and too deep to contemplate it. Jimmy glanced over his shoulder in the direction of the flow. There was no sighting of Ghosty. "Follow me!" He lorded, mounting back up the levee.

"Look!" commanded Pepper, directing his men towards an overturned tree. The trunk was horizontal, bridging its way across the stream. Footprints decorated the snow, revealing the skin of the blackened bark.

All five men stood in position awaiting Harry's arrival like toy soldiers, each adopting their own unique position along nature's bridge.

Jefferies checked the safety on his rifle and removed the bayonet blade. Clutching the barrel, he crouched and dangled down the stock so that it was subaqueous. Everything was set. Now just pending two hypothermic hands to rescue.

"Grab us a long branch, Wilf," ordered Jimmy, laying his stomach flat against the trunk of the tree. He had less than a metre to the surface of the wild stream. If he could hook the raft from below, he knew that it would rotate and level off. Wilfred rummaged in the bushes for a suitable device.

"Quick, Wilf, he's coming!"

"Here… he… comes," announced Jefferies through chattering teeth.

"Hold on, Harry, we gotcha, boy," Smith declared optimistically. Harry's shuddering hands held the stock of Jefferies' rifle. The men reached down and clambered around Harry's shoulders. The identity disc tore from his neck as the first shell cracked through the wood below their boots. Jefferies' gun fell from his grasp and was swallowed up by the raging river.

"Tommy Atkins," barked a sharp German accent behind the rustling bush.

"Huns," howled Smith. "Split!" The troops scrambled their way across the tree to the other side of the bank. Hundreds of spasmodic shells ripped through the air, splitting the bark of the tree at their dancing feet. They scurried like tightrope walkers. Doomed if they fell; fated if they were hit. The five men made it across, springboarding over the mound; their limbs heaped and coiled in the ravine. Continuous shots fired over the top of their heads and unearthed the rested soil. They weren't even wearing helmets. They hadn't intended to meet the enemy, let alone engage in an attack.

Harry's body floated lifelessly past, unseen by the German eye.

"*Freund*," mustered Private Pepper. "Please. Please."

The shooting subsided.

"*Wir sind nicht dein freund!*" responded the cold voice.

Pepper took a moment to decipher the words. "No, no, *our* friend! *Unwer freund…* he's in the river… er, *ist im fluss.*"

Silence.

What felt like minutes passed. The privates, following Pepper's actions, removed the safety from their rifles.

"Please, he will die. Er, *wird… sterben*." Smith looked towards Pepper for the next move. More uncomfortable seconds passed. Inaudible mumbling from the German soldiers. Jefferies lay breathless and dejected without his rifle. What was he supposed to do now? Collect rocks from the ditch to stone them with? They must have been outnumbered three to one. And that was just the troops who had opened fire.

"*Sehr gut Tommy*," came the enemy.

"Huh?"

"Very well. Go getch your *freund. Wir schienßen nicht*."

"What did he say?"

"He said they won't shoot," translated Pepper, looking deeply into his friend's terrified eyes.

"That's horseshit," snapped Reynolds.

"What choice do we have?" added Rice, hugging Harry's uniform into his chest.

More seconds passed.

"Harry hasn't got the time for us to contemplate!" Pepper left his rifle where he lay and stood to his feet, arms raised with his back to the river. They were just kids; all of them.

"Jimmy?" Wilfred challenged for the umpteenth time. His friend was unresponsive, still arranged on his belly against the bark, his arms suspended, weightless over the water. "What's wrong, Jimbo?" he persisted from the shore, a little more solicitous.

The Harry doll had long since drifted past. Jimmy had dropped the branch Wilfred had bestowed upon him, devoured by the water. He had been staring downwards ever since. Lost time.

Wilfred was now in a predicament. He was too scared to negotiate the bridge to find out if his friend was still breathing.

"Jimmy, please," he attempted one last time. He placed one shoe on the corner of the beam. "If this is your idea of a prank then you have another thing coming." He gazed at the corners of Jimmy's mouth to see if he found any of this comical. Nothing. Jimmy's rebellious curls continued to sway with the breeze.

"OK… here goes," he announced without taking another step. Wilfred predicted that Jimmy would animate and wrestle him off the trunk. Still nothing.

As Wilfred approached his friend, he saw a single tear on his cheek.

"Jimbo?" He ruffled at his coat from the shoulder. Trying to keep balance, he attempted to roll him over.

"W-w-what's happening…W-where am I, W-Wilfred?" garbled Jimmy.

"Ha, ha, very funny, Jim."

"W-w-what?"

"You don't fool me, pal!" The moment he said it, he saw the look on Jimmy's face, jumbled like dropped puzzle pieces. Wilfred reached out to offer him a hand. "Are you hurt, Jim?"

"N-no. I d-don't think s…" Once to his feet he scratched his head, wiped the tear from his cheek and stumbled around to see where Harry had got to.

"He's long gone, Jim," said Wilfred, detecting his friend's thoughts. He looked into Jimmy's glazed eyes, like the fog resting on an ocean of translucent blue. Jimmy caught the slight flicker from his friend.

"What, what is it?" Jimmy looked down at his crotch. There was a wet patch.

"Oh… Christ," said Jim. He rubbed at it, hoping it would go and Wilfred could un-see everything. Even though they were best friends, Jimmy couldn't conceal his embarrassment at the situation. Jimmy hadn't the faintest idea where he had been for the past few minutes. He still felt far away, like he had been off someplace else. His mind roamed some more amongst the mist. "Jimmy John Ford, Jimmy John Ford," he muttered to himself.

When his senses were restored, he stepped off the log and grasped a handful of long reeds from the side of the stream. He did the best he could to wipe away the moist patch that decorated his trousers.

He had lost time. He searched his soul for recollections. He remembered moments before the blackout, the scent of rain. Rain. Did it rain? He looked around him. The floor wasn't damp, still frosted like cake icing. He definitely smelt rain. He remembered that much.

Night fell as quick as a blown-out flame. The regiment were treading lightly on their feet careful not to crunch the new snow. The river was swimming with German battalions. Pepper felt a responsibility for the safety of the other four men. The chance of the boys bumping into a forgiving Fritz was highly improbable. Next time it would be *their* lives.

Private Harry Needham hadn't been sighted for hours.

The sound of tins opening and the scent of stew pervaded the crisp, black night. Steam rose from the enemy trenches as the silent footprints of ten boots crept back towards base. There was bound to be repercussions for such foolhardy antics. Not only had the six men abandoned their post, they would return at nightfall with one less. The war wouldn't wait.

The privates crawled beside the mound of slush they had departed hours before. The search was off and if they made it past this last ditch undetected, they could carry on living their lives. *Living*, if there were such a term.

Smith wept. The Hun sung across the moonlit expanse of no man's land.

> "*Stille Nacht! Heil'ge Nacht!*
> *Alles schläft; einsam wacht*
> *Nur das traute hoch heilige Paar.*
> *Holder Knab' im lockigen Haar,*
> *Schlafe in himmlischer Ruh!*"

The five men clambered down into the parapet not at all relieved to have made it back. They knew a hickboo was overdue. In the safety of the trench stood a sign: 'Do not stand about here. Even if you are not hit, someone else will be.' Someone else. Anybody else. But not Harry. Not anymore. Beside the post, Billy Needham was there to receive them.

Billy slammed his helmet down on the table. The noise of the Brodie steel startled them all. Billy placed his right hand down. It was purple and swollen; stitched and marred like a surveillance map.

Through seething teeth, Billy listed their names one by one and a separate order for their sentence. His words forced the air to smoke.

"Private Smith. Where is Private Needham?" Smith gazed pop-eyed, his pupils still moist. He gulped. "Private Smith. I won't ask again. Private Smith, where is my brother?"

"Missing, sir," he finally declared. "He lost a bet, sir. Attempted to swim the Douve, sir."

Billy's eye's widened with rage. "And whose idea was it for Private Needham to attempt something so foolish?"

Smith looked around at the other men in his line. "H-hi-his, sir."

"It's my fault, Billy," proclaimed Private Pepper, breaking convention. One would only have expected to break convention when somebody's sibling was concerned.

"And why would this be your fault, Private?" muttered Billy, avoiding breaking rank.

"I bet him, Billy. I bet him that Taffy IV wasn't a black Canadian bear as he thought. I bet him that Taffy IV was a goat."

"Of course it's a bloody goat!" raged Billy, saliva forming around the corners of his mouth. "Taffy was the goat, Winnie was the bear and Methuselah was the fuckin' tortoise pleading for more shells!" The boys looked at Billy, rather enthralled.

"Well…"

"Well, what, sir?"

"Where is he now, Private?"

"He drifted, sir."

"Drifted?"

"Downstream, sir. We tried to find him. He went under. We had him and then the Hun opened fire."

"Hun? Where were these Germans? Tell me exactly. Where were they, Private?"

"A hundred yards from the rivers fork, sir."

"You will pick back up your rifles and follow me. Private Jefferies, where is your rifle?"

"The river has it, sir."

"You better start making sense, Private, or I'll have the lot of you court-martialled!"

"I dropped it, sir. Attempting to… attempting to rescue Private Needham. Before the Hun, sir."

"And where is Harry's… Private Needham's gun?

"Billy?" said Pepper.

"Never mind. Grab a gun and assemble back here."

"Billy?"

"What?" spat Officer Needham.

"That was hours ago." Between muddy fingers he revealed Harry's round, metallic disc.

Billy's face collapsed in front of their eyes. "H-h-hours ago?" His face folded inwards like a walnut as he gripped the identity tag.

"I'm sorry, Billy. We followed the right fork. The current looked like it would have taken him that way. Night fell and there were too many Germans."

"B-b-but it's freezing out there, Private," muttered Billy, trying to grasp his racing thoughts. "I-I-I don't understand.

Why would he swim the Douve? He… he—"

"I know, Billy. It was Harry… moment of… well, of…"

"He can't swim!" exalted Billy, his eyes darting like ping-pong balls. "I have to try, damn it," he finally spluttered.

"Billy, they're everywhere!"

"You!" Billy pointed, now pacing. "You… you don't tell me what to do… ever, Private!"

Private Pepper raised his defeated hands. Billy was now up in his grill. Pepper could barely face him.

"Look at me, Private. This isn't training camp now." Pepper took a deep breath and burrowed into Billy's charcoaled eyes.

"Do you have a brother, Private?" Billy seethed.

"N-no, sir." Pepper calmed himself. "But I'm going to help find yours!"

Billy nodded, loosening his grip from Pepper's collar.

The six figures hopped the bags and slowly dissolved into the white horizon.

"Let's go find them," he finally uttered. Jimmy was ashamed, but Wilfred wouldn't question his leader; he simply followed him along that bank in search for the two soldier dolls.

1916

*"One ought to hold on to one's heart; for if one lets it go,
one soon loses control of the head too."*

FREDERICK NIETZSCHE

CHAPTER ELEVEN

DOWN WENT THE HOUSE LIGHTS

SATURDAY 23RD SEPTEMBER 1916

Myrtle Road cottage was small but everything it lacked was made up for in cosiness. It wasn't clean or tidy by any means, but the charms of its inhabitants trickled through its imperfections and every fault was forgiven. From the outside the cottage had its bottom half dressed in sandstone brick and its top in black weatherboarding. Jimmy felt that the position of the windows and doors made the house look as though it was always yawning. Not because it was tired, nor because it was bored. It couldn't be so, for its occupants had never been bored a day in their lives. Not for a single moment.

Inside it was brimming with patriotism, especially from George. He paraded around the kitchen table to 'Pack Up Your Troubles' with poor, bewildered Poppy being sucked into his vortex of unrelenting energy. If he could pierce his own heart with that gramophone needle and for a moment live between the grooved streets and dance inside the vinyl houses... he would.

As the needle lifted for the fourth consecutive time, he rubbed his hands together and summoned another family meeting.

"Jimmy, my boy!" he hollered between cupped hands.

"Here, Dad," came the close, cavernous voice.

"Right, so you are. Now, if you would kindly ungrasp Oscar Wilde from your firm grips, my wife and I have a proposition for you!" Jimmy's eyes were still fixed resolutely between pages when his father closed the spine of the book against his fingers. What was revealed was the first poor excuse of a puerile beard. "Blimey!" jumped back George. "Almost two years into an English lit scholarship and he's turning into Chaucer... or was it Tolstoy?"

"They both had beards, Dad, if that's what you mean? They just grew them several hundred years apart." Jimmy gave George the look of a disdained adolescent.

"Right... well," he continued. "In celebration of recent antics, performed by none other than the courageous Lieutenant William Leefe Robinson... wait, you are aware that such an event has occurred, aren't you?"

"You read it to me, aloud, on several occasions... whilst I was reading!" he quipped.

"Right, of course."

Jimmy secretly loved hearing the latest war news from his father's harmonious chords. It was the way he passionately praised and commended *his boys*. It was the way his tongue waltzed with the words, the sounds tapped and twirled, creating a mesmerising beat bop of melodious noise. Jimmy gave a wry smile. He wouldn't dream of telling him this, of course, he was an adolescent, for Christ's sake. "And you have been informed of his VC, have you not?" Jimmy nodded and caught Poppy's anticipating eyes.

"I've got the photograph on my wall Dad, you cut it out for me!" George lifted the paper from the table and laughed through the cut square missing from the middle of the page.

"Of course!" he tutted. "The first zep shot down on British soil. That's got to cause for some celebration, right, Birdman? Cuffley! I'm surprised we didn't see it. Next time son."

"Just tell the poor boy, George!" laughed Poppy.

"Well…" George twirled his moustache to build the suspense. "Poppy here has got us four tickets to see… drum roll, please, dear…" Poppy reluctantly started palming the table. "*The Battle of the Somme.*"

"Brilliant!" chuckled Jimmy with honest elation.

"Tonight!"

"Ah." Jimmy's head dropped. "But, Dad, I have to finish this book tonight. Pleasants will kill me. Assignment is due next week and I'm already behind thanks to the last outing."

"Well," muttered George, "I'm sorry if during these turbulent times I want to inject some love and laughter into my family's home."

"George, if Jimmy has to work tonight, then perhaps—"

"No," smiled Jimmy. "I'd love to come."

"That's my boy!" George enveloped the pair. "One more gift." George exposed a brown paper parcel with a thin rope entwined around it. He placed it down on the oilcloth tabletop and gestured.

"For me?" said Jimmy.

George's dimples revealed themselves. Jimmy undid the knot and sliced back the paper carefully.

"Come on, boy, tear it!" exclaimed an excited George.

"George!" Poppy calmed the man down.

"We aren't leaving this house…" Jimmy peeled back the contents of the kit: the wooden handle of a straight razor. "Not before I teach you how to shave, laddie."

Jimmy reluctantly met George at the white enamel basin. George was waiting with all the necessary props laid. Jimmy stepped forward towards the mirror.

"Take a long good look at that reflection, my boy, because now you're fourteen, it will almost change in front of you."

Jimmy rolled his eyes.

"Now then—"

"I know how to shave, Dad," said Jimmy, half-sighing the words from his lips.

"Let me have this moment, would you, Jimbo? After that, you shall be left alone!"

He reluctantly obliged. The scene was silent as he watched his dad unfold the corners of the paper and reveal the shaving soap. He warmed his hands and massaged the soap until it formed a lather. He took the brush and dipped the bristles from the badger hair into the foam. Everything was done so delicately, so cherished.

"Come," he said, beckoning his son closer. The bristles left behind a trail of white on Jimmy's jawline. He then clasped the wooden handle of the straight razor from the basin and quickly swiped at the whiskers on his cheeks.

"Shaving is about confidence, my boy." George rinsed the blade in the warm, soapy water and turned the handle to face Jimmy. "Here," he said. "All yours." His mouth reached both corners of his face. Jimmy studied the blade in his hand, looked into the reflection and began.

Blood trickled and exploded in splatters against the white porcelain. Jimmy looked at his dad, eyes wild.

"No need to panic," said George calmly. "Just a flesh wound, is all." He removed a square of tissue and placed it on the hole Jimmy had opened. "Happens to the best of us." Jimmy nipped himself a few more times on his first shave and George obligingly applied more tissue when required. He pulled a stool beside the basin and sat there so still and proud, watching his son. "She can't complain about those kisses now, can she, boy?"

"She never complains." Both men shared a smile.

"Shame she can't make the show, Jimmy," said George. "Be good to see Wilfred, though, lad, be emotional for him."

Jimmy looked at his dad through the mirror. He agreed.

"Yesterday is nebulous," said George, passing Jimmy the towel to wipe away the remaining blood and foam. Jimmy glanced back over at the profound man. "Redundant, another life away. It's what you do today that counts!"

"I know."

"We were all born to be someone, Birdman. One day, you will know what that is."

"Thanks, Dad," said Jimmy. His dad departed and Jimmy spent a moment looking at his new reflection in the mirror. He wiped his hands across his new smooth jaw. Indeed, there would be no complaints from Grace.

One red and one blue bike leant against the railings outside the Electric Palace. The cinema was once a drapery shop. George was doubly happy. From a business point of view, he was glad that the competition was gone. From a leisurely standpoint, both Fords were mesmerised with what they witnessed on screen. It was a black-and-white portal into another world. A darkened room filled with strangers, yet everybody's experience was unique and intimate. Everyone believed that for an hour or more, it was only them and the screen. Jimmy felt that the secrets he shared between himself and the screen were the most sacred and deific of all. They were anything your imagination could make it and, "Imagination is the most powerful thing we have," George would say before every production.

On Saturday 23rd September, George, Poppy, Wilfred and Jimmy found themselves in the back row of this packed-out place, devouring a bag each of sweet popcorn.

"A double date," George mocked, taking his chair. Jimmy simply snarled on the matter.

"Shame she had Brownies, Jimbo." Poppy was quick to tame George. This had become quite the role since moving in with the two men.

"She isn't, actually," said Jimmy, rising to the occasion.

"She's on call this evening." He glanced sideward and watched as Wilfred guzzled the popcorn. The buttery balls disappeared between those bloated rosy cheeks. Jimmy smiled sympathetically. He hadn't seen him as much as he had liked since the move. But he was still his best friend, he knew that much.

Since leaving school, Wilfred had taken over Harry's route on the postal run; he was now responsible for giving others the bad news that his family had received. Two years had passed. Nearly two years since his mother took the telegram with trembling hands.

You could trust Wilfred to get each letter to its destination, that was unless, of course, they were in green envelopes. Repressed, adolescent Wilfred had a wonderful time sitting under an oak tree making out the explicit nature of some of the censored words. He couldn't read well, but he knew enough by now to get a racing ticker.

Jimmy felt strange asking him to join them this evening, especially as his dad and Billy were still out there. The group had a late-night showing of the production, mainly because half the country was queuing to see it. Unlike the films that Jimmy was used to watching, which were usually between fifteen to twenty minutes, this was a full feature documentary and Jimmy knew it wouldn't fit on a single reel. Jimmy loved looking out for the cue marks, the small round dots in the top right-hand corner of the screen. The first appeared eight seconds before the end of the reel. Seven seconds later, the changeover cue appeared, and this gave the projectionist a final second to make the swap. Jimmy and George would be forever pinching one another when these marks appeared, and their ears would flex in anticipation for the sound of the second reel motor. But neither had time for games tonight, not during this production. Besides, Poppy sat between them now.

A layer of smoke hovered a few metres from the tops of their heads. "All sorts of punters filling the velvety red chairs tonight," said George. The front row mainly consisted of blue lax soldiers with their legs in casts and their crutches piled; special guests at their own production.

Jimmy drew a long breath, as he did every time he wanted a moment never to pass. The scented haze of the cinema filled his nostrils with mystical exhilaration. Every time Jimmy sniffed in a moment, he also flew upwards, above himself like a movie camera being winched. He would travel out further as if he were anchored to the Earth, higher and higher until he was a flashing beacon on the map of his own country. Then beyond, a dot on the map with the entire world surrounding him. He was in this place, at this moment, experiencing it all.

It was cosy for Jimmy to think that when he was up there, everyone he loved was in this single place on his map. The entire Earth surrounded them, keeping them safe like the amniotic fluid protecting a baby. There would be one marker for the four of them in the cinema this evening, another just down the hill where Grace and her little mole lived, a beacon beside Alfred's home over in Shenfield and some sprinkled over The Avenue, where the Needham household stood. Only now, there were a few more stray markers; pulsing, panicking over the middle of nowhere France. It was Mr Montrose, it was Edward and Billy

Needham, both alone and lost; nowhere, amongst the black void, spanning the rest of this dark planet.

Outside, the last remaining light traced the ochre pillars of the cinema. Punters staggered their way in from the taverns under the blurred light, courtesy of Georges Méliès' misty moon. The stars, one by one, began to fold. The streets were finally silent and ready. Down went the house lights.

The silence in the cinema was deafening. The reel motor turned and that wonderful rotating hum tickled Jimmy's ears. It truly was a spectacle.

"All those poor folks before who have lived and died without ever seeing a single film!" he whispered to Wilfred, who continued submerging his red, plump hands into the popcorn. Darkness enveloped the theatre. The screen turned black and a bordering white frame emerged as if by magic.

Within it beamed out the words from another world:

BATTLE OF THE SOMME
PART ONE

PREPARATORY ACTION
JUNE 25TH TO 30TH

SHOWING THE ACTIVITIES
BEFORE FRICOURT – MAMETZ.
SIMILAR ACTION TOOK PLACE
ALONG THE ENTIRE BRITISH
FRONT IN PICARDY

The jovial music from the pianist ricocheted around the room and the screen was filled with wide landscapes, queues of waving soldiers and parades of horses pulling carts full of ammunition. A member of the second row stood and clapped two coconut shells together to the timing of galloping feet. This was followed by the echoed laughter of the auditorium and continuous questions from Wilfred asking Jimmy, "What happened?" and, "What's so funny?" Brentwood too was in full patriotic spirit, as were the small speckled towns and villages watching the very same spectacle across *Great* Britain.

The next half hour saw the audience witness the smiles of valiant soldiers and chivalrous armies, marching in nationalistic harmony in preparations for battle. The melody from the piano keys sauntered with every soldier on screen and opened the hearts of the voyeurs, filling each of them with a generous cupful of jingoistic glee.

Then, just like that... the pianist stopped. Jimmy uprooted from his seat to see if she had passed out. She hadn't. The screen poured black. Etched between its white borders read:

THE ATTACK

AT A SIGNAL. ALONG THE ENTIRE 16 MILE FRONT. THE BRITISH TROOPS LEAPED OVER THE TRENCH PARAPETS AND ADVANCED TOWARDS THE GERMAN TRENCHES. UNDER HEAVY FIRE OF THE ENEMY

The first charge was a scene branded on the brain of everyone to witness. A line of soldiers faced the muddy banks of the trench, beyond that, the white mist of no man's land loomed. The moment was futile, and no words or sounds could capture the fragility of such a thing as life. Silence said it all.

One by one the soldiers charged. One by one the soldiers fell. One man slid back down the face of the trench towards the horrified audience. A single bullet from a gun, aimed and fired by a fellow man. Life was there one second and taken the next. *Gustav's eyes took aim*, thought Jimmy. His fingers pulled the trigger not realising that his target was behind an author's brain, a musician's brain, a poet, a postman, a lawyer and teacher. The tiny flex of a finger would remove hundreds of generations from hundreds of men. Bloodlines that had been flowing for thousands of years. Unborn babies wailed the world over. Jimmy couldn't comprehend this. His hands turned clammy and his heart began to race.

At a signal. Along the entire sixteen-mile front. What about all those soldiers? He thought of Edward and Billy. He thought of Harry.

I wonder what I was doing when they were filming this, he pondered pensively. *I wonder what all those soldiers are doing over there right at this moment.* The film continued to roll. The piano keys talked but never sang. There were images of the dead and the dying. Wilful men struggled along, carrying stretchers of wounded friends and brothers. There were piles of motionless bodies and perhaps the most distressing for Wilfred was the image of a lonely soldier lying next to his lifeless comrade, his pet Alsatian. Not much imagination was required to visualise their last shared and silent moment together. It could have just as easily been Harry and Pippa.

The two boys were as stiff as corpses in their seats. Neither wanted the confirmation that this was real. *Cinema conquers death too!* thought Jimmy. He wished his mum had been filmed. Captured by the great machine, living, breathing. The soldiers before him once were. The next thing, they've copped it, like a broken watch. But now shot on film, they can be referred to for the rest of time.

The reel changed, and it went unnoticed to Jimmy's eyes.

Jimmy smelt rain.

He breathed in to confirm his senses. He was in the cinema; why could he smell rain? That was his last thought for a while.

Urine trickled down his leg.

Jimmy's mind was as blank as his expression. He couldn't see, he couldn't hear, he couldn't talk. Tens of minutes passed by, but not on his clock. Lost time, a void with nothing but nothingness. He was neither in a cinema, nor in Brentwood; vanished inside the portal.

Up went the house lights.

Jimmy's vision returned from behind the blurred wall of vapour. A single tear toppled down his cheek. He quickly composed himself and covered his damp legs with his long, woollen jacket. He was jumbled and embarrassed beyond words.

Poppy was wailing on George, losing liquid for lost love on the shoulders of a man who had become her next. George angled his mouth over her cheeks and sucked those salty tears right where they had fallen. Jimmy too heard Wilfred spluttering; his dear brother, Harry. In fact, the two Fords seemed to be the only two in the cinema without waterworks. Not from their eyes, anyway.

Upon coming around, the last thing Jimmy remembered was the distinctive smell of rain. It was as if a shell had exploded and had slowed everything down. The tinnitus in his ears was fading fast, but the motions around him were askew, as if, for that moment only, he was living inside a raindrop looking outwards at the world.

Jimmy was so tangled beyond words that his tongue

could not muster a sound; his body was trembling and tired past command. His heart, beating like the engine of a jumpstarted biplane. He bent round into the eyes of his teary friend. *Jimmy John Ford, Jimmy John Ford*, he recited in desperation. Jimmy's words felt slurred, even in his head.

Jimmy turned and eyed his father, who was still consoling Poppy. Over her shoulder, George winked towards his son. Jimmy knew then that he was all right. He had experienced various moments like this since the day on the log. Nothing quite as poignant, but then his body was changing all the time. He was becoming a man.

"You know for a second there, I thought I saw Walter Tull?" George stood and stretched, as he did following every production, regardless of length.

"The Tottenham player, it couldn't be…?" said Poppy, wiping the last tear from her long, black lashes.

"Yeah, I could have sworn it was him. He's in the Football Battalion for the Middlesex Regiment. He always was playing his game left right, left right!" Both boys laughed. George always had deployed his words at the right time. "You've just witnessed a little slice of history there, boys. We read about it enough in the papers every morning, ain't that right, Jimbo?" Jimmy was preoccupied, wondering if the smell of urine had permeated the air. "Back on July 1st, Jimbo and me were in the garden watering the phlox and heard the guns over there. Just think, twelve weeks later and there still at it. Poor boys. The papers then, they said it was a great success. Well, if that's so, if it's such a great success, then how comes they are still at it?" No one responded. Poppy looked around to ensure George's words weren't taken in context. "I get it. Boys won't enrol if the press is bad, but there's bending the truth and outright lies!"

"Hush now, George," said Poppy, gathering her coat. "You're getting excited!" George ushered the four of them down the steps and passed the screen, which had taught each of them more about life than anything except experience could.

The sky was charcoal when the pair made it outside. Knots of all manner of people were departing the foyer. The blue lax soldiers began hobbling back in the direction of Coombes Lodge.

"Where else can we go, Jimbo? The pubs are all closed, compliments of Mr Lloyd!" George was still on his bitter mission.

"I can't stay out, Dad—"

"Right, right, your precious book…" George ushered his hand out for Jimmy to take a seat. "Well, let's at least wait for the wives, shall we?"

Between the two men, the bench meant more to them than the town itself. It was where George had planted his knee the night he had proposed to Poppy. It had also been witness to Jimmy's first date with Grace.

George leant over and pulled the blooded shaving tissue from Jimmy's soft upper lip. He showed it to him.

"Oh, Christ," laughed Jimmy.

"It's all right, son. It was dark in there, nobody would have noticed." George winked. The pair leant back, observing the sea of stars.

"Well…" said Jimmy finally, stretching out his arms and

yawning. "Today he did shoot down Lieutenant Herbert Bellerby! And he already shot down Lionel Morris and Captain Tom Rees back on the seventeenth—"

"Mark my words, son, this Manfred von Richthofen… he'll come to nothing… not like our Leefe Robinson." George nudged his boy. "Besides, he's nothing but a Fokker!" His dimples expanded next to his whirly moustache.

Jimmy laughed softly. "Yeah, perhaps you're right."

George gazed into his son's identical eyes. "I'm always right." He smiled. "Albert Ball will bring him down soon enough. You know he's on twenty-three already?"

"It's not a competition, Dad!"

"Yep." He ignored Jimmy. "He'll paint him red all right!" He was lost in his own head. "Say, the sequel to *The Somme* will have those armoured cars in it, boy… they used them last week at Flers–Courcelette!"

"Not sure they'll be a sequel, Dad. Besides, aren't those tanks meant to be a big joke?"

"They were," said George. "Fired back at our own men. Not now, though. Perhaps the pigeons didn't translate the message, eh?"

"You read the papers far too much, Dad!" Jimmy smiled.

"Yes… well. I haven't got a thesis to write like you, laddie." George placed one hand on his boy's leg. Jimmy moved it away quickly in the hope that he wouldn't feel the dampness. "Oh, Christ," said George. "Can't a man tell his son he's proud?"

Jimmy lifted his head. "It's not that… I—"

"Actually, Jim, there has been something I've been meaning to show you." George reached into his back pocket and showed Jimmy the white envelope.

Jimmy's face turned pale; he already knew. "No," he whispered. "You can't."

"I have no choice, Jimbo. It's compulsory."

"But, Dad—"

"Don't worry so much, Poppy will be here to look after you."

"It's because you married, isn't it? It's because she—"

"Marrying Poppy was the best thing that has happened to me." Jimmy stood to his feet, he was frantic, he felt disorientated. His dad pulled him back down towards the bench. "We knew it was a possibility and now fate has summoned me. Fate in the shape of this white envelope." He raised it up.

"Fate in the shape of a wedding ring," Jimmy snarled.

"Now, now, son." George raised a stiff finger. Jimmy looked into the mouth of the torn telegram and wanted it to swallow him too. "You think I want to leave the two of you? You think I want to be posted in some muddy trench, spitting orders at kids barely older than you?" Jimmy couldn't help the tears forming on the surface of his eyes. "I'm doing my duty, Jimmy. I owe that much."

There was a silence that could fill a tomb.

"How long?" said Jimmy finally.

"It'll be months yet. There will be training at Warley Barracks. Nothing will change, Jimbo, except my clothes!" George held his son's gaze in his. "But for now, I don't want any fuss around Poppy. Can you do that for me?"

"She does know?" said Jimmy, eyes startled.

"Of course. She's… she's not taken it particularly well."

"I thought she was, well, quieter than usual."

"Yes, well. She thinks history is repeating itself, with what happened to her previous husband."

"And she thinks it's her fault?" said Jimmy.

George nodded. "But it's nobody's fault. You can't help who you fall in love with. Isn't that right, son?" Jimmy wasn't so sure. He couldn't be sure of anything. "Poppy, she feels fear beyond her bones, but she won't show it. She will bury it, deny it, like she has the memory of poor Paul. But, Jimmy, she will get there. She will come to terms with it because now she feels she has a responsibility far greater. She will be here for you, Jimbo."

"For me?"

"I've raised you the best I can, but you haven't had a mother."

"I still haven't," snapped Jimmy.

George lifted another stiff finger towards his boy. "You—"

Jimmy raised his arms defensively. "I'm sorry, Dad. It's just a shock is all. I know what you have to do." The two men talked and talked, or rather George did the talking for both of them. Repeating words for exhausted ears. Jimmy had sat there silently, picking apart his options, nodding in agreement every time conclusive decisions were made.

"Ah, here they are…" George doffed his cap as Poppy and Wilfred ambled through the double oak doors and out into the street.

What other choices were there? He was a boy, he had none. Or so he thought, at first. But it was what Jimmy had not said, not agreed with, that would be his fate.

CHAPTER TWELVE

L 32

H AD WHAT HAPPENED TO him in the cinema been the same thing that had occurred on the log almost two winters past? Had he imagined the entire conversation on the bench during this dream state and in fact his dad was not condemned to leave? His mind was as hazy as the fog-filled night.

He had given Wilfred a limp goodbye and was going through the motions of unshackling his own bike when a giant shadow darkened the gas-lit corners of the town. Brentwood fell silent and from over the cinema, it reared its bulbous head. Like a silvery, tapered cigar, it shimmered under the moonlight in what looked only metres from the tip of the roof. For a moment, it was as though the three of them were all living on the seabed and a great ship was

passing over. Their faces gawked upwards, missing the stars. Their view interrupted by the bloated hulk of a floating zeppelin. A bladder of blood waiting to burst.

It was so low you could smell the kerosene. Filling the entire surface of the sky, the zeppelin would have been majestic, beautiful even, had it not been utterly harrowing; the predator fish inspecting ragworms in the sand between shells. Women who had been nattering on the corner after the film screamed and ran for cover. Most of the townspeople just gawped as the whirling propeller could be heard parting Brentwood's air supply.

Bells echoed from St Thomas' Church and constable's whistles screeched all around. The air raid bellboys awoke from quiescence and peddled between the cobbles, hurling, "*Take cover, take cover!*"

George rounded up the herd and shouted, "Wilfred," in every perceivable direction. It was to no avail. The boy was long gone. Jimmy thought of Grace and her little mole and for the first time in his life, *prayed* they were both safe.

"Look, Jimbo!" George was pointing at the back of the ship. A small, pink light wept out from its undercarriage like the sore on a wounded piglet.

"It's getting redder," yelled Poppy.

"Wait…" quietened Jimmy. "What's that noise?" The chug of another engine could be heard beyond the soft glow of the cinema. From behind its rooftop emerged the wings of a Be2c aircraft. "Leefe!" shouted Jimmy in utter awe. He was joined by a thousand cheers or more.

Everyone had their mouths fixed on the exhilarating duel. As the plane chased the zeppelin, the battlefield rose higher, making it difficult to tell hero from villain. Flickers of coppery red brushed against the clouds. The three of them shambled their way after the two great machines and towards Myrtle Road.

"Christ, they will end up in our garden soon, Jimbo," roared George, as excited and wild as ever. "Mind the phlox, boys!" he chanted. "Come on, Poppy, do keep up, love. You don't need a seat in the cinema to see this action, eh, boy?!"

The Be2c sure was putting on a spectacle. Its nose would tip vertically as if riding an elevator made entirely of warm clouds. Once it reached the penthouse overlooking its prey, it would manoeuvre in the most stupendous of fashions.

"Barrel rolls," Jimmy yelled, proud that he could identify the trick. "Reverse half-Cuban eights, English bunts… bell tailslides!"

The biplane ascended for a minute or so and dived downwards at seventy miles per hour towards its target. Once in line, like a shot bird it spiralled downward towards the Earth again.

Poppy gasped. "George, no, it can't be…"

"The fallen leaf. I've read about this in my magazines," Jimmy screeched. "It's OK, Poppy, he'll be back up again, you watch…"

Poppy couldn't move; she observed through narrow white fingers as the plane dropped at a remarkable speed. It disappeared behind a line of conifers and Poppy grimaced in preparation for the smoke and eruption of colour in this now seemingly black-and-white world.

Silence.

The boys watched the zeppelin claw its way towards the fatherland, drifting home on their eastbound breeze.

"Come on… come on…" Jimmy muttered through gritted teeth.

"Get the bastards!" yelled George, overcome with chauvinism, forgetting what either outcome truly meant.

The conifers purred. The engine reignited, rustling the leaves from bottom to top. Louder got the chug of the Be2c as its double wings became visible. "Wooooooo," George called between his paws. Jimmy joined him and even Poppy contemplated. Up, up it climbed, until the plane's silhouette branded the face of the white moon as it passed overhead.

The image was now stamped on Jimmy's brain every time he blinked.

Playtime was over. Incendiary ammunition was deployed. The pink flame on the monster's backside turned from cerise to scarlet to crimson. It whimpered its way further east. "Surely it won't make it home?" asked Jimmy, squinting at the ascending machines. Both the zeppelin and plane climbed higher away from onlookers. Through slit eyes, Jimmy made out the red chaser bullets leaving the Be2c and shredding through the black air.

The three made it back to Ford Street. Throngs of neighbours gathered in rows outside their doors, all peering up in jubilation.

"Did he get 'em?" George excitedly grabbed Mrs Hallmark at Number 8.

"He got 'em, my dear," the seventy-year-old spoke gruffly, nuzzling elated into his arms.

"Birdman, start up the engine!" George threw him the keys to the Red Indian, to which Jimmy plucked out of the air like he had no earlier fit at all. "You take the side cart, Birdman. Poppy, wear this…" He closed the red door behind him and threw her a sandy pith helmet covered in cloth.

"George, this is cork… where did you get this? You fought in the Boer…?"

"Another time, my love… hold on tight now!" Within seconds they were all aboard the cherry-coloured Indian PowerPlus.

"The three musketeers." Jimmy gleamed.

"The three musketeers," said Poppy.

"Yup," said George above the roar of the motor.

She rumbled over the bridge at Brentwood Station and hummed her way up Queens Road past the chapel towards Ingrave in pursuit of the plunging inferno. It was a 998cc flathead v-twin with white wheels and nickel fixtures. What a beauty she was.

The road was powder-white for miles around, as if someone had taken the pastels from the day and painted the night with them. Jimmy tilted his head out his side cart and watched in astonishment as the flames grew. He wished that Grace was observing the spectacle from the safety of her window, but he wanted no pane between him and the action, an uninterrupted view. The motorcycle enabled that: it was cool, it was romantic and it sure knew how to move. *Sod the book*, he thought. *This could lead to my own story!*

Jimmy glanced around into the changing wind. His hair was trailing behind him like a wisp of cloud at the back of a propeller. He eyed a speck of white on his lap, pinched it between his fingers as granules of grey dust stained his tips.

"It's snowing ash," he said. "She's dying!"

Poppy had her face sheltered behind George's shoulders, her arms interwoven with his and her hands resting gently on his abdomen. She wasn't afraid; she was grinning in Jimmy's direction, displaying that famous gap. Her expression was one of contentment, of gratification and of peace. Her black hair pitter-patted against her cheeks, most of its strands held in place by the pith helmet. Jimmy thought she looked beautiful at that moment, against the falling flakes.

"It's coming down!" called George over the sound of

the roaring Red Indian. "Won't be long now…" The fireball glided across the sky like a comet; the last howl of a dying star. The bike whirled left through the rural rutted lanes of Herongate village.

"Just keep following that yellow road," Jimmy whispered, convinced that there would be a goldmine at the end of it.

The wheels bumped and bopped against the unmade road. Poppy gripped George.

"Hold me tighter, my love." George took both hands from the bars and changed gear – thank God there were no rocks. George, like Jimmy, was fearless… especially on a night such as this.

The zeppelin was so low now that the three began to lose sight of her. George pulled up at the crossroads between Great Burstead and Billericay.

"Right!" ordered Jimmy, pointing towards the retreating Be2c. He saluted the wings as they passed overhead and back towards base.

"Think it's Leefe, Dad?" he shouted. George didn't hear him.

"I smell smoke," muttered Poppy.

The skeleton of the zeppelin was oozing black blood into the skies for miles around. George had darted from his Red Indian to assist the burning body of a man who was wandering deluded amidst the field of flames.

"My, oh my," screeched Poppy, clasping Jimmy's ruffled hair into her breast.

"Stay here, Poppy," he said chivalrously, running over towards his courageous father.

"Jimmy, wait…" Poppy shambled after in her heels, one fell from her foot as she rambled on with the other.

"Dad?" George was crouched over the smouldering body of the German officer around a hundred yards from the crash site. With the flames as violent as they were, Jimmy could see all the niceties. The man's flesh was as black as brittle pieces of bark. He was spluttering and wheezing, but his body looked too stiff to bend with all that was growing on it. George was frantically attempting to remove items of the man's clothes, but clumps of skin were falling off the bone like slow-cooked meat. The man wasn't screaming; he simply watched all the efforts George was making. He removed his own white T-shirt and laid it over the man's abdomen, gently patting the cotton against his smoked carcase. The fire was already inside him.

"Dad?" said Jimmy, mouth wide. His words were hollow. He was paralysed. He would be no use.

The young man absorbed George's hand in his. His fingers were like twigs to touch. He couldn't have been many years senior to Harry. "Sssssss…" His body quaked. The whites of his eyes folded inwards and it took all his might to focus them back again. "Siiir…"

"Don't talk," said George, observing his helpless condition.

"Sir," he mustered.

"*Nicht… Reden.*"

"No, sir." The boy gripped George's fingers tighter.

"English?" George jumped back.

"Yssssss…" He spluttered his s's with splashes of deep red. George had to turn his head and hover his ear inches away from the boy's cremated lips. "Yes, sir. Born in Beccles… sir."

"Then what the bloody hell are you doing in this uniform?" George enquired, realising there was barely any branding left of it; barely any human left in it.

"M-m-mother's E-E-English… fa…fath…father's German, sir… that way… I got the best of both… sir."

"Or the worst of it," replied George.

"Eng… England looks so pretty from the clouds… sir."

"You don't have to call me sir, laddie, that's quite all right."

"Sss… Sorry about all this bombing."

The boy's eyes folded closed for the last time, leaving behind the only white he had left. Death came slow, like roaches over a fallen quince. He had died in that English turnip field, all the colours of the German flag.

"Jimmy… pass me my coat, would you, lad?" George calmly and respectfully laid the black jacket over the dead boy. Without a word, he marched hurriedly towards the shell of the burning zeppelin.

As the last of the flames dampened, smog glided across the surface of the Earth as if that too had been on fire. Like the flesh of the burning boy, the surface of Billericay only felt skin deep that evening. Hundreds of people now gathered around and many more were turning up by the minute. As dawn broke, soldiers armed with bayonets circled the aluminium bones. The fields were littered with motorcars, bicycles, motorcycles and traps. People didn't seem to care where they left them, and the nearby brambles were turned to metal.

"Anything we can do to assist, officer?" asked George, gesturing towards his wife and son.

"Stand bloody back if ya know what's good for ya! I'm losing my voice from saying so." The vein on the constable's head swelled. The imprint of an officer lay charred in the mud below his feet. Nothing remained of the man, a mere outline, a diaphanous shadow fallen from the burning zeppelin only moments before. Jimmy didn't understand what he was looking at.

"What if there's more men in there, Dad?"

"Ha! No men in there, boyo… only Germans," said the irritable constable.

"It's OK, Jimbo," George intercepted, glaring directly into the eyes of the law. "There's all these firemen see… If anyone is alive, they'll be the first to know." George ushered the three of them over towards an empty patch of grass. "Why are people so terrible at being human?" he whispered to Poppy.

"Why, George, what a profound question."

"Well, it's the one thing they should be good at really, isn't it?"

Once the remains of the twenty-two men had been gathered and carried down to a local shed, everyone could have a good time without a conscience. Jimmy was a two-headed boy that morning: rapturous and joyful at the patriotism that had evolved, sullen and grave about the bodies he had seen. He had never seen a dead boy before. Even with the masses shown on the cinema screen that evening, it was something he could never imagine his eyes getting used to in real life. He knew that he would never quite be the same again after that. He had been passive; he hadn't helped anybody. He felt like it wasn't his place, like he was observing nature take its own path. As for his dad, proud wasn't a strong enough word. Jimmy made a pact: next time, next time he would help. Next time, he would act!

The sun rose, and the surrounding fields were teeming as yet more onlookers arrived. The only vehicle heading in the other direction was the rusting back of an open-air truck with the entire rudder of the zeppelin strapped in.

Cleaved pieces of brown rope held it loosely in place as they rolled around the corner and departed Billericay.

There were tradesmen carts and lemonade stalls. One merry band had a makeshift sign: 'Stocks Souvenirs'. Young lads were selling parts of the metal organs they had collected from the wreckage, all at a week's wages. There were burnt fabrics in silk and cloth, aluminium chips.

"Well, look here… here you go, Birdman, a little souvenir…" George lifted a compass from the edge of the mangold field. It was roasted by flames and hardened by the cold, left looking like a fossil that had rested there for a million years. Jimmy rubbed away some of the soot and the glass shimmered silver in the rising sun.

"That'll save us a few pennies. Better the compass than the cross, eh, lad?" The device was laid out in his hands. Jimmy watched as the dial danced naively north, doing its job despite what it had been through.

Looking around it seemed the whole country was at Snail's Farm this morning, yet more and more kept turning up. Policemen were having a terrible time controlling the scene.

"If everyone is here, who is fighting for us over there?" George asked. Smears of black ash and dried blood criss-crossed his chest.

A young man in uniform arrived at the address of the flabby constable. "Second Lieutenant Sowrey," he exclaimed.

"I don't care who you are, you're not coming any closer, laddie! I have enough soldiers on guard!"

"I am a pilot for the Royal Flying Corp and I demand

to be escorted through."

"All right, Sowrey… don't shit yourself!"

"Well, that's it, you see, I can't… the chloride, blocks us up before the flight."

"Huh?"

"I was the one who shot it down."

"You did what?"

"Chased it all the way from Leyton, sir. The Huns don't go down easy… it took three of my drums and almost all my incendiaries… right up the Aris… sir."

The constable looked flabbergasted. "You mean to tell me you were responsible for killing these twenty-two Bosch?"

"Twenty-two? Is that how many there were? Oh, my."

"Well why didn't you say so?" the ebullient constable took his hand and shook it so that all the rolls in his chin were jiggling.

Jimmy was starstruck, he hadn't seen a true, gallant war hero before, not outside the printed press and certainly not alive. He studied the man in uniform as if he was from another planet. He bounced in and clasped the stranger's hand as if wanting to feel the physical form of the person who had saved hundreds of lives.

"Oh… I—"

"Thank you," said Jimmy, his adolescent voice fleeting between tones.

"The flying is fun, kid, but the killing… not so much, I'm afraid."

Jimmy finally let go and drifted back to admire the man in full view.

It was George's turn. He leant in and firmly shook the pilot's hand. "You were doing your duty. We are forever indebted." Sowrey gave an accepting nod as he locked eyes with George. All gratified men held such manners when addressing serious matters such as these.

"If only I got there sooner…" he said.

Poppy gave a curtsy.

As the three departed, one of the uniformed guards approached the constable.

"A lady's heel… must have been some crumpet on board, Sarge…" He held the article in his muddied hands, his face black with slag. Poppy gripped George's hand tightly as they followed Jimmy through the crowds; she was clutching her remaining shoe.

Jimmy didn't sleep a wink that morning. Last night, he had experienced a newsworthy event first-hand. Until that moment, Jimmy hadn't witnessed a real scene strong enough to make the history books or newspapers before. That, he thought, was the greatest thing: comparing what actually happened to how he actually felt, as he himself was there. That way, with confidence, he could write it up in the *School Gazette*. *No, bigger*, he thought, shaking his head at how small he had been.

Beside his bed hung the harrowing bleached image of a zeppelin gliding across the London skyline. Illuminated in searchlights, the firmament was a murky pallid blue. The silhouettes of St Paul's and Big Ben were in jeopardising positions. Below the scene, read:

Had he left his idol in that field?

He stared at the words he held: *The Picture of Dorian Gray. What was life?* he questioned. What was he to do with the one he held? Life was short, at least it was for Harry. Sure, he wanted to be a writer. But as he knew, writers need to live through the event, not just read about it in some paper. His dad was off to fight for his country! And what was he to do? Sit tightly at home scribbling underqualified critiques of other authors who had made something of themselves? No, he wouldn't stand for it. He would take his pen and carry it with him, beyond the viaduct, beyond Brentwood.

CHAPTER THIRTEEN

YOUR COUNTRY NEEDS YOU

H E SAW HER SEATED there the moment he dipped his head below the chapel ruins, her almond hair poking from her white nurse's cap, resting against the nape of her neck. She turned, the mole on her cheek sensing him as he approached, the roundness of her breasts silhouetted by the setting sun. Her instincts were right, she stood and clasped his hands in hers.

"Oh, Jimmy, I can't help but smile," said Grace, her plum lips spread across that soft, rounded chin. "It excites me so much to see you every time. How did your assignment go, when is your father off? Do tell me everything, you must?! Oh, but sit down first, sorry…"

Jimmy dropped his brown leather satchel under the

bench and positioned himself with one leg on the floor, the other folded at right angles on the wooden slats so that he could take her all in. He leant forward and kissed her little round mole. Her soft cheek rested against his a while before he started to feel the weight of her turn. Their lips met. Grace parted hers just enough to let him in. The tip of her tongue twirled around his and then retreated back to be all lips again. Jimmy leant back; her eyes were closed, her lips were two eager, red pillows waiting to be kissed again. Jimmy obliged.

"I haven't seen you since… well, last week!" She laughed. "It feels longer. Work, it's been… I was so tired sitting here, waiting for you and now that you're here, I feel… I don't know what all my fussing was about."

"Hush now," said Jimmy, leaning back in. "How come your skin is so soft? Your face, it's never seen a spot."

"It has… it's seen yours!" Grace giggling between kisses, wrapped her arms around the back of his head and began bunching and scrunching at his curls.

"I've missed you, Jimmy Ford!" she said, her crocodile eyes glowing like lamps.

"I've missed you, Grace Bergman!"

Streetlights dimmed throughout the town, casting dark shadows which made love against the cobblestones. Blackout regulations were in full swing and the lawless flames were seen waltzing from behind the windows. The Palace Cinema was shut today and only a few people milled between the closed shops. "Now… what was it you wanted to know first?"

"George, your dad, when does he leave?"

"Next Wednesday."

"Oh, Jimmy, you will miss him terribly."

"Yes… well. I know he has to, I know it's… compulsory."

"Doesn't make any of this right, does it?" Jimmy retracted in thought. "What was that you put in your bag as you walked over?"

"Oh, that was nothing… gas mask."

"You can't fool me, Jimmy Ford, that wasn't your gas mask. It looked, well, like a soldier's cap?!"

Jimmy reached down and lifted the leather flap. "Yes," he said. "It is—"

"Is that… his?" Jimmy raised his eyebrows. "Your… dad's?"

"Yes! Yes… it is. I wanted to, er… well, take it to school today, before he embarks, you know, silly, really!"

"No," said Grace, looking directly into his periwinkle eyes. Jimmy went to speak out but was interrupted. "No, it's not silly at all!" She smiled.

"You know, Grace, you know how I've always said, that to write about something, I mean to truly write about something, you need to experience it—"

"Yes, you do make me laugh, Jimmy. I can't believe you went to all those lengths, sneaking off to see the street where those two poor Jewish girls were killed in the raid—"

"Christian Street!"

"Right! Anyway, what were you saying? I need to slow my mouth down. We don't get to speak at the hospital, you see, not much, only on our breaks, and even then—"

"Oh, I don't think that mouth needs slowing down…" He leant in and Grace parted her lips for him.

Taped against the double oak door of the cinema hung a poster. The illustration showed a long line of khaki soldiers with a single space filled by a white billboard. The board read: 'This space is reserved for a fit man. Will you fill it?' Grace caught Jimmy looking at it through squinted eyes.

"Are you thinking about him again, Jimmy, your dad?" He nodded. "You know, you need not worry. He will do wonderful things and return to you with lots of tales… you can fill that notebook of yours!" She gestured to his satchel. "I'm sure he will write to you every chance he gets. Besides, I know it isn't the same, but I'll be here, I'll come by yours and see Poppy and you. Every chance I get…" Jimmy nodded. "You know. Seeing that dead German boy in the field last year, Jim, that can't have been easy."

"No, well—"

"I can't believe they are still showing that film." Grace gestured towards the billboard. "Surely everyone in the town has seen *Battle of the Somme* five times?"

"Yes. I have." Jimmy smiled.

"Ah, before I forget…" Grace was changing subjects faster than she could find the words. "There is a dance on at work, and it would be really nice if you could come with me… together, you know?" She lingered. "Jimmy, are you up to something?" Her eyebrows were shaped like two black question marks. His head bowed. "What is it? You can tell me anything, you know that."

"I can't let him go alone," he said finally.

"George? But isn't it compulsory, Jim, he has to—"

"Yes, I know all that. But I still can't, I have to find a way."

"A way? Jimmy, the war has no place for us yet—"

"I'm hardly a child," snapped Jimmy, knowing full well what she was going to say next.

"Well… you're acting like one." He could have guessed that too. Grace ushered her body away from his. "The war is real, Jim. It's not something you can just fabricate for one of your stories. The men I treat every day, you think they wanted to lose a leg, a lung, for some story to tell, some sort of experience?"

"That is the risk I will have to take."

"Jimmy, that's crazy."

"Then perhaps that's exactly what I am. But if I never go, Grace, I will never know. You're doing your bit, now let me do mine!"

"And what about your writing, your scholarship?"

"This will teach me more of life than any scholarship could!"

"I can't witness this happen, Jimmy, I just can't lose you… I love you, Jimmy Ford!"

Jimmy was taken aback. He knew it, damn, he felt it himself, truer than any sensation that had entered his body before. "Grace. Remember that day on the beach."

"Your dad and Poppy's wedding."

"*I'll go with you, Jimmy*, that's what you said. *I don't want to be left behind*—"

"That was Paris!"

"Then Paris it is."

"Jimmy!" Tears streamed down her rosy, inflated cheeks.

"Don't you see? There is nothing left for me here. After he goes, I'll have—"

"You'll have me. Jimmy. Isn't that enough?" she babbled. Before she could gauge any reaction, he leant in and kissed her soft, salty lips. He drew her close and her forehead tilted against his, their eyes angled as they whispered.

"OK," she muttered.

"OK?"

"I'll do it, Jimmy."

"Grace, I don't want you to do anything."

"Just tell me the damn plan, Jimmy Ford, before I change my mind."

Cricket legs conducted the forest orchestra. The colour of spring leaves turned grey below their feet.

"That should do us," said Jimmy, placing the last log diagonally against their wooden tepee. "That will hold us up for the night." Jimmy stood back and admired their entire bivouac. "Fit for a king, that is," he said, pressing against his construction and scraping the broken bark from his hands.

"Two kings." Wilfred smiled, his Cheshire Cat-like mouth the only object visible in the fading light. "What time do you think it is?"

"Not sure, Wilf."

"I bet it seems later than it is!"

"How can it seem later than a time we don't know anything about?" Wilfred shrugged.

"They have that new BST, don't they? That took effect again last week!"

"Dad calls it BS time. He says it was only introduced so people could work longer hours and not feel short-changed."

Jimmy got the fire roaring. He had little difficulty. Sticks of dead willow and clusters of dried bark sat on a nest of rounded white stones.

"Fire is the greatest invention of man," he said, echoing his dad's words. His friend couldn't agree more as Wilfred bravely dared the orange flame. Jimmy wrestled with the bottom of two tree stumps and placed them around the crackling embers as Wilfred watched.

"You want to be careful getting those sausages too close to the cinders!"

The pair sat opposite, with the dancing flame between them. Jimmy reached into the depths of his coat and removed a tin of Maconochie. He suspended the mess tin containing the collected river water above the fire and placed the can inside the bowl.

"Gawd. That fire ain't half hot against my head. Think that sun got me all burnt up," bleated Wilfred, shuffling his seat a little further away.

"Probably the reflection off the water."

"I don't think we will ever find 'em, Jim. I mean, 'ow far does the river go?"

"No idea, but it must stop somewhere... the sea, obviously."

"If the rivers all flow into the sea, why isn't it overflowing?!" Jimmy shrugged. "How much longer can we really look for, do you think?" Wilfred started calculating, using his red fingers. "Almost two and a half years it's been, Jim!" Both boys knew that this wasn't the real reason they were choosing to sleep below the stars that night. Initially, the boys had spent every weekend from winter

1914 through spring 1915 looking for those damn dolls, searching every fork, bank and tributary. But Jimmy got busy with his studies, the two of them were growing up and, although Jimmy didn't like to admit it, growing apart.

There was a fizz as a moth dived into the flame.

"Shall we play the sentence game?" requested Jimmy as the aroma of turnips, carrots and potatoes imbued.

"Here?"

"Here is as great a place as any. Just because we are in the woods now doesn't mean men haven't been telling tales on this very spot before us. Besides, let's not play the *same spot version*. You get points for saying things nobody has ever said… ever before, anywhere in the world. The fewer the points the better!"

"2,305," stated Wilfred boldly.

"I hadn't started the game yet, Wilf!"

"I know, but I think 2,305 other people have said that exact statement that ya just said there… if we are playing the *world version*."

"OK… so for you to get zero points, we both have to agree unquestionably that the sentence we say has never ever been said by any man…"

"Or woman…"

"Or woman. Or beast before… anywhere in the world, in any other language. That clear?"

"Clear," assented Wilfred, leaning readily inwards. "Although, I did like the version we played the other week when you have to say a sentence that someone else in the world was saying at that very instant!"

"I know, that was funny, Wilf. But this… this is harder…

think of all those who have ever lived before us. I mean, it's unfathomable… truly." Jimmy leant back on his tree stump with his hands behind his head and gazed towards the black ocean of stars bobbing between ship-shaped clouds. The boys both knew that there wasn't any real way of telling if their sentences were truly uniquely spoken but it would lead to some riveting laughs whilst they waited for their al fresco dinner to heat through.

"If animal bones… or our own bones dissolved, that would be the end of history, wouldn't it?"

"Wow," said Wilfred, in awe of his friend's first attempt. "Hmm… scientists would have been saying that for years, though, Jim," he concluded. "People would've said that before. In hundreds of languages too… I'm certain of it."

"I hadn't started, Wilf! Wait a second, would ya? I'm just trying to tell you something." Wilfred sighed a hiss between his gapped teeth. "Think about it, Wilf. There would be no fossils, no discovery… just clothes and tracks… actually, the clothes would even dissolve, wouldn't they?"

"Animals don't wear clothes!"

"Our clothes!" Jimmy chuckled. "Without bones, we wouldn't know how big anything was or what anything looked like… no dinosaurs, no dodos."

"No dogs…"

"Of course, there would still be dogs… Pippa would still be…" Jimmy paused, realising his mistake too late. "I just mean everything that has been extinct, we wouldn't know it had existed, if bones dissolved!"

"Hmm…"

"There's this one animal, a fish in the Amazon…

Montrose… he had been! He said that the locals are terrified of it. Apparently it's really tiny—"

"Then why they so scared?"

"It can swim up your wee stream and insert itself right in ya japs!"

"Ewww." Wilfred burst his supressed laughter and grimaced in pain at the thought of it. He held his crotch and rolled his legs side to side.

"Would it go on flapping?"

"I don't know, Wilf, think it just burrows in there."

"Ask Montrose!" demanded Wilfred, still squealing as if he wouldn't stop until he found out the truth.

"He's still out fighting, Wilf." Jimmy stared into the cluster of trees. "Anyway, let's start the game, shall we?" A gnat buzzed around the bubbling stew.

"I've got one!" Wilfred screeched.

"Proceed, Professor Needham," mocked Jimmy.

"OK, OK… If that gnat doesn't stop, I'm going to… shoot it."

"Oh, come on, Wilf, that has got have been said a million times!"

"Na ah! Think about it, to shoot you need a gun and guns haven't been around forever."

"OK, I get that, but you could also *shoot an arrow*, before that! Besides, all the wide world over people are annoyed by gnats. Every single day. That must have been said at least a thousand times, by thousands of tongues!"

"It would be pretty impossible to shoot a gnat, though, eh?"

"That may be. But you don't get fewer points in this

game for making the task impossible. It's how common the sentence is."

"OK, OK," said Wilfred, dejected. "You try."

Jimmy leant back and took inspiration from above. "If I ate every star at the size they look from Earth, I bet I would wind up the same weight I am now."

"That's positively bonkers," giggled Wilfred, joining Jimmy's glance up to the sky.

"Do ya reckon ya would, Jim? That sure is a lot of stars."

"But look how small they appear from down here." Jimmy's legs were jittering. He needed to go to the toilet, but he didn't want to miss a thing, even though weeing outside was his favourite of all. "We should play this game when we're older and wiser, Wilf. We'll have more words then," said Jimmy.

"Nonsense, Jim, that was a good one, zero points."

"Really?" Jimmy expressed with real surprise. "OK, so that's zero points to your thousand. There was another fizz. "The moths sure like our fire," said Jimmy as another grey pair of suicidal wings took the plunge.

"'Ow close do they have to get before they realise the heat will fry 'em?"

"Too close, by the sounds of it," giggled Jimmy as another one sizzled in the inferno.

The steaming can brought the game to its natural conclusion. The boys took turns to scoop out chunks of beans, onion and veg. If they were lucky, they caught a clump of beef.

"Vile," laughed Wilfred. "Utterly vile!"

Jimmy got the giggles as he scraped into the far corners.

The inside of the tin was as ridged as a whale's mouth.

"Tolerable," he said between breaths.

"Tolerable my arse," guffawed Wilfred, letting off a guff of his own.

"Bssssssst," the boys exploded. Jimmy felt more himself with Wilfred than any other being. "Ah, Wilfred. I've missed this."

"Shhhh," quelled Wilfred. "What was that?"

A tawny owl hooted and took flight. A squirrel disembarked a tree and froze against the firelight.

"Just a squirrel, Wilf."

"What if it's a wolf?"

"You don't get wolves in Brentwood, Wilf!"

"Go check Jim…please," his anxious friend pleaded. Jimmy rose to his feet and wandered into the darkness. He waited a while, observing the stillness the night brought with it. Then came a sudden crunch. Stepping into the clearing was the small face of a majestic fallow deer. She had dainty precision; barefoot as in cold snow. Her face was soft and delicate under the swaying moonlight. One ear flexed, the other folded. Jimmy suspected she had been wounded.

Closer, closer she neared, turning her head, distracted by a smaller sound in the darkness. A dormouse sniffed and scurried off through the wood sorrel. Against the firelight, the deer boasted her dusted spots; circles of sieved white flour against gilded fur. Jimmy gulped and stepped towards her. She was noble and gracious. She snapped her supple neck back at the sound of his footsteps and stared right through him.

"You poor thing" he whimpered, his own face reflected by her milky eyes. She was blind. The deer sprang into action, pinned legs bashing the sides of trees as she attempted escape. She stumbled and fell through a burgundy bush, her scut; white and pure. Composing herself the deer scampered away. Just like that, she was gone.

"Well, what was all that commotion?" said a startled Wilfred as his friend returned.

"Nothing," said Jimmy, not wishing to share the poignancy of the deer with his friend. "I told you, just a squirrel."

The boys moved out their stumps to make room to lie down. Their camp was suitably positioned in a dead-end patch of forest, blocked on three sides by a perimeter of dense coppice; their very own treeline cul-de-sac, roofed with leaves. The moonlight spliced light through the gaps, lighting the canopy with white lanterns overhead.

They looked up through the canopy towards the universe. Jimmy locked his fingers behind his head and took the deepest breath, his attempt to swallow it whole. The air was muggy and the weight of it smothered them both like a heavy cloak. He thought of the deer.

"It's difficult to distinguish the floor from the sky, don't you think? Like Van Gogh himself has decorated his own trench, without a single gap to ponder the horror."

"Jim?" Jimmy flashed his eyes over to his big friend and back towards the stars.

"Wednesday," he said before his friend could ask. "And before you say it, Wilf, it's compulsory service, he has to fight."

"Yes, but why not before?"

"He was widowed, Wilf... after my... so that meant, it wasn't compulsory then."

"Think they'll have a baby?"

"Wilf, no! He will be at war next week."

"Well, it might be in the range already!"

"I don't think so." Jimmy contemplated for a while.

"Yer Pa will be all right, Jim," Wilfred said, finally plucking up the courage to reassure his friend. "Look at mine. This is the fourth year." Wilfred cocked his eyes away from his friend and gazed upwards.

"Four years," whispered Jimmy. Both lay silent. Jimmy's way of thinking had changed, he knew he and Wilfred couldn't relate in the same way they could as children. But they were children together once, and that was enough.

"It's like I don't exist anymore, Jim!" Wilfred had been waiting for this moment. "Back home, that is." Blankets of water filled his podgy eyes.

"Ah, Wilf, your mum just has a lot on her mind after—"

"Harry. Yeah I know." He paused. "But he wasn't the only one living with us, Jim. She ain't the only one suffering… he, he was my favourite brother, Jim!" He lifted his body, arched it like a chrysalis and wept. Jimmy inclined, crossed his legs and sat silently beside his friend. He was waiting for him to transform into a beautiful butterfly. There were no words. Not that could change the way things were. His butterfly wings had been torn off.

But this was Jimmy's moment.

"I have an idea, Wilf," he said finally, placing his hands on his friend's curved shoulders.

"Yeah," Wilfred spluttered. "Another one?"

"Yeah. One you'll like, Wilf… sincerely." Jimmy held his gaze. Wilfred lifted his head and Jimmy wiped away his tears on the sleeve of his coat. He knew it would work; he knew his friend didn't have anything to stay home for. Not since his mum had stopped talking. How the war had taken everything from her, how she had longed for daughters.

Jimmy jumped to his feet and paraded back and forth in front of his meek friend. He adopted a thick German accent.

"You English. We have come, and we'll come again soon. Kill or cure." Wilfred stared vacantly forwards. "That was the note Linnarz left on the unexploded shell he dropped over Essex!" Nothing. "You remember the story about Jack Cornwell right?" Wilfred shook his head. "Well, he was fifteen years old when he joined the Royal Navy... he was an Essex lad too. Well... he was born here, Wilf."

Wilfred half-smiled. "How did he go undetected?"

"He didn't. He got a letter of recommendation from his headmaster!"

"There ain't no way I would get one from my boss!" sniffed his husky friend. "Too many letters to deliver." He preoccupied himself with scraping lines in the mud with a twig.

"Just listen, Wilf... his older brother served in the infantry, that's why he wanted to fight, you see. Just like you. He probably lost someone." Jimmy added solemnly, "Like us."

"Is he still alive?"

"And get this... at sixteen, he was awarded the Victoria Cross!"

"Is he still breathing?" Wilfred demanded.

"I don't think so. But that's not the point. He was only

a few months older than us and he got out there. He fought for his country. What can we say, eh?"

"We can say we didn't die like your mate Jack... like Harry... like Leefe!"

Jimmy dipped his head a little. "Wilfred... Leefe isn't dead!"

"He is. His plane was shot down in April."

"Wilf, didn't you hear? They received a letter home. He's in a POW camp," said Jimmy with sincere exuberance. Wilfred peered back upwards. The whites of his eyes glistened in the dying firelight. "Listen, Wilf. I've been busy at the shop most nights. I've made us uniforms." Wilfred looked up at his friend like a rounded hedgehog who had tasted sour milk. "Listen, Wilf," said Jimmy again. "Pa is catching the eleven o'clock train from Brentwood to Liverpool Street on Wednesday. He's heading for the front!" Jimmy tugged at his pensive friend. "Wilf?" He rotated his big body towards him. "You, Grace and I. We have to be on that train!"

CHAPTER FOURTEEN

WAX DIAMONDS

W EDNESDAY 13TH JUNE 1917 was a stupendously
bright morning and Jimmy's disposition married it
well. It was one of those comfortable hazy days, when, for
the first time, you admire the clouds over their mother sun.
Gilded rays flew through his bedroom window and dappled
in luminous pearls of light. The stained glass of a broken
cathedral window fragmented in all its beauty.

Jimmy paused with his door ajar, absorbing one final
image of the place.

"This isn't goodbye. It's farewell," he whispered at all his
harmonious things. No Ghosty, no Buck; no companion
to travel with. As his door clicked closed, he got an
overwhelming sense of never opening it again. So, he did, one
final snapshot to ensure he could return whenever he needed

to. He grabbed the burnt-out compass from the zeppelin and removed his mother's photo from its frame. "You're free now," he said, replacing it on the side table with a letter he had written to Poppy. With piety and honour, he followed downstairs the dispersing footprints of many soldiers.

George and Poppy were standing outside the cottage, allowing the sun to take them. George was robed in full uniform and the weight of him reminded Jimmy that the gravity of war was infinite.

"Well?" George spread the wings of his Burberry Tielocken and gave an approving nod. "Give those Germans a run for their money, right?"

"Sure do, Dad." Jimmy smiled.

"Tailor first, soldier second." George winked. This was the second time he had dressed in his nation's cloth but only the first time that he'd altered it himself with needle and thread. It suited him as well as his own naked flesh. "It's my second war, kiddo," he said. "I'll have musket breath when I return!" Poppy giggled like a schoolgirl. "I've left the key in the usual spot, Birdman. Pops will only be a few hours, all right, lad?"

Jimmy nodded. He wouldn't need it. He imagined poor Poppy knocking and calling his name through the letterbox into the empty house. It's only then she would notice the unmoved key dangling there.

George looked at his inside wrist.

"Train departs in twenty minutes. Let's take a slow walk, shall we, my musketeers?"

A slow walk it was. The station had never seemed so far. Jimmy toed the path as if it was for the last time in his life, taking in every tree, bird tweet, post and person. Their local faces nodded at George with pride as he passed them by.

Jimmy had everything meticulously planned. That morning, before the young lovers rose, he had packed his battered case with his and Wilfred's uniforms. He'd spent the last few evenings stitching them by candlelight, getting the measurements just right. He didn't stop until the reflection in the mirror gave him back that approving nod. "You'll be the best dressed on the front, Private Jimmy Ford."

"Why thank you," he answered himself. Alfred was bound not to notice two missing uniforms in that mess. For the past month, Jimmy had been hauling the surplus cloth in his pockets and discarding them on the way to school. Grace had her uniform already and would be where she had promised.

That morning, Jimmy had placed his luggage bag under the bench in the corner of the station waiting room. Wilfred had strict directions of where this treasure was located. After the send offs were concluded, Jimmy would knock three times and the pair would race towards the back carriage, where Grace would already be waiting. Once aboard, they could use the toilet to change and, "The rest is like falling off a log," Jimmy affirmed. *Providing none of them were caught by George or Poppy, that is.*

As the three musketeers slowed on the platform, the new Mrs Ford fell quiet. She let Jimmy take centre stage; she knew that the relationship between a man and his boy was unbreakable, even through war. Besides, she had her husband all last night, and for forty-five-minutes more. The dragon-toothed awning hung over them and Jimmy felt the heat of its breath. He calculatedly stopped outside the red waiting room door. This was it.

George went to perch down onto one knee like the night he proposed to Poppy under the pillar of the Palace Cinema. He stopped, deciding it better to talk man to man. He reached forward and removed a dried, bloodied tissue from his son's upper lip. The pair of them laughed.

A hospital train slowed on the opposite track; its painted red crosses were as conspicuous as blood. Heaps of mangled and maimed men disembarked with the aid of stained, covered nurses and loyal station staff. The soldiers were once dressed the same as squeaky-clean George here. Some were blessed, placing the feet they had left back on British soil. Others should have been left back there, remembered for who they were.

George took Jimmy's hands in his. Jimmy glanced down. His dad's hands had lived a life. A life with him and a life before him.

"Be kind, Jimbo," said George. "Everyone you meet has their own demons. Don't add to them. They are all going through tough times in some way or another. You stay kind and you can't falter. Life will take care of the rest."

Jimmy nodded. The reality of his father's departure hit him, the magnitude of what he himself was about to embark on.

"Be wise, be just, be reverent... but," said George, shattering Jimmy's ambivalence, "take every experience and don't regret a thing, because life is now and not the end of some road or that track." George pointed towards London. "But right now!" Jimmy beamed, his fate reaffirmed by his old man. "Now, I'll be back before you know it, Jimbo, but I don't want you counting down the days either. Poppy will be with you for all that boring adult stuff. "You're in the prime of your years, son. Go be a kid, kiddo!"

Jimmy could tell he'd been rehearsing; it was endearing beyond any measure. The importance of a fair goodbye had always been of high priority in the Ford household.

"Always try and find meaning behind things, Jimmy, not just reasons. Some things happen for no reason, no purpose at all." He looked at the boy and knew they were both thinking of his mother. "But the meaning behind things, that's different, it's what you take from it that makes it worthwhile, son. Today you are alive; tomorrow you rest. When tomorrow comes, it will be today, and you'll live again. Apply that every day, Jimbo. Except, of course, on the day you die. But that's a long way off yet." He winked.

The Pullman whistled as it cleared its lungs of steam and slowed beside the platform edge. Their view of the injured men was wiped clean. Time was running out. He undid the brown strap from his watch and placed it around Jimmy's wrist.

George hoisted his shoulders, rattling the contents of his backpack. Jimmy had helped him organise the kit only yesterday evening, what now seemed light years ago. Its contents: a greatcoat, mess tin, wash kit, groundsheet and entrenching tool. Perhaps the most important to George, or so Jimmy thought, was the trench pencil.

"Dad. Don't try and make the other soldiers laugh, OK?" George looked at his curious son, more curiously. "Harry was always like that and he… he—"

"Look here, Birdman. I will return in one way or another. I'll be back here with you, talking movies and reading stories. By the time I'm back, I want you to have written your own Birdman, you hear?" Jimmy nodded; he sure would have enough material by then. "Keep Pops involved too, won't you? Take her to the pictures occasionally… with you and Grace. You're the man of the house now!" Jimmy bowed his head, knowing he wouldn't entirely except the title. "Look, Jimmy, there are a lot of injustices in the world. Some we mere humans will never sort. One is wealth. Wealth is measured in different ways, not just in money. I am rich, as rich as any king because I have you in my life… and I have Poppy." George used his thumb and forefinger to pinch the left cheek of Mrs Ford. She smiled the saddest smile Jimmy had ever seen.

"The worth of a man is not in his wallet but in the people he meets along the way. The people he loves and who love him."

"I wish I could come with you, Dad," said Jimmy. "I'd make a good soldier."

"I'd follow you over the top, Sergeant Ford!" George saluted. Jimmy smiled. Overnight, he'd been promoted from private to sergeant. "Goodbye, Birdman." George clasped the most precious thing on Earth into his chest. Jimmy got one last whiff of Creola biscuits. He could feel the pounding of his dad's heart. *Stay beating forever. Wherever you beat.* He closed his eyes and heard sniffling.

"It's only farewell, Dad," corrected Jimmy.

George nodded in agreement and tipped his hat. He had veiled his emotions long enough. His mouth was next to go. He scuffled Jimmy's remaining hair. It was a short, curly, crew cut. Jimmy had insisted it had needed trimming, to match his role, of course.

"Ah, come back here!" ordered George, unable to conceal his tears. "I don't care who's looking. You can never be too old to give your old man a squeeze." Jimmy's head was now burrowed back into his dad. This time his heart was faster. Poppy clasped her arms around the two of them like a cowgirl with a lasso. They stayed there, closed and as impenetrable as a rugby scrum.

"Remember what I always tell you, Jimbo?"

Both Fords repeated the sentiment: "Fear nothing in life because living in fear raids your time away."

The train whistled.

"All aboard," yelled the conductor. If only he knew how precious moments at stations were. George placed his left hand on Jimmy's and Poppy added hers on top, their diamonds glistening in the sunlight. They inspected each other's flushed faces and smiles prevailed; they always did.

"Farewell, my dear boy."

The end carriage, as planned, was empty. The panels were lined in a fine wood and the seats a beaten brown. Jimmy saw the little sign of Brentwood and the house he was born retreating on the plain. This was it! The fields, endless, golden wheat fields. He wondered if the pastures on the front would be as lush and smell as sweet. The train picked up speed and thumped along, roaring like a wild beast ready for battle. The hum from the tracks brought the bustle of life into his soul. The pair of them sat silently as they passed over the wooden viaduct and the brook either side where the treasures of their childhood rattled inside a mess tin. Jimmy imagined the plane below his seat orbiting in wide arcs, just as excited as he. Then there was Ghosty, long-lost Ghosty. *The doll will have to find his own way now*, he thought. And Buck, whatever had become of his white wolf?

The boys had taken turns in the toilet and were back seated as soldiers before the next station.

"How do I look? It's a bit tight around the legs, Jim," said Wilfred, attempting to separate the khaki cotton from his chunky thighs.

"You look younger when you smile," said Jimmy. Wilfred's heavy lip dropped to cover his jagged milk teeth. He was rosy-cheeked like he was teething again. "Couldn't you have at least worked up a small beard?"

"You know I can't grow hair, Jim."

Jimmy looked down at his crotch. "Yes, I can believe it."

The boys giggled.

"Well, you can't exactly call that fluff on your face… a beard."

Jimmy stroked at it self-consciously. In all the initial elation, Jimmy had forgotten.

"Uh, Jimmy… where is Grace, wasn't she suppose to…?" Jimmy's heart jumped into his throat and he rotated in all directions until he was dizzy. "Perhaps she got the wrong carriage?" offered Wilfred innocently.

"No," said Jimmy. He knew full well she hadn't. He bit his lip so hard that it drew blood on the inside. He wiped it with his khaki sleeve, leaving a red smear on the brass button.

"What do we do now?" Jimmy sat silently, steering at his solemn reflection in the glass. He felt a fool. A fool in costume. There was a creak as the carriages parted. He saw a soldier walking. Time stopped. The compartments parted and he caught another glimpse.

"How long will it take us… to get to the front? I didn't even bring snacks," said Wilfred, his back to the action.

"Not now, Wilf…" Jimmy caught another sighting of the man in uniform. There was someone else with him: a woman.

"Why the windy face?" said Wilfred.

"Wilf! Do not turn around. I think my dad and Poppy are walking right this way!" Wilfred's eyes leant to one side, awaiting the door to open and the lecture to commence. "Why the bloody hell are they walking all the way to the end carriage?" said Jimmy between gritted teeth. "We are for it now, Wilf." He turned quietly, secretly glad he got to see them both again.

"Well? What's happening, Jim?"

Jimmy breathed for the first time. "They've sat down. They are at the other end of that carriage." He nodded. Jimmy saw his dad remove a white handkerchief and wipe sweat around his eyes and forehead.

"That was bloody close, Wilf!" He play-punched his friend in the arm.

"Hey! You can't do that… I'm a soldier now!"

"There is no reason they will come this way now, Wilf. When we pull in to Liverpool Street we will just have to wait a few minutes and they should walk that way… forward!" Jimmy gestured with his hands.

"How long will that be?" asked Wilfred again. Jimmy checked his inside wrist, his dad's brown watch.

"Forty-five I reckon Wilf… it's nearly eleven!"

"Think I'll see Billy or Pa first... when we get to the front?" Jimmy shrugged. "When you think we'll get our guns?"

"Minor details, Wilf. Let's just get there first, shall we?"

Jimmy's mind drifted. It only felt like yesterday he was picking out pear drops in the sweetshop for Grace. Grace, beautifully safe Grace. Of course, she wouldn't come, and he knew now how unfair it was to expect it of her. She had her life and that was here. Where this train was heading was no place for her. He wished he hadn't been so foolish. He shouldn't have asked that of her, put the weight of it upon her. If he had just taken a breath and thought of the consequences of it all. *She will wait*, he thought. *She will wait for me to return.* He looked out over the folding green fields and smiled. *If I had known, I would have filled her entire letterbox with pear drops. Pear drops and a note. 'Suck one a day and I will be back before the last enters your mouth.' Grace. If only you knew. I'll write to you soon... my love.*

"Captain!" interjected Wilfred.

"That's right, Private Needham. I am your captain."

"No... there, captain boarding the train at Harold Wood." Wilfred pointed behind Jimmy.

"Ah, Christ. We're stuck, Wilf. If he asks questions, we're done for!"

"Again?"

"You know what the punishment is for impersonating a..." Jimmy's voice trailed off.

The door slammed shut. The boys sat as stiff as boards. Jimmy watched Wilfred's fat, frantic eyes as the hard clunk of boots got closer. A large man with a moustache swayed and belched and almost fell into the adjacent seat. Behind him glided a slimmer version of himself, shoes barely stirring the floor. The thinner man was a private, wearing khaki which matched the uniform worn by the two boys. He placed himself on the seat directly in front of his captain.

The scent of scotch permeated the already cramped cabin. The captain leant across with a grunt, offering the boys a swig from a ruffled brown bag. His eyes were puffy, squinting slits of lid. Jimmy shook his head on behalf of both of them.

"Not for us... sir."

"S-s-suit yourselves, young'uns," he said, eyes rolling about the place. "S-S-Scully, you take another tot, boy." The private obliged. "None of you can judge. You ain't seen nothin'. Look at ya, look 'ow clean ya all are. How c-c-clean those minds are. I was like you all once." Scully ignored the captain. He had heard it all before. He took another glug and retired his shoulders. He removed the captain's hat and slouched back with it covering his face. The captain didn't even notice; he was almost blinded by drink.

"He's a darned foo-ool!" said the captain, loquaciously looking in all directions. "If he wasn't in charge, half our boys wouldn't be comin' home in wooden boxes."

Jimmy checked; the captain was talking *at* the sleeping private.

"Take Loos, for example, over sixty-thousand of *our* men, triple the Huns... only a fool would obey the French commander and do exactly as he was told!" The captain fell onto the window and propped himself back upright. "I bet Haig still did it with that o-op-optimistic smirk on his face too. Give me

George any day," he slurred Scottish. "Men, I'm ain't ordering you to fight, I'm ordering you ta die." Jimmy's eyes lit up. He'd heard his dad recite that one before. "That's w-what he may as well a' darned said!" The captain slugged his scotch and flopped his head onto his chest like a newborn baby. "The only man on either side who could lose the war in an afternoon. Wasn't that what Churchill said after Jutland? Well... he said it about the wrong man, he must 'ave meant Haig!"

In the brevity of silence, Jimmy peeked through the carriage door and watched the two lovers wrapped around each other. If only George knew what his precious son was getting himself in for.

Jimmy turned sombre. He knew he could never reveal himself to his old man; he may never get the chance again. He observed as the lovers twirled their rings in each other's palms. He spied those white flecks on the back of George's head, suddenly overwhelmed by the sense of a wasted goodbye. The urge to get up and run through the carriage and sit beside his new mother was too great. The Earth was vaulting, suffocating him. His dad turned his head to the side and curled the corners of his moustache. It was like he sensed his son somewhere nearby.

George had taken Jimmy down the White Hart last night. He said that if he was to leave and never return then he needed Jimmy to be left with the first taste of beer on his lips. He at least wanted that honour.

"She was a delectable woman, your mother," George had slurred after his sixth. "You know. She would always read to you when you were in her belly? Maybe that's where you got your passion for books. Do anything for anybody, she would.

Could talk the hind legs off a donkey. But she knew how to listen too. No one will ever replace her, Jim. Poppy and her, they aren't alike. Your ma was never lost, not like Poppy and me. I need a companion for the remainder of my years, Jim, and I need a mother, a mother for you, you understand that, don't you?" Jimmy also found out why his mother had died. "You were breached, weren't you! Bloody legs first, as always!"

After recent events, Jimmy wondered what was so good about beer.

The captain realigned himself on the seat and startled Jimmy out of his own dreams.

"Some of those casualties was from our own g-g-gas! We used it, killed most of our own. That bloody a-accessory. And why were we wearin' fucking kilts? Gas travels to the sweatiest part of the body, don't it? The Germans started it and we've been ordered to use it tenfold s-since. Fucking turnip eaters… I mean, what the fuck happened to all the potatoes, that's what I wanna fucking know!" Another pause as he lost his train of thought. He was still directing his drooling speech towards the sleeping private. "Our men would be better off in the trench they've dug in Blackpool, Scully. P-penny a time and a wounded soldier with VD!"

Jimmy had little comprehension of what the captain was saying but deep down he wanted to know it all. Wilfred stared with heavy eyelids out the window. Trees chased cattle across boundless fields. The rumps of pigs sprayed black, adhering to regulation. Light flickered the shade of walls and poles and signal stands into their cart as they passed.

"They should've listened ta Kitch, stuck the wine, not the women!" Another sup. "My, my, least they had a jolly good ol' time beforehand, eh?" He nudged Scully, who grunted.

The captain finally focused his attention on the boys. "What 'bout you two young whippersnappers... are you having a good time?" Jimmy pursed his lips. He didn't need to answer. "Blimey, they make them young nowadays, dunny they?!" he said, leaning in towards Jimmy as if collaborating. Wilfred's baby face blushed red. "You look as young as Private Condon. J-John Condon. Too young to shave. Younger, in fact." The captain shrugged. "I was there, you know... Second battle of Wipers. I saw the yellow gas, the chlorine mist that took him. I mean, what d'you think a soldier even is? Hardly any of the boys who sign up are soldiers. They just die that way! This ain't just war against an enemy, it's a war against ourselves. All that sinful shit we been doing here at home. War is correcting the wrongs of our past." The captain pinched Jimmy's cheek. "The three L's." The captain prepared each finger. He had a few failed attempts at finding them. "Luxury, lust and... er, oh, liquor. It costs four times more during war and it is the same diluted. So, I must save up ma money and drink more of it!" The captain's eyes rolled back. "This w-war will end where it started, lads. I was at Mons when the first shot was fired. I see the angels. I signed the fucking tablecloth. You mark my words..." His plump body slumped across the seats. "Mons." He chuckled. "Our fucking gas. A change of wind... sometimes that's all it takes!" It wasn't long before he too was snoring.

Jimmy and Wilfred didn't talk for a while. They couldn't risk being exposed. Besides, what on Earth was there to say after that? Jimmy could tell what Wilfred was thinking. They had made a mistake. They should turn back. Jimmy looked through the compartment to his dad. He couldn't turn back now, even if he wanted to.

Their eyes darted from left to right as they admired the silent view through the window. The carriage passed fields of yellow wheat bending in the gallant breeze. Particles of falling dust danced and crackled around them under the flickering sun. It had been years since Jimmy boarded the train towards the city. Life was nearing.

At the next stop two more men boarded and sat with their backs to Jimmy. One wore blue naval, the other a red cross.

"Doughboys!" whispered Wilfred, listening to their faraway accents. And boys they were.

"He kept us out of the war?"

"Yeah, right," the soldier bleated. His voice was nasally and irritatingly loud.

"And I voted for him too!"

"Peace without victory, eh?"

"Unrestricted subs are what done it for me, Ernest. That, and the fact they are in our pockets… quite literally."

"You have our pal Zimmerman to thank for my enrolment."

"Where you heading to, anyway?"

"Italy, Humphrey, you?"

"France, to start with… on to Paris, most likely."

"Reckon I'll join them in Isonzo."

"Decimation! Let's hope you're not tenth in line, eh, Ernest?"

"No Italian is shooting me. We've only just got there… my fate can be decided by the Good Lord!"

"The Heinies may have something to do with it as well, eh?"

"I could see myself living there, you know?"

"Isonzo? What on Earth for?"

"No! Paris, Humphrey. Once this is all over with. Find myself a fine little Chicagoan and make a Parisian princess of her!" The two men wouldn't have had anything in common if they weren't fighting in the same damn war.

As the train slowed into Stratford, the Americans were replaced by two more: a young nurse and her boyfriend in blue. It was romantic hearing their exotic accents. Jimmy's ears erected as they discussed a comedy they had just seen: *The Cure* starring Charlie Chaplin. The stench of scotch from the snoring captain was fitting given that Charlie played a drunkard who checked into a health spa with a suitcase of alcohol. Jimmy had seen it last week with his dad. He smiled wondering what impersonation George would have conjured for that production.

The boyfriend nudged his sweetheart and encouraged her to look at the slumped captain.

"We'll give him the benefit of the gout, shall we?" The pair bellowed with laughter, referencing the scenes from the movie.

"Oh, I do wish you could stay, Johnnie. Just another night or two. We could see *Easy Street* tomorrow or *Butcher Boy* with Buster Keaton."

"It's no use, Annie. If I'm not back by three, there will be no tomorrow for me."

Jimmy smiled. He couldn't imagine a world without the movies. *When I return it's the first thing I'll do, take Grace to the cinema. Then, I'll ask her to be my sweetheart. Properly, that is, with a ring. She'll have to say yes, there is nothing more romantic than a film!*

"Be careful up there, Johnnie!"

Jimmy whipped his head round, witnessing Annie point towards the sky. He was a pilot, a real pilot!

"Bloody April," wept Annie. "Tell me there won't be another bloody April, Johnnie!" Jimmy felt a pang in his chest. He knew what Annie meant. It felt like centuries ago when his father read the news to him. It had only been a matter of months. April saw hundreds of pilots shot down. It made Jimmy feel lucky that his legs were firmly on the ground for once.

"Annie, I've written something."

"A letter?"

"A poem. Here, I want you to take it home and—"

"Oh, Johnnie. Read it to me now, dear."

Johnnie opened the sealed envelope. "It's not finished yet, it still needs a lot of work," he defended.

"Johnnie!"

He checked around the carriage and cleared his throat.

"A Soldier's Son,
By me, Johnnie B."

Annie reached for his hand, interlocked his fingers in hers and placed it onto her lap.

"I am a soldier's son,
Startled by the thrall of guns,

> **Terrified I'll never be a man,**
> **The man he was once."**

Jimmy leant his head to the side, opened his ears and watched his father's every move.

> **"He was a Tommy,**
> **But I am a fighter,**
> **He ran further,**
> **I flew higher."**

The train rattled between blocks and towers. The city was coming. Jimmy looked at the captain, who was coughing out his snores. He thought about what a waste of time sleep was. Blinking is bad enough, but you miss out on so much life when you sleep unnecessarily. The poetry of it all.

> **"There was an April once,**
> **This one fled,**
> **Not this time,**
> **This one bled."**

The deafening sound of planes squawked like pterodactyls overhead. Everyone on the train rushed to the windows. The formation of them matched that of the birds: perfect diamonds. Pigeons flew westwards in messier swarms.

"Johnnie?" Annie questioned. "Is that us or… them?"

The train entered the dark tunnel of Liverpool Street station.

> "Up above the trees,
> The albatross soared,
> Black Maria screamed,
> Woolly bears roared."

"Johnnie?"

Johnnie was somewhere else. The torpid train slowed into platform nine.

> "Between the swarms,
> An iron cross,
> A Gotha's nest,
> Paradise lost."

The train stopped.

"Johnnie?"

Shadowed wings expanded, obscuring the station roof. Black painted the walls from the top down. Below the Gothas, the hatch doors opened. *Whiizz.*

> "Knock, knock,
> It's me at the roof,
> I'm here to maim,
> I'm here to spook."

The train doors parted and out stepped George and Poppy, white diamonds flashing between their linked hands. *Whiiizzz.*

"I once was a soldier's son,
But now,
Now I am no one."

The point of the black bomb scythed the station roof. Concrete folded like liquid waves. Lead and blood and flesh in all directions. Trunks and limbs of skin like wax dummies laid.

Jimmy ran in motions so slow, like a giant net had been cast over him. Inaudible begs from Wilfred died on silenced ears. He fell to the platform, losing his cap. He crawled through dust and grey clouds of smut and smog and smoke which he now inhabited. Coughing, spluttering, he disappeared like a soldier seen amongst the mist for the last time in no man's land.

Masses scurried over one another like louse. Some were upturned in shock; others, unrecognisable doll parts. He crawled and crawled, clasping his hand around the ankle of a man rocking back and forth. His bare torso spotted like a red and black leopard.

"S-s-secret m-m-ission, S-S-Sergeant S-S-Stone." He was surrounded by the fabric of old clothes.

Silence.

Plane engines.

Animal screams.

The train was hit this time. The carriage wood splintered like bone. Glass blasted into atoms. Pillars toppled. The world crumpled inwards. No memory of a life outside the blast radius, only purgatory within.

More engines. Passing planes.

Jimmy unclasped his hands. His face was speckled with blood and ash, inanimate and human.

"*Dad!*" he yelped from the sooty cords of his throat. Wet tracks of tears parted the black mounds his cheeks had become. "*Dad!*"

He crawled to the lip of the platform edge. The track below was hollow. Up against the wall, empty eyes stared back. Two buckled, dead corpses.

The bodies had melted together to become one. A soldier and his wife. A father and his new love, their arms wrapped around one another. Their spines coiled like two white snakes. There were flaps of lung where skin should be, brains where skulls should. Their left index fingers sparkled from a myriad of diamonds.

Jimmy didn't respond. He was nowhere. Carted away from London, four tons heavier; he was living inside the raindrop.

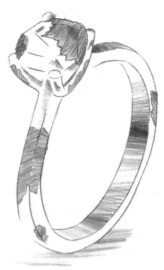

CHAPTER FIFTEEN

DAD

JIMMY COULD SEE HIS arms when he crawled, but with each movement, a new ghost of himself was born. Double vision, triple vision and so forth. He crawled until he didn't know who the real Jimmy was and who were the intruders his mind had created. All he could smell, and taste, was rain. As he swallowed, a metallic paste occupied his palate. The more he swallowed, the harder it became to do so. He felt panic, fear, impending doom. His tears flooded the cracks of the concrete platform as he was carried away on its current.

Disconnected, like a cord being snipped from a baby. For a moment, everything silenced.

The floor disappeared. He hung, suspended on the end of an anchor being lowered. Down into the dark he was taken. He had never felt so alone.

A round screen receded on the plain above him, distorted, like he was seeing everything through a wall of water which kept cascading. His thoughts raced, but he couldn't make sense of them.

The porthole narrowed. A round frame of colour and life. Distant. Everything surrounding it was black. Further, further he descended away.

Slow, muffled music played like it was being wound backwards through a phonograph. The thunder of train tracks, the flicker of passing light. The sky moved like a zoetrope.

Inside the round portal, an electrical tempest surged. The lightning crackled and blazed like bright phosphorus bulbs. Blinding like camera flashes that popped and sparked. Faces flickered like a projection. They moved so fast that his brain couldn't comprehend who they were. *Dad? Poppy?* Rotating backwards, random, jumbled. He recognised them one second, then the next they were strangers. Terrified, he couldn't think. He didn't know who he was.

Lower he foundered into the darkness. He felt a strange rising in his chest. A sensation that his body was sinking through water, cloying and gloopy, black tar. Lightning whipped the water with its long tentacle. Jimmy's whole body shook as the electricity howled from inside. His body flopped, limp.

The sensation of falling had ceased. He'd hit the bottom of his well and the raindrop surrounding him had burst. His legs curled gently towards his chest into a foetal position. He felt drowsy, peaceful. He just lay there, floating in the tar. The screen was humming somewhere way off overhead.

Then there was silence and darkness, like the hatch of the well had been covered. He no longer had a porthole.

The well began to fill with more liquid. Jimmy heard gasping breaths ringing from inside. The liquid underneath propelled him upwards. The darkness blocking the hatch dissipated. He charged towards its opening. He could see the screen again. Bigger, brighter.

"Can you tell me your name, sonny?" a man with an imperial moustache echoed down his well.

Jimmy was numb. He could barely lift his head. "Jimmy... Jimmy John Ford," he whispered back from the darkness, a stranger to his own words.

"Can you hear me?" came the voice again.

"Jimmy John Ford," he repeated, his voice languid and meek.

"Let the young lad rest, Betsy. He'll come around soon enough."

"Shall I restrain him, Doc?" There was silence whilst the doctor was thinking.

"Yes, restrain him."

Jimmy's arms mechanically formed a cross against his chest. His legs stretched out and forced together.

"Remove his uniform too, we don't want his first thought to be embarrassment when he wakes."

"I'm awake!" Jimmy blubbered from the bottom of his well.

"Christ, they make them young, these soldiers."

"Shell shock again, Doc?" cooed the gentle, feminine voice.

"We won't know until he wakes." The doctor fiddled

with the curls of his moustache. "I'll send Doctor Turner in. He knows more on these matters."

"Right you are, boss."

"Offer him something when he is lucid, Betsy, it'll help with the nausea. This man has seen hell over at Liverpool Street Station. Probably a damn sight more if he had made it to the front."

"What time the Norfolk and Naspburys arriving, boss?"

"Ah, don't remind me. Six, I believe. This relief is only short-lived. We'll end up back with the worst cases."

"What to do about the overcrowding?"

"Right, well, leave the lad in here, Betsy."

"This is the children's ward, boss."

"So it is. Who is he bunking with?"

"Oren."

"Very well. Brief Oren."

"Brief Oren?"

"Tell… Oren, not too many questions when our soldier wakes. He knows how it feels when you first come around."

"Good day, boss." The squeaking of shoe soles.

"Oh, and Betsy, don't call me boss."

"Sorry, Doctor Campbell, sir."

Doctor Campbell nodded. "Frederick will do."

The sound of footsteps receded. The muffled voices dispersed.

Jimmy could see himself as if from another camera angle, out of body. Clothes began to slip from him, a mannequin being undressed in a store window. His sooty khaki uniform was replaced by soft cotton pyjamas, white.

After the transformation, there was a groan, a heavy

door sealed like the entrance of a great vault. Then, reticence. Not harrowing, nor deathly, more the sensation one could expect from the womb, the ebb and flow of amniotic bliss.

He breathed as if for the first time, born again.

Jimmy checked the brown watch on his inside wrist: 11:40. How could it be so cruel? The time the bomb had fallen. The time his dad's heart had ceased. He watched the hands until they ticked forward an extra minute and closed his eyes, letting the darkness take him once more.

Jimmy couldn't tell if he had slept. He tossed and turned in the strange room like a caveman protecting his grotto. From beneath the sheets he heard the bird chirping his lonesome call. He tossed the duvet, stood to his feet and approached the small, lead-laced window. There were red cinders in the clouds like the sky was on fire. The clouds crackled with the sound of falling bombs.

Behind him, there came a shuffle. Jimmy cranked his head to see Oren silently breathing under sheets.

"*Birdman!*" whispered the invisible voice.

"D-Dad?"

"It's me, *Birdman!* It's your old Pa!" The soldier stepped into the light from the shadows. He stood in front of the heavy closed door. Immaculate uniform, hair waxed and moustache neatly combed; clean as a whistle. Jimmy stood paralysed by the window, watching him with strange intrigue.

"*Dad!*" said Jimmy. "How did you find me?" George didn't respond. He slowed his step. "Where have you been?"

"I've been at home. I've been waiting for you, Jim!"

"N-no, it can't be. I saw you. I saw Poppy and you... you were de—"

"Dead? Never! Your old man doesn't die, Jim!" There was something different about his dad. He was changed somehow. Not his appearance, but his mannerism, his tone.

"Why can't I see you anymore, Dad?"

"You just can't, son."

"Was it me? Something I did?" George didn't reply. "Did I not make you proud?" Nothing. "Can I come live back with you, Dad? Please can I?"

"I can't, Jim."

"Why not? I'll be good. I'll study, I'll write, I'll make something of myself—"

"It's impossible," his dad said coldly. "You have to listen, Jimmy."

Silence filled the room.

"But you're not saying anything." George just stood there. "Dad!" Jimmy panicked. He didn't understand why he was acting the way he was. "Dad, it's not you, is it? Dad?" Jimmy was overwhelmed. He embraced him, hugged him round his middle and felt nothing but cold air. Ashes from his father crumbled from where his body had been. They scattered and tumbled to the floor. "Dad!" he wept.

"You have to listen, Jimmy."

"But you're not saying anything!" he cried. He reached up and placed his hand on George's lips. They crumbled and fell, adding to the pile of ash. "Dad!" he said desperately. "Dad, don't go, don't disappear!" The rest of his remaining limbs turned to dust and dispersed, nourishing the room.

Jimmy fell to the floor and wept like his soul was being burnt from the inside.

Jimmy gasped and bolted forward in his bed.

"Gaaaaarrrrrr, geeeeeerrrrr," he choked. It was light, and the room was empty. He fought for his breath from the force weighing on his chest. Once he caught it, he laid back against the firm mattress. His heart was thumping faster than ever. Tears came and went. He felt so hopeless. It was all just a terrible nightmare. But he'd woken up to another. A real one. Still here. Still in Warley Lunatic Asylum.

Wednesday 20th June 1917 was the longest day of the year. Quite literally; it was the summer solstice. For Jimmy, though, it was the longest for another reason. It was the day he would bury his father.

Another funeral was to be held today, to honour eighteen infants killed at Upper North Street School. Fifteen children to be buried in a mass grave. 'Louise, John and Grace are to be put to rest at their local cemeteries', read the accounts. Rest.

As Jimmy straightened his black tie in the smeared mirror, he thought of *his* Grace. He debated whether she knew where he had ended up. She would have heard the news of the bombs. She may have been sitting at their bench at the time the bomb was released. The bomb that had killed his dad! Jimmy imagined what fragments of memories George had watched before his body was blown apart. He buried the visual deep inside of him, only causing the feeling of pain to surface alone.

A florid complexion peered back at him from the

glass. He looked deep in the mirror and could tell it was thinking. His cheeks blanched of all colour, contrasting those red, bloodshot eyes. It was true, what Doctor Turner had said: his symptoms were more somatic, his seizures more frequent. There had been seven in the past four days. He felt drained of himself.

Jimmy popped a large whitehead on his neck and contorted at the noxious sensation it caused. He took the straight razor from the side of the murky sink and plunged it into the tepid water which swirled in the bowl. As he lifted the dripping blade towards his face, he remembered his dad teaching him this very accomplishment. His eyes filled like buckets and behind the tears he watched the entire scene play out as if it were in this very mirror it had occurred.

He wished the memory, although a wonderful one at the time, would wash away by itself, but he was too tired and apathetic. It played on him, plagued him, poked and picked like an infected scratch.

Jimmy splashed his face with the water and wiped the remaining foam from his tender cheeks. He pressed the plump parts of his palm against his eyeballs in attempt to keep them inside his skull. He readjusted his black tie, a gift from Turner. The suit was provided by the asylum's lost and found. Not that there were many things *found* in here. With delicate fingers, Jimmy organised his short curls and gave a subdued smile to himself. He knew his dad would be proud to see him dressed in such attire, like he was on his wedding day. Jimmy's smile faded. He no longer had his own clothes, his own identity. Only those items left in his vacant wardrobe on Myrtle Road. No longer his home. He poked at the bags below his eyes one last time, took in a deep breath and blew at the curls that dozed against his forehead. He marched out the room, attempting the valour of his father.

Jimmy hadn't attended a funeral before, his own dad's would be his first. Doctor Turner had met him at the asylum entrance and together they travelled down in a horse-drawn cart, an experience he would have once revelled. Not today. Today, he was seated in a dark black box. Today, he felt suffocated.

In came the rattle of the coffin containing his dad and Poppy, pulled from behind as if there was a reluctance greater than life to be buried. The galloping feet of the horses reminded him of that night at the Palace when the coconut shells clanked. Jimmy's days felt grey and his memories full of colour. Everything before his dad had died was painted in wonderful luminosity. Everything since had a darkened hue; the clouds were deflated, fluff-less wisps. The sky had lost its blue, stolen by Jimmy himself.

The cortege trotted through the iron gates, out the death bells tolled. From inside the dark, black box, Jimmy spotted the freshly dug grave. It took the sight of the hole to make the whole thing, finally, real.

Jimmy bore the weight at the front of the coffin. It sloped down with his slight height. Five strangers he hardly knew filled the remaining places. He waded down the aisle, barely seeing the faces of those attending.

Down the wooden casket was lowered. Used spades patted and flattened the soil as if nothing of any significance was below. How many last farewells had they bore? They were part of it all now: Poppy and George. The earth, the grass. The graves of men would soon sprout and cover them both. Jimmy looked upon the soil. Since the beginning of time, have more people died or has more grass grown? How heavy heaven would have to be to accommodate them all. *Now that they are dead, are they not interested in us?*

From amongst the strange faces came hobbling one Jimmy recognised immediately. It was the white, mossy beard, the large nose; it was Alfred. The old man shambled and embraced Jimmy with the warmest clench. Jimmy gripped him back just as tight, like he was greeting his dad returning from war.

"Oh, Jimmy, Jimmy, Jimmy… you're alive!"

"I'm alive, Uncle Alfred," choked the boy.

"Let me look at you!" said the old man, pulling back to take him all in. "I thought… well, the papers, there were still two unidentified bodies… after I found out about poor Wilfred… well… I…"

"Wilfred?" muttered Jimmy. He could feel his legs going before the question left his lips. "Wilfred's… dead?"

Jimmy's body tumbled to the floor. His hands stiffened like claws; his neck braced backwards. His whole body violently convulsed. The congregation screamed.

It was a struggle to open his eyes with the throbbing weight of his skull. Light flickered between the branches, casting dark lines across his face.

"Here. He. Comes…" Jimmy made out the face of the hairy doctor first. As his vision began to clear, he saw the mossy, white beard. Alfred came forward towards him.

"Wait, not yet," said the doctor. "Let him be. He'll come around soon enough."

"Doctor Turner?" said Alfred. "What's epilepsy, really?"

"Well… it's like a storm in the brain," said the doctor, keeping one watchful eye over his patient. "But it's not like clouds build, they turn black, rain comes and the storm erupts. It's more complicated than that. There are triggers and different people have different triggers."

"So, was it me that triggered Jimmy's?

"Highly unlikely. Triggers don't really work like that. It's more, a chemical imbalance."

"If you found out what the right balance was, could he be cured?"

"In theory. It's a lot of experimentation of doses. We can't necessarily avoid the seizure happening."

Alfred nodded solemnly. "Why does his body shake like that?"

"It's electrical, a misfire in the brain," said the doctor, tapping his temple. "The brain gets confused. If the brain is jumbled, then the body has no hope. It convulses, uncontrollably. That's what we call his grand mal seizure. That's what you just witnessed."

"He must be exhausted!" said Alfred empathetically.

"He is. Not every time, though. Sometimes, we've noticed that Jimmy has absent ones too. Don't you, Jim?"

"W-wh…?" muttered Jimmy. He wasn't yet back.

"See!" The doctor laughed. Alfred looked concerned. "Oh, don't worry," said the doctor, posing his hand around the old man. "He's nearly back with us! It's absent because he can just stare off into the distance, you see. Be completely lost inside himself. No thoughts, nothing. Then he comes around and he is confused, faded with tiredness, nausea and has a headache like you wouldn't believe."

"Sss…" Jimmy quaked.

"Jimbo!" said Alfred. The old man exerted all his effort to balance his frail body. With his wooden leg unable to bend, he attempted the best crouch he could. "So, he isn't mad?" asked the old man.

"Jimmy Ford… mad? No more than the rest of us!"

"Why is he in an asylum then, doctor?"

"Because it's a mental defect, a disorder. Doesn't make him mad—"

"But he's contained, with all those mad ones?" The doctor lifted the rim of his hat, slipped a finger through and scratched his itchy scalp. "I shall be his first visitor then," added Alfred.

"Oh... but if you come down to the asylum, I can't guarantee you will leave with your mind intact," laughed the doctor. Their conversation stopped in its tracks.

Jimmy's lips quaked. "T-tired!" said Jimmy. Alfred leant in closer.

"We should get you back," suggested Turner. He knelt beside the boy and slipped his arms under his shoulders.

"No!" said Jimmy. The doctor removed his arms and gently propped Jimmy up, his back against a tree. "Not yet. P-please."

"Oh, dear me," said Alfred. "Do as the doctor says, Jimbo!"

"He's OK," defended Turner. "Alfred... it is Alfred, isn't it?" The old man nodded. "Grab him some Creola biscuits, won't you? They are in my coat pocket."

"Right away!" Alfred hobbled back towards the mausoleum.

"Here's your tie back, Jim." The doctor handed it to him. "Choking hazard, that!" Jimmy went to clench the blurry black object. "Here, allow me..." The doctor crouched down to his level and began turning his collar.

"Do you remember anything when that happens to you, Jim?" asked Alfred, returning and reaching down with the brown biscuit. Jimmy took it between his fingers and languidly shook his head.

"It's a little like being lowered down a well," he said, focussing the little energy he had. "Everything above, like you, grows further and further away. I forget who I am. Who you are…" The old man looked concerned. "Don't worry… it returns. It's actually quite peaceful… for a moment, down there. But then, I come back, and I feel exhausted. Tired and battered, like I've been away on the longest journey and everything from before, directly from before, feels so far away now."

"Very good, Jim," said the doctor. "Most people, they don't remember anything of that stuff in between. Yet, you describe it so eloquently, so well! *Ha!* So, *well!*"

Jimmy smiled, but Alfred remained anxious. Jimmy must have been the only person on the planet who understood the doctor's sense of humour. He read the lines on the old man's face and remembered the conversation before he had fallen into the darkness.

"Wilfred…" he moaned.

"I'm afraid so, Jimmy. They buried him yesterday… that's why you see, I thought, your fate… was…" The last visual of his best friend flashed before his eyes. Jimmy slammed his head down into his palms.

"It's all my fault," he spluttered. "I made him get on that train!"

"Oh, Jimmy," said the old man, his tiny teddy bear eyes glaring into his. "You can't blame yourself. How were you to ever know? There was no warning… no…" The old man trailed off. What was the use in words?

Jimmy reached into his inside pocket. There was some rustling and out he pulled the furrowed paper.

"I'm not sure that's the best idea right now, Jimbo," advised Doctor Turner.

"What's that?" asked Alfred.

"His speech."

"No, I... I want to do it, I *need* to... do it."

The doctor smiled. "Very well." He knew that some things must be said.

Doctor Turner helped Jimmy to his feet and together with Alfred, the three small men ambled back towards the congregation.

Jimmy searched the mausoleum of strange faces.

"My dad," said Jimmy. "My dad. You were my hero! Growing up, you were everything that I wanted to be. You still are. Now you're in the ground, it doesn't change that. It just means you're in here now instead!" Jimmy punched his heart and looked to the back of the congregation.

The hairy doctor tipped his bowler proudly in the midday sun. He had helped him with some of the words. He was honoured and delighted to have been asked.

"You, you were taken so sudd... s-suddenly... that I still see you in everything." His hands were rattling the paper he held. He rested the sheet back on the podium and knitted his trembling fingers tightly together. "I-I see you in the bath water, at the asylum. Bath time was always a ritual, at home, on a Sunday, you see. That's w-where you would read to me. I a-also see you in the moon at night. That moon you always pronounced funny, the waxing gibbous! You would always reassure me that there wouldn't be a raid. At the beginning of every evening, you promised me that!" Jimmy breathed deep. "I-I guess you never thought that one would come in the d-daytime!" His wet tears fell over his cheeks. He left them there, right where they landed. "No matter how busy you were, you always dropped what you were doing. You always had time for me. You taught me how to ride my bike. I remember because I was waving and shouting for you, you were doing the same back to me. You were so proud!" he spluttered. His mouth creased downwards in a crescent; he fought it until it was straight. "The reason I was waving and shouting so much was because you hadn't taught me how to use the brake!"

The audience let a laugh pass by their lips.

"You taught me how to shave. You always made time to play this and that. Time for cards and draughts. Time to read. You always encouraged me with my reading. You were the reason I got so far in school. Without you, I wouldn't have wanted to be someone. Without you, I wouldn't have been anyone!" Jimmy looked up towards the clouds; on the horizon, one formed like a beautiful snow-peaked mountain. "We made model planes. You believed in me, you believed that one day I could be a pilot!" He used his trembling hands to mask his face. "You…" he attempted, tangled on the word. "You always made me laugh… now look at me… you're making me cry!"

His audience sobbed with him.

He took some time regaining the rhythm of his breath. "To me, you're the scent of soap, of pears. You're the scent of Creola biscuits, moustache wax and hair oil. Ha!" he sniggered, looking away from the paper. "I enjoyed a kiss from you... because I liked how the bristles felt." He drew another deep breath and found his place. "I'm reminded of you in the lawn and in the flowers that I helped you grow in our garden back home. I'll be reminded of you when I go to the cinema or when I'm older and go to the pub and try that ghastly stuff you called beer!"

Smiles unfurled across their earnest faces.

"You weren't just a dad to me. You, you were my best friend." Jimmy paused and looked down at his shoes and the green grass beneath them. He wanted the soil to surround them and take him. The words felt like giant pills that he could no longer swallow. "You... you always took me to zoos, to museums, to funfairs. You were always the best dad you could be. You... you helped people. You stitched clothing they needed. Clothing they needed to fight, to serve, to become the profession which kept them paid and fed."

Nods came from all around.

"You were always joking and larking around, playing pranks. So much so that I was scared in my own room at times. You were always up to no good, but you were always solicitous, giving, candid... generous with your time. If there were more people like you in the world, Dad, perhaps it would be a better place. A place without war. It's only now I realise how easy you made things for me. How you sheltered me, protected me so I could be a child and not care for the woes of the world." His blue eyes scanned the scene. Their sad, wan faces poked out from black clothing; everybody was a victim. "Growing up... you were everything I wanted to be. You still are. To people here, you were the greatest friend, the greatest colleague. To me, you will always be the greatest dad!" He lost his cadence.

Doctor Turner wolf-whistled between fingers. Alfred squeezed at his shoulder.

"You can do it, Jimmy!" The crowd started to cheer.

"I would have followed you anywhere, Dad! I tried. The moment you were drafted, I wanted to follow you to the front!" Members of the audience nattered. "Growing up, I was so desperate to leave this town, to leave Brentwood, unlike all those Fords before us. I was so desperate to become someone, to make you proud. It's only now I realise that everyone I love and everyone who is left are right here. Now… now you're always be here and I'll always stay. I wish I didn't waste our last goodbye. I love you, Dad."

Jimmy let the words tarry a moment whilst he turned the paper. "And P-Poppy. I hadn't known you long enough. I wish you had have walked into Dad's shop sooner. I-I wish you had of been my mum for longer! My last…" He choked and waited a while. The birds started to chirp. "My last memory of you both. You were holding hands. You were… both h-happy. You were together. A-and now you can always be!" Jimmy gurgled and wiped the slime from under his nose. "Goodbye, Dad," he finally mustered. "I'll always visit you and Mum, and Poppy. I'll always be close by. I'll always be listening…"

Jimmy closed his eyes.

Drawn blinds and flags half-mast. Six hundred wreaths. Fifteen little coffins laid out in a row below the steps of the altar. A sixteenth coffin, scattered limbs of unknown.

Whose ankle? Whose ear? Pink and white blossoms held in tiny hands of classroom friends which lined the silent road. The futility of that day.

The mausoleum applauded. Jimmy wept.

People laid flowers on top of the new soil. The procession lined up and squeezed the life out of him, offering their sympathies. Words that meant well but fell on muffled ears.

Once they had said everything worth saying, Jimmy looked down at the brown dirt and beyond. He imagined a six-foot hollow drop, the coffin resting at the bottom in the dark, the casket hinges squeaking open and them both there, melted as they were, diamonds glinting from their hands. The bodies shuffled aside and between them a new face ambled through the mud. It was red and bloated, covered in ash with burnt lips, black like bark.

"Wilfred!" he screamed.

The old man gripped his cuffs and drew him in. He embraced him a while without words. Then, he said finally, "There *are* people, like your old man, making this world a better place, Jimbo… there's *you*! You did them so proud," said Alfred. His little walnut head, creased and red. "*I'm* immensely proud of you lad!" Streams of tears poured from Jimmy's face. Alfred rotated him from the shoulder and embraced him again for the longest time. Alfred had squeezed him tightest of all, which was extraordinary given how frail he was. The mossy, white beard draped across Jimmy's shoulder and tickled the nape of his neck.

"Enough now," whispered Alfred.

"Enough now," Jimmy babbled back. He relaxed his muscles and closed his swollen lids.

Upon opening them, he saw an angel, a real one, standing in front of a cluster of trees. The short hairs surrounding her flesh glowed, a halo of white. Her hand was curled, carrying in her palm a ball of light that she had stolen from the sun, like the pair were playing catch. From this distance, he couldn't make out her freckles. Only the auburn curls that the sun lit the gaps between. It was Grace.

As he got closer, Jimmy spotted her lovely mole and noticed her plum lips were trembling. She reached around him and planted a delicate kiss on his cheek. He felt the damp, she had used all her tears.

"Haircut looks nice," she said, biting her quivering bottom lip. Jimmy half-smiled. "Oh, Jimmy. You poor thing! I am… truly, truly sorry!" Jimmy didn't know what to say. He was delighted to see her, of course he was. But his body and his mind were both equally weary and weak. "I thought the words you said, Jim… they… they were just perfect." He gave another hollow smile. "I can't believe it," she said, cupping his chin in her soft hands, hands he had fantasised touching him for so long. "I thought… I thought you were… dead." Tears like effortless raindrops fell from her almond eyes. "You're alive. You're here. You're here with *me*."

"For now…" Jimmy mustered. She leant in and her moist lips met with his. He felt the wet of her freckly cheeks on his and tasted those succulent droplets of pear. "What do Jews believe of death?" he asked.

Grace was a little taken aback. "*Olam ha-ba*, Jim… the world to come… the soul lives on, in another form."

"Like an animal?"

"Well… reincarnation, yes. But also, in heaven. Your father was a righteous man, which means he would have a greater share in the world to come."

"But he wasn't Jewish?"

"Doesn't matter. It's not about being Jewish or being owed anything for good deeds. It's living selflessly and how you are in this life, you get rewarded for… in your next."

"Well, why can't I see him? He's not up there sitting on some cloud!"

"Not sure it works like that, Jim."

"Then how does it work? Nobody knows. You're just here, then you're gone. That's it!"

"In body yes, but—"

"And Wilfred. He's dead too! I'm sorry," he shouted.

Grace knew he wasn't talking to her. "Jim…" She lowered her head to his and took his eyes in hers. "Don't ever say that. You have nothing to be sorry for!" Grace didn't know what to do with her arms; they weren't much more than children, after all.

"I hope they all come back as something," Jimmy said finally. "Whatever form they take. It's too lonely here. Here, without…" Grace smiled. "I wonder what he would be?!" Jimmy wiped his sore cheeks. "My dad?" She nodded. He looked up on the crook of the tree and there stood a yellow-breasted songbird.

"A bird," he said. "Then he could fly anywhere, do anything, see... everything."

"And sing as loud as he wanted!" quipped Grace. The bird chirped for her on cue.

"I can't help but think, if I hadn't have got the train that day, if I hadn't have forced Wilfred on with me. My dad, Poppy... they would still be—"

"You can't think like that, Jim. Of course, it would have happened. It would have happened that way, every time."

"Not for Wilfred, it wouldn't!" Jimmy's head sunk. "It's all my fault, I killed him, I killed them all!"

"Don't say that, Jim. You weren't flying the plane, you didn't open the hatch. Your dad, Poppy, at least... at least you got to see them one final time, Jim," she said. Jimmy looked about the dispersing crowd over where generations of his family lay buried.

"I just think it would have been… easier, if I had gone with him, you know… like George and Robert Lee."

"Don't talk like that, Jim!" demanded Grace.

"I am a soldier's son."

"Pardon?"

"But now, now I am no one… the poem. A man was reading that poem on the train… just before…" Jimmy noticed the bird had gone from his perch on the tree. His face solidified into stone. "I want to join a squadron," he said with the utmost conviction. "I want to train to fight. I want to meet those raiders head on. Next time they come, I want to be ready for them!"

"But, Jim—"

Jimmy interrupted her. "No," he snapped. "I've stayed here doing nothing for too long."

"But, Jim—"

"I have to. I must. To honour Dad and Poppy, to honour Wilfred."

"You must get better—"

"You're just like the r-rest of them," he spat. "Nobody can tell me what I c-can't do!"

Grace took his hand in hers. "Jimmy, I will wait for you. Wait until you're better, until we can be together. Let's take a stroll, Jim, like we used to. Let's go sit on our bench and for a moment, forget all these terrible things."

"No!" he said, slipping his hand away.

"Jimmy I can't help you if you don't let me in."

"You don't want to help me, you can't help me. You

weren't there. You were never going to be. You're not extracting a piece of shrapnel from my leg or... what was it, lung?" Grace gasped. "Let you in? Like I did, Dad, Poppy, Wilfred—"

"Jimmy!"

"What? What?" he pleaded, half in desperation, half in anguish.

"You can't bear it all, Jimmy. Let me in—"

"Why, so I can lose you too?"

"Jimmy!" Grace wept.

"If you had have come with us, if you only had of listened to me, your fate would have been the same too! The things I see when I see your face. I want them to be beautiful, the way I saw you before, but now... now it's replaced by things that could happen to you and it causes me pain, boundless agony!"

"Jimmy, that doesn't make any sense, nothing is going to happen to me."

"I know!" he raged. "Well, I think I do, but then my mind, it bleeds! It runs away with things, overruns with visions. I know it doesn't make sense, but that's what I see, it's what I feel, and I can't let you in because it causes me more suffering than you'll ever know."

"But, Jim, by thinking things that haven't happened and probably won't ever happen, you're basically making them so."

"Then so be it."

"Jimmy, you can't mean that, you can't... we can't just give all this up!"

"I'm not thinking anything. I look at you, Grace, and

all I feel is pain and the fear of losing you like I lost them."

"Jimmy, by not giving over to me, you're losing me anyway."

"At least you won't come to harm. If I can't have you—"

"Don't you even say that, Jimmy Ford. I don't want anyone but you!"

"I'm no longer me."

"Jimmy!"

"I have to go—"

"Jimmy! I'll visit, I'll—"

"*No!* Promise me. Promise me you will never come and visit me. Not there, not in that place, promise me, Grace."

"I… I…" Jimmy felt his body take over. It did the only thing it deemed itself capable of. The place, the situation; it escaped.

Jimmy found himself running. Running faster than his body had carried him before. He shattered through the crowds, body colliding against their black silhouettes. He stumbled down the stone steps of the cemetery and hurtled himself over the fence and into the woods. He was a shadow.

CHAPTER SIXTEEN

HOME

WHERE DO YOU LOOK for someone who does not wish to be found, even by themselves? Patients escaped from the asylum all the time. Many for reasons beyond their own understanding, others with a sole purpose: to end the misery bestowed upon them by the cruel mistress of life. Most of them were free to come and go as they pleased. But this was different, and everyone knew it.

It was Doctor Turner who had arranged the search party. An assembly of staff gathered outside the entrance of the asylum for the second consecutive day. The hospital could scarcely afford to do it, but it was Jimmy; the doctor had to try.

Alfred had been back and forth to Myrtle Road, to the cottage the Fords had once called their home. Nothing had been disturbed there. The key still dangled as it was left that day.

The general consensus was that Jimmy had fled the town. His attempt to start anew, somewhere else, where nobody knew him, or his condition. That was what the majority of cases did. But Jimmy wasn't like the majority of cases. His father had been taken from him in the most heinous way; he wasn't about to leave him here, buried only days past. Not unless, of course, he was seeking his revenge.

The murmur overhead dislodged the raindrops from the steel tracks and splattered them across Jimmy's forehead. He shuffled his body across the beams in an upwards motion, attempting to land them in his mouth. His lips were cracked from dehydration, his skin pastel from lack of sun. Squinting at the sharp, white rays of the sagging moon through the slats in the viaduct, he stared, disoriented, towards the rope which dangled from the horizontal trestle. Ghosty had hung from that very rafter in 1914. How different things were then, oh, how different things were now! He looked out and up towards the stars. Even with the expanse and solitude of it all, he felt suffocated.

After burying his father, he had run as far as his legs could carry. But what good was running when the thing you're running from is yourself? Jimmy had clambered the muddy banks in search for his hemlock and with empty hands, he had retreated, withdrawn behind the khaki curtains of the viaduct.

The stars overhead turned cold; they'd been dead for years. His body trembled in shock with them. Jimmy looked back at the empty noose. *Could I take my own life?* He wondered. It wasn't a question of why. That part was obvious. He would join Dad, Wilfred, his mums, who had twice died. Do people have to be their conscious self at the time they do it? Or is the deed done during the height of their madness? Jimmy couldn't be sure which category his mind currently fit.

His head lay on the piles of wet books. The flying magazines of his childhood, damp reminders of the person he once thought he was to become. He sifted through the articles in the mess tin, the treasures he and Wilfred had collected over two long summers. There were rank insignias, cap badges; the markings of true soldiers. He clasped at the wound stripes. He didn't even deserve those. Not visible ones, anyway, not unless he could stitch one across his heart. His best friend, his dad, Poppy, they deserved them all right. Their deaths were the price they owed to the war and they paid it, in full.

The tracks rattled; a train was approaching. The shell of the Be2c oscillated. Jimmy felt nothing, numbness. He already knew. He hurled his body up and pushed his head through the slats. This time he wasn't trying to trick his friend. This time he wasn't trying to find the reverse track.

As the headlamps lit up the surrounding forest, Jimmy got an ethereal glimpse of the train which would take his life. It was bound for the city. Life would go on without him, as it had for him the past week. As it did for everyone left behind on this rust-covered marble.

Jimmy shuffled himself over to the right side of the track so that his head was central between the sleepers.

White, viscous steam dispersed, shredding into pieces by the shiny black face of his killer.

Jimmy looked at his trembling hands, the hands that had touched everyone he had loved in his short lifetime. The hands that had not yet written anything of merit. His life was no shorter than those soldiers who had made it overseas. He was grateful for all he had experienced. For all the love he had received in this speckle of time that was proudly his.

Jimmy closed his eyes and braced his body for impact.

He saw his dad, the plane they had made together in the garden shed with balsa wood, shavings and glue. The plane which now dangled below his feet. He saw his dimples as he smiled and raised a glass on his wedding day. He saw he and Alfred, the pair of them, two adults, laughing with wet eyes on the floor of their grown-up shop. And Poppy, the way her dress danced without music, the way her hair pitter-pattered against her cheeks on the roaring Red Indian motorcycle. He saw Wilfred, his wheezing best friend, his podgy frame standing below the gates, behind the burning embers of their campfire, wet tears reflecting back the cinema screen. He saw her mouth, always her mouth. She parted her lips and planted a kiss on the toy doll she held. She parted her lips and popped in a rose-coloured pear drop. He watched her tongue as she licked the dusting of sugar. He saw her rounded cheeks and nose, that generous sprinkle of freckles. Then her eyes, the flecks of green and brown that glowed like lanterns.

"Grace," he whispered sweetly.

The leaves rustled, the trees split, closer the beast came. He took in one last long exhalation. This was it.

What would his obituary say? He was mad. He was epileptic, bereaved, he gave up. What a waste of life when he could have added to the effort overseas. Nobody begrudged a soldier from dying. But Jimmy was no soldier. The horn blew billows of white smoke into the air. Above the thunder, a familiar voice cut through the sound.

"Train!" Jimmy felt a rush of blood as his skin pimpled. He turned to the side and looked down over the bank. No one was there. The brook glistened under the pandemonium moon. He turned back to face his killer.

"Jimmy… get down… t-train!" Jimmy snapped back his neck. He saw the ghost of his best friend on the banks of the river; he saw him as he had been all those summers past, frightened, with porky fingers shielding his face to avoid his best friend's head from striking him across the shoulder blades.

The treetops soughed as the heavy load of the train clattered and roared. The river gurgled as it swallowed.

Doctor Campbell blew from his pipe, billowing great plumes of smoke up the red and brown brick of the main tower. Tonight, he was out on the lawn, seated opposite an officer in full uniform. The night was calm and clammy; the only sound was the soft rattle from the officer's fingers which jittered against the wooden frame of his wheelchair. The search party had all returned empty handed for the second day running. Campbell had to reluctantly order Turner to give up hope. From his experience, if the patient wasn't found within the first twenty-four hours, they would have to wait for that person to be pronounced dead. The body, if still intact, would be carried back and incinerated in the asylum mortuary. The train, that's what usually did the trick. Given the proximity of the asylum to the railway tracks, it didn't take a sane mind to work that out. Twenty unfortunate souls must have made that same trip within the last year, one or two staff included. Doctor Campbell had assessed Jimmy, only briefly, on account of his bad dreams. He had hoped to have more time with the young soldier, but, with almost fifty hours since sighting, he had lost any hope. Another life wasted, the killer, war neurosis. That was his conclusion. That is what he would write in the report. Besides, if the train didn't get him, it sounded like his epilepsy would. It was a double blow and the doctor felt saddened by the result. He wondered about the debilitating condition, if it hadn't have surfaced, would Jimmy still have suffered the same fate with the horrors of war alone? Would he even have wound up here in the first place? He knew how Turner felt; he saw it in the doctor's eyes. The blame he bestowed upon himself, the unfinished treatment and conversations he would never administer. He could see it in the doctor's eyes. He hadn't lost a patient; he had lost a friend.

Campbell felt something mildly resembling guilt. He remembered he was with his own patient. He leant across and, with a white handkerchief, dabbed at the beads of sweat which trickled down the officer's brow. Campbell always made an effort to have the officer's back to the asylum building, so that, for a moment, he might forget where he was. *Perhaps that would trigger him to talk*, he thought. Not tonight; tonight he was done with talk.

The officer had been a lost cause since his admission a month after the war had started. The only audible command his body had made in all that time was at those damn bells, and even then, screams were not exactly seen as progress. He simply sat, hand trembling, a distant gaze in those black, sunken eyes.

It wasn't particularly common for officers to lose their voice, Campbell had deducted. Privates, perhaps, the inability to make decisions, to command anything. That was the usual outcome. But Campbell had soon learnt that there was nothing usual about this place.

He was more than aware of procedures that had been carried out in the city asylums. Electricity had recently been applied to the mute patients' vocal cords; that would do it! But Campbell wasn't one to try such torturous practises until there was proof, and that alone was questionable. If Campbell was honest with himself, on nights like this, he preferred to inflict no attempt of cure at all. He sensed that the officer preferred it that way, to just sit here in silence, nobody probing or prodding him, picking apart his brain.

The moon illuminated silver stripes across the manicured lawns. The doctor was thankful for the solace. Rest from the relentless therapy sessions, the paperwork, analysis and incident reports. He hadn't had a single day off since the war broke out. The pangs from his body reminded him of that. He certainly wasn't getting any younger. But it wasn't the physical ailments that bothered him; he knew that his mind was exhausted and what good could become of an exhausted mind? He knew the results all too well.

The night was rhythmic with the constant rattle of the

officer's hand. Between that and the ribbiting toads from the nearby water tower, Campbell almost felt at peace. After all, the asylum had become his home and the noises it respired were his responsibility.

There was an abrupt interruption as the Officer's tapping became louder, more spasmodic. The doctor looked down at his wart-covered fingers and back up at the man's face. His eyes had burst open. *Another haunted memory*, he thought. Campbell noticed that his black pupils were shifting; unlike their usual glaze, there was some life in them. He looked back down at his hands. With the officer's index finger lifted higher than the rest, it could have almost passed for pointing. The doctor followed its direction, but there was nothing there, just the tangled roots of a giant maple tree. The doctor sighed and listlessly drew from his pipe.

Then came the rustle and stumble of feet. The doctor leapt up. He saw the silhouette of a small, dishevelled figure approaching. The shape shifted from the tree, out into sight on the moon drenched grass. Campbell could see the ill-fitting suit hanging from the man's shoulders. The rings surrounding his eyes were grey, the face pale. Curly brown hair was matted on the side of his skull. He tripped on the corner of one the gravestones.

"Jimmy!" shouted Campbell, running towards the falling figure. "He's here, he's home. The boy's home!"

CHAPTER SEVENTEEN

DOCTOR TURNER

JIMMY WAS FATIGUED FROM his jaunt. His body ran a fever, spiralling him into a delirium which merged days. Every time he was pulled towards the light, he was greeted and choked by a pill or the end of a needle. What did he care, they could do what they wanted to his body; his mind, it was no longer his. When he was dragged back into the darkness, he danced with the shadowy puppets of his family. He saw the hazy face of the buxom nurse as she squeezed a dampened flannel over his forehead. He caught blurred glimpses of the hairy doctor perched at the end of his bed, and the outline of an elderly pirate with his mossy, white beard. But even then, these outlines would soon merge into the face of his smouldering best friend, his solidified parents.

The moon had orbited the Earth five times before Jimmy

finally tore open his bloodshot eyes. The insipid rays lit the darkened corners of the dorm. It took him a long while to adjust. His forehead was still throbbing with heat, his temples pulsating with an ache he hadn't experienced. Even after a fit.

He heard the soft tick of the watch. He looked down at his wrists; they were bare, nothing but white cotton cuffs hung from them. He turned his heavy head. On the bedside table was his dad's brown wristwatch. It would have witnessed the last five days from there, indifferent to its surroundings. With tremendous effort, he rolled over the cold coiled springs and lifted the face towards him: 11:40, of course it was.

Jimmy heard the squeaking of shoe soles below the heavy white door. He no longer feared them. He lifted his corpse and made for the hefty white handle. There was a creak and a groan, then the floor flecked with firelight. The corridors were empty; he stumbled out of the room, chasing after shadows that weren't there.

Jimmy strolled the passages with light feet. He wasn't sure if he was looking for his own soul, lost amongst the corridors, or whether he was hunting the soul of someone else. Some of the doors to the dorms were ajar and the gentle rustling of patients could be heard inside. Violet light danced softly on the white tiled floor. Those melancholic, those who managed to keep their eyes closed and the horrors out for most of the night; the medication. Then, there were the other doors, those which were firmly shut. The noisy hysterics, the deranged, confused, tremoring, stammering, night terrors. Those patients barely saw the blue light. Jimmy felt part of this place now, now more than ever. What separated him from them?

314

The corridors unravelled and elongated in front of his eyes. It felt as though he was walking on the spot and no matter which direction he took, he would never get anywhere. He found it difficult to breathe, as if the lungs in his chest didn't belong to him. He opened one door after another, after another.

At the end of one corridor, there was another door. This door looked different to all those on the wards. Different, but not in the way the suicidal ward looked different. There was warmth, dark brown oak barred in a gold trim; inviting, even. Jimmy attempted the brass handle, it was locked. None of the doors on his ward were locked, but perhaps he wasn't on *his* ward. He checked in with his mind – no use, it wasn't there.

"I believe this is what you're looking for!" came the voice. Jimmy turned; the moonlight swam inside his thick specs. It was the hairy doctor. He unravelled his furry hand, revealing a long-toothed key. It glimmered gold under the tremulous crescent.

"How did you know I was here?" asked Jimmy.

"How did you know I was?" said Doctor Turner. A smile unfurled underneath his brown moustache. "It's good to see you back, Jim!"

"Am I in trouble?"

"Trouble?"

"For trying to…"

"Escape?"

Jimmy nodded passively. "I wasn't actually trying to escape… I—"

"I know," said the doctor. "Come, let me show you something!"

Jimmy hesitated. "I've seen it all… on the tour."

"*Ha!* The tour."

"Nurse Harrison, I mean, she wasn't really—"

"I know, dear boy. You don't have to tell me. Mildred Harrison has been through a lot in her life too, Jimmy." The doctor gave him an empathetic nod. "If Doctor Campbell can make it as pleasurable as possible, he will. If we can make life here as pleasurable as possible for all our people, we will." Jimmy looked into the doctor's large, magnified eyes. "And Jimmy… you are one of our people!"

"I know," said Jimmy. His forehead was still burning, but the pain in his temples had dwindled to a light throb. "Doc, about Nurse Harrison," he said. "You mean to say that Doctor Campbell allows her to go on with that—"

"Escapade? If it means that or shackling her to a damp wall… yes." Jimmy bowed his head, ashamed to have asked. "Now, Jimmy, where were you? Ah, yes, that's right… your tour."

"Doctor Turner?" Jimmy quivered as the doctor fumbled with the key.

"Yes?"

"Why is this door locked?"

"Some rooms in the asylum just are, Jim. This one, for good reason. *This* room is not down in any map; true places never are!" He winked.

Jimmy gave a meek smile. "*Moby Dick*." He was amazed that in his condition, he had any recollection at all. The white whale swam fathoms through the depths of his own broken mind.

"Very good, Jimbo. It's one of my favourites." He

looked at the doctor through transparent eyes. "It is OK if I call you Jimbo, isn't it?"

He nodded. The little man used two hairy hands to push the doors wide apart. They creaked and moaned, giving way to a huge expanse of darkness.

"W-where are you taking me?"

"Don't you trust me, Maddox? I am your doctor..." Turner grinned, gesturing for Jimmy to proceed.

"Doctor Turner?"

"Yes, Jimmy."

"I-I'm not too sure about this. Shall I go back to my dorm? Is this so I can't escape?"

"Escape? *Ha*, that's exactly what this room allows you to do!" A pungent odour filled his nostrils. Jimmy became cautious with every step. "That's it, you won't bump into anything, Jim."

"Why, because there's nothing in here?"

"Oh, there's plenty in here, Jim. Entire worlds are in here."

"I-I don't understand."

"I just need your help putting them back together again," said the doctor, now too surrounded by the darkness of the room. Jimmy was tempted to run back towards the passageway light, then, he heard the flicker of the match. *Fsssst*, the small flame danced.

"Smells like we're going back in time, doesn't it?" said the excited doctor. "Not only time... but dimensions, boy!"

"What is that smell?" said Jimmy.

The doctor lit the mantle and the room came alive. "The most liberating scent of paper and ink... books!" Jimmy's mouth fell open. He hadn't quite seen anything so grand in all his life. "Welcome, dear boy, to the asylum's very own library!" The little hairy man celebrated with tremendous joy, running into the bright room, jumping and tapping the heels of his feet together. The spines ran from the chequered black floor to the white arched ceiling. Everything in between was flecked in browns and golds. The shelves, the books. The occasional flicker of yellow and peach, of warmth, like the inside of a hearth. There were balconies made of ornate wood, gullies and tunnels littered with pages. There were globes and skeletons and scrolls. Egyptian relics, sculptures of Greek gods and various other antiquities. Piles of brown battered suitcases and old clocks sprawled on an oak desk, with silver candlesticks on either side.

The sight of the books awakened something in him that had been dormant for so long. His soul was projected with colour, carefree reminiscence of home.

"I don't believe it?!" Jimmy muttered. "I can't believe it… I must be dreaming, I must be—"

"Oh, but you must," said the doctor jubilantly.

"This is bigger… better than the library we have at the Brentwood School."

"Well… I sincerely hope so, dear boy. I've worked extremely hard on this in my years here."

"You?"

The doctor nodded proudly. He ran and jumped onto the wooden ladder which leant against the bookcase. He and the ladder sauntered across the room on its squeaking wheels. "Use this to reach the highest rafts. The best of books!" The doctor dipped his head and his brown hair flapped across his face. He blew.

The ladder lost momentum beside a gold-rimmed clock embedded in dark wood, with two cherubs touching hands over the face.

The doctor noticed Jimmy spot it. "Replica of the one on the Titanic," he said, jumping back down onto the chequered floor. "There is dust, and there are cobwebs—"

"Shh! It's perfect," said Jimmy. "Where do you start?!"

"Why, at Austen, of course." The doctor pointed over to the first shelf. "Then you get around to Barrie, the Brontë sisters, Burnett, Carroll, Collins, Conrad, Dickens, Eliot, Fielding, Forster, Graham, Melville, Milton, Shakespeare, Stevenson, Stoker, Swift and Wilde. Oh, and I do believe we've had some Woolf just in…" he pointed around the alphabetised shelves like a madman. "And that's just the fiction—"

"What's the best?"

"Best?"

"But you just said—"

"Poppycock! There are no best books, my dear boy. They are all the best. It all depends where you want to go?"

"Go?" entertained Jimmy.

"Yes. Which will it be: Neverland or Wonderland? Treasure Island or Lilliput? Toad Hall or Thornfield Hall? Bleak House or Lowood? Limmeridge or Blackwater Park?"

"Well… all of them, eventually."

"Right answer, my dear boy! And, who do you want as your guide? Captain Ahab? Captain Smollett? Doctor Jekyll? Mr Hyde?" In the doctor leant with a terrifying smirk. "You want to witness the demise of Mr and Mrs Lennox or Howard's End?"

"All of it," shouted Jimmy, his face glowing for the first time in weeks without tears.

"Then you've got to stay!" Jimmy's smile fell from his face and he wiped the floor with it.

"I—"

"Look, Jim, I know what you're going through. I don't intend to ask you where you went for those two days. I don't care. I'm just glad to have you back."

Jimmy let his shoulders drop. "I'm not sure I know where I've been," he said.

"Jim, before you ever consider something like that again, you must listen." *Here it comes*, he thought. "You go out there and… Look, Jim." The doctor's face turned heavy. "Your condition. It is severe. You could have a seizure one day and it *will* be your last. It's not a matter of if. They are getting more frequent." Jimmy looked defeatedly at the doctor. "In the meantime, they will send you to a workhouse, you know?! An infirmary!"

"I'm sorry," he said. "I didn't know what to do, I didn't know—"

"Now, now. That's quite enough. I can't replace your dad, Jim, but I am responsible for you. Besides, if they send you to an infirmary, who am I going to share my books with?"

Jimmy smirked. "Charlie went to the workhouse," he said, proud to have a part of him back. "Charlie was already making films by fourteen!"

"That's the spirit! Charlie Chaplin conquered it."

"He wasn't here!"

"He was somewhere worse! Let me tell you something, Jimbo. Charlie's mum is a music hall performer under the name of Lily Harley, did you know that?" Jimmy shook his head. "Yep, and you know where she spends a lot of her time?"

"In music halls?"

"*Ha!* Very good, Jim. Yes, in music halls, but also in places like this."

"You mean she's crazy too?"

"Not crazy, Jim. Disparate. Unique. What is society to tell you to be the same as everyone else?! If Hannah Chaplin had stayed the same as everyone else, then there would have been no Lily Harley and certainly no Charlie Chaplin! One day we will all be celebrated!"

"It's so hard to be someone. It's hard enough just being me!" The doctor slanted his head. "It didn't have to happen like this!"

"It could have happened a million other ways, Jim. Your father. He wasn't a religious man, was he?" Jimmy shook his head. "Me neither," exclaimed the doctor. "I think we would have got on." Jimmy nodded. "Look, I don't know why bad things happen to good people, I don't believe God is pointing his big stick and striking you over the head with it. But I do believe that sometimes when your number is called, you must get in the line and accept what you've been served. It's how you take it that counts, Jim. It's now. I'm not going to tell you that your dad is up there on some cloud looking down on you. But you must choose to live a life that your dad would be proud of you for. You be the person you know that your dad would like to follow. Then you can't fly far off course." The doctor scratched at his itchy beard.

"I wanted to be a pilot," said Jimmy.

"Wanted?"

"I have epilepsy!" Jimmy bowed his head.

"Don't do that."

"Do what?"

"Remorse. It's an ugly course."

"I do want to be a pilot then. More than ever. Those pilots killed my dad… they killed… Poppy… they killed… *Wilfred*!" Jimmy wept.

"Don't do that, Jim. Your head is filled with flame."

"Shame. How can I not feel shame?" said the boy.

"No, not penitence, Jimmy, flames, fire! Enmity at the

322

situation… anger! You don't need revenge. 'Living well is best revenge', revenge is making your life stupendous, revenge is you waking up each morning and making choices."

"Choices? I can't make choices. I'm here," he spluttered.

"You're here because of circumstance, Jim, because of your condition. This wasn't a decision you were responsible for making. You're not imprisoned because of some crime you've committed. You've got epilepsy, it isn't you, it's just something that you have."

"I feel trapped!"

"We quite often do. But you're not trapped. By your illness? A little. It will get worse if untreated! By these asylum walls? Possibly. But you come in here and read betwixt these pages and you can be anywhere you want, 'for the pen is much mightier than the sword, dear boy'!" The spirited doctor gestured up with a clenched fist. "Some of the books in this library have centuries of dust pressed between their pages. Until now, mine have been on the only hands to stir it! Look, Jimmy…" The doctor paused, gathering his thoughts. "You'll pass the time here. You'll heal those wounds. Your sorrow, Jimmy, it's a crown, a shroud that will lift freely one day." The doctor wiped the boy's wet and withered cheeks. "Madness, is it inherited? We don't know. Is it contagious? Almost certainly not! 'There is wisdom that is woe, but there is woe that is madness'." Jimmy looked at the little profound man. "*Moby Dick* again." He winked. "I could tell you knew it," said the doctor. "Jimmy, you stay here, let me treat you and together we will make this asylum sing with what we've learnt. Cognisance. Knowledge. They're gifts, Jim. You're young, but you have a lust for it. I see it in those blue eyes of yours, oceans, waiting to be discovered!" He stretched out his arms and scoured the imaginary landscape in front of him. "Whether or not you like it, you are confined here. You're not confined…" He tapped his forehead again. "Not, in here!"

Jimmy tilted his head to face the doctor. "My dad, he said. Before he died, that by the time he returned from war, I should have my own story to tell. Some story, eh? Being locked up in a nuthouse?"

"The best of stories." The doctor praised. "As good ol' Walt says, 'stand up for the stupid and crazy, devote your income and labour to others'!"

"So, I'm not just crazy." Jimmy sulked. "I'm stupid now too, huh?"

The doctor laughed. "Not at all, dear boy…" There was a slight pause. "Stupid and crazy aren't the same thing at all!"

A gust of wind bellowed from the open window, creating an arc with the tasselled curtains that stung Jimmy's sore, damp cheeks.

"If you let it eat you, it will consume you. It will take every last piece of the boy you are."

"Were."

"Pardon?"

"The boy I was. It's not just the epilepsy," said Jimmy. "There's something else. Something darker I can't quite grasp. I see things. I feel things. Like there is a shadow of a stranger on my shoulder. Someone else controlling my emotions. Waves of fear creep through my body like poison. I experienced it when I was at the funeral. When I was with… Grace."

"Is that why you ran?"

"Yes. I fear, I'm turning into…" The boy bowed his head. "A monster."

"Jimmy Ford, you are no monster, you are merely human, I'm afraid."

"All the things that make us human. I feel are at a distance now, a past life. A life without them, without my dad." He slumped down at the desk and rested on his knuckled hands, his face broken. "Where is he? Is he alone there, is he with my mum, with Poppy?" The room lay listening.

The doctor put his arm on the sobbing boy. He had rolled his sleeves up since being inside, but with all the excitement, his arms were soaked in sweat. All those hairs were deemed useless.

"He's in here," he said, thumping against his heart. "I know you feel your life has ended, winding up here, losing him. But time will heal! You will find a way. These books, they are temporary. Paper plasters for your wounds, but your wounds, eventually, your wounds, they will repair."

Jimmy's face exploded. "But it hurts so much!" he exclaimed.

"Love does," said the wise man. "Loss does. Life does. It can boot you, scratch you, spit on you… and that's just my patients." Jimmy laughed through the wall of tears. "You're fourteen, Jimmy, your dad has just died, your best friend has just died… you're a boy on the cusp of becoming a man. That's life, kid! I still don't know if the path I chose was right, but I know sure as hell it could have been worse. You must turn this extremely negative thing into something worth living for. If you focus on what you've lost, then you end up leaving your entire life behind you. You don't even have to look as far ahead as the future, but now, this moment, that's what counts. If you can live in that, it's like having your very own home. Not many people will crowd you in there, not many people have such ability." Jimmy pulled his hands away from his face to look at the doctor's huge, kooky eyes. "Jimmy Ford…a monster…piffle. Some of the so called 'sane' should be here in this asylum. Some of the staff should be patients!" The doctor pulled at the strands of hair below his lip. "Certainly, some unsavoury characters," he mumbled. "Nesbit! You watch out for that man Jimmy. He isn't…well, he isn't like *us*. Jimmy let a smile pierce through. *Us.*

"Let me tell you a story about a boy I once knew".

Jimmy nodded for him to proceed.

"After his daughter died," said the doctor, "he developed this phobia, if you can call it that. Obsession. An obsession that he couldn't cope with anything negative happening, anything dying, anyone he loved departing, any sad news. Even saying goodbye would tear pieces out of him. Because, he thought… he thought that saying goodbye each time would be his last." Jimmy gulped. "That person, who he loved dearly, that person he would no longer be able to see, no longer be able to touch, to exchange words with. The fear of being left here alone with the same pain he felt losing his darling daughter, just consumed his daily life. Films, that he loved to watch would always have content which caused him great pain. To the extent that he stopped watching them—"

"Even Chaplin?" asked Jimmy innocently.

"Even Chaplin…" The Doctor looked deeper into the boy's moist blue eyes. "Newspapers! The harmful headlines damaged him, psychologically convinced him that he was a murderer, an imposter, a fraud, a liar, a cheat. He would absorb it all like a sponge. He would hold that negativity in so close that it was coming out in his own thoughts. He confused his thoughts with his feelings and felt more pain and horror than he ever thought possible. He lived his days terrified. Even books, books he loved to read. Poems. Words would always arise that would haunt him, force his hand to stop turning, his eyes to look away. When he stopped reading, he would leave characters in strange, dark, frightening places. He subsequently started reading multiple books, always ceasing when the protagonist got himself into some sort of trouble. He left one fisherman in the middle of an ocean storm, one lady at the bottom of a well, one man sharpening his blade for the kill, he was convinced he himself, as the reader, would go on to commit."

"Why are you telling me this?"

"Everyone needs company," chuckled the doctor. He shrugged. Jokes over. "For my own therapy, I suppose. Isn't that how these things usually work?"

"I don't understand."

"You see, Jim. The most harmful thing of all was that he thought those feelings were his true beliefs. They consumed him." Jimmy knew exactly why the doctor was telling him this.

"And… what happened to him?" he asked.

"Oh, he became a failure, a wasted, washed-up alcoholic." The doctor chuckled. Jimmy couldn't hear the humour. "He had a wife once. Not anymore. He's alone. Drove everyone away because he was afraid he would cause them harm. In his head, he became that monster. Afraid of his own brain. Do you know what it's like to be afraid of your own mind?" The pimples on Jimmy's arms raised. "It's suffocating. The most petrifying experience imaginable. Your mind becomes a predator, but you can't run. It's inside you, devouring the person you once were, eating away at your deflated corpse."

Jimmy couldn't breathe. The doctor had hit his mark. "Was this one of your patients?" he finally plucked up the courage to ask. "One of your patients… that this happened to?"

"No, Jimmy. This was me!" The boy looked at him, studied him. "I am telling you this because the books, they saved me when I was in a similar predicament. The same way the movies do. The escape of our own lives. But it wasn't until I managed to finish the stories, got through the negativity and faced my own life. My own truths. That was when I was able to finally move on. To finally find peace, peace for dear Annabelle." The doctor's eyes turned watery. "If you look at your fears in the face, they are nothing more than yourself, mere shadows. And shadows can't hurt you, especially not your own! Don't live in fear, Jim, because—"

"Fear raids your time away!"

"Right! And you. I see you, Jimmy… you have a fire burning in there. You may not be where you want to be. You may not be Mozart at eight creating his first symphony or

Charlie Chaplin at fourteen making his first movie—"

"No, I'm fourteen, and I'm in an asylum!" He laughed.

"Well, I'm forty-one and I'm in an asylum!"

"But I'm the lunatic!" The doctor ignored the provocation. "I… I don't want to cry anymore! I'm not, it's not manly."

The doctor stood silent for a while, his fingers toying with his top lip. "'What is a man, anyhow'?" he said finally. "'What am I? And what are you'?" impersonated the doctor. "Whitman!" He winked. "Hmmm… or how about 'Flower in the Crannied Wall'?"

"Huh?"

"Don't they teach you poetry at that fanciful school of yours? Tennyson… Alfred Lord Tennyson." The doctor ran over to the alphabetised shelf and removed the dusty book. He licked his finger and began peeling back the pages.

"'Flower in the Crannied Wall,

I pluck you out of the crannies,

I hold you here, root and all, in my hand,

Little flower – but if I could understand

What you are, root and all, and all and all,

I should know what God and man is'."

"I've never read poetry!" stated Jimmy, shocked at his own lips. "I mean, we were planning too… next term… this term, I guess."

"Well… that's something we will have to remedy then, isn't it, young Ford? You see, poetry allows men to feel, Jim. Breaking down is nothing to be ashamed of. Nor is enmity, not after what you have been through. What happened to you, you can't repress it. The tears are part of grieving… lamenting. Your soul is grieving, Jimmy!" said the spirited doctor. "Can a man not feel fear, tenuous or tenderness? Let yourself feel it, Jim, then that shadow looming over your shoulder, that shadow will disperse. You must accept your emotions, accept your thoughts. Don't put lids on them and bury them in jars in the garden. I did that, and I was further from being a man then than I ever was!"

Jimmy wiped his cheeks. "I thought you were a doctor who treats epilepsy, not—"

"An alienist? No, well… that's Doctor Campbell's role. Philosophy and medicine do not mix."

"Is that what you believe?"

"On the contrary. The only view Doctor Campbell and I share is the one of the inside of our spectacles."

"Why did you become a doctor?"

Turner thought for a moment. "To help people, of course."

"People like you?"

"Eventually I want to help people like me. But for now, epilepsy is fine!" The little hairy doctor peered back down at the book he held.

"Is he your favourite?"

"Tennyson?"

Jimmy nodded.

"'I am a part of all that I have met'." The doctor shook his head. "Whitman, it's got to be Walt Whitman!"

"Why Whitman?"

"Well. In his own words, dear boy…" said the doctor,

getting ready for a performance. "'The greatest poet hardly knows pettiness or triviality. If he breathes into anything that was before thought small it dilates with the grandeur of life of the universe. He is seer… he is individual… he is complete in himself… the others are as good as he, only he sees it and they do not'."

"Did you memorise that?"

"You see *it*, Jimmy!"

"Poetry?"

"Life!" He looked at Jimmy and flicked some more pages from the book he held. "Oh, so many favourites, though, Jim. So many saviours!

'How dull it is to pause, to make an end,
To rust unburnished, not to shine in use!
As though to breathe were life! Life piled on life.
To follow knowledge like a sinking star,
Beyond the utmost bound of human thought.
The lights begin to twinkle from the rocks;
The long day wanes; the slow moon climbs; the deep
Moans round with many voices. Come, my friends,
'Tis not too late to seek a newer world.
We are not now that strength which in old days
Moved earth and heaven, that which we are, we are-
One equal temper of heroic hearts,
Made weak by time and fate, but strong in will
To strive, to seek to find, and not to yield.'

Ha! Tennyson is pretty damn good, though, wouldn't you agree?"

"Beautiful," whispered Jimmy. With his two hairy hands, the doctor gently pressed the lips of the book to a close.

"Oh, but then there's Blake, Wordsworth, Keats, Yates, Dickinson... Po! Anyone who wishes to live, to love, to suffer... to feel, needs it, dear boy."

"Can you read me another?"

The doctor walked over to the wall of books, where the ladder lay listening. "Hey! You know what makes that fire of yours burn longer? *Paper!*" he exclaimed, jumping for joy. "What adventure shall it be first? —Blake!"

"Is he one—"

"Of my favourites?" The doctor smiled. "I'll let you be the judge of that!" The doctor pressed the ridge of his small, round specs into his nose and drew a breath.

"'To see a World in a grain of sand,
And a Heaven in a wildflower,
Hold Infinity in the palm of your hand,
And eternity in an hour'."

Doctor Turner looked at Jimmy who had his head low.

"What is it dear boy? Too beautiful to warrant response?"

"Yes, but ... Doctor Turner... there is something I need to confess."

"You can't confess anything to me that I do not know already, dear boy!"

"Perhaps, but this is different—"

"What? You're not a soldier?"

Jimmy's face folded. "Yes, well there was that, but how did you—"

"You expected me to believe that you, Jimmy Ford, were a soldier?" Jimmy looked a little offended as the doctor barrel laughed. "You wouldn't have the discipline, boy!"

"I would!" he argued.

"Poppycock! Stick to your dream of piloting that plane, Jimbo. That is your raison d'être. You need to be out there, flying!"

Jimmy's insult gave way to reverie. "Is that it?"

"What should I do? Reprimand you? Send you to the firing squad for impersonating a private? I think you have enough on your plate boy. Your secret is safe with me." He winked. "Now, was there anything else?" Jimmy thought for a moment and shook his head. "Well boy...choose a damn poem!" The doctor watched as the boy's soppy eyes gleamed with life. "OK, let's see... there are words in here for every occasion," pondered the doctor, looking back amongst the shelves. "Even when no words will do!" He licked the tip of his finger. "*Leaves of Grass*," mumbled the doctor, searching for his prized possession. "You know Whitman and Tennyson died in the same year? 1892. Worst year of my life. My heroes... both dead!" said the sobering doctor.

"Me too," said Jimmy glumly. "1917." The doctor was too distracted, finding a poem to fit.

"He was a transcendentalist, you know?"

"Whitman?"

The doctor nodded. "He focuses on the inherent goodness of people and nature. Society!" he coughed.

"Institutions," he coughed. Jimmy laughed. "Ah!" he said, clearing his throat. Jimmy leant in.

"'There was a child went forth every day,

And the first object he look'd upon, that object he became…

His own parents…he that had propelled the fatherstuff at night, and fathered him…and she that conceived him in her womb and birthed him…they have this child more of themselves than that…

The village on the highland seen from after sunset, the river between,

Shadows, aureola and mist, the light falling on roofs and gables of white or brown two miles off,

The schooner nearby sleepily drooping down the tide, the little boat slack-tow'd astern,

The hurrying tumbling waves, quick-broken crests, slapping,

The strata of color'd clouds, the long bar of maroon-tint away solitary by itself, the spread of purity it lies motionless in,

The horizon's edge, the flying sea-crow, the fragrance of salt marsh and shore mud,

These became part of the child who went forth every day,

And who now goes, and will always go forth every day'."

The doctor flattened the pages inwards towards his chest and took a long, deep breath.

"And what child will I become?" said Jimmy. "Fatherless, in here, with these—"

"And have you even acquainted yourself with *our people*?" said the doctor.

Jimmy bowed his head. "Well, yes... Oren, Nurse Harrison... Mildred," he corrected.

"That all?" spiffed the doctor. "Well... I think you should make that your calling, don't you?"

"I'm afraid."

"Afraid madness is contagious?"

"Afraid I already have it."

"Fear of life, that's what gets most folks in here. Fear of madness, now that's something else entirely." The boy observed the doctor curiously. "You wanted a story, didn't you? Get to know your subjects first!"

CHAPTER EIGHTEEN

THE VISITOR

THE DINING HALL MUMBLED; the buzz of stammering could have passed off as conversation. Only a few mouths could feed themselves.

Jimmy had made his excuses to Oren. He needed to be on his own a while. He sat timidly over his food, startled every time a tray was flung, or someone screamed involuntarily.

He buttered to the stale corners of his bread using the one-inch blunt instrument bestowed upon him, keeping one watchful eye on the spare brown chair. He wouldn't give in, wouldn't accept the madness around him, inside of him. He didn't dare breathe too deep.

The lack of awareness they all had, that was in his favour. Each of them in worlds of their own, one that was detached and didn't seem to overlap with his. *Not yet, anyway*, he thought.

He took one bite, spat the mushy grains back onto the plate and picked the remaining acrid pieces from his teeth. It didn't taste of traditional floured bread; it tasted of turnip, the least appealing vegetable he could muster. He idly stirred the soup, lost in its fluorescent green appearance. Lukewarm nettle, pea and sorrel. Alone it was tangy and acidic, but after combining it with the turnip bread, careful experimentation brought the balance of flavours and the meal became piquant and rather pleasant. Gladdened by his own company, he mopped the last of the congealed green gloop. As he was about to stand, he spotted it there in black and white: the crumpled newspaper.

Jimmy turned the headline and was paralysed. There on the front page were the terrors of 13th June. It flooded back to him like a wave surging through narrow corridors of a sinking ship. As he read, a horrible bitter taste entered his mouth and nose. It was the taste of that tormenting day. He knew it was a taste that would fade but never really expire.

Having witnessed the scene in real life and comparing it to what he read, this was not, as he presumed, the greatest thing to witness; far from it. It was the most disturbing and devastating thing imaginable. Jimmy was caught off guard. He was used to reading articles as facts, as he had done all those times in the paper prior to this moment. It was impossible to remove himself from the situation; the humanity was overbearing. The words weren't words at all, but menacing, serrated pieces of shrapnel tearing clumps from his heart.

According to the sources, twenty Gothas had entered

at the mouth of the River Crouch. The first bomb had dropped near the Royal Albert Docks. At 11:40am three others hit their mark over Liverpool Street Station. One of the train coaches took a direct hit, read the accounts. Another two were ablaze. Sixteen reported casualties. Four unidentified bodies. *Himself?* Jimmy shook off the thought. No other names were listed. Not even a name.

His dad always commended his boys, always asked where the heroes were hiding in the headlines. Jimmy's hero was hiding well, all right, not even reported missing, not yet anyway. 'It is the worst home front fatalities of the war, but it won't dampen our spirits!' Jimmy wasn't damp; he was drowning.

Jimmy was there. He knew that much. But how could it all be so prescribed? These weren't stories. They weren't sharing the souls of people at all. Jimmy read on. Further bombs had landed on Fenchurch Street, Aldgate, Bermondsey, Dalston, Limehouse, Tooley Street, Silvertown, Stepney and Saffron Hill. Sterile statistics and locations. One hundred and twenty-six bombs in all. One hundred and sixty-two casualties. Some hit stables, others hit sundry domestic works, a brewery and private homes. But perhaps the most harrowing of all were those infants killed at a school in Poplar.

The gravest of incidents, infuriating cowardice, unaccountable malice. Sixteen were under the age of six. The sources said that the children had truly suffered for their country. Whose country? Theirs. But what did children know of war? What did they owe? Their lives? Jimmy wept in his chair. A tear for every deceased.

Finally, the heroines. Two teachers recovering the dead and alive bodies of the children buried beneath the rubble. Lamenting mothers, busy nurses and skilled surgeons. Jimmy saw right through it. The skewed accounts of comradery, collaboration, the community spirit. He wasn't sure what he wanted but it wasn't this.

The article included a photograph: the school caretaker, Benjamin Batt, clearing the rubble from the ground floor where the bomb had exploded. It had taken the life of his son, five-year-old Alfie.

Seeing the image made Jimmy hate the Germans. No, it made him hate humans. Those behind the murder, the mutilation of innocent infants and Alfie. Alfie, who had attended the Upper North Street School.

Jimmy's mind lingered on a memory of his school assembly, where they would remember those who had lost their lives. The list of former pupils at the Brentwood School had grown and grown in the last few months. What must the list now say at Poplar? Where would it even hang from?

According to the news, the bomb tore through the roof where the girls were. It scythed its way through the second-floor class of boys before exploding in the infants down below. *Why there?* thought Jimmy. *Why did that bomb have to land right there?* The accounts mentioned the proximity to the East India Docks. Perhaps that was where the Germans meant to strike. Perhaps. What good was that? Did men know the consequences once that button was pushed? How could they? They were just men.

Jimmy sighed. He felt strangely relieved that he wasn't

alone but then riddled with guilt at those who too had lost their lives, their beloveds. Why Liverpool Street? Why platform nine? Could it have been someone else? Did it have to be someone? Jimmy heard the hatch opening, the whiz as the bomb tumbled out. He smelt the smog, he tasted the blast, the ash; a flash of two coiled spines.

A commotion began in the dining hall. Everyone in white rummaged over towards the bright Georgian windows. The whole right-hand wall was embossed with colourful boxed panes. The floor cast in dark square shadows like a chocolate bar. Jimmy was hesitant on his feet but relieved to turn the paper down, slithering through the sea of cotton until his hands were pressed firmly against the glass. He turned and saw the patients had closed in around him. Panicked, crazed eyes enveloped him.

With tilted heads, the wanderers peered out over the lawn. The green blades drenched orange in the haze of the rising sun. In the distance, a red vehicle with a whaling brass siren could be seen whizzing between the hedges. As it circled back, Jimmy caught sight of the wooden ladder which ran the full length of the vehicle. A Model T fire engine. Wooden spokes with red rims and enough brass tanks to refill a castle moat.

Two men in firemen's uniforms were seated on the black leather seat. The driver's movements were hurried as he slipped the steering wheel through his gloved hands. The truck dipped down the undulated turf and across colourful flower beds which slept in the asylum gardens. Soil sprayed up in all directions from the thin, bobbling tyres.

Balancing beside the two firemen with his foot on the

side panel, a man dressed in white cotton was pointing enthusiastically, arms fully stretched. His movements echoed the erratic motions of the truck. One sharp turn and he was gone! The man wasn't fazed, more so, elated.

"That's the second time they've come around," muttered one of the patients.

"Third, I think, Slugs," said another. Jimmy was amazed that they were conversing with one another. He turned and saw why the man was called 'Slugs' – his eyebrows! He had one hell of a bulging brow and protruding from it looked like two sleeping slugs.

"Fairlop's taking them for a ride, all right!"

"Whose Fairlop?" asked Jimmy.

"The biggest joke that ever walked these wards."

"Ah, and here comes another!" The fire engine came to an abrupt stop in front of an outstretched palm. It was the orderly with pond weed for hair. "Nesbit!" sneered Slugs. "He puts a stop to anything that gives you a break from this place."

"Always had it in for Fairlop," nattered the man beside him.

"Nesbit," whispered Jimmy, eyes widening. He watched as Nesbit sneered his instruction to the two firemen. Nesbit clicked his fingers and Fairlop was pulled forcefully from the engine by two other burly orderlies.

"I don't get it," said Jimmy. "Where is the fire?"

"Fire?" tutted Slugs. "I'll be damned if there's even smoke. He's pulling their leg, kid. There's no fire. Fairlop just wanted a free ride about, that's all!"

"Fire? Fire!" shouted one of the patients, excitedly

slapping his hands over his bald forehead and choking on his own mad laughter.

"Fire!" bellowed another, jumping up onto the table, eyeballs popping from his swollen skull. "There's a fire, Betsy, a fire!"

"Get down from there, Brian, there's no fire!"

"Fairlop, you festering fuckwit of a man, what in God's name?" One patient hurriedly removed his white cotton at an alarming rate, patting his busy hands against every inch of his body. He rolled across the floor in his undergarments.

"Get up, Patrick!" yelled Betsy, arms swinging. "Get dressed!"

Another patient darted towards the wall and yanked the fire chain. The piercing shrills of the alarm tore through the hall. The loud noise palsied some and excited others. One man with round specs, messy brown hair and a sere, white, scraggly beard, dived into the corner and rocked.

He began mumbling to the wall, "A thousand drenched puppets dancing in dry rain. Yes, Alex, I've read *Revision of the Echini* fifteen times. Concrete sardines for supper. Wind tunnels filled with tentacles. The lion. Bitch. Whore. Droves of black doves. Males can give birth, see? I'll never change *my* gender. Eyelid chandelier. School of bent railings, pail, pale, pardon? Battery. Smack. Seagull policeman arresting poltergeists. Penguins. Emperor's feet washed in holy milk. Bleached musket. Lost the battle, lost the war, lost his mind, I'm afraid, lost my sandwich, 1912, lost sight of the pickle, found the cheese. The curiosity of the situation is this… coral atolls lead to subsidence. That's an awful lot of barnacles. My spectacles are starving, my hernia hurts, my home is haunted. No more leaches, more blood this time, I'm awfully listless – no, languorous. Yes, sir, tortoise shells are mostly empty, why do you ask? It's just a common cold. They always flap in June. How many buttons? One single eye on the end of each arm. It only cost a penny, Father, supper will be late tonight. I told you already, you can't harpoon a horse like that!"

"What on Earth is he saying?" asked Jimmy.

"Allen? Nothing of this Earth. Anything… everything! He does this when he's afraid," added Betsy.

"But what does it mean?"

"Absolute nonsense, dear… it's just his escape, dear… from the fear of the situation."

"What situation?"

"Exactly!"

"How do we make him stop?"

"That's it, dear. You can't. Have to let it run its course!" Betsy wrangled up some of the patients who were tied in knots on the floor. Lost shoes, lost causes.

Jimmy stepped towards the man with the nibbled beard, trapped on a rocking chair of his own mind. Jimmy perched beside him, crossed his legs, leant back against the wall and just sat, listening.

"It was like that when I found it, honest. Be kind. Eel's light. She's fatter than I. I'll find her the finest pearl. The plankton always paddle north. How many times must I tell you, Agassiz? Her laces always were undone. No turtles in Antarctica. Just one nostril. Mucus masks the smell. Disseminate pheromones. Pee-pee eyes. What a peculiar shape. Of course, the whale shark is not a mammal. I'm sleeping on my awaken side—"

"These words cannot have been spoken by any man," whispered Jimmy. "In this place or any other across the entire globe, across the whole of history. He would get zero points every time! Wait until I tell W, Wilfred!" The lump in Jimmy's throat silenced him.

"After careful consideration, my conclusions are this…!" The man cleared his throat. "I only do that because I have a rather large nose." Jimmy giggled. It was true, he did. "Lakes underwater, it cannot be?! Three hearts, blue blood. Thank you ever so much for carrying my child all this time. One hundred and eighty-eight decibels I think to be precise. I have three shillings for your mermaid's purse. Ah, the hermit crab. I would share a shell with you any day, my love. *Balaenoptera musculus*, say it with me. *Tepre Pacificum*. The whole town was underwater. It's a pleasure to meet you here…"

The shrill of the fire alarm ceased. The man stopped rocking almost immediately, removed his glasses and pinched the ridge of his nose. He rubbed his eyes and replaced with his porthole specs.

"It's a pleasure to meet *you*, Allen!" said Jimmy boldly, slanting his head.

The dishevelled man turned and looked at him strangely as if awakening from a deep slumber. "Do I know you, young'un?"

"Uh-uh!" He shook, startled by a normal reply. "I'm Jimmy. It's the first time we've met!"

"Ah, I see. You're with the Norfolk lot?"

"I'm not, actually. I'm from here. From Brentwood, I mean!" Both sat there tacitly. "Who is Agassiz? Can there really be lakes underwater?"

"*Ha!* I see. I was babbling off again, was I? Not the greatest of introductions, I'm afraid."

"I liked it…" Allen looked at him more strangely.

"Well, glad *you* did. I don't remember a thing… never do!" He began to find his feet.

"That happens to me!"

"The gibbering?"

"No. Afraid not. The memory loss. I'm epileptic."

"I see," said Allen. "I'm an unknown. A congealment of bafflement… one of the crazies!"

"Is that all that happens to you? The conversation thing?"

"*Ha!* Conversation is two-way Jimmy!"

Betsy and the other nurses now had back control of the room.

"It was very interesting!"

"What was?" Allen's eyebrows leapt up his high, bulbous forehead. He had a large white cranium receded by wiry black hair.

"What you were saying… well, I found it interesting."

"Barr. Take no notice."

"Had a kind of melody to it."

"*Ha!* Harmonious. Whatever next?! Some song I could sing! What did I say this time?" Jimmy shrugged. He wished for the life of him he could remember it all. "That's what the doctors are trying to decipher. I wouldn't bother. Sounds like absolute gobbledygook if you ask me. Words from a time gone by. It's only a visitor now. And it comes when it's least welcome!"

"A visitor?"

"I was a marine biologist… once."

"No?" said Jimmy in admiration. The skeletal face smiled. "You seem very wise for… for a p—"

"A patient? You can say it! I know what I know, and I don't much about much else. That's all there is to it. Have you got acquainted yet?"

"Not really."

"It gets easier."

"It feels strange because I didn't come through the entrance. I just kind of appeared here."

"Yup, I was absent when I arrived too!"

"Absent?"

"Yes. That's what they call my mumblings. I just sort of go somewhere a while… then I come back." Jimmy pondered this. "Somewhere down the line our great-great-grandad's would have talked and drank beer together!" said Allen. He stretched his sea legs. "Now, where was I?"

"The dining hall," obliged Jimmy.

"Right, yes. Breakfast…" The madman swanned off with his mumblings firmly buckled inside his luggage. He had a sense of calm Jimmy hadn't witnessed, nor could put his finger on.

"That man is a prodigy, a prophet, an oracle," he concluded. "Marine Allen. Allen Agassiz. Allen the Great. Allen… in Neverland!"

Jimmy sat against that wall a while, trying to make sense of everything which had led him here. The paths he had travelled, those he chose, those he didn't. Did they all really lead right here? Under this wall in the dining hall of an asylum he had no idea had existed just three years past, suffocated by a malady he had barely any knowledge about?

CHAPTER NINETEEN

BUCK

Evenings were drawing in quickly now that the summer was coming to a close. There had been a heatwave all week, its own microcosm of weather. You'd have thought his dad had been cremated with the heat he had brought the past two months. The night was sultry and whistled with wind and crickets.

Jimmy wandered under the scarlet night, between the cloistered courtyards and out on the open grass. He leant over and felt the floor, retracting his dew-covered hands, soft palms covered in pine needles. As he crept across the clearing, a screech startled him. Jimmy looked over towards the darkened outline of a children's play area. A court with empty swings and a vacant see-saw. He thought of Lolola and was saddened by her existence. The existence of all the children here at the asylum. Of Oren – patient, loyal Oren. Oren with hollow words and endless supplies of Creola biscuits. Oren's condition was ameliorating.

"I'm afraid there is no set cure which works across two *people*," Doctor Turner had insisted. Just because a certain recipe had worked for Oren, didn't mean it would be of any benefit to Jimmy. In fact, Doctor Turner put this into practice after Jimmy's persistence, only to be proved correct. The medication Oren was taking only exacerbated Jimmy's condition. "It's simply not time for the fits to leave you," preached the Doctor. Words laid out like colourless flowers on deaf ears.

"All of us here are people," the doctor had said.

A wise man, thought Jimmy. He reminded him a lot of his dad. *My dad.* The wound still felt fresh, but now he held a defence against it, a plaster that stopped the breeze from aggravating it.

He tip-toed with his notebook around the graves, avoiding the moonbeams as he went, blending and dissolving into the shadows like a kodak reel. The doctor had issued Jimmy with the brown book and pen on the condition that, on occasion, he was able to read some of its contents. Jimmy was happy to oblige, if only Jimmy had something bigger to write about, a real event.

"You said it yourself," the doctor had said. "It's all around you, Jimmy. You *are* living through that event... right now!"

Jimmy felt at peace beside the graves. Perhaps because he wouldn't be judged, perhaps because his best friend had once been there, on this exact spot. Surrounded by the solitude of the still air, he found a secluded patch where all the windows of the asylum were visibly facing, the all-seeing eye. There he watched small capsules of existence unravel in front of him, until they either sparkled or burst. They were like little cubicles of light where life reverberated, and there was nowhere bustling with life quite like an asylum at night.

Jimmy, once the boy who slept oblivious, safe, warm in his bed at home, was now here, observing, learning; people. Just as the doctor had ordered.

In each window were his subjects, his shadows. They were like shop displays; he could browse them all. In one, the grey face of a drunkard, a restraining nurse and a medicating doctor. Jimmy panned his eyes, another, the lonely chronic imbecile, an unwanted housewife who was forced mad from sectioning, lost it all, mind and all. Jimmy peered down at his shoes. He found it all so difficult, all so distressing. Then, from the soft glow of one of the rooms, he spotted the smouldering face of the neurotic war hero. It was the officer. He appeared to be staring knowingly out of the window, aware that Jimmy was there.

Jimmy felt strange, watching the man do nothing, bound to his wooden wheelchair inside that glass box, bound to the confines of his mind, to the memories of purgatory and the hell he had seen, only to be thanked by the night visits of fallen comrades and dead brothers. Displayed there like he was, *he wasn't far removed from an animal in a zoo*, thought Jimmy. He wasn't far removed from the white wolf he once possessed, confined to that sulphide marble, desperate to howl.

"Buck," he whispered.

The moon illuminated one tiny corner of his desk.

With his eyes tiring in the candlelight, Jimmy placed his copper fountain pen in its holder, rested back on his chair and glided his fingers through his long, brown curls. The breeze from the open window licked between the pages of his open notebook.

"I wonder if the real officer was anything like this?" he whispered, imagining the mute man in uniform staring back at him from the window. Jimmy looked at the ash-covered compass as if it were a fossil from a world long ceased. He tossed it down and replaced it with his dad's watch. He turned it to face him; he had been up writing a long time.

He observed the photograph of his mum and dad, which now occupied his dark, smoked tabletop. His mother's smile, that supple skin of snow white. He opened the frame and discarded the photograph into the drawer. He picked up another from the sideboard and replaced the paper in the frame. It showed three people gaily dressed: George, Poppy and Jimmy on their wedding day. *Take a photograph and for that snippet of time, they are alive*, he thought. He leant towards the glass and saw his own tired face stare back at him, the grey rings round his eyes. How the reflection had changed from the young, naïve boy smiling in the photo. He thought of Grace, their argument at the church, their first kiss on the sand. He thought of her often, about their last fleeting conversation at the funeral, the anger he had felt which had now passed and was impossible to conjure back up.

Alfred had visited him at the asylum many times in the last few months, but Grace, she had solemnly stuck to her promise. He often wondered what she was doing, who she was with. His mind threw him over the wheat fields to her house, but he could never truly imagine her there. He felt she was somewhere else, some far-off place, nursing, treating, aiding the war effort he so desperately longed to join.

With an index finger, he twirled the propeller of his wooden Be2c. Jimmy had been back to the viaduct last month to collect some of his possessions. It is hard, revisiting a place that you almost ended your life in. He felt a mixture of sadness and nostalgia. He had also gone back home. Although the most painful experience imaginable, he now had some comforts to tame him.

His fits had somewhat subsided. Perhaps it was closure, perhaps it was progress? It may as well have been the weather for all he knew. Doctor Turner had strongly recommended he stick with the books, but what proof was there that his state of mind could suppress his epilepsy? Regardless, reading wasn't a hardship for Jimmy. And now, in this asylum, he had all the time in the world to write.

There were still the nightmares. Doctor Campbell had taken it so far but could never get past the moment the bomb hit platform nine. His dad had visited his room on numerous nights, during that half-awoken state that Campbell so often insisted on calling hypnagogia. Sometimes Jimmy wouldn't play along; he would lay still in his bed and watch the ghost of his dad, torpid and numb. Other times he was vulnerable and weary and couldn't contain himself. He would engage in short, repetitive conversations about how his dad was living down the road but to see him just was impossible given the new... situation. Often, Wilfred would join in the party, forgiving Jimmy for his premature and ill-timed end. Nothing that Wilfred said could ever repress the guilt he felt. Jimmy hoped that if he stayed up writing, he would sleep more soundly, draining his mind of all that harmful matter. After all, writing was his only therapy now. Jimmy folded back the spine of his brown notebook, leant over the wax candle and blew out its flame.

The next morning, Jimmy was in the rec room. He looked around, noticing the silvery film which enveloped the patient's skin, that extra layer babies have after being pushed through the birth canal. Martha was in her usual chair, staring vacantly out of the window and across the manicured lawns. One of the orderlies had placed her there. Supposedly – according to the doctors, at least – she could see perfectly well. Martha would never be able to express this; her arm had been stuck in that damn raised position all the morning long. Outside the window, one mighty great tempest was brewing.

Jimmy drew his attention back to his book.

It's truly fascinating. I can turn and land on any page and there is guaranteed a zero-point sentence! Jimmy began to flick through, his finger falling on a page. He closed his eyes and slid his tip up and down, calling a stop in his own head.

"'The youth lies awake in the cedar-roofed Garret and harks at the musical rain'." *Not only unique but beautiful,* he thought. *I must improve my writing!* Jimmy wasn't entirely sure of each meaning, but he loved the sound the words made in his brain. Another, *another.* He closed his eyes.

"'I bequeath myself to the dirt and grow from the grass I love,

If you want me again look for me under your bootsoles'."

That one he did understand. He pivoted his feet inwards below his chair. Again, again he went, carrying out the same meticulous task. When he opened his eyes, he saw his finger pressed down on the next caption and began to read:

"'Where burial coaches enter the arched gates of the cemetery.

Where winter wolves bark amid wastes of snow and icicled trees'."

"Buck! Where is Buck?" he yelled aloud.

"What on Earth are you doing, young'un?" interrupted Allen. He had been sitting quietly beside Jimmy a while, just observing everyone and everything happening in the rec room. He could have passed entire days that way.

"Just a game," said Jimmy. "My friend and I used to play it." He noticed that Allen was still awaiting a real answer, the skin on his great skull taut and salty as seawater. "You try to think of a sentence, you see. One that no one would have ever thought or said ever in the world!"

"Gotcha," said Allen. "And you feel this Whitman fellow here, he has what it takes?"

Jimmy nodded. "He certainly does. You know, I think you do too!"

"Me?"

"Yes, your… mumblings," he added cautiously. "It's like nothing I'd ever heard before."

"Ha! Is that so. Well, next time they arise I will be sure to let you know. And if you can do the same for me in the process, that will be equivocally, and well… equally marvellous too, young'un." The pair fell into comfortable silence a while.

"You know, I often wonder if this clinical smell will always pervade."

"How so?" Jimmy closed his book. When conversing with Allen, he didn't need it.

"Well, will these halls always have this stench, even long after us patients have gone? Even in years and years to come, when children are exploring them as haunted corridors. You know, larking about in play... whatever mischief you kids get up to nowadays!"

Jimmy thought that maybe Allen didn't need his mumblings to win the game.

"Or, beyond that!" said Allen fiddling with his tousled beard. "Imagine when the sea level rises, the Earth falls, and the entire town is underwater. Divers swimming *through* the corridors, the dormitories with their rusty spring beds, this very hall! Those people trying to piece together what happened here, who *we* really were!"

"Whose people?"

"Why, the future people of course!" Allen laughed until his eyes sweated.

Over in the far corner of the room, below an open window, a card game was in hot pursuit.

"Say hello to my two ladies, ladies! That one there makes me a little ménage à trois! Three of a kind. Three queers, in your cases!"

"Fairlop, you festering fuck..." came one beat patient who stood to his feet, hunched his back and trampled off. He was all out of smokes.

"You had that last time," said another. "What do you do, keep it in your pocket?"

"I admit," said Slugs, who Jimmy recognised from the day of the fire engine, and from his eyebrows, "that does seem rather strange, Fairlop, considering it was your deal. The last one was luck, this one—"

"You boys callin' me a cheat, are ya?" accused Fairlop, who continued scraping down his winning cigarettes. The men retracted.

"I'm just saying, that can't be happening for a third time, you know?" warned Slugs, his thin voice tinged with nerves.

"How d'ya figure that? I'm tipping off old Chat here too, am I? Bungin' him a smoke on his next deal?"

"I-I'm just saying is all. Most men play their hand. You just seem to play your cards."

"Well, ain't I the lucky one?! Make your own in this world, boys, stop grouchin'." When Fairlop played cards, his feet were never on the ground. Today he'd adopted a crouched position on his chair like he was the lead rebel in some kind of youth club. He looked towards Chat with his sunken eyes, sun reflecting off the top of his pallid head.

"I'm bored of ya backstory, boys," he said flopping down the pack. "Now then. I think it's about time we got ourselves some new blood, don't you?" Fairlop bounced to his feet like a coil released from a tightly wound spring. "Listen up, everyone," he projected across the rec room, "I here need to get me a couple of new recruits!" Those who were able to gazed the other way.

"Who is that?" whispered Jimmy with a sprinkle of admiration in his voice.

"Fairlop... he's a Palaemonetes," said Allen.

"A what?"

"A ghost shrimp. He doesn't cast a shadow, leave a trace, but take a real close look and you can see most of his workings. I got him all figured out!"

Fairlop advanced on Martha first. "That's it. Raise your hand if you want to play!" His body bent back under the weight of his laugh. A few smirks came from some of the patients who watched Fairlop with an unworldly intrigue. Poor, catatonic Martha. "Letchy!" continued Fairlop, approaching the officer hunched over his chair, back curved like a boomerang. The officer's eyes jittered nervously in their craters. "Come on, Private, you must know how to play!" The officer mumbled and retreated far back into himself, like the neck of a tortoise.

"He isn't a private..." came Allen unexpectedly. "He's an officer. Why do you think he's in uniform? Show some respect!" Fairlop walked with long lazy strides, his large, flippered feet clanging against the rec room floor.

"Well, well, if it isn't the brainbox bi-ol-ogist. The muttering mollusc. She speaks after all." Fairlop fanned his large, comb-like hands through his red hair.

"Cut it, Fairlop, I've known bullies like you all my life."

"Me? A b-b-b-bully?" stuttered Fairlop purposefully, catching Jimmy's eyes. "Ah, look what we have here... not seen you round these parts before. Got a name, curly?"

"Jimmy... Jimmy Ford."

"Well, well. You know how to play poker, Jimmy Ford?"

"Not very well. I played with my dad a few times," he said courageously. "But I'm sure he let me win."

"Ain't that somethin'? Come on over. I'll teach you a thing or two and be sure *not* to let you win."

"I…" Jimmy looked over at Allen for affirmation. None was provided. "I don't really have anything to offer."

"To offer?"

"To bet with. I don't smoke."

"You hear this, Slugs? The kid says he don't smoke. Well ain't that one mighty old shame." Slugs rolled his eyes, waking up those sleeping brows. It seemed everyone was exhausted with Fairlop's show.

"I've got you, Jimmy," said Allen. He reached haughtily inside his breast pocket and produced a packet of Kenilworth. "Now go beat Palaemonetes!" he said, looking directly at Fairlop.

"You what?"

"It's a shrimp," said Jimmy, proud of his new knowledge. "You can see right through it." Fairlop's eyes squinted warily, not sure what to make of it. "I don't smoke," mentioned Jimmy again, "so why would I want to win all his cigarettes?"

"Ew!" came the crazed crowd. Fairlop smirked the width of mouth only a madman could muster.

"Let's play!" he said, snarling at Allen.

"Bring your sanity, kid, you'll lose it with this lot!"

Jimmy clumsily held his borrowed cigarettes and followed Fairlop the length of the rec room towards the card table. The tiled window ledge glistened. The sunlight was tempered by the drapes, casting a soft shade of red hue.

"Jimmy… Fairlop is the name," said the man, almost dancing with the energy that rocked inside him. "And a fair game I play too. Don't let these boys fool ya none!"

Fairlop gestured for Jimmy to take the seat between him and Chat. He placed his behind down and nodded in acknowledgement to the other players.

"Hey, I know you! You're the kid we met during the fire drill?" accused Slugs. Jimmy nodded. "Excuse Fairlop here, he pulls pranks like that all the time, you get used to him and his…improprieties."

"Yeah, like the furniture!" barked the square-eyed man across the table.

Fairlop was busy shuffling.

"Where are you from, F-Fairlop?" asked Jimmy.

"Well, ain't this swell? This here youn' whippersnapper de-tects an accent. The one and only US of A, sonny… Salt Lake City… Utah, yee-haw!"

"I've never met someone from America before… not… in person."

Slugs chuckled. "You won't want to meet another after Fairlop here!" The other patients all joined in.

"Go on… laugh!" said Fairlop. "We'll see whose laughin' when you have no smokes to toke tonight! You must be mistakin' me for Woodbine Willie!" The man sure had a lot of energy. If he wasn't flicking his cards, he was tapping his feet; if he wasn't tapping his feet, he was drumming the table; if he wasn't drumming the table, he was searching the room. And damn if he wasn't doing it all at one time.

"Two stick blind, my boy. That's two fine smokes here if you be big blind, one if you be small blind. You got that?"

"I understand," said Jimmy.

"As you boys are all nervous of my triumphs, I'll let the young lad here cut the deck, well, how about that? Yes, yes,

yes." Fairlop kept the pack steady whilst Jimmy counted down five cards and cut.

"Hey, what's the deal, sonny?"

"Well, I figured, if you are cheating, as these gentleman claim, then you would have calculated how many cards down your picture would be. By counting out a card per person, I should now be dealt the card you intended for yourself... I figured that you asking me to cut was just a rouse and providing you got a read on where it was, which I assume you did, you would be placing my cut directly back on the top of the pack before these gentleman here saw! Oh, that's also providing you are now somehow dealing again, of course!" Jimmy sat back smugly, but inside, his heart was pounding. Allen applauded from his distant chair. The players each looked over at the scene with open mouths. Their eyes darted back and forth in anticipation of Fairlop's next move. Fairlop dragged indolently from one of his cigarettes and blew smoke in Jimmy's face on his smirking outbreath.

"Well, well, well. Ain't that somethin'?" he sneered. "I'll be damned. You hear that boys? Jimmy here called you lunatics, gentleman!" The table all erupted in laughter. Fairlop ruffled Jimmy's hair and, cautious that the attention was on his hands, began to deal. He curled the worn cards out across the table in a frenzy. "Now then," he exclaimed, shrugging off any attempt to be embarrassed by the young boy, "before we proceed, allow me to introduce you Jimmy, to some of the potential threats we have here! This *gentleman* to your here left who will blind you with his rather oversized cranium, in the shape of what some may describe as a beluga whale, is the loveable, uncalmable, uncontrollable chatty man… you can call him Chat for short." Chat gave a sideward nod at Jimmy. Jimmy caught the silent irony. "Chat in his past life was a pig."

"A pig?"

"Yessss, sir, a damn near cop, a po-lice officer. Seems he got hit in the head one too many times." Jimmy looked back at the man sympathetically. He was busy trying to decipher his cards. "This here next to Chat, the man living with slugs above his eyes…" Jimmy giggled like a schoolboy before sensing the man's disposition. "Slugs, it would seem, has been dunked in boot polish and stuck there to dry," he added. "Well, what do you know… his name is Slugs!"

"Yes, thank you, Fairlop," said Slugs, his hands shaking uncontrollably as he picked up his cards.

"Ah, yes, I almost forgot, we call him Shakes too, or Shaking Slugs… in here for alcoholism if you couldn't figure!"

"Yes, thank you, Fairlop," seethed Slugs between grinding teeth.

"Old schoolmaster," added Fairlop relentlessly. "I mean, just imagine the looks he would have given *you*, boy!" Jimmy smiled meekly at Slugs. "And this here is the finest of fine fellows, this here…" Fairlop pulled the man directly beside him and ruffled his thick hair. "This here is Wilkie. When he closes his fat skin lids here, the purple appearance on said closed lid versus the white appearance underneath rather delicately and ever so sweetly conjures up an illusion of a pill, or as you Limeys may call them, a capsule or tablet, wouldn't you agree?" Jimmy couldn't either agree with or deny the accusation. "Wilkie, you hear? Not to be confused with Milkie, because you're right, I knew you got to thinkin' it... he also possesses what you would consider a ghost-like complexion, but hell, most of the gone-cats in here have. You see, Wilkie here, if you haven't already noticed, has tics. He was a farmer, so wouldn't you know..."

Why does a profession always define who somebody is? thought Jimmy, acknowledging the wise doctor's words. If that was the case, who was he? How would he be described at the table to the next recruit who joined? "Yup," continued Fairlop. "He must have fucked too much, got himself too many sprogs and not enough food, that would have led him to the bottle too, see, ain't that right, Slugs?" Fairlop winked. His observations weren't without sacrifice. "Yours truly here has had the pleasure of timin' these tics on various occasions and I here can confirm that they range between precisely thirty-three to one hundred and seven seconds apart. Now, given that he had one prior to my deal and calculatin' I deal at a rate of approximately fifteen seconds, before then here givin' you a brief introduction to Chat and Slugs. I would say, we lucky folk are due a sighting of one riiiiiight about..." As if on cue, the man snorted and rolled his protruding eyes towards the back of his head. Fairlop was balled over by this accuracy and his belly folded double. Jimmy looked away from Wilkie to save his dignity. Instead, he watched Fairlop with a wonder of a firefly. A firefly, that in all its beauty, needed swatting.

In his quiescence, Jimmy attempted to identify why a man like Fairlop would have been admitted. He did remember him for the stunt he pulled on the fire engine.

Maybe an action like that was enough to keep you here?! Perhaps he was pulling all sorts of stunts on the outside?!

Fairlop's laughter continued to roar. "Ha-ha, you see that crazy son of a bitch right there?" Jimmy's intrigue fell away to indignation. *Why do people have to be so mean to each other all the time?* He remembered his father's wise words as if they were scratched on the walls of his soul: be kind. Everyone is going through a tough time at some point or other.

"That's not fair!" said Jimmy abruptly, words surprising himself.

Fairlop took a break from his laughter. "What ain't fair?"

"Well…" Jimmy inhaled, knowing he had to continue. "Wilkie probably only tic-ed because you went and mentioned it… he… he was far more likely to tick *because* you mentioned it…" His voice trailed off as he saw Fairlop wasn't entertaining the logic. The other patients looked at Jimmy with an air of admiration. Wilkie's pupils flicked between Jimmy and the table, a small smile unfolded.

"Hell to it," said Fairlop. His large fingers scraped the stubble on his rugged, square jaw. "Let's play!" *Hell to it,* thought Jimmy. Even a fellow like Fairlop might have been going through a tough time, although he did a mighty swell job of concealing it. *He is here like the rest of us, isn't he?* Jimmy turned his palm to reveal the two ruffled picture cards: a pair of kings. He glanced over at Fairlop, who had already folded his hand and had busied himself with smoking. Jimmy paid his small blind and folded. He was no cheat. The first card on the turn was also a king. Jimmy looked over at Fairlop again, who now got to distracting himself with swatting a fly. This was the worst kind of conman; you only had to look at who he was conning to know that.

Not many hands were played when Fairlop asked the question, "Say, Jimmy... what you in for?"

Jimmy searched his mind for a suitable answer. This wasn't like prison where the most heinous crimes earnt you respect. Although, perhaps the crazier you were, the better it was.

"I have epilepsy."

"Say, epilepsy, isn't that the one where you..." Fairlop insensitively shook all his limbs in one go. Jimmy grudgingly nodded.

"And you?" His eyes met with Fairlop's; it was like nobody had ever asked him before or he didn't even know himself.

A plump man with sparse wiry hair, wearing nothing but his underpants, burst through the doors and squirmed around the rec room. He stopped beside Jimmy, wide eyed, incessantly rubbing his bare red torso.

"Excuse me... " said the man earnestly. "Are my legs on fire?" Fairlop couldn't contain himself. His face folded in laughter. Jimmy looked the man up and down.

"What's your name?"

"P-Patrick," he said, eyes pleading for an answer.

"It's ok Patrick" said Jimmy. "No, you're not on fire".

"Oh..." the plump man stopped patting himself down and calmed. "Thank you," he said gripping Jimmy's hands between his. Jimmy felt how drenched with sweat they were. An orderly came by to collect Patrick and ushered him calmly out the rec room.

"Well, I never," said Fairlop.

A small girl in her white rags now approached the table. "Hi! I'm Jimmy," said Lola.

"Not now, Lola," whispered Jimmy.

"Well, check this crazy-gone chick," said Fairlop.

"Hey, she's not crazy, she's not gone anywhere," defended Jimmy.

"She's not crazy, she's not gone anywhere," repeated Lola.

"Whatever you say, Captain," smirked Fairlop. "The boy sure knows how to pick em…" he said, addressing the table.

"What do you expect?" said Jimmy, a rage boiled inside him. "We're in an asylum," he shouted. He stood to his feet. "*You're* in an asylum," he pointed at Fairlop, heart pounding once more. This man sure knew which buttons to push.

"You're in an asylum," pointed sweet little Lola. "You're in an asylum, you're in an asylum."

"Shut that bitch up," snarled Fairlop.

"You're in an asylum, you're in an asylum," continued Lola.

"I said—"

"For speaking some truth? It's the only bit of it I've heard all day!" laughed Slugs. With that, loyal, bald-headed Oren appeared.

"Come, Lolola, the boys are playing cards. Let's get some air." Jimmy nodded at Oren and took his seat back at the table. Oren ushered Lola towards the outside world, her white hair spread across her small back.

"You're in an asylum, you're in an asylum…" Her words trailed off.

Thunder gargled in the clouds, forcing open heaven's door. Nurses ran to the open windows, snapping back the catches before the rain crept through. With the thunder, Allen retreated into himself, mumbling about the territorial habits of Wobbegongs and Cookiecutter sharks.

Jimmy sat flustered, palms sweating, veins pumping with adrenaline.

"Cool it, kid," said Fairlop over the roar. "I merely make observations around here, that is all." Streaks of lightning cracked their whips across the face of the sky.

"Yeah, well, don't. Ever tried that?" Jimmy crossed his arms in a huff. "What are we even doing playing cards anyway? Pretending… that's what!"

The table sat silent. Each of them turned to watch the world crumble outside. Inside the rec room, agitation swept across the aroused patients.

"Deal the damn cards, Slugs!" demanded Fairlop. "Before Jimmy here has a fit."

"Something the matter over here, boys?" said the shadow from a man who crept towards the table. "Heard me some sort of altercation." It was a limping orderly, his posture that of a scraggy alley cat.

Fairlop rolled his eyes. "Seems that altercation you heard is happenin' outside Nesbit, why don't you go investigate?" Jimmy's mind gasped. *Nesbit!* The doctor had warned him. His eyes flicked up at the man and back down at the table.

Nesbit looked at Fairlop with disdain and Fairlop back at him in equal measure. Nesbit's hand was gripped around a wide black instrument, as black as his polished hair.

Fairlop saw this but wouldn't let the intimidation surface. "Now get!"

"It's a free country, Fair-lop," said the predictable man. He chewed his tobacco with a monotony that made everyone around him instantaneously irritable.

"Free country. Right, I'm just as entitled as you then, ain't I?"

"Titled," laughed Nesbit. "Only, Fair-lop, we ain't in your country, are we? And even if we were, ya ain't in the free parts, I'm afraid, ya confined here."

Fairlop sighed; he had been here countless times before.

"Nesbit, I just want to play some cards with my boys here."

"Didn't sound that way from way over there."

"Well, why don't you go back way over there and listen to what it sounded like?"

"As I said, free country!" Fairlop nodded for Slugs to start the deal. His freckled hands remained still. "Ya see, Fair-lop…" Nesbit strolled over and stood beside the seated man. "I can wander all I like, where I like… you see…" He jiggled the metal teeth. "I got the keys!"

"That so?" said Fairlop vacantly, sliding up his cards.

"Yeah, that so, Fair-lop."

"It's light outside still, Nesbit, don't you usually wait until after dark to harass your victims?" Fairlop didn't even look at him as he spoke. He coolly slid his two sticks into the centre of the table. The black club was now out of its holster and twirling around Nesbit's knuckles as if it were only a coin. His eyes shifted round the room for witnesses. Only the sane ones mattered to a man like Nesbit.

"No victims here, Fair-lop," Nesbit gripped Fairlop's head and bowed it down towards the floor. "Ain't any in white rags, anyway!" The vein in the middle of Nesbit's forehead was pulsing. "You see this leg? Do ya? Fair-lop?" Fairlop raised out his arms, signalling he didn't want any trouble, but Nesbit continued tugging his head closer, his grip tighter. "I'm the victim here! *Me*, that's who!"

"Well, congratulations," mocked Fairlop. "Now, if you're quite finished kindly messin' with my hair wax, I'd like to get back to playin' cards with my boys." Fairlop wriggled from Nesbit's grip and pushed him back a stride. He repositioned his red hair.

"Why ain't you out fighting, Fair-lop?" demanded Nesbit. Fairlop didn't give him the gratification of an acknowledgment. "Is it because the doughboys ain't involved?" Nesbit began panting under the strain of his exertion. "Let me see, no, it isn't, is it? Because the doughboys joined back in April, didn't they?"

"Raise, two sticks," announced Fairlop to the table. The others sat anxiously looking between the two men.

"My knee!" continued Nesbit. "I'm no coward!"

"Jimmy, your play," said Fairlop. Jimmy stared through his cards, not really seeing them. His eyes flicked towards Nesbit and back at his jacks. "Jimmy!" prompted Fairlop.

"I hear you, Fair-lop…" Fairlop received a ball of spit as Nesbit spoke. He raised his arm to wipe it off from his lip. Nesbit swiped it. "Ha! Almost," he said. Fairlop looked at the man pathetically, loosened his arm and attempted to get back to his cards. "I hear you and the boys all saying it! My knee, Fair-lop, that's my excuse… what's yours? What brings a man over for war one month and in an asylum the next? A deserter, that's what. Nothing but a run-away piece of scum I wouldn't waste the time scraping off me shoe." Fairlop sat silent. Silence that only seemed to exacerbate things. "One day I lasted," he spluttered, coating Fairlop's face in spit. Nesbit raised one finger up, "One fuckin' day! Because of what? Because of this!" He signalled back down to his wounded leg. "You think I wanted the bullet? I wanted to fuckin' fight for my country, Fair-lop!" Nesbit's face was dripping with sweat and his polished hair loosened some dry black strands which creeped along his forehead like ivy. Fairlop separated his palms and began to applaud Nesbit. Nesbit's face turned the colour of raw meat. He raised his voice over the claps. "I was injured, Fair-lop... where are your wounds? In here?" He pointed to his temple. "That's horseshit and you fuckin' know it!"

A tattered wire-haired lady shuffled over. She was dragging a giant wall clock, hands long ceased. She stopped between the two men.

"Well, ain't this a parade of Warley's finest?" mocked Fairlop.

"What is it, Ethel?" demanded Nesbit. The lady didn't stop long; she sneered in the orderly's face and started shuffling away again. Fairlop chuckled like a circus clown.

"You want veneration, Nesbit? You want respect? Worship? You're bottom of the food chain in here, even with these crazy cats!" Nesbit's flow had been interrupted. He was frustrated, infuriated. He knew that Fairlop had back the upper hand.

"Ethel," he commanded. The lady turned and sneered

again, holding her dear clock, warding off any potential threats like a mouse might hold its sacred cheese. "The damn thing is only right twice a day, ya got that? And the hour moves faster than the minute hand!" Nesbit placed the instrument back in his holster, checked his wristwatch and leant over the big clock.

"Nesbit, I wouldn't do—"

"You wouldn't do what, Fair-lop?" The aggravation of the man's tone led Fairlop to his next move. Jimmy and the rest of the table had thoroughly abandoned their hands.

"Nothin'," said Fairlop calmly, gesturing his arm out for Nesbit to proceed.

"Nothing is right." Nesbit double-checked his watch. He marched a few more steps to catch up with the old lady, leant over and began winding the hands forward.

Ethel's face instantaneously transformed into one of sheer torment. In her anguish, she pounced on him with claws readily sharpened, tearing and scratching away at the orderly's face.

"Get... get off me... ya crazy whore!" screeched Nesbit. He fumbled around for the black instrument, but with the weight of Ethel and her clock, the three tumbled to the floor. Jimmy was knocked from his chair and rested back on his hands, eyes petrified. Ethel sunk her head into Nesbit's shoulder, split white hair like dry bramble, thorns cutting through cloth and skin and sucking around the marrow of his neck. Fairlop giggled from his throne. Ethel was hysterical; Ethel was crazy.

Nesbit regained the upper hand. He rolled Ethel onto her side, clambered on top of her and successfully removed the black club. Fairlop's face dropped. Without hesitation Nesbit raised his arms over her like a lumberjack and began swinging down against her skull. Jimmy closed his eyes in horror.

Fairlop was first to leap upon him. He got in one good blow, knocking Nesbit's head sideward. Nesbit wiped a streak of blood against the back of his hand. His smile, sinister and wry. He had been waiting for that moment a very long time. Still straddling the old lady, he turned and swung his club, giving Fairlop one almighty thump. His eyebrow unstitched from his forehead and he flopped back onto the table like a discarded joker. Nesbit stood over his limp body and brought the club down. Again, and again. The cards bespattered with Fairlop's blood, spades soaked red. *Crack. Crack.* The thunder outside continued. The rain trying to get at them through the cracks in the window.

"Stop!" Jimmy yelped. He shuffled his body below the table, pressed his fingers against his tragus and shielded his eyes with half his palms. From a distance, Allen could be heard, restrained to the rocking chair of his own mind, prattling on about single-minded limpets suckered to rocks.

Through the gaps, Jimmy witnessed in silent horror the legs of the nurses sliding across the rec room floor. Ethel was cleared unconscious from the wreckage. Her head hunched back flaccid against her frail and bony shoulders. Others attempted to wrench Nesbit away from his workbench. As his arm raised, Betsy tried to grip it. Her hand slipped through the thick liquid, club and hand shimmered vermillion against the glint of the window. Her body hurled across the floor.

"You're killing him!" she screamed. Jimmy heard that much.

A second orderly, of large stock, managed to get a firm grip up and through his shoulders. The orderly clasped his fingers and pressed against Nesbit's pulsing neck. With one leg firmly pressing against the table, he used all his strength to lift him. Nesbit and the orderly slammed against the rec room floor. The club fell from Nesbit's bloody grip and reverberated. A small round ball burst from the seams of his pocket and rolled towards the hollow table.

Underneath, Jimmy slowly removed his hands from over his eyes. Fairlop's legs slumped lifelessly above him. He heard dripping. He turned his head; Fairlop's big hands were hanging over the back of the table. He must have been sprawled over it like a drawn and quartered peasant. Beads of blood slowly trickled down each finger onto its tips. Running as thin as water, it reached the end and cascaded. *Drip. Drip.* Upon the floor, droplets exploded like red raindrops, forming a large puddle of blood. Between the cracks in the wood, a small, red river ran.

The silver marble kept on rolling. Slowly it stopped beside Jimmy's shoes. He reached down and between his fingers was a glass sphere with the small statuette of a white wolf inside. Areas of the ball were smudged in blood. As Jimmy rotated it, the kaolin clay shimmered silver as it refracted the light. For the first time in nearly three years, Jimmy held the wolf in his hand.

"Buck!"

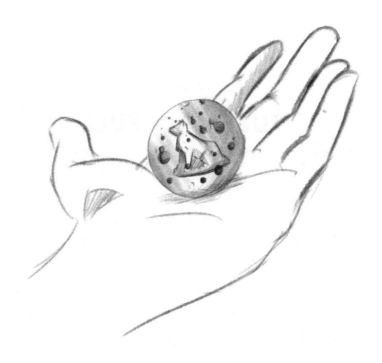

CHAPTER TWENTY

TUBE HALF FULL

H E WAS DEAD. FAIRLOP was dead. That was the rumour whispered around the walls of the asylum. "Chat saw his body carried to the mortuary." That's what the others had said. Nobody had heard Chat say it himself, of course. No one had heard Chat say much of anything.

Between tics, Wilkie had regaled the group with the news of Nesbit's exclusion. Even with the issues of understaffing, Campbell knew full well that there wasn't a choice to be made on the matter. 'Do no harm', that was the motto. Campbell had been secretly gladdened by the result. He had been looking for a reason to dismiss Nesbit for a long time now but even he hadn't wished for it under such circumstances as these.

It wasn't until a week later that Ethel was seen back

in the rec room again, her head bandaged and the pointed features of her face blue with bruising, a leaking pen with its ink congealing below the surface of the skin.

It was thought, by the group, that with the slow recovery Ethel had made and with far fewer blows, Fairlop was sure to be dead. The sad truth of the matter was that the asylum residents were used to it, death.

"Chat had seen them carry his body to the mortuary," or so they say.

Fairlop was no longer a good man; he had become a great man. A man regarded as a true American hero.

"You remember when for a dare he took all Wilkie's medicine and didn't sleep for a week?" Slugs would boast on the deceased's behalf. "Or the time he streaked the cricket pitch with only a copper cup to protect his manhood? Oh, and there was the time..." Slugs creased over, eyebrows reddening around the tips. "He sent poor Lolola down the other end of the hospital asking for those fallopian tubes!" The table erupted in laughter.

Without Fairlop, Jimmy had accumulated quite a fortune in cigarettes for Allen. Allen was ecstatic; he could smoke a pack a day if he so wished. Jimmy, on the other hand, gained no pleasure from his poker victories. He couldn't help but look across the table and imagine Fairlop's limp and bloody body sprawled out over it. *Jimmy John Ford, Jimmy John Ford*, he repeated in repentance.

Since the incident, Jimmy hadn't written a word, hadn't read a single line of a book. He knew he must get better, get out of here for himself, his own sanity, for Grace. Since the incident, Jimmy had found that he was, once more, a noxious bag of nerves. Sometimes he was equipped with the glue to fix the cracks which scarred his brain. Other times, he wasn't. Some days his glue tube was half-full, so he could quickly repair some of the intruding thoughts but not others. Today was a tube half-full day.

"That doesn't make any sense. Why would he be in the suicidal ward?" demanded Slugs.

"Wouldn't you be suicidal, Slugs, if you'd been beaten within an inch of your life by Nesbit?" Wilkie gestured towards the empty seat. "You saw him, he had a…" Wilkie's eyes bulged, the snorts came first, then his skull swelled and surged backwards like a retreating tide. "Club!" he announced. "He had it in for him from day one. He had a club!" Slugs stood and precisely placed one card down at a time in front of the four players. This was when Fairlop was missed the most, during the deal. Everyone thought it was a fair game now at least. Really, it was Jimmy's game. The other two were there for the conversation and the occasional lucky draw.

"He's alive… I'm telling you," persisted Wilkie.

"You saw them, Chat, didn't you?" Slugs shouted to the player directly beside him. Chat picked up his cards and grunted. "Yeah, see, Wilkie, Chat saw them taking his body into the mortuary." Chat turned the cards in his hand and frowned at them as if he believed they were upside down.

"Doesn't prove a thing! Say Chat is right. That could have been any number of bodies!" offered Wilkie. "The rate they are dropping around here—"

"The rate *we're* dropping," added Jimmy, his face hidden behind his pair.

"Right…" Wilkie looked disturbed. "*We're.*"

"I tell you what," said Slugs, jaded by the perpetual conversation. "Why don't we have a wager on it?" Jimmy looked at Wilkie, Wilkie back at Slugs. Chat picked up some cigarettes from in front of him to gesture that they were already betting something. "No more smokes," said Slugs. "Not on this hand!"

"What you have in mind, Slugs?" asked Wilkie.

"Well, how about we find out what happened to poor Fairlop, once and for all. Let's say, on this next hand, if I win, I get to nominate one of you three to head over to the mortuary and take a look for him?" He leant in and smirked. "His body." The table fell silent under the gravity of the dare.

"And if you don't win?" demanded Wilkie.

"Then… then I'll do it!" Slugs collected their cards up before any objections mounted and began shuffling the deck. "The odds are in your favour… gentlemen." He looked over at Jimmy and winked.

Jimmy felt somehow alive for the first time in a week. Alive but petrified. "You're on!" he said.

"All right." Wilkie nodded cautiously. "Slugs… let's go!"

"Chat?" prompted Slugs. Chat reached out his arm. Slugs placed the deck in Chat's hand and he cut. It was settled.

Jimmy's heart was pounding when he reached down and lifted his cards. He kept the two in line with one another, to gain a slow reveal of the back one. The first was the eight of clubs. Jimmy squinted his eyes tightly and rustled the cards together between his fingertips, slowly coaxing out a single pointed spade, the ace of spades. It suddenly dawned on him that there was no skill involved in this hand. The back of the five cards which faced down, red against the table, they were his fate now. All of their fates.

Slugs looked around the table as if to raise suspense. He leant over and turned the first three cards: ace of clubs, eight of spades, king of diamonds. *Two pair!* screamed Jimmy's monologue. He checked his cards again to be sure.

"Everybody happy?" said Slugs, who proceeded with the fourth card. The fourth card was the queen of hearts. Dried blood stained the face of the queen: Fairlop's blood. Their consciences riddled.

"On their backs, gentleman!" ordered Slugs, ignoring the brutality this evoked. Wilkie was first to toss.

"Na-da! Fancy dealing me a seven two, Slugs... I couldn't have even bluffed it if we were playing raises!"

Chat was next to grunt. He flipped them over in a slow wide arc: eight, six. One pair, Jimmy had him beat regardless. Jimmy was next to flip. He bit the corner of his lip in attempt to conceal a cheeky smile which found its way through anyway.

"Well, well..." Slugs slumped back in his chair. "Looks like you have this one, Jimmy!" Slugs turned his two cards, revealing a red ace and a black ten. Jimmy's teeth became less shy and he could no longer hide his smirk.

"Except..." added Slugs. "We do still have the river card and the odds are now in my favour."

"And how do you figure that one, Slugs?" said Wilkie. "The kid has two pair."

"Correct," said Slugs. "Jimmy here does have two pair

and I'm merely chasing a straight. However, let me point out that Jimmy here has himself a hand known as dead man's!" Even Chat leant in with intrigue. "Bill Hickok, or Wild Bill as you probably know him by," continued Slugs. "According to Fairlop, he was said to have this very hand the night he was shot dead at the poker table… all black… just like you, Jim! That was five card stud, of course, but same rules may apply." Jimmy looked intently over at Slugs. Although it was Fairlop's story, it checked out. Slugs brows remained bushy and as stern as ever. "They never did find out what that fifth card was… shall we?" Jimmy nodded slowly, now unsure of anything. Slugs leant over and slowly pinched the corner of the remaining card. "Well, I'll be damned," said Slugs, adopting an American accent. "Uncle Jack turned up late and drunk to the party after all… and he brought his diamonds!" Slug's lips creased in triumph. "Straight!" he yelled. "How about it, boys… dead man's hand! Maybe there is some truth in it, after all!"

Jimmy slapped his palms across his face. It couldn't be.

"Wallow no more, me blighter," said Slugs, gathering up the discarded hands, and in true Fairlop style, he added, "You, boy, have yourself a date with a dead man."

Jimmy knew he couldn't just expect to be able to walk into the mortuary unannounced. He needed a plan. He realised where he was: the rec room, her favourite room. It didn't take long to spot her. Her with blonde locks and satellite ears. Her with her machine-like ways.

"Nurse Harrison?" called Jimmy politely, approaching behind the lady in her stage clothes. The patient appeared to be counting the cracks in the wall. Up went her finger, signalling that the young boy would have to wait. After what seemed like minutes, she turned, slowly, mechanically. "Yes?" she said softly, staring above his head. Her eyes finally darted down to meet with his. "What is it, patient 130617?"

"130617?"

"That was the date of your admission, was it not?"

"Right… yes, my admission, my tour. That is what I came to ask you about."

"No patient after a tour is allowed a second tour."

"Right… yes, well. Nurse Harrison, I'm Jimmy. You did give me a tour already, Oren joined, remember? That was his second tour, was it not?"

"Patient 130617, no patient after a tour is allowed a second tour."

"Nurse Harrison. I don't need another tour. I just want to see the mortuary!"

"The mortuary?" The nurses' head tilted on its crook.

"Yes, the mortuary."

"Forbidden!" she said quickly.

"But—"

"I never take a patient to the mortuary on a patient tour."

"Right… I see." Her wide eyes were making Jimmy a little uncomfortable; he gazed away for a moment and realised his mistake. "Ah," he said, placing his hand coyly across his forehead. "How could I be so foolish?" he whispered.

"Speak up, patient 130617!"

"Nurse Harrison, you can call me Jimmy."

"Speak up, patient Jimmy," she said abruptly, as if her words had not been replaced.

"I just want to see the brewery!"

"The brewery? Where Timmy—"

"Yes," he interrupted. "Where Timmy fell into the copper and died from lockjaw."

"Well…" said the nurse, her seriousness slacked and evolved into a confused smirk. "Why didn't you say so?" she added, eyes wild again and focused above his head. "Follow me… this way patient Jimmy." The nurse glided along the rec room floor and out of the side door.

Jimmy looked back at the table; Slugs and Wilkie gave him a thumbs up. Around five seconds later, Chat raised his.

The nurse swung open the large creaking door.

"This is the… brewery!" Jimmy entered the enormous, dark room; it was still clammy.

"We used to have so much fun here until Timmy fell into the copper. Made a right old fuss…" The nurse was repeating her statements word for word from the tour Jimmy had back in June. "Lockjaw… died!" she added. "Before that, we had beers every mealtime. Gin and water, or lemonade… my favourite. Every patient got an allowance."

This time, Jimmy engaged in conversation. "Where was the copper?" he asked. The nurse frowned at him. He had disrupted her script; there was no way back. She gathered herself.

"Over… there." She pointed, eyes drifting to the far end of the dank room.

"Can I see?" said Jimmy. The nurse ushered out her arm. To his surprise, she didn't follow.

As he approached the rows of tables, the smell became overbearing. He lifted his clothing and clasped the cotton up and around his nose. This somewhat subdued the fetid, decaying scent of rotting flesh, but not entirely enough. It had been a hot summer. Jimmy turned to see if the nurse was watching. It appeared she had busied herself with another cracked wall and was beginning to count. As he neared the first body, he noticed a small, brown tag dangling and twirling from the end of a toe like the packages at a sorting office. Jimmy didn't think of it in terms of a body at all. He knew he couldn't allow his thoughts to surface. He dabbled on some of that mind glue, held a deep breath in and checked along the first row of tags. In canonical order they read: Mary N, Annie C, Elizabeth S, Catherine E and Mary K. All women. He was a little relieved not to be forced to discover what lay underneath. Without hesitation, he approached the next row of five. He hadn't yet allowed his imagination to visualise what was under the murky brown cloth. Maybe he was mad. At that moment, he remained unafraid of life, unafraid of suffering, of death. Jimmy didn't know if he was any longer sane but for now, he didn't care. That was the beauty of it.

The next tag: 'Nicholas K', he read. It suddenly occurred to Jimmy that he did not know Fairlop's first name. He would have to look for the initial 'F' listed as the body's surname and take the chance. The next four: 'Floyd N, Louis B, Oscar C… and… Theodore W'. Jimmy rechecked the nurse. She was crumbling off some of the wall and massaging it between her fingers like lotion. The third row only had four bodies on it: 'Melanie P, Ruth T, Virginia N… and… Laurence F'.

"F… Fairlop!" gasped Jimmy. He attempted to stabilise his thoughts, but it appeared he had run dry of glue. Fear came knocking once more; he was a child again. He was marginally thankful to get some feeling back. Perhaps he wasn't mad after all? Or was he partially enjoying the intrusion? Sadistic, perhaps? His throat closed; his mind raced. He'd opened the flood gates; the thoughts came pouring. A thousand phosphorus photographs of Fairlop's bloody face splattered against his brain. He felt sick. "Jimmy John Ford, Jimmy John Ford," he whispered, his voice quivering alongside his hands. He reached out, slowly, clumsily. His fingers met with the edge of the dampened cloth. He began turning it reluctantly, like forcing over the pages of a book he was scared to read. As the cloth uncovered a white cheek, he saw the curls of a moustache resting gently against it. His lips began to quake, he knew instantly this wasn't Fairlop. The hair was as black as boot polish and slicked back with a glug of petroleum jelly pomade. The occupant of such hair had combed either side to form a regimentally straight whitewall down the left of his scalp. The occupant certainly wasn't Fairlop. The occupant of this body was his dad!

Jimmy looked along the line of bodies. The cloths were all draped, so he saw them all: Poppy, Wilfred, Harry.

The heavy door squealed open.

"What on Earth are you doing in here?" came the husky voice of an orderly. "Miss Harrison!"

"It's OK, Doctor, he is with me, I am giving patient Jimmy a tour. Strictly speaking he isn't allowed a second tour, but it is only a tour of the brewery, you must understand."

The orderly shrugged off any conversation, any hope. He darted his eyes across the dark room, squinting to make out the silhouette. Jimmy was breathless and bewildered; he glanced back down over the body. It wasn't his dad at all. Gazing sternly upwards was the face of a large, bloated man with receding mouse-coloured hair.

"You there!" shouted the orderly, interrupting any logical thought. "Boy! Come here now. What are you doing with my bodies?" The orderly began to widen his stride. Jimmy turned frantically and spotted a door at the end of the room. He dropped the cloth and ran for it.

The brightness of the outside world startled his sight. Jimmy could waste no time adjusting. He hopped across the pig pen and over the cow gate. He stumbled to regain his balance as he passed under the big oak tree, ran the length of the gravestones and bent around the corner of the asylum wall. He leant back against it, catching his breath but soon enough the orderly's voice trailed behind. "Boy! Come back here now!" There were no patients out on the lawn to blend in with. He had already gained tired of running; his epilepsy had not been kind to the state of his health. Jimmy knocked his head back in defeat. The rear of his skull echoed like wood. He turned and saw the black and splintered coffin-shaped door; the suicide ward. The door was slightly ajar. He didn't have any decision to make. Forcing two hands around the knocker, he yanked it open just enough to slip inside. He pushed the door closed and through its weight heard the knocker slam back down against the wood. Silence. Darkness.

Jimmy's breath began to return to its usual rhythm. He

was alone. Square pools of light sat still in straight and equal distances along the length of the long corridor. As he began shuffling towards them, he heard music, soft and sweet. He reached the first square window and placed his face up against the glass. A layer of steam hovered over a ceramic white tub. Jimmy curved his hands to make binoculars. He made out the side of a lady's face. Her head turned slowly towards him; Jimmy gasped and ducked down below the frame. He gave it a few seconds before raising it again. The lady was back facing forward, her hair draped over the lip of the basin. Her body appeared to be wrapped in a white sheet and was submerged underwater. Steam seeped from the bath on the sweet melody rising from the scratch of a gramophone needle. Jimmy shrugged and continued his journey along the corridor. As he approached the next window, he heard similar classical music playing. He cupped his hands once more and looked in. A similar set. This time it was the side of a man's head and he did not turn. His hair, shaved short around the ears, appeared jet black against his pale complexion. There was no steam in this room, the small green tiles below the tub coated with moisture. Again, the music wept. *Maybe the suicide ward isn't bad at all. Everyone just seems to be having a long soak in the tub.*

As he neared the third window, he heard a muffled pounding sound. Again, he cupped his hands and peered through. This time it was a small padded white room. The sonorous sound was louder now but Jimmy couldn't see its cause. Suddenly, the square pane fell dark, blocked by the back of a patient's head. This startled Jimmy and he too jumped back. The patient hopped two-legged away from the door and in full view. The arms of the man were bound across his abdomen by a white jacket, a straitjacket. Legs shackled together like cattle, a posey.

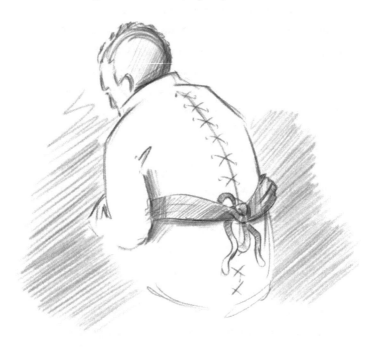

Jimmy panted as the man crashed to the floor and coiled like a stiffened wolf mid-howl.

"We must pacify patients due to our understaffing issue," came the tender voice from the far end of the corridor. Jimmy turned his head startled by the sudden sound. "We wouldn't usually use restraint. But Edwin here is a special case... among some of the others we have down here." Jimmy couldn't conceal his disturbance. He was going to make a run for it, back out the wooden door, but then what? The orderly would have him. The nurse was now only strides away.

"I'm sorry, I'm Millicent… and you are?"

"J-Jimmy."

"Nice to meet you, Jimmy. What brings you to the suicide ward? I'm afraid I can't let you stay here…"

"A-a friend," he said quickly.

"Oh?"

"Yes, he… he was attacked, you see. Some of the others, they thought he might be down here."

"Your friend got a name, dear?"

"Yes. It's Fairlop."

The nurse shook her curly bun. "Nope. Afraid not. Although may be that's a good thing, right?"

"I suppose," said Jimmy. "Why are they having baths?" He gestured down the corridor.

"Well, hydrotherapy is used in all sorts of circumstances," said the nurse. "Alice at the end there has insomnia." Jimmy looked at her dimly. "It means she can't sleep."

"Ever?"

"Not as much as she needs. She is easily agitated."

"She doesn't look it."

"That's what the water does. She soaks in hot water for a few days."

"Days?" gasped Jimmy.

"Yes, well… the water needs time, to set in and relax the patient."

"And why the music?"

"It's soothing. Audio stimulation helps her to relax."

"The man… there isn't any steam in his bath."

"It's cold," said the nurse.

"Cold?" Jimmy grimaced.

"That's Jack. He has… well, an overactive mind!"

"Why cold?"

"It slows down the blood flow to the brain, decreases mental and physical activity."

"So, you stop him thinking?"

"For a while, until he is calm and ready to again." His skin crawled with pimples. "Jack has manic depression psychoses."

"What about him?" Jimmy pointed back to the third door.

"Edwin? Well, he is suffering, like many here, from general paresis of the insane. He's not well." The nurse looked empathetically through the door at the man on the floor. "Not well at all."

"I'm not surprised, he's tied up, like… like an animal!"

"At least he isn't shackled up with ropes and chains. This asylum is one of the good ones."

"Good ones?" said Jimmy sceptically.

"If you want to untie him dear, by all means…" She gestured out her arm. "But it's your funeral. Poor Edwin needs malaria."

"What good would that do him?"

"The Viennese swear by it, dear. Doctor Wagner. He is a neurologist. He insists on treating a patient with malaria-infected blood."

"Wouldn't that make him worse?"

"At first. He would develop one hell of a fever. But then it kills off the syphilis bacteria and after administering some quinine, he would soon recover, and both the malaria and the syphilis would be gone. That is the theory, anyway…"

"Then, what are you waiting for?"

"Where to get some malaria blood. There is a war on, Jimmy, if you hadn't noticed. The Austrians aren't exactly our friends right now."

"Yes. But they can't be the only ones with the blood."

"No, all in good time, Jimmy. It is only a theory."

"But he will die!"

"We are all going to die, Jimmy."

"Not like this, not this way…why does it have to happen this way?" Jimmy let his emotions get the better of him. The nurse gripped his wrist; he whipped his arm down and ran back the length of the corridor. He would take his chance with the orderly.

CHAPTER TWENTY-ONE

MUTE

SINCE THE STORM HAD silenced itself, the weather was more tolerable and the pungent odour which previously occupied the rec room had subsided. It had been almost two weeks since Fairlop was seen, and Jimmy could not bring himself to lift his pen. Jimmy could not bring himself to do much of anything. This place was getting the better of him, and he knew it. He felt his old self slipping away. Fairlop was attacked and yet again he didn't act. He was far too frightened, but it wasn't a fear of getting hurt, not physically anyway. It was the fear, as the doctor had stated; the fear of himself, the fear of going mad. By accepting therapy, by accepting this place and its occupants, he was accepting madness. But by rejecting it all, would he go mad anyway?

He had the strange theory that by finding Fairlop, by finding him alive, he would, in turn, find himself. It was but a theory, after all. The writing was working before; it had subdued him, provided an outlet. After all, he wasn't going to be flying a plane anytime soon. But every time Jimmy even spied the nib of his copper pen, he felt the fear grip him, like two hands clasping around his throat. He had come to acknowledge that it wasn't real events he wanted to witness and write about. He just wanted things back, back the way they were before. He had spent his entire life finding ways to escape, to leave the town of his childhood. Now, he just wanted a portal back and he would be satisfied, if only he could find a way.

"I wouldn't have put it past Fairlop to get himself a spot beside all those women," joked Wilkie, just in time before one of his tics.

Jimmy startled himself, waking up from his thoughts at the poker table.

"Well, I did tell you he wasn't on the suicide ward, didn't I?" Slugs had to wait a while before Wilkie could join back in the conversation.

"That d-d-doesn't prove a th-thing," said Wilkie, attempting to take back control over his own body. "He wasn't in the mortuary either. I wonder where in the hell that American fool got himself to?!"

Jimmy sat, pensively looking around the rec room. He felt exhausted after the fit he had endured over breakfast, and his temples were hot and throbbing. It had cut Alfred's visit short and for that, he was sad. As his dehydrated eyes scanned the windows, he spotted the officer sitting over the lawn.

"I wouldn't bother, kid," said Slugs. "Officer Letchfield, he's a mute!"

"Officer Letchfield," whispered Jimmy. It took a while for his brain to compute.

"Ere. What happened to his sister? Visited him every week at the beginning. Pretty little thing she was, I miss her. What was her name?"

"Katherine" whispered Jimmy. He tossed his blind in, folded his hand and walked out.

"Where's he going?" said Wilkie, already claiming the two smokes. Allen scuttled over to the table to gather his morning profits.

The waft of lavender permeated the summer air. Jimmy clambered down the two steps and onto the patio where Officer Letchfield sat twitching. The wooden spokes on his wheels rattled quietly under his bony backside.

"You mind if I...?" Jimmy gestured. He clumsily wheeled over a white garden chair. The heavy legs scraped along the slabs, leaving behind a chalky trail against the stone, a shrill like itching cutlery. Officer Letchfield turned away. "Sorry," muttered Jimmy, abruptly lowering the chair where it stood. He sat down and rested his arms across his lap. He couldn't believe it; he was sitting here at the asylum he had broken into almost three years ago, sitting beside the officer he had read in the letter he had lost beyond the viaduct.

At this intimate proximity, the officer seemed more vulnerable. Jimmy noted how young he looked, his cheeks filled red with rosacea, still possessing that fat that puppies have.

Jimmy glanced around the pruned gardens, a concoction of bloomy odours. A few wandering patients were scattered out on the lawn. He spotted Stephen under the Japanese blossom, his rake clanging against the stone fountain with the statue of the Virgin Mary. The graves were drenched in the orange glow of the morning, the sprouting grass below softly glistening with dew. Jimmy watched lethargically as two buff-tailed bumblebees passed between flower heads.

"That can't be a bad job... can it?" he said, pointing to the workers who hovered purposefully above clusters of pink-blushed stonecrop. Jimmy smiled languidly and turned to face the officer. It was difficult to tell if Letchfield could hear, but he was back and calmly facing forwards at least, his hand rattling against the wooden armrest. "We used to grow runner beans at home. I... I used to salt them, keep them... fresh." Jimmy couldn't imagine the scene, for it took too much energy. He looked back over at Stephen, the endless raking, too much energy. He slumped back in his chair, pasty and weak. The sun was being gentle with him this morning, like the warm tongue of a soothing cat. Jimmy peeked over the treetops. "I only used to live down the hill there, with my dad. Where are you from, officer, originally, I mean?" He spoke to the side of Letchfield's face; he looked too young to be an officer. His strawberry hair, fluffy like a baby chick. He was surprised how well he looked, his skin almost sun-kissed, even. Jimmy found it miraculous that even though his mind had given up, the officer still blinked, still squinted those grey lids when the rays were too bright for his husky dog eyes. His body still rocked ever so slightly; a small reminder that not all was lost.

Jimmy drew his attention back to the bees who now occupied the same flower head, another joined them.

"It was just me and my dad, growing up... well, then Poppy, Dad married her before he embarked. If he hadn't, he wouldn't have been eligible for compulsory sign up. Love, eh? He was a soldier too, you know? Fought in the Boer." Jimmy let a smile peek through. "He never talked about his time there, though. He was a good man, you know?! The best man."

Jimmy busied his mind back on the bees. Two of them with loaded saddlebags moved towards the yellow face of a black-eyed Susan. They clambered over one another for a taste of that sweet pollen.

"I had a sweetheart on the outside. She came to Dad's funeral! We fought. I... I wasn't myself that day. I'm not sure I will ever really find myself again." He cleared his throat. "She is a nurse, you know?! Not here, physical cases. Oh, can you imagine if she had to treat us?" Jimmy studied the officer as if their circumstances were the same. He wondered what it would be like to be confined, not only to an asylum, but to a chair. What was the difference? All of them were confined, really. He wanted to change the subject, the subject he was discussing with himself. "This weekend we're off to Southend for that trip. Day before my birthday! You're coming too, right? Be nice to get out a while, won't it? I use my books as an escape sometimes… and my writing. I've only just discovered how powerful it can be. I know it's good for me, psychologically… it's just hard to, sometimes, when my mind's… well…" He hesitated. "Grace!" he said, looking at the gawking soldier. "My sweetheart's name was Grace!" For a while, Jimmy was left with his memories of her, and for once, he wasn't trying to fight them.

"I haven't spoken to an officer before, about the war, I mean. It's hard to imagine a war being on now that we're in here, isn't it? But both of Wilfred's brothers were out fighting in France. Wilfred… he is my best friend. Or was… he, we found a letter back in 1914, it brought us here, it mentioned you! I left him on a train… a train which was hit by…" Jimmy unheeded the thought. "I think Billy is still in France…" he said. "I hope so. Harry was killed a few years ago, at Christmas, they were in the same battalion. It wasn't a PALS or anything… but they were stationed together… at Messines. I wonder where they… where Billy is now. I wonder where you were, maybe you knew Harry, Harry Needham… Private Needham, that was his name, the one who... died." Jimmy saw the officer's milk eyes shift in their deep-set craters. "I heard why you're here and regardless of what they say, I think you are the bravest of men. I truly believe that anyone who wears that uniform is. Besides, it must be nice wearing your uniform... over these rags!" Jimmy pulled at the white cloth which sagged pendulously around his thighs. "I wanted to be a pilot, you know? So, I could do my bit too. I saw a real pilot once, a real hero, like you. Second Lieutenant Sowrey, he shot down zep L32. This war, it's brought trouble, hasn't it? Not just over there, over here too! I mean, if it wasn't for the war, my friend Wilfred, he would still be here. I wouldn't have left him on that bloody train! He wouldn't have been... and, and my dad... and Poppy. Plus, you wouldn't be here... not in this place, anyway. Because you... you wouldn't be m-ma... well, you just wouldn't be here." Jimmy flushed a little. He didn't want to accuse the poor man any more than he wanted to be accused himself. "And Fairlop, he wouldn't have been called over from America and got his brains all bashed in by Nesbit, who wouldn't have been so bitter about being shot in the knee. He wouldn't have been shot in the knee because there wouldn't be a war on!" Jimmy exhausted himself in all the conceivable parallel possibilities these lives could have taken, a lost generation.

"Hey, I wouldn't be here either!" he concluded, starting back up again. "My dad, he would have taken care of me, I know he would. I should have told him sooner... sooner, about my condition, my epilepsy. I think that deep down, I knew that I had it. Just that I... I was ashamed, you know?" He stopped a while, wallowing in pity. "Maybe if I had, he wouldn't have gone off to fight... off to die!" Jimmy wiped his tears away as automatic as a body would shiver in the cold. "Ah, what's the use? What good is it all now?" He wept wearily in his chair. He thought of it all, life, like a game of chess. There were so many possible moves he could have made, any number of plays he could have made, but inevitably he would be left here right where he was, as a king, a king being protected by a mere pawn at the end of it all, life.

Minutes passed; the bees buzzed on. Jimmy observed as the pair moved on to the white heads of snowdrops. The first bee remained. "*My* best friend... Wilfred. He didn't ever know what happened to me... winding up here... a madman!" He chuckled. "I'm only here because of my epilepsy, and now... now I'm grieving, but I feel like *I am* going mad. But... but it's here that's made me so, or it's losing him, Wilfred, Poppy... my dad. My mind won't stop. I'll end up in one of those baths like Jack, I know I will. How do you do it? How do you shut down, stop thinking?" Jimmy turned his head to face the officer and, to his surprise, Letchfield was staring right at him. The ominous, sneer of a man who had seen it all and was fine with it. "You hear me, don't you? You understand me?" he said as if an animal had just spoken to him. The officer's head slowly rotated back, facing forward over the lawns. Jimmy joined him.

"Lavender," came the gruff voice. A voice that could make a corpse move.

"What?" Jimmy spun his head around so fast that he almost witnessed the officer's lips bite down on the last letters. "Did you say something?" Jimmy looked over his shoulder to see if there were any nurses or orderlies, anyone sane enough in the vicinity of where they sat... talking. There were none. He concluded that he must be going mad. Jimmy sat silently a while longer; no more bees to distract him. They had left, left like everyone else had left. Even the flowers hung their heads over their graves.

Above the officer's head, he spied two great stone faces worn down by the April rain. Sculpted on the skirting of the asylum, they protruded out as if what they had to say was more important than any doctor. *What more could you know with moss and bird shit growing out of your mouths?* he thought.

He removed Buck from his pocket and began to swirl the marble between his thumb and forefinger. He scraped some of the congealed blood from the surface and then removed it from under his nails. He observed it closely, the last remnants of Fairlop.

"Lavender... quietens the mind," the voice said, still rasping. Jimmy didn't dare turn. He looked down at Buck, the wolf unreactive, howling at yesterday's moon. "Slows down our thinking. Ha! So *they* say..."

"You... you're talking?" said Jimmy, pivoting round to face his superior. The officer nodded. "But you don't..."

"Don't?"

"Won't... didn't! Not since, since you've been here..."

"Nothing worth saying, kid. These doctors can't help me!" The officer rolled up his khaki sleeves, brass buttons glistening in the sun. His actions were perfectly competent. "They've put me here every day for a year, you think I can stop thinking? Ha! Lavender. It will take more than lavender to stop seeing their faces!"

"Whose faces?"

The officer didn't answer straight away. He stared vacantly forward. Jimmy worried he'd lost his voice again.

"My men," he said, finally. The smell of vomit lingered subtly on his breath.

"H-how many did you...?"

"Kill?"

"Have!"

"What's the difference?" sounded the strings from his hoarse throat, slowly adjusting to real conversation. "Too many, kid. You know, whilst we are at war, the penalty for not killing is death; in peace the penalty for killing is death... go figure!" Letchfield removed a dirtied white handkerchief from his pocket and proceeded to wipe the sweat from his brow. "Death... did you really look at it. Into its eyes?"

"Its eyes?"

"Those that died, your dad. Did you see his eyes?"

"I—"

"It's all I see when I imagine my men. It's how you tell."

"Tell? If they were ready. All men welcome death at the very end, but that glint just before it takes hold, that glint reveals everything." Jimmy sat startled, paralysed to his chair. "I heard what you said, kid. I'm no hero, I'm not sure what that letter led you to believe, but I'm no hero." Letchfield's shaking hands managed to push the last of the handkerchief into his trouser pocket. "Me? Ha... I'm barely a man, let alone a good one!"

"I'm sure you did something heroic out there?" Jimmy said boldly.

The officer limply shook his head. "A hero saves lives, a

hero doesn't watch powerlessly as his men scream, lie scared whilst his men are buried and silenced after a bombardment. A hero doesn't stand back and observe his men mutilated, torn apart by shells, charred by flames, blistered by gas, sunk and left to drown in mud, struck by clubs with nails, bleed to death whilst shrapnel is removed from a wound so deep you see others lose their hands inside." The officer's acorn-shaped eyes drooped, the weight of his voice, the weight of his own haunted memories. Jimmy dropped with it; it was all too true. He let out a foiled outbreath. "What makes me any different from the Kaiser?" Jimmy was shocked. How could he possibly relate? In a strange sense of obligation, he felt it his duty to try.

"You're… you're taking orders," said Jimmy. "He isn't!" Officer Letchfield squinted. "Anyway, I keep hearing rumours the Kaiser's dead."

"Rumours. Right, keep us hopeful. Keep us busy to keep us sane. *Ha!* How that worked out!" His tongue creaked when he spoke, uncurling in his mouth.

"Have you… have you spoken to Doctor Campbell? He… he's helping me, at least, I think he is—"

"He's spoken *at* me, too many times. Persistent bastard, ostentatious old fool. I've known smug spectators all my life. I was an officer, remember!"

"Was?"

"Yes. Well, not exactly fit for duty now, kid…" The officer removed a medical wallet from under his rear, its creases as red as Satan's rolls.

"Want some?"

"What is it?"

"Opium for your stomach, cocaine for your cough, quinine for fever and coca for when you're lethargic," he mocked.

"No…" Jimmy raised his hand, "…thank you."

"Suit yourself." The officer folded the red wallet and put it back into his secret hiding place.

"Why haven't you… been talking?" Jimmy asked.

"Talking, talking… it's all we humans do. It's overrated, if you ask me. I've been talking all my life, kid. Look where it's got me. It was talking that killed my men." The officer waited a while, taking in the sound of his own lost words. "I gave the orders!"

"B-but why now? Why… me?"

"Don't flatter yourself, kid!" The officer frowned. "Always wasting words," he grumbled.

"What?"

"Forget it!" He swiped the air. "If I was a good man, I would tell you that I'm touched. Is that what you want to hear?" Jimmy didn't know how to react. "All right, in fact, I am touched," said the officer, bored of his own irritable disposition. "I'm touched that someone so young can feel so much… has gone through so much, over here, that is. There was me thinking that all the horrors of war were fought on foreign soil," he added, a little more sincerely.

"Well… now you have told me!" smiled Jimmy.

"How is it?"

"What?"

"Smiling. I forget how it feels."

Jimmy's smile faded.

"Don't listen to me, kid. I'm nothing but a coward, see?

You were smiling and now I've gone and taken that away. That was the problem, you see? I never knew when to stop… talking!" The pair ceased conversing and observed the white figures scattered around the grass. "It's like the stillness of a rural cottage in the fields of France before the German army arrive…" muttered the officer. "This place… it isn't so bad."

"It isn't?"

"No comparison," he said, shaking his head.

"You dive from an exploding sausage, then you'll know!"

"Sausage?" chuckled Jimmy.

"You know, a rum jar, a Minnie… a flying pig? It's the heaviest mortar!" Officer Letchfield started motioning at the horizon with his hands. "A tail of light trails across the sky behind it. We soldiers, we all watched it with intrigue. Then the light goes out and that's when you take cover!"

"Minnie?" laughed Jimmy.

"That's right. Not so funny when you're there!" Jimmy's face turned stern. "Nor are the pip squeaks, the plum puddings, potato mashers, the stuttering aunts!"

There was a long silence.

"Rats…"

"What is it?"

"No. Rats, scurry on your face at night when you're sleeping. They eat your light!" Letchfield screeched the words out like they were etched onto his scalp. "You wake up in the morning and all the wax from your candle is gone…" He paused. "We shot at them each dawn. Sometimes we missed and smote a Hun having breakfast by mistake."

"Mistake?" questioned Jimmy, curious at his turn of phrase.

"Rats are worse than Germans, Jimmy. And collection duty—"

"What is that?"

"Collection duty," repeated the officer from some place far away. His eyes rolling back towards the dark projector inside his skull. "Corpse collection!" ordered the officer in a loud shrill. "Winter's the worst. Only frost stops the stink. Bodies swell with the rain. The rain smokes. The smoke settles around them like their souls are escaping. No flies. No maggots to erode them away…"The officer's eyes turned glassy, filling black like secreted squid ink. Black, with his memories. "They stay sighing," he whispered. "They are dead, but their souls still go on screaming. There's an open mine of corpses and worms. No tombs. Their bodies just lay there, mangled in the mud. The stench of them taints the air. Rotted, naked flesh. You can't tell who is human, who is Hun. A frozen hell populated by foreign ghosts… You can taste them."

"The dead?" gasped Jimmy.

"They don't look the same anymore. Don't look like they should anymore. You collect them at night, that's when they watch you…" Letchfield's eyes burnished behind the panes of a mask. "The gas. Chlorine. Sweeps through the trench, a sea of green mist like we're all suddenly on the bottom of the ocean." Jimmy thought of what Allen had said in the rec room. Even he would have struggled against the officer. "Men trying to remove their clothes like they are going swimming!" Jimmy thought of Harry. "They drown on their own blood and clumps of burnt lung—"

"Stop," whispered Jimmy. "Stop!" he screamed. A few of the patients looked up from under that towering oak tree.

Jimmy's mouth was wider than his open ears.

"Will you talk to the doctors now?" he asked as quickly as his words would come.

"You leave the doctors to me, kid!" Officer Letchfield folded his arms and relaxed back in his chair. "I heard them conversing, you know? Something about having to fry my chords with a metal spoon if I don't start soon." Jimmy's mouth widened further. "See… don't flatter yourself." The officer pointed towards his torso. "Nothing but a coward here, kid!" The pair watched as a pigeon landed on the patio and began pecking foolishly at the trail Jimmy had made with his chair.

"Listen, kid."

Jimmy took a deep breath. "I'm listening."

The sun hid behind a cloud, casting shade over the asylum.

"The world, it's a terrible place, a dead place." The pigeon took flight. The officer's skin turned grey with leaden recollection. "A place where enjoyment is only given out in rations. Then these rations, they are distributed, unfairly to the ones with money, the ones with power, the ones whose names mean something to somebody, somewhere else, with money… or power!"

"I-I don't understand."

"Then I suggest you keep it that way, kid. The wealthy rule the wise… the wealthy rule everyone! But what right do they have? A birthright?" crowed the officer.

"Wealth doesn't have to mean money and power," said

Jimmy, reciting his father. "Even the Kaiser must stand naked!"

"Excuse me?"

"My dad… when I was unnerved about something, or rather… someone. He told me to imagine that person naked. Because, deep down, we are all the same, all flesh and bone, all human, all in this together… *in this marble of a world*, he would say, *everyone gets a throw*."

"Sounds like one of the wise ones…" Jimmy nodded. "One of the wise ones being ruled by one with wealth!"

Jimmy studied the white wolf inside the ball he held.

"I don't know. Perhaps we are all just upside down on this marble, scrambling around not knowing what we are doing…"

The sun re-emerged; the officer looked out over the lawns for a very long time.

"I'm sorry to hear about your dad, kid. Mine used to beat me blue," glowered the officer. "The longer he lived, the more misery and pain he inflicted on my mother and me."

"I know."

"You know what?"

"I know I was lucky to have him, before losing him. I know that now. I-I just wished I knew that at the time, you know?"

"Same goes for my men. The men I was ordering to die. They weren't much older than you." He turned to face the boy. "I lost the damn near best men you could ever meet. Had their whole lives ahead of them."

"But what can you do now? They are dead, and you're not… you survived!"

"God is the only survivor in war! And why do people say that? I didn't want to survive... not in body... it was my damn mind that betrayed me." Jimmy didn't know how to respond. He didn't need to. "*Ha!* I'm not dead? I could say the same to you, kid!" Jimmy nodded. The officer sized him up. "Don't be tricked into thinking that because they are here, or we are here..." He flicked his eyes back and looked down over the mad patients in their rags of white. "They or we are any better off than people out there... or down here." He pointed to a place below the ground. "Victims of war are not just soldiers, kid. Most wounds aren't publicised with white crosses!" Jimmy gulped. "You know?" said the officer. "I was at the Somme."

"You were?"

"That's what got me back here a second time. I did a stint in '14 and another now."

"I was here in 1914 and now in 1917!" said Jimmy.

"You said."

"Yes. Although, the first time, not as a patient..."

The officer frowned. "The Somme... we were in this nowhere town, I can't remember its name... Albert, I think. There was a statue of the Virgin Mary hanging from a shelled church. Just like that one..." The officer nodded down over the grass. "She was broken up pretty bad, half her face was missing. When she falls—"

"The war will end," said Jimmy enthusiastically.

"Ha! Admire your optimism, kid. How much madness those statues have seen... all those Virgin Marys in prominent positions in churches, in war... in asylums. She must wonder what the hell we humans here are doing!"

"Yes, I suppose she must." Jimmy relaxed. "She was here the night Wilfred and I broke into this asylum."

"Broke in?"

"Yes, that's why I was here in 1914!"

"He was the kid brother?"

"Of Harry and Billy Needham, yes, did you?"

"I was at Messines," said the officer quickly.

"You were? You were there the day Harry—"

"Drowned." The officer nodded gravely. "Nice kid."

"But I thought you were here in *1914*?"

"Come on, kid, I thought you were smart. How can I be in two places at once?" Jimmy looked bewildered. "It was you, the letter. It was written to your sister, to Katherine!"

"I don't have a sister, kid," said the officer, matter of fact.

"This letter, it was hurled from the train, *you* were mentioned. We came here because of *you*!" The officer's eyebrows triangulated. "We were over there, right by those graves." Jimmy outstretched an arm. "From there, I could see the room I'm in now." He pointed out his dorm to the officer.

"You weren't here because of me, kid," sneered the officer. "You were here because of you. Nobody comes through that door because of someone else." There was silence. Jimmy's skin pimpled.

"There was a German boy..." said Jimmy, hastily changing the subject. "He... he died in a field, over here, in England. He was flying in the zeppelin that was shot down by that pilot I mentioned, Sowrey..."

"The hero," seethed the officer. "But suppose all that a hero is, is one who achieves his orders?"

"What?"

"Suppose he was following orders, as the German boy was following his. Haven't you just labelled him a hero because he was the one who kept his promise?"

"Well… yes… and saved… I mean, he shot down the zeppelin which was bombing England… which… which killed people!"

"We're out there doing the same," said the officer. "It's just someone else's friend, someone else's family…"

"I guess…" said Jimmy passively.

"Look, I'm sorry about your friend, your old man… but bringing personal attachment… weakness, that's what got me here. Hell, thinking is what got most of these poor buggers here!" The officer stretched out his arms.

"Not me!"

"Right… your epilepsy!" Jimmy nodded. "I've seen plenty men die in fields, kid. In fact, that's where most of them end up doing it."

"Heroes can be made in death too."

"You really believe that?"

"There is a plan for us," said Jimmy. "And, it might not include death just yet, so we should make the best of it."

"God's plan?"

"I don't think so. But don't suppose it is just a lonely world full of frightened people. There is a plan for you too. How are you supposed to become who you are meant to be if the events of your life don't… sculpt you?"

"Ha! That so… how old are you, kid?"

"Fourteen."

The officer coughed. His cough arced into a horrible wheeze. "Fourteen?"

"I'm nearly fifteen!" added Jimmy. "You don't look too old yourself… for… for an officer."

"That so?" Letchfield chuckled for the first time.

Jimmy noticed that his eyes looked old. He wasn't surprised. What he had seen and stored behind those panes had been engrained involuntarily on the windows of his skull. Those scenes could force a calf to become a bull within a week.

"I just wondered where you got your words from, that's all. But I guess age is but a number, eh? No doubt your words have come from your own experiences, kid! You have your reasons for carrying on, I have mine."

"But, you can't—"

"Can't? Carry on?"

"Can't… give up."

"I gave up living the day after I was born, kid. From then I was busy preparing myself for this."

"I don't believe you!"

"*You* don't believe *me*?"

Jimmy shook his head. "You're wearing that uniform because you have some fight left in you!"

"I'm wearing this uniform because someone else makes up the rules. I'm following an order."

"But what if we could live in a world without unnecessary death? What if we could change the rules, the order?"

"You got wealth I don't know about, kid?"

"No." Jimmy sunk his head. "Yes, well, it depends how you defy wealth. What if the world isn't as dead as you say? Or, even if it is at the moment, it doesn't always have to be. Reincarnation. Rebirth... we can change it!"

"You and I... from here?"

"Yes!"

"In the face of adversity, eh, kid?" The two of them watched Stephen, eyes squinting towards the sun which had poked its head through the distant line of poplars. Two squirrels tussled over an acorn below the giant oak tree. Jimmy let out a long-relieved sigh.

"There must have been some fond memories... of the war?" said Jimmy.

The officer looked at him as if he dwelled on a different planet. He swallowed and retired in thought. "Playing cards by shell light," he finally declared.

"But I thought you hated the shells?!" said Jimmy, oblivious to it all.

"Not star shells, they're silent." He turned to face him. "On a clear night, you can hear the Hun's harmonies." Letchfield's eyes glazed over again as he watched the scenes play out on a projector in his mind. "Everyone's faces turn colourful in sync with their music, as the shells pass. Red, white, green..." Jimmy broke eye contact and fixated on the bushes as if he could see it all. "It's the clearest night sometimes and the stars just... are." The officer trailed off across the sky, like his consciousness. He uncovered more things than he even thought possible. "The smell of damp wood in the morning, the smoke after a left-over fire" he said. "The SRD." Jimmy looked back, muddled. "Service Ration Depot..." he offered. "Or Seldom Reaches Destination... it's diluted rum, but it does the trick on a cold night. The planes purr overhead. Sometimes, they dropped whisky down… the *Princess Mary's* gift boxes, all sparkling in gold. That's about the only time you feel contented… like you could be amongst real friends in a public house celebrating. You take it in turns to open up a tin and each face lights up gold at the sight of tobacco and chocolate." Jimmy's face lit gold. "You swig from the bottle and pass it to the next man. You don't even have to go to the bar… and the games…" Officer Letchfield tilted his head as if emptying the vision. He sniggered.

"What… what's so funny?" asked Jimmy.

"You know. I started talking because it sounded like you could use some help. Not sure it was you who needed it, kid!"

"I think we helped each other."

"Talking, eh?"

"It's what separates us from the animals!"

The officer looked at the boy. "Who are you, kid?"

"I'm Jimmy, Jimmy John Ford!"

"Well, Jimmy John Ford. I suggest you hop to it, don't you?" Jimmy looked over his shoulder. Nobody had been witness to their conversation. Nobody at the asylum knew that Officer Letchfield had his voice back. It wasn't Fairlop he needed to find at all. It was Grace! He needed to find Grace and live their days in solitude, in the solitude of Brentwood even; he didn't care, as long as he had her back. A hero doesn't stand there and watch. A hero doesn't let his life disintegrate before him until he can no longer even swallow the crumbs. He needed that piece of him back. He was sick and tired of being the spectator in his own life. He was going to fight to the death until he got it. Until he got her *back*.

CHAPTER TWENTY-TWO

THAT TO BE

S UNDAY 12ᵀᴴ AUGUST 1917. It was the first time
Jimmy had taken the train since the incident. There
was a strange sense of exhilaration, not for the train ride
itself but to be nearing the seaside. The claustrophobic
weight of the world diminished, houses beside the railway
tracks lessened and gave way to an expanse of sun-soaked
fields. Those freshly ploughed to their west were flanked by
ditches, dotted with stocky brown bovines, wooden cattle
gates and wriggly sandy paths. The turf to the east rolled in
carpets of green and peaked in tufts overlooking a medley of
millponds. Boats with staves and masts with gulls balancing
on crests, nodding aboard in time with the sultry wind.

"You know what game I loved to play?" said Jimmy
to his fellow passenger, Oren. "I pretend I am running

alongside the train here." He tapped on the glass. "And in order to get where I need to go, I clamber and spring off objects from the landscape at lightning speed. Like this tree here, I'd mount that and dive across the sky to this hedge, which I can run along until it ends and find a gate or a post or apex of a house and glide along the roof—"

"But wouldn't the fall from the roof hurt?" asked a confused Oren, looking to his friend with the cottony beard.

"Yes, but I'd have special... abilities, special soft shoes that cushion my landing... hey, look!" A Canadian goose glided beside their carriage at equal speed. "Now, I could ride on him, see..." Oren nodded as if he understood. Jimmy took a while, taking in the strange child with his large, golden, egg-shaped head. He smiled. He was pleased for Oren's good health. But just as often, it would cause him great distress, understanding the reality that he too would one day soon abandon him, like Wilfred, on this very train. Jimmy now found temporary solace in the memory of his best friend, regaling dewy-eyed reminiscence to Oren of all the adventures they'd had growing up. All those bases they built, all those journeys across the brook with burnt palms from rope or tyre, all those times they had been up to no good, caught egging or playing knock down ginger. Well, Wilfred was the one who got caught, of course, but Jimmy would never have let his friend go down for a misdemeanour *he* had caused. At the end of these conversations with Oren, Jimmy was never sure which direction he wanted to grow in, torn, in part, between the longing of his recent childhood and the burden of adulthood which had been forced upon him.

"Oren?"

"Yes, Jimmy."

"What did you want to be when you grew up?"

"What do you mean?"

"I mean, what kind of person? I wanted to be a pilot, a writer, direct films."

"Direct?"

"Yes, direct movies, in the cinema. You've never been?"

"Nope." Jimmy gasped. Oren turned back to face him, eyes flicking between him and the view outside. "Where I'm from, we... well, we were very poor. There was a cinema, but we never got to go. I tried to sneak in once and was caught with my legs dangling out the toilet window." Jimmy laughed. "The guard who caught me pulled me legs through from the outside. I caught me head on the window frame and... well, that was when I had my first fit, outside, right there on the floor..." You could tell that Oren was there himself. "After that, my mum, she couldn't look after me too good. I have three brothers, two sisters. She has to work a lot."

"Is that why, she doesn't visit?"

"They are a handful. Well, they were..."

"We will go!" said Jimmy.

"Where?"

"The cinema. There's one called the Palace up in the High Street in Brentwood. We will go and see a film together."

"Together?" said Oren.

"There's bound to be a Chaplin production on."

"Chaplin?"

"Yes, Charlie! He stars in all his own movies. He also directs them. They are comedies, you see, he's really ever so funny. You'll wet yourself laughing, Oren, really, you will. This one time… Charlie in *The Fireman*, he squeezes the firehose, but he accidently blasts it out all over the other men and they can't get up because the water is so strong."

"That does sound funny, Jim."

"It is. Truly! My dad, he and I once acted out the scenes Charlie featured in his films, he's…the greatest." Jimmy's voice trailed off, saddened by the prospect of never playing that game again, saddened by the prospect that with Oren's mum still alive, she hadn't even come to the asylum to visit her boy, her *son*. Jimmy made a note that he would go and visit Mrs Needham. When they were back from the trip, he would go. He owed her that much.

It must have looked strange to the other passengers boarding the train, seeing clusters of patients in their white rags. Jimmy always ensured to give a sincere nod, a reassurance that they were behaving themselves. And they were. The intrigue of the outside world was almost too great. Many had their silent eyes shoved up against the glass, pupils shifting back and forth with the passing scenes. Their tranquillity, however, did not stop the other holidaymakers from being cautious. Many caught sight of the group and pivoted on their heels, travelling back towards the other end of the carriage. Curious children would get their arms guided by their wary mothers, bucket and spade in hand, clanging clumsily against the seat lip.

It wasn't just the scenery they all found mesmerising, it was the people too. Elderly couples with their matching

Waverley deckchairs, or the Hygienic model for those constipated few. Those with packed lunches, soft cheese sandwiches, which would no doubt later be dropped and devoured together with crunchy granules of sand. Some carried fishing rods equipped with lines, reel, hooks, float and tackle. Boxes of bait airing the stench of the sea which filled Jimmy's lungs first. It seemed every passenger had the same agenda today: to forget that there was a war on.

But, unlike the so-called serenity provided by the asylum walls, being back in the real world made the realities more obvious than ever. At Laindon, a group of young soldiers had boarded their carriage. It didn't take long until they had spotted Officer Letchfield in his chair and shortly after ensued in pointing and muttering. They couldn't fathom why an officer who was dressed in uniform the way he was, was surrounded by all these ghosts in white sheets. Lucky for Letchfield, he had his back to them, not that he seemed particularly talkative this morning.

The trip itself had been months in planning. One had to ensure there were enough staff per head to orchestrate such a feat. Then there was the matter of who would attend to fulfil the needs of the patients joining and who would stay behind to look after the thousands of others with immediate care. It was Doctor Turner's idea, of course, and one doctor was a requirement as a precautionary measure. Betsy had volunteered her name and various other lucky orderlies were selected from a random hat draw. As for the patients, those who hadn't showed signs of their condition deteriorating got first allocation. As for Jimmy, well, he was the doctor's favourite.

Upon passing a great green plateau, the ruins of an old castle became visible.

"You know, that castle was once prisoner to Ralph de Binley," said Jimmy proudly, poking at the window. Oren looked at him. "He was in love with Princess Beatrice, but they weren't allowed to be together".

"Not allowed?"

"He fell out of favour from the King. He had to board a ship for France and leave her here to marry another man".

"How do you know all this Jim?"

"An old friend." He smiled.

"*Warley Wanderers!*" shouted Turner. "Gather your things, all off, next stop… Leigh-on-Sea."

Jimmy was infatuated. After his conversation with Officer Letchfield, he had spent the entire day and all the next evening writing. He had borrowed books on local interest from the library and old newspapers the doctor had collected. His subject had combined his two passions: writing for starters, flying for mains. It was the first of his works he was proud to share.

"An utter triumph," Turner had concluded, almost hugging the words from the boy's notebook. "It makes a delightful read, Jimmy. Lieutenant William Leefe Robinson would be honoured to have this in his hands at a time like this," the doctor explained. "If only his POW camp would receive letters?! 'This is the house that Jack built' indeed, we need to get you a typewriter, dear boy, get this down in real ink. You, Jimmy Ford, are building more than that…"

Jimmy was charmed with the glowing appraisal, but what lead to his exhilaration this morning was the fact they were visiting the very town he had written about the previous evening. In his scene, Leefe flew over the barracks at Shoeburyness, the pier at Southend and the Old Town of Leigh-on-Sea, the same town his dad got married in, the same town Jimmy had experienced his very first kiss!

Many of the patients were distracted as heaps of emerging cockles appeared like alpine mountains on the horizon. Their nostrils flexed as the liberating fragrance of the sea imbued. As the brakes squealed, an automatic response informed their legs to stand, but with the unpredictable rhythm of the train, some gave way and tumbled into the gullies. With the helping hands of the orderlies, they dusted themselves down, mostly unaffected. Lolola mooed at the cows behind the window to the sound of Oren's relentless laughter. Jimmy thought it was funny that she seemed less mad this side of the asylum walls. They all did, although perhaps society had its own perception of them.

"Right, quick head count," said the doctor, helping Betsy lower Officer Letchfield down on to the platform in his chair. "Nobody move!" Hordes of holidaymakers navigated their way through; they had no choice. Jimmy observed as they glanced upon the madding crowd and just as quickly flopped and turned their heads.

"They ignore us," whispered Jimmy to Oren. "They all do."

"So what?" said Oren blissfully.

"You'll be one of them soon, Oren."

"Yeah, guess I will. And you will... one day!"

"But I'll never forget that once... I wasn't."

"We will go to the cinema one day, won't we, Jim?"

Jimmy thought it sweet that the boy was holding on for the trip. "We will. Once you're out, we will!" he reassured himself. Turner's hairy hand interrupted the boys as he planted it down on their crowns.

"Thirty-five... Thirty-six! Righto, all present and correct. Let's move, shall we?" He skipped ahead like an excited schoolboy, a hairy one at that.

Once everyone was safely over the level crossing, the doctor pointed over towards Bell Wharf, a concrete construction jutting out over the mudflats.

"That's it, this way, follow me." Letchfield's chair reverberated on every cobble. It was strange. Since their conversation, the officer hadn't muttered another word, not to Jimmy, not to anybody. Every time Jimmy had seen him, he was surrounded by other patients, other doctors, and he simply sat, hand rattling in that chair, a distant gaze across his eyes. It was almost as though his condition had worsened overnight and he was back, confined inside his haunted mind once more.

"Sorry, officer," obliged Doctor Turner. "Duty calls us over that way... away from these tourists!"

The bells chimed eleven times.

"Yes, thank you," said the doctor obligingly. Some patients laughed; others stared vacantly out across to the shores of Kent. "Listen up, everybody, this is rather important, we have some business to discuss." Whispers. "Who here, of age, would like a beverage of the alcoholic variety? Raise your hands."

The group of orderlies cackled. "Yes, boss; yes, sir!" The

majority nodded, some stretched and raised both arms. Jimmy peered at the officer; he didn't budge.

"Very good. We shall firstly then, take a trip thataway." He pointed back towards the direction of the travelled train. "There is a more than satisfactory little public house at the end there, known as the Crooked Billet. One fine pint of ale per piece, washed down with some seafood from the Osbourne Brothers. No chancers or there will be consequences," he warned with an outstretched finger. Nobody cared. One was plenty. "Jimmy Ford, where are you, lad?" The boy raised his hand amongst the patients who still held there's high. "Ah, there you are. Take Officer Letchfield here, you can pilot your way across a few cobbles, can't you?" Jimmy stepped forward proudly and gripped the two handles. "Very good, steer this ship to dry land, my little powder monkey," encouraged the doctor. "Boatswains…" He nodded to the orderlies. "Quartermaster." He tipped his hat at Betsy. "You know the drill."

They bowed back in unison, earnest smiles proudly upon their faces. "Yes, Captain!" They split into pairs and rounded up the patients like sheep.

"That's right… you can call me… Captain." He winked at Jimmy who frowned in recollection. "Well, what are we waiting for? Full steam, gentlemen… ladies." He doffed his imaginary cap.

Jimmy was baffled by the officer's lack of willingness to partake in any form of conversation. On the way to the pub, without the other patients in earshot, Jimmy had attempted to start a discussion. But even with his favourite topic on the table – the war – he received little more than a wrist rattle. He regaled Letchfield with new knowledge of a patient grave at the asylum, a white stone that had joined the others below that towering oak tree; the grave of a John William Tebble. Jimmy informed the officer that John had been an honoured stoker, 1st Class of the Royal Navy when his battleship HMS *Russell* was steaming off the coast of Malta. Last year, on April 27, it was struck by two sea mines that had been laid by German Submarine U-73.

"Just imagine it," Jimmy had said. "Gustav hard at work on that torpid seabed, laying twenty-two moored mines, waxed in black skin. The Kaiser fastening the triggers for him to fire. Those iron monsters of the deep just waiting there until the moment *Russell* crossed their path. Kind of ominous don't you think?! Nothing sentient about that, is there? No matter where Gustav placed his pieces, the rules were already written, their fates marked. Mere pawns in the game and this time, Gustav had checkmate!"

Still the officer gave him nothing. "Most of the crew escaped you know. John escaped! At least his body did. He was placed in care at Warley, I thought you may have known him?" But it was no use, the officer gave him nothing in return; Jimmy thought Letchfield to be discourteous, plain bad-mannered. Jimmy propped him alone in his chair overlooking the estuary and moved on. He joined the patients queuing for seafood at the Osbourne Brother's and afterwards joined Allen over the seawall.

"Not bad beer… whilst we wait for this high tide," said Allen, licking the moisture from his lips.

Jimmy looked out across the flats. "Is it *in* or *out* if you can see the mud?"

"Out. I think. Look, nobody knows the answer, Jimmy."

"I thought you were a marine biologist?!"

"It's just one of those things, young'un, like how people think sushi means raw fish!" Jimmy looked lost. "It translates to sour-tasting."

"I see, and what else?"

"What else what?"

"Are there any other…misconceptions?"

"Tons… you know a goldfish has a longer memory than three seconds?" Jimmy looked at Allen who nodded.

Jimmy prodded his wooden fork into his pot of crayfish tails.

"Bulls!"

He almost dropped a tail from laughing.

"Don't be daft." Allen chuckled. "Bulls, I say. They

aren't angry by the red they see. In fact, they don't see red at all!"

"Fascinating."

"Oh, and penguins!" said Allen. Between the conversation, the creek-side view and the beer, he was enjoying himself. "Despite what people think, penguins don't have a mate for life… they may do for a season or so… but by next year, they move on…" Allen proudly swigged the remainder of the head, leaving a trail of creamy foam across his already bushy moustache.

"How do you know all this?" said Jimmy.

"I've been here and there, young'un."

"On your ship?"

"Once upon a time. More of a boat, really." Allen stared across the marsh; the rivulets were starting to fill with estuary water and the small vessels rose on the encroaching tide. Their reflection upside down in the water below mirrored scenes of what had been. Jimmy offered Allen a tail.

"No, thanks. Never ate what the mistress served me."

"Suit yourself," he said, soaking one end of the tail in vinegar and popping it into an open mouth. "What is that, seaweed?" Jimmy was pointing at the clumps of black and green washing up with the tide.

"That's bladderwrack."

"Why do they have those balls hanging from them?"

"Well… they are its vesicles."

"You what?" giggled Jimmy.

"Very funny, young'un. They are simply pockets of air is all."

A hypnotic ball of birds spiralled overhead. Jimmy was mesmerised, squinting until his eyes gave way to the sun. Squawks from nearby hordes of gulls got louder as they fought over mud snails in the soft sand. Sanderlings skipped along the shoreline, their spindly black legs blurring against the white of the new waves.

"Ah! Sand-ploughman's," said Allen. "Must be searching for lugworms before the tide takes them!" Jimmy looked up at the wise man in approbation. Behind him the sea wall was lined with people wearing white. What a sight they must have been. Jimmy looked down below his shoes, dangling above stacks of cracked shells. A bird with a black and white plumage glided down and landed silently on the shingle.

"Watch… it's an oystercatcher," said Allen excitedly. "See him? Opens even the tightest shells!"

"You must have been out at sea a long time to know all this… stuff," probed Jimmy.

Allen simply hummed.

"Is it true that there is a pearl in every oyster?"

"Ha! If only, young'un," laughed Allen. "I would have been a rich man. I would say the odds are more likely to be ten thousand to one."

"Ten thousand? How does it get in there?"

"The oyster makes it."

"Makes it?"

"Yes. It all begins with a grain of sand. The sand, or any other form of floating debris, gets inside the oyster shell and to protect itself, the oyster will cover the intruder with layers of nacre, which in turn, forms the pearl."

"Is it quick?"

"Not really. But then, most good things aren't. Can take twenty years!"

"Twenty years! *I* grew quicker than that."

"Yes. But then you have the largest, most beautiful pearl, Jimmy!"

"And will removing it from the shell kill the oyster?"

"Never. Not if you are careful. The oystercatcher, on the other hand… he's only after one thing… food!" Jimmy tilted his head to observe the ingenious bird. "Who is she?" asked Allen.

"Who is who?"

"The lady, you would like to give your pearl to!"

"How did you—"

"Ah, behind every good pearl hunter, there is always one fine lady."

"The finest," said Jimmy. He plonked his empty pot onto the sea wall, swung his legs back and forth from the edge and gazed out over the horizon. "Her name is Grace."

"Well, good things are worth the wait, young'un." Allen's wise beard floated weightlessly on the sea breeze.

"That's just it," said Jimmy, bowing his head. "I just don't know if she will… wait."

"She will," said Allen with a certainty that brought a smile to Jimmy's face. "You know, a bird of paradise woos his mate by making his surroundings dull? He then showcases a truly dazzling display…"

"Huh," sighed Jimmy. He realised that life, no matter where it befell, never really had a dull moment, especially when seated here beside Allen, especially in an asylum. The pair sat for a while, taking everything in. Jimmy closed his eyes and took another dose of sunlight.

"Look young'un, that's a Brent goose. See him?" Jimmy opened his lids and lazily nodded; he did see him. "A dark-bellied one. Must have flown here from the tundra of Arctic Russia."

"Russia? Really?"

"Yes, they migrate here during the winter, he must be early!"

Jimmy pondered all the sights it must have seen on its journey. "Do you ever think that the world only spins in the part you're in?"

"You mean is there a world beyond us right now?"

"I can't imagine that there is a war on. But that's because I haven't seen it. Well, I have, the zeppelin, the planes... but I've only seen the front, the trenches... in films and on posters—"

"Not on the faces of those that return, not on... Officer Letchfield?"

"Right. But it feels, if I made it to the front, low and behold, there the war would be. But, if I am not there, not a part of it. What proof is there that it really..."

"Exists."

"Exactly. Like this goose. Has he ever really been to Russia? Or did he just land here... because we were here?"

"Well... why don't you ask him?" They both laughed. Allen excited his beer, the froth dripped down his nose and back onto his bushy moustache. "It's funny, people always look upon a place for what it is, rather than what it was or what it would one day become."

"I used to try and imagine what places and people looked like!" Allen nodded at Jimmy to continue. "It was more of a game really. I called it 'now and then'. I would stare at a place and really try and imagine what it once looked like, through history. Like outside my dad's tailor shop on Brentwood High Street— I would rewind my mind back a hundred years or so and watch the characters passing by, changing their clothes in my mind. Men in knee breeches, linen shirts and thrills, wearing tricorne hats with upturned brims," he laughed. "Motor cars would transform into horse-drawn trams, bicycles: penny farthings!"

"How curious."

"It was easy because I just imagined the paintings in the station waiting room.".

"I bet young'un. But I mean individuals specifically. You know those blue plaques fixed around the city? They remind everyone of who has been. You know Napoleon III has one?" Allen wiped his moustache clean. "Funny, eh? Some people get buildings and streets named after them and others die without a single footprint!"

Jimmy let the thought wallow a while. "Hey, what was the best thing you saw, on your… explorations?"

"I've seen a lot, young'un, more than you could imagine." He turned and faced the boy. He could tell he wasn't going to settle for that one. "Well… we were in the Poles," he said, his eyes glazed. "I can still hear the sound of the sonar." Allen rotated his finger round and round. "Beep… beep… beep. We used them in our subs, to detect icebergs, you see. And down there, in the Poles, there were monsters, ice seven hundred feet deep! So, one ear on the sonar, one eye on where we were heading. Then, all of a sudden…" Allen rotated his finger faster and faster. "Beep, beep, beep, beep."

Jimmy leant in. "Icebergs?"

Allen shook his head. "We ran to the portholes. In the Arctic, you can see for what seems like miles. Rods of light beaming from the surface to the dark depths. Then we see these shadows, gigantic, they were. Rounded at the top, then at the bottom, they narrow, pointed, like a tail. Beep, beep, beep. We saw a few at first, then more and more. Tens of these colossal masses of black… shapes." Jimmy gulped. "As we neared, we saw them… sperm whales, vertical, facing upwards towards the surface, like a mass grave, like they were worshipping some great god, being summoned by the light. Pods of something unearthly waiting to hatch! They were just floating there, bobbing in this isolation of deep blue of nothingness. Then…" Jimmy jumped back. "All of a sudden, they move." Allen gestured with his hands like the cracking open of an egg. "Then their tails propel like a ship, they turn away, flatten out… all we can see is the level black wings as they dissolve into the bars of light on the horizon. Then, they were gone."

Jimmy's mouth was wide with wonder. "Rebirth?" he said finally.

Allen looked at the boy curiously. "More like they were… waking up." There was a lonely silence. They were speechless; they had both been there.

The pair watched as the goose flew away.

"You know, I saw manta rays do that once." Jimmy's eyes glided. "In the Sea of Cortez. There was this beautiful stillness, like just before a storm breaks. The surface of the water there, it was like a mirror. Then all of a sudden, the glass, the surface shattered and out fly these majestic rubbery wings. There were so many, they were so… focused, so…" Allen carved the air, using a tilted hand. "So certain of their purpose." Jimmy peered at the wise man through squinted eyes. "There they were, these fish, these cartilaginous fish, these eagles of the sea just… deciding to take flight in the air, and… just…" A tear fell down Allen's salty cheek.

"Go!" Jimmy breathed as if for the first time. He had felt everything Allen had said. He had seen the whales; he had witnessed the rays take flight.

"It must be nice Allen. To have been everywhere."

"Not everywhere young'un, and not anymore."

"But to have the memories of somewhere. To have been, *somewhere*." Jimmy looked up to the sky. "What happened to you, Allen?"

The old man turned slowly. "To me?"

"Yes, to wind up here…"

"In Southend?" He smirked.

"You don't have to tell me…"

"I couldn't, young'un, even if I wanted to." Allen stared at the boy. "You know, I like you, Jimmy. You are one of the few in here. You have heart. Ha, more heart than an octopus!"

"An octopus?" Jimmy frowned.

"They have three!"

"Wanderers!" projected Doctor Turner. "Finish up your drinks and wander thisaway. Next stop, the open-air swimming pool!"

And just like that, their moment had been washed away. Never to return to the shores of anywhere.

The open-air swimming pool was a sheltered inlet of water within the main estuary. The group couldn't stop long because on a day like today, it was brimming with life. Intent children held crab nets, their by-standing grandparents at the ready with half full buckets. Those there to swim in the depths, the masses wading in the shallows, and those sunning themselves on the dry lip of the pool. Most of the patients cupped a handful of saltwater and dabbed it across their forehead and around the nape of their neck. Not much room for much else.

Even Turner recognised the risks of thirty-six asylum patients mixing with water.

"Wanderers!" he yelled again. "We have a fair walk ahead, we shall stick to this side of the railway tracks, hug the coastline and take in all the sea air and sights the promenade here has to offer. Wet those whistles and follow me... next stop is the longest pleasure pier in the world!" He rolled his shoulders and angled his back straight, like a wealthy punter holding a cane. "Betsy, dearest, I do hope you've brought your costume, beaches the whole way along!"

The buxom nurse blushed.

The pier at Southend was not a disappointment. They had walked there, thirty-five pairs of shoes and two wheels, clobbering against the wooden struts. Either side of them, graveyards of boats sat stranded in the mud. A pool of turquoise water surrounded the end of the pier head like a little green island. At the end were penny arcades and Jimmy joined Oren in his excitement. They rustled together the coins they had between them.

"Let me see that!" said Jimmy, snatching the flattened shilling from Oren's palm. He twirled it between his fingers, doleful eyes for a time gone by. "That's been run over by a train, that has!"

"And how would you guess that?"

"It's not a guess," said Jimmy gravely. "I did it… Wilfred and I…" Jimmy disappeared a moment.

"*For keeps?*" came his best friend's voice.

Jimmy was astonished how easy he could flit between being a boy one moment and a man the next. A man haunted by memories of the boy he no longer knew. He straightened his thoughts, compelling himself to be present.

"Submarine lung tester," read Oren walking below the canopy of the arcades.

"It's a spirometer," said Jimmy, joining him overlooking the transparent tank. "See these divers?" He tapped against the glass treasure chest. "You have to blow into the machine, using this hose and see if you can raise them all to the top. My dad, he did it once, his face went red… then blue… but he did it!"

"Think I'll pass," said Oren wisely. "What's this one?"

"Electric shock…?" Jimmy tipped his head so that the back of his skull rested on the hinge of his neck. A disturbed clown peered down from the top of the great, towering machine. It had a painted red nose, bloodshot eyes and thick, static hair. Jimmy gripped the two silver probes which pushed through the plate, and read the words suspended above them. "Electricity kills many ills, electricity is life. Drop coin in slot, grab handles…"

"Well, you're already doing that." Oren took the thin side of the penny and rolled it into the slot; it rattled on its journey into the abyss. The machine lit up like a Christmas tree. It rumbled and Jimmy unclenched his fingers.

"Hey. It tickles." The clown chuckled with him, goofy and gay with his nose slowly flashing red. "Look," said

Jimmy, nodding upwards. "His nose must indicate the speed… of the electricity."

"Hold it tight!" ordered Oren.

"You hold it, it's your penny!"

"We both can." With their outside hand, the boys took a handle each. Jimmy felt fuzzy. He clasped it tighter and a shockwave ran down his wrist and knocked his elbow out of joint. "Wo—" Oren jumped back, frightened, letting go of his handle.

"It's OK," reassured Jimmy. "It's just warming up. Here, take my other hand." Oren cautiously lowered his onto Jimmy's and immediately felt the jolt.

"I… I'm all right. Think I'll watch…" Jimmy gripped the empty handle with his other hand and dug his legs in as if riding a horse. The music was building, and the red nose of the clown blew brighter.

"*Vvvvv…*" Jimmy's teeth chattered more and more vigorously. The clown cackled, nose now blood-red and throbbing. The louder the music built, the faster the light pulsed, the quicker Jimmy's teeth chattered. "*Vvvvv, vvvvvv…*" All three hit their crescendo, the clown gave one last sinister cackle, then all the lights went out. Jimmy dropped to his knees in good time, his body let limp.

"Jimmy!" Oren tucked his arms through and attempted to lift his lifeless frame. "Jimmy… wake up… wake up, Jimmy!"

His head turned in Oren's hands and a smile cracked through. "Gotcha!" Jimmy's periwinkle blue eyes burst open and exuded. Oren dropped his large mass to the floor.

"Not funny!" Jimmy helped himself up and stood tall

above the young boy. "I thought you'd had a f-fit!"

"Where to next?" said Jimmy, washing away the scene. "Look… there's a kinetoscope over there with photographs of the seaside!"

"But we're already at the seaside—"

"Hey, and over there, a strong man. Bet I can beat it! Or look, a fortune teller. Maybe she can tell me when my next fit will be. Better not be today, I'm having too much fun. What a day to be alive!"

"You're nuts, Jim!"

"That's right. Isn't that why we're all here?"

The slide glinted a gaudy red and white in the late afternoon sun.

"What's that pink stuff in your beard?" laughed Jimmy.

"Fairy floss," said the doctor. "You know this stuff was invented by a dentist? Here… take a mouthful. The seaside experience wouldn't be the same without it." Jimmy obliged. "Nor without fish and chips soaked in far too much vinegar!"

"Nor without crayfish tails, penny arcades and boating lakes," laughed Jimmy. "Nor the pier, the fun fair, goldfish—"

"Precisely, dear boy… give me a cup of ocean and a dose of sunshine daily and I will die a happy man! Wait, goldfish? I thought Allen caught whitebait?!"

"He did. Fifteen. And he threw them all back. The goldfish is Wilkie's, he won it on Tin Can Alley."

"Good for him. Poor fish. Ha! An asylum within an asylum, eh?!" The pair stood a while. "You see that ship out there Jimbo?" The doctor pointed.

"The one with the red funnel?"

"POW ship!" Jimmy double fluttered is eyelids between the ship and the Doctor.

"You mean to say…"

"German's are aboard. The war is closer than you think dear boy!" Jimmy nodded. "Vinegar bottles!" declared the Doctor with a pointed finger.

"Huh?"

"The German prisoners, there were complaints from the ship that they didn't receive news from the front. They wrote letters and put them in empty bottles of vinegar. Didn't make it mind. Most just wash up on the shore here and the residents of Southend get delight in decoding them."

"Down on the shore there? We must try and find one before we leave."

"Marvellous. We'll take it back to the asylum." Jimmy's face turned sober. "What is it boy?"

"It's just at the asylum, the war, it's so far away, so non-existent".

"Isn't that good?"

"I don't know."

"That place does funny things to a man."

"Doctor Turner?" said Jimmy. "It would be nice to add some painting to the walls, of the asylum. All the ones I've seen around feel unfinished, the artist just gave up…" The doctor frowned at the boy. "Once Oren has gone, you think I could move in with the residents at Brentwood Hall? I hear that there are men there who tend to the farm. I used to help my dad with our garden. It's a little more land, but—"

"Thirty acres," obliged the doctor.

"Right. Well, I can do that." The doctor smiled. "You know, at home, we had this giant chestnut tree. I would lie on my back underneath it during the summer, my legs up towards the clouds. It's funny." he chuckled. "I thought I could fall from the ground into the limitless sky, cast off, away from the house. If I missed the cloud, then I would just freefall."

"Then…" added the doctor, "if you missed the stars?"

Jimmy shrugged. "Well, I would be falling for all eternity." The pair of them turned their heads, looked at one another and smiled; they had both been looking up and hadn't realised.

"Doctor Turner?"

"Yes, Jimmy?"

"Now that he is talking, will Officer Letchfield be sent back to the front?"

"Talking?"

Jimmy nodded. "He spoke to me, out on the patio. He hasn't since, but—"

"You sure he wasn't just grunting? Or screaming at the bells?"

Jimmy looked at the doctor quizzically. "I'm very sure," he said.

The doctor pointed his two bushy eyebrows. "Well, I wouldn't worry about that just yet, dear boy. Doctor Campbell is assessing Officer Letchfield. He will keep his best interests at heart."

"Doctor Turner?"

"Yes, Jimmy?"

"Is it strange that I'm fourteen years old and I've got the pressure of carrying on the bloodline of my entire Ford name?"

The doctor was taken aback by the weight of the question. For once he didn't have much of an answer. He gave a staccato laugh. "Well… you're a little young to be worrying about such things, Jimbo!"

"I think that," said the boy, squinting into the sun. "But then, so much has happened and time… well, it sort of feels condensed and all of a sudden, I'm older, I have duties."

"Duties?" Jimmy looked over at the glistening shingle on the beach. "How do you make a footprint in the sand and hope it doesn't get washed away?"

The doctor's face took him all in. "Well, the war started when you were still a child—"

"And as it continues, I haven't quite become a man. More someone lost in between. Who knows what I'll be by the end!"

"It's like autumn, Jimmy, the leaves turn lavish in colour."

He smiled. "Yes, but they're dying."

"Only temporarily," said the doctor. "Until spring—"

"Once they return, they aren't the same leaves, are they?"

"You've had a lot of time to think about things, haven't you, young man?"

Jimmy nodded. "One day I was building model planes and reading flying magazines, I was digging trenches in the woods and fighting with rifles made of sticks". Doctor Turner chuckled. "We kidnapped the Kaiser once and threw stones at spiked helmets we had made from buckets!"

Jimmy paused. "I guess the realities were a little different."

Doctor Turner looked at him. "I am as romanticised as the next man. Providing that next man is you!" he crooked his elbow.

Jimmy smiled. "You know, I once asked my mum, what does it feel like on your last day being a child? Well... I guess... this year, on that day, I found out..." The doctor's kooky eyes accessed his patient. "Every time I look at the clock, it's 11:40, morning and night. Twice it happens, pretty much every day. That was the time the bomb fell. The bomb that killed... some joke, eh?" he said in infinite jest.

The doctor cupped his hand on Jimmy's. "A mere coincidence is all. Would you keep note how many times you looked at the clock and it wasn't 11:40?"

"I suppose not," said the boy woefully.

"I had a birthday surprise for you, Jimmy, but perhaps I should give you the news now."

"News?"

"No. Not sure I want to—"

"You can't say that..." Jimmy smiled. "Please...is it Grace?"

"No, no." The Doctor shook his head. "I think you should wait and see for yourself."

"See what for myself?" He laughed.

"Your dear friend, Alfred—"

"What about him?" asked Jimmy, now looking alarmed.

"Nothing to worry about, Jimbo. He's decided that, well, without your dad, his little shop isn't the same, he wants to work but doesn't want to... well, we've decided between us, that—"

Jimmy couldn't wait. "What?" he said, sizing the doctor up.

"Well… he will come into the asylum as our tailor!"

"Tailor?"

"Yes, our other one left to fight in France and, well, we are never short of uniforms to stitch and repair—"Jimmy couldn't contain himself; he grabbed the doctor with both hands, arms resting around his small hunched shoulders. "Ah, I'm glad…" He patted the boy with his hairy hand and straightened back out his arms, Jimmy with them. Jimmy had lightened his load, or rather, as always, the doctor had helped him.

The pair observed the queue of patients inside the struts of the slide.

"Now then, I have a question for *you*…"

Jimmy nodded. "Go on…"

"You wanted to use the air raid shelter for what?"

Jimmy smiled. He hadn't thought the doctor heard his request on the train down. "A cinema," he said obligingly.

"Yes. That's what I thought you said! And why exactly?" asked the doctor, his arms folding with the railings.

"Why a cinema?"

"Of course not why a cinema. I was sold on the cinema, dear boy. Why the shelter?"

"Well," said Jimmy, now excited, his pitch fully prepared, "you know how many of the patients get rather… upset, with the noises caused by the raid? I thought that the cinema could provide entertainment, take their minds off what is happening."

"You mean the fact they are in a nuthouse?" chuckled the wild doctor.

"No, well… yes, and the fact there is a war on. The films could give them something positive to focus on."

"Escape from. Indeed," the doctor steadied his excitement and toiled his beard. "Chaplin?" The boy nodded. "A viable distraction. Not so much a viable location, though, I'm afraid, Jimbo. Not all our people can make it out to the shelter, some are… immobile."

"Yes, but not immovable!"

"It's too much strain on staff, I'm afraid. I love it, Jimbo, in principle. But I could never get it agreed."

"From Campbell?"

"No, the superintendent. Campbell isn't the boss, you know. Everyone answers to someone."

"But, the patients…" Jimmy looked at the doctor. "The people here, they could use something—"

"The people *here* are doing just fine by the looks of things." The doctor smiled. He nodded at the hordes of them lining the inside of the great slide, each holding a proud pink ticket in hand. "But you want it as inclusive as possible, right?"

"Yes," said Jimmy dolefully.

"Well, I have just the place!"

"The library?"

"Piffle," said the doctor. Jimmy laughed. "You aren't making a cinema out of my precious library, Jimmy Ford." Jimmy laughed louder. "Where else could you write about the antics of Lieutenant Robinson, eh?"

"Then where?"

"Patience, Jimbo!"

"Yes, that's who we're doing this for… the patients!"

"Ha! Very good, dear boy." The doctor watched as the spindly legs of patients emerged from the bend in the slide and landed with delightful thuds against the red crash pad. "I tell you what. When we get back to the asylum, you got yourself a deal. When we get back, we will build this cinema… together!"

"…together." Jimmy smiled, his eyes stretching long over the pier they had walked. "You know, it's been a good day. The best, the best I've had since that day."

"That's because, Jimmy… you have learnt to be."

"I have? Am I not just, you know, distracted?!"

"Perhaps…"

One by one the patients retrieved their mats or sacs and stepped back inside to queue again.

"*'The lunatic is carried at last to the asylum a confirmed case. He will never sleep any more as he did in the cot in his mother's bedroom'.*" The doctor turned his head in recollection and caught Jimmy's affirming nod.

"'Song of Myself'."

"That could have been written for any one of us," said Jimmy. The hairy man nodded. "Doctor Turner…? Can you learn… to be mad?"

"Learn?" Jimmy slapped his forehead. "As much as one can learn to be homeless. And you, Jimmy Ford, are like a homeless man taking refuge in a storefront he can ill afford an item from." The doctor winked.

"I don't understand. I mean, can you learn to live with it? The madness?"

"Jimmy—" said the doctor.

"The strange thing is, I fit in here more than I do out

there, and that once scared me more than anything."

"Fit or *fit?*" gestured the doctor. He refrained his laugh surfacing. "And now?" Jimmy smiled. "That's what I thought," prodded the doctor. "Learnt to be…"

"'*That to be*'," whispered Jimmy.

"You know, he would be proud of you Jimmy." The doctor ruffled the boy's hair. "He would be very proud indeed." Jimmy smiled. He let the words linger, then inflate and lift his floating heart.

"You know, I've been thinking?!"

"What, again?" mocked the doctor.

"My dad, perhaps *he* was the one to die because he couldn't take the grief of losing a son. Perhaps I was the one to remain to uphold the…suffering, the pain for those lost because being here is a greater burden on those living than those lost." The doctor waited, wide eyed.

"You know Jim, that may be the wisest anecdote for death I have heard in a very long time…Whitman included," he winked.

"My attempt of justification, I guess. Either that or madness…"

"No," said the doctor. He searched his mind for a lighter path. "But you want to know what *is* mad? The system is mad. The reasons for admission are mad. You know, when I joined this asylum two years ago, there were patients here—"

"People," corrected Jimmy.

"Right, people, locked up in that place because of immoral life, laziness… masturbation!" Jimmy laughed. "Oh, I'm quite serious, dear boy." The doctor laid out more fingers and continued his list. "Supressed masturbation." Jimmy erupted again. "Over study of religion, political excitement, bad habits, bad whisky, egotism, jealousy, women trouble, greediness, studying too hard, oh, and my personal favourite, novel reading!" The doctor looked at him for a reaction. Jimmy simply shook his head side to side for a long time.

The pair stood silently a while. The sea, now fully present, crept up the shore, bringing the first rations of its cream from Kent. As the tide subtly exhaled, bubbles and jellyfish were left stranded on the shingle. With an inhalation, they were collected, turned upside down and replaced. The boats lifted their bellies from the mud and their bells rattled with the waves. Jimmy's eyes wandered back to their place, and the doctor and he exchanged a notation of peace.

"My fits," said Jimmy, "they aren't always terrifying you know?" He had Turner's attention. "At least, occasionally I even see them as edifying and rather... prophetic."

"Prophetic? Are you telling me you are receiving messages from the great beyond Jimmy, informing you of our fate down here?"

"Not quite" he chuckled. "But for a moment, just before the seizure takes hold, suddenly, amid the panic, the sadness, there is...I don't know—"

"Spiritual darkness," said the doctor, his specs reflecting the sunlight. Jimmy looked at him.

"Yes! Exactly. Spiritual darkness. I don't know whether it lasts for seconds, or hours. In that moment, there is no such thing as time and whilst there, I wouldn't exchange it for all the delights of the world!"

With that, the two men sunk satisfyingly into silence.

"Now," said the doctor finally. "Where is Wilkie? I should ensure that fish doesn't come home with us." Jimmy pointed to the top of the helter skelter. "With the fish?" shrieked the doctor.

"Ha. Imagine… ah, yes, here, I think this is Wilkie!" said Jimmy, searching for the familiar sound of his grunts nearing. A man in white rags came racing round the corners of the slide, his sharp, knobbly knees bent double on the coconut hair. As his speed built, his hoots lessened. On the last bend, the mat he was riding shot out from underneath him, hurtling both the bag and fish into the air. Neither Jimmy nor the doctor could help, for they were on the wrong side of the railings. There was one almighty splash.

The fish flapped golden against the concrete, splatters of water surrounding the murder scene. Jimmy peered over and watched anxiously as the fish floundered and squirmed.

The madman stood to his feet. "Jimmy, Jimmy you're not going to believe it…" Jimmy's eyes widened with wonder. "It's Fairlop Jimmy, he's here!" the madman muttered.

"What?"

"He's up there!"

"He can't be," said the doctor. The pair crooked their necks and traced the curves of the slide to the top. In a break of colour from the white, they saw some glistening flesh.

"Is that man… naked?" shouted the doctor, cupping his hands around his eyes to see.

"Sure is!" said Wilkie proudly, picking up his fish and

popping it into his wide-open mouth. Jimmy double took between the madman on the ground and the one at the top of the skelter.

The naked man bent over, his cheeks shimmering like two plump peaches in the sunlight. Throngs of holidaymakers gawked up with outstretched arms and murmurs.

"Yee-haw!" exuded the red and curly man.

"It is Fairlop!" shouted Jimmy fervidly. "He's alive!"

"He looks alive all right," chuckled the doctor. "Just not

sure in how many pieces." A gilded brown object fell from the top and crashed to the ground like a comet. It was the coconut mat used for riding down on. "I must get up there," philosophised the doctor.

"It-it-it's t-to-too late for that, D-D-D—" Poor Wilkie had one of his timed episodes.

"Too late," affirmed Jimmy. The bum of the naked man planted down on the slide and his arms reached wide as an eagle. "Here he comes…" That man flew faster than anyone before him. His muscles pulsated, the veins tracing the length of his biceps swelling in the heat of the day and moment.

"Yee…" he shouted on one side of the slide. "…haw!" he clinched in a faded voice on the other. As the man neared the end, his skin squeaked. He landed gracefully on his two legs and bowed to a muddled audience. Little girls pointed out his trunk and screamed. The old wounds on his face were visible, as were the new burns he had acquired on his ride in.

"Well, hi-ya, Doc!" greeted Fairlop, as if nothing were the matter. The doctor jumped the railings like a racehorse and collected up one of the sacs. He stood inside it and yanked the coarse brown fabric up above his waist until it tore. He stepped out gracefully and handed it to Fairlop.

"Put this on immediately!" he ordered. "Are you mad?"

Fairlop jumped straight on it. "My clothes were given to me by a German spy. They want me to join them on their secret missions!" The man sure laughed like a madman. "Well, well, you don't look too happy to see me, Doc," obliged Fairlop, lifting the sac over his manhood.

"I am… of course." The Doctor nodded, partly satisfied certain areas were now covered. "Where have you been these past weeks? And where are your clothes?"

Fairlop gave a goofy grin.

"Well, I've been at our nation's capital, Doc. I had been meaning to catch up with our dear friend Nesbit for a while."

"And… did you?"

"Well, that would be telling now, Doc, wouldn't it?" Turner tilted his head in attempt to read the lines of his face. Fairlop was a difficult one to read.

"Well, you're back. It's good to see you again… Neal."

CHAPTER TWENTY-THREE

FERRIS WHEEL

THE FERRIS WHEEL WAS the main attraction at Sunken Gardens. There was time for just one more ride before the patients had to return and be patients again. Fairlop had been handed his clothes and was back where he belonged amongst the crowd in white.

"I thought you'd say I wasn't dressed proper for the occasion, Doc, so I took the liberty of bringin' here with me some fine civilian clothes. You didn't figure I came all the way down by train in this attire, did you, Doc? Bet you would love that, you dirty bastard, you!" Doctor Turner was distracted handing out the last remaining pink tickets. Without his audience, Fairlop regrouped with his poker friends. Jimmy drifted over to join them.

"Neal?" said Slugs, brushing down his eyebrows. Fairlop

finished tying his shoes, taking his time about it.

"Well… everybody. Now I am dressed, let's get one thin' straight and proper." He pulled from a cigarette which dangled carelessly from his lip. "It took me only a few days to recover… Nesbit hits like a damn girl." He looked around the group and made sure his words were heard. "I was, however, rather perplexed by the whole encounter and decided to seek out our friend. Unfortunately, he must have seen me a-comin' due to the fact he got a few days' head start an' all whilst I was busy recoverin'. I snuck his records from the ward, see, and found his squat up in the high street of Brentwood there, that very day, in fact. Sensin' the little coward had fled, I got to enquirin' regardin' his whereabouts. Didn't take me long to follow the scent of the little rat west into the city. The problem is, the city is full of rats, and I lost his tail." Fairlop got a good look at each of their faces.

"Fairlop… this was weeks ago. Why come back now?"

"Because, Wilkie…" he grabbed Wilkie around the head and ruffled that thick black cap of hair, "I missed you!"

"No, really, Neal?" asked Slugs. Fairlop loosened his hold around Wilkie but carried on the conversation with his head locked.

"I found me a little back alley tavern and had me a few games of poker with some soldiers. I got to drinkin', fightin' and gamblin'… not to mention my trips down Whorterloo, wooo-hah, I tell yer. You really want to know why I'm back here, Slugs…" The group remained his faithful listeners.

Fairlop let go of Wilkie and with it, he dropped his half-smoked cigarette. He removed another from his pocket and lit up. "To cleanse my soul," he said.

"Pffft! You have no soul to cleanse, Fairlop," laughed Wilkie. The group joined in.

"What you fools doin' here, anyway?" he said, observing his surroundings. "A kiddies' funfair."

"Kiddies? You seen the height of that thing?" Slugs gestured up to the big wheel.

"All right," said Fairlop, no arguments, flicking another semi-burnt cigarette and bouncing it off Slugs' head. "You're on!"

Jimmy was delighted to see Fairlop back in one piece. Not because he loved Fairlop, not because he particularly liked Fairlop, but it gave him hope, a glimmer of hope that just maybe the world was readjusting its orbit and things could turn another way.

As Fairlop was about to trudge on, he spotted someone in the corner of his eye.

"Well, well, well. Who is this little dame here to see?" Jimmy felt two taps on his shoulder.

"Happy Birthday, Jimmy!" chimed the sweetest voice. There she was, adorned in a pretty white dress, holding a delicately made sponge with a small wax candle on top. There she was, Grace!

"I… I—"

"Come on, boys," said Fairlop. "Leave our curly-haired Casanova here…"

"How did you…?" said one flabbergasted Jimmy. He saw the doctor over her shoulder give a surreptitious smile. "I see…"

"I know that it isn't your birthday until tomorrow, Jim, but I thought, well, this way I keep my promise, and I… you like surprises?!"

"I do, I mean… I do!"

"Did you want to make a wish? We would need to light it first, but I bought matches with me."

"What could I possibly wish for?" He smiled. "Thank you… so much, Grace." The innocent girl grinned, and her crocodile green eyes gave way to a flash of almond.

"I brought a knife with me. Here, let us sit on this bench and have some cake, shall we?" The doctor dropped two pink tickets in Jimmy's hand and winked.

"I have a better idea," he said.

Their basket twirled gently with the sea breeze.

"I feel like an acorn hanging from a tree," said Grace.

"Well, let's hope a squirrel doesn't pinch us!"

"This goes high, Jim."

He nodded. "It's nowhere near started," he said, tapping the globular bench for her to take a seat. "You're not afraid of heights, are you?" Grace shook her head languidly. "I assure you, we won't fall. I've been watching it go round all day." The girl lifted her underdress, sat beside him and safely placed the cake onto the bench. The conductor clicked the compartment door shut behind them, so they were surrounded by thin white bars.

"What's this part for?"

"I think it's to steer," said Jimmy, leaning forward and gripping the white wheel with both hands. "Yeah, look, see… it rotates the basket. Which way shall we face?"

"The sea," said Grace. "Always the sea." Their suspended basket rose higher on the giant wheel. Jimmy felt the weight of Grace's bare leg touch his. His heart skipped a beat. He couldn't comprehend that she was really here, seated beside him. He wanted to pinch himself, but if it was a dream, he equally didn't wish to wake.

Below them the unfurling waves churned at the shingle. Grace used her hand to tame the hair which was now blowing into her mouth as she spoke. "Sorry I'm so late. It was the cake, you see. This was my fourth one!"

"You made four... for me?"

She swiped the air. "Promise me, Jimmy, promise me we can come back here, when it's just us, when you're... you're better!" Grace nestled her head onto his shoulder, and he smelt her hair. His heartbeat found the rhythm it had missed for months. Just like that, she had forgiven him.

"I promise we will come back here, Grace, when I'm better," he said without hesitation. It was the easiest promise he had made. "You know, Grace, I am sorry."

"Jimmy— "

"No... please." He ushered his hand to silence her. "I spent all my energy thinking... believing that leaving this town would make me *become* someone." Grace combed her auburn hair and tucked it behind her ear. "But I never stopped... stopped to think what that really meant if it was without you." Grace skimmed her pupils across the surface of the sea. "It's like the particles around us when we are born, they become part of us, and we can never really leave without missing that thing we call *home*. And that home Grace. That home wouldn't have ever been. Not without you. I would have spent my entire life searching... running. Running towards something whilst falling further away from myself, the self I can only be whilst I'm with you."

"Jimmy— " Grace dived through the blue of his eyes. She had no words. She leant in and cushioned her lips between his. They stayed there. Minutes past. The basket neared its highest point before it would start descending. She pulled away and a smile stretched the far corners of her cheeks. Jimmy's mouth joined hers.

He caught a view of the other pods and sighted Fairlop, Slugs, Wilkie and Chat. The four of them looked sombre and pensive, overlooking the horizon, which, on a day like today, merged the sky and sea, so it was an infinite expanse of powdered blue. He saw Oren, Lola and Betsy, and in the basket beyond theirs, Allen sat contented and alone. He watched him looking out over the bay, joined by a grey-blue naval ship which had emerged close to the pier. Jimmy smiled sympathetically and pondered the act which had confined him. As they lifted, nearing the peak of the great white wheel, he got a good look in the cabin behind: Officer Letchfield and Doctor Turner. Their backs were to the land and the doctor pointed out across the estuary. Jimmy thought about the sorts of conversations they would all be having. He hadn't felt like this since June, when the innocence of life was still a part of his being. His soul felt nourished, drenched in sun and the emotion he had recently reclaimed, the sensation of love.

His mind scurried back to his own basket with Grace; there was nowhere he would prefer to be. He stood to his feet in elation and gripped the bars, bending his body backwards. "'I too am not a bit tamed... I too am untranslatable, I sound my barbaric yawp over the roofs of the world'."

"Jimmy!" Grace giggled.

"What?"

"You're…"

"Mad? Genius? Walt Whitman!" Jimmy's hands clammed up, he sat beside her and took hers in his. "Grace, I've been meaning to ask you something," he said. "I was going to wait until I saw you… well, and here you are. I swore that when I saw you again, I would say… what I am saying now…" He sunk his head into his palms.

"What is it, Jimmy, it's OK, you can tell me."

"It's not telling you, it's… asking you. I haven't got you a pearl," he said. "At least, not yet… I haven't even got you a, but—"

"A pearl?" She removed her head from his shoulder and faced him; her movements turned erratic. "Ah, Jimmy, look! We are approaching the top. You *must* blow out your candle and make a wish at the top!"

"I must?"

The girl ardently nodded. "Here, I have a match." Grace fumbled inside her bag and curved her hand around the wax candle to protect it from the wind. There was a hiss and the little flame danced. She presented the cake in front of him, with the perfect backdrop of the sea. Jimmy closed his eyes. He heard the waves pounding the beach below them, heard the squawks of seagulls, the murmur of children and the sweet music from the amusements. He heard the distant hum. He pursed his lips and blew. Smoke billowed and dispersed with the sea air.

"Jimmy, you must tell me your wish, but first I have an I spy for you, one you'll love. But we must be quick!"

"OK…" he said. Grace sure was full of surprises today.

"I spy with my little eye, something beginning with… P."
Jimmy rotated his head in all directions. "Patients?"
"No," giggled Grace.
"Pier?"
"No!"
He caught her gazing out to sea. "Prison…ships".
"No!" He heard the humming get louder.
"Planes!"

His body immediately trembled.
"Yes!" shouted Grace. "I thought you—"
"Grace, what if it's them?"
"Who?"
"What if it's the—"
"Germans!" bellowed Fairlop from his compartment, his hands clasping round the bars like a bear inside a circus cage. "Those are German Gothas!" The patients scuffled

within their suspended cabins. They were too high up; they would be forced to watch.

The hums grew; the pointed black shadows swooned across the face of the clouds.

"Nine!" spat Fairlop. "There are nine Gothas and they are headin' right this way! They are low, they're goin' to drop!" His words were serrated and true.

The gardens fell still. A harrowing silence as crowds of people stood like statues below the great Ferris wheel, Jimmy and Grace at the very top. He pulled her close; he held her tight.

"I've got you, Grace," he said, periwinkle blue eyes fixated through the bars. The black wings of the vultures crossed the pierhead. Time stopped as if this place had never existed.

Engines rumbled to the cry of the Ferris wheel, obeying its helpless orbit, its entire eye of wheel, watching. Jimmy heard her squeals. He clenched her hand in his. Powerless, they sat like voyeurs in front row cinema seats. The Gothas traced the wooden struts, they were half the length of the pier now.

"Arrrrrrrr," roared Fairlop from his cage, his possessed red fists wrapping the bars. The pitch of the planes deepened with his growls as if the devil himself were responding. Jimmy clenched her hand tighter, pulling her closer inwards like a puppet he could command. He gritted his teeth and began to mumble:

"Up above the trees,
The Albatross soared,
Black Maria screamed,

Woolly bears roared.
Between the swarms,
An iron cross,
A Gotha's nest,
Paradise lost."

The hatches were pried open like forceful dentists. Jimmy drew Grace's head into his chest and felt the moisture. He raised her face to his. She was crying.

"I won't let anything happen to you, Grace," he said, sucking the salty tears right from her cheeks.

The black crossed wings were now upon them. Grace closed her wet eyes. There was an almighty whoosh. Then another. And another. Nine planes whistled over the Ferris wheel and climbed with the slope of the cliff. A hundred heads turned with them and watched as small black shells tumbled from their bellies.

Whiiiizzzz! In joined screams from the onlookers. *Whiiiizzzz.* Plumes of sulphurous yellow smoke curdled up from the rooftops and building blocks. The formation split in haphazard siloes. Amongst them teared the bullets from the anti-aircraft guns.

"Here's our boys!" hollered Fairlop from the cage hanging almost above them. Jimmy kept his eyes wide. Black wings overlapped one another as the planes darted ungainly, like a mass migration of geese.

Grace whimpered; Jimmy held her. There must have been forty planes filling the sky now, one giant game of noughts and crosses. Bullets from below, bullets from behind; the show must go on.

The battlefield rose higher, the small black shells continued to fall, the acrid flames continued to bellow from the town. *Whiiiizzzz!*

"They're emptyin' out…" commentated Fairlop. "They're going to scarper!" No one else dared speak. One of the seaplanes began to smoke; it left a smear of charcoal against the white, chaotic clouds. It whined and spiralled above the Ferris wheel like a clumsy firework. It neared their basket. Jimmy calmly wrapped his arms around Grace, who was now tunnelling into his tummy. He closed his own eyes, only for a second. He squeezed her tight. The shrill from the plane was deafening; it was sure to hit. He applied pressure to the side of her head, forcing her tortured thoughts to burrow deeper into her skull.

Then… the wailing faded. The plane was spiralling in all directions like a wounded bird, black wings plummeting downwards. Jimmy watched until the very end.

The sea, as if blinking at the unfolding scene, split. There was a tremendous crack. The shell had hit the naval ship. Neither chain nor anchor kept her grounded and like a boxer; she was stunned and delirious. The vessel spiralled from the shock, thrusting her weight left and right in the liquid. Jimmy watched as men on deck scurried like crabs. The ferocious waves caused by the bomb pounded with the steel and the wet formed a wall of bitter spray which merged and made rain. Men scurried beneath the funnels, scampering desperately for life rafts. Groans were thrust, tapered off below the sea's swell. The waves bit down on the ship with gnarling teeth before soothing and silencing the screaming men.

There was a second crash. This time it was the plane that had collided. Wood from the deck tore in two as torpedo shells rolled out through the splints and into the salivating foam which swallowed the fuselage whole. Once the tide calmed, there was no evidence a ship with an entire village now lurked and lived on beneath.

Eight of the Gothas remained. They swarmed and dived like tumultuous bats, still spasmodically releasing those deadly black shells. Yellow powder coated the tips and walls of some of the town's dwellings. Rubble and great clumps of concrete lay strewn in the streets with shattered glass from the store fronts. Grace watched in terror as people ran in every direction, not knowing if it was their number next.

Jimmy remained steady. As their basket descended, he saw less and less of the carnage up in the town. Their compartment slowed into the station.

"Some ride, kids…" spat the sweat-covered conductor. He forced open the door. Jimmy guided Grace out, her legs barely able to connect with the concrete. "Your friends," said the conductor, "they are gathering over there!"

Jimmy observed the masses of hysterical patients in white. Betsy and the other orderlies, there was no difference between them and the patients now; they were one great congregation of naked madness. Jimmy clasped his hands firmly around Grace's shoulders. He pulled her with conviction, ushering her away from the crowds. He guided her below the baskets of the great white wheel and into the green gardens. *Whiiiizzzz.* A shell, waxed in black, scythed through the spokes of the wheel and exploded against the side of the ticket booth. Jimmy turned back; amongst the parting smog he saw him, part of him, the conductor. His legs were nowhere to be seen. Intestines hung from the railings like Christmas decorations. Viscous red poured like wine from his spleen. Expressionless, Jimmy burrowed Grace's head into his neck so she couldn't turn to face the horrors. He gritted his teeth.

"Knock, knock,
It's me at the roof,
I'm here to maim,
I'm here to spook."

The pair hobbled beneath the floral arch and into the square where there stood a stone fountain. There was another great whizz. Grace blabbered and tore from Jimmy's grasp. She dived away from him. He tried to regain his grip, but it was too late. She laid there, face down on the floor, hands gripped around her ears.

Jimmy Ford stood beneath the great wheel.

Below the crosses of the Gotha, the fairground was silent. Masses of people lay strewn out over the floor with their hands cupped around their ears. Above the stone fountain, it opened.

Jimmy looked up, the mouth of the hatch; black, wide, screaming.

The shell tumbled out.

"I'm listening" he whispered. "I'm listening" he said. "I'm listening!" he shouted.

He saw the shell spiral. Inside its point, he saw the face of his dad, of Poppy, of Wilfred. He saw the face of his love, his sweetheart; he saw only her face now, the face of Grace Bergman.

PART THREE

1944

*"He shall cover thee with his feathers, and
under his wings shalt thou trust: his truth shall be thy
shield and buckler"*

PSALM 91

CHAPTER TWENTY-FOUR

BIDMAN

A LANGUID FOG DRIFTED across the beach of Omaha. It suckled dried sweat from the flesh of a dead soldier whose body was bloated and face down in the sand. The fog glided over carmine puddles and absorbed the blood of an entire battalion wiped out by the shell of a Granatwerfer. It wrapped like a white ribbon around a mortar whose barrel was being reloaded over and over. The fog swallowed the residue from the gun and meandered through the trenches, collecting billows of cigar smoke from the men leaning idly against the parapet. It slurped the steam from a flask of tea and imbibed the fumes from a tot of rum; courage before another charge. It roamed rivers and piloted streams, snaking its way back through Normandy, cooling in clouds and rising over the channel. The nimbus smeared the mouth of the Thames, borne heavy on a western wind. It soared over Brentwood, over the cemetery on Woodman Road. The cloud blinked and released the first thousand tears, all it had seen. Droplets fell and toyed with the grey stone, trickling into the creases and filling the letters of the ageing epitaph.

IN MEMORY OF
GEORGE FORD
1862 - 1917

POPPY FORD
1871 - 1917

BLESSED BE THE MAN THAT SPARES THESE STONES
AND CURSED BE HE THAT MOVES OUR BONES

The man with grey-flecked military hair looked large in front of the small headstone. He placed his brown leather pilot hat and goggles on top of the grave so that they dangled effortlessly. He knelt on his navy-blue trousers, long black boots covering his shins. Using gloved hands, he cleared the colourless flowers from the floor and replaced them with a fresh batch of spotty white lilies. He stood back to admire them, kneecaps circled by dark wet patches. He stood tall and thin on his toes, hair combed either side to form a regimentally straight white wall down the left of his scalp. Using his teeth to grip the tip of his index finger, he removed his hand from the leather glove. Once free, he checked his inside wrist for the time; you could tell he was a military man. Using the same hand, he rifled inside his brown Irvine sheepskin jacket. He removed the crumpled paper from his pocket and began to gently unfold its corners, the summer breeze lending its thin fingers.

"I've still got it!" said the man in a deep, virile voice. "The letter…" he said. "I'm off again shortly. Back to France, I'm afraid, back to fight. Don't worry, you won't miss out, I'm still writing it all down for you!" He uncurled the last of the folds, cleared his throat and began to read from the old, withered paper.

"Dear Dad, I don't know where to start. Today is my birthday; I'm fifteen!" The man let out a small laugh, remembering the naivety of the young hands that had written those words. "I don't know if you saw, but yesterday, I nearly joined you and Poppy here…. and you, Mum!" The man looked beside him towards the old crumbling grave of Anne Ford. "The Gothas, they came back! They came to Southend and now more people are dead! I'm lucky to be here. We all are, us that remain. Apparently forty bombs were dropped. It felt like hundreds more, I can tell you. The sounds... the screams... thirty more people were killed, half of those were down for the day, like we all were. Blown to bits at the station, where we would have walked had it not been for good timing on our part. Grace and I..." The man stopped and took a beat to observe the sycamore trees and how the light tickled through onto the dew-drenched grass. "We were suspended inside the Ferris wheel... But I wasn't so afraid, Dad. Not truly afraid. I don't think I could be truly afraid. Not after what I went through. The papers said the whole thing lasted ten minutes... it seemed like a lifetime passed. As they left over the sea, we were all still in Sunken Gardens. The last plane, it dropped one last shell, right over us all; yards away, it was. The others, they all dived to the floor. They all closed their eyes, they all waited for the end. But I couldn't close my eyes, Dad, I couldn't just wait. I have been waiting for something to happen these past few months, waiting for someone to miraculously save me, from my condition, from the asylum. But then I realised, nobody can save me, but me. And finally, I had the reason I needed, the reason for living; I had Grace!" The man tilted his head down as a raindrop splattered against the paper and smudged the black ink.

"The bomb, I watched it, the whole journey, from leaving the hatch to tracing it down to the very ground in which we stood. I watched it the entire time and I held her close to me, whispering all the lovely words I could muster into her ear. I just knew, Dad, I just knew that this wasn't it for us, this wasn't the end. It didn't explode, the shell. It hit the ground with an enormous thud; it cracked the concrete! We looked at one another, Grace and I. There was nothing to say; we both knew. Life. It's a funny thing. It's quite often cruel, yet we crave it the crueller it gets."

The man shook his head, cracked lips and dimples smiling at the recollection. "Our planes took down one of theirs, it's sitting at the bottom of the Thames with the pilot. But, Dad, they're come back, they always do! I came here to tell you that I have epilepsy. I've been living in an asylum since you left."

The man let a tear fall from his eyes. The fading sun appeared from behind a heavy grey cloud and tipped its hat back across the line of sycamores. He began to read before the words receded in front of him. "When I've got walls around me, my head feels smaller, my mind suffocating. Maybe that's why I've always liked being outside? Even in the rain!"

The man smiled, laying his large palm flat and letting the raindrops explode against his skin. "I often feel like I'm on a long, relentless road and all I want to do is pull over or take a small, unmade path and feel some rest... rest from myself, I guess. The sun, it rises over us all and we feel like we are it... life. But there are so many other people here, Dad, yet we don't consider them. Not all in one go, we can't. We just aren't that intelligent. Or, at least... I'm not!"

The man lifted his head to see if the stone responded.

"How can there be so many pockets of people in the world, Dad? All with their own agendas, own ideas, all actioning their own things. It's nearly dusk here, yet somewhere on this planet, people are getting up and others are already asleep. I find it all too huge… the world!" He looked around, taking in his tiny pocket of it, sympathising with the young writer. "But at the same time, it feels so suffocating living inside only my own mind!" More raindrops detonated, and the paper ran grey. "If we could… if we could take everything and everyone in all at one time, maybe then we would be more considerate, more human! I mean, what are the raiders thinking? What do they see when they look down over us? Can they not hear our screams, is that it? Seeing our limbs blown apart in silence makes the whole situation, acceptable? Do they see us as humans at all? Butcherbirds, Mantises, Black widow spiders. They all kill their own, just like we do. Are we really all just animals at heart? And what about those in charge? What does that make them? How do they know they are the ones who are… right? Or maybe, maybe they aren't thinking. Sometimes, I wished that I wasn't! But just maybe, for all its harm, there brings some good… some appreciation and gratitude… for things, for others…"

The man sank the paper, shaking his head at the weight of the words. "I found this poem before I ran down here. Well, Doctor Turner, he found it. He let me borrow it… so I transcribed it for you here. It's called 'Choric Song of the Lotos-Eaters'." The man cleared his throat.

"'There is sweet music here that softer falls
Than petals from blown roses on grass,
Or night-dews on still waters between walls
Of shadowy granite, in a gleaming pass;
Music that gentler on spirit lies,
Than tired eyelids upon tired eyes;
Music that brings sweet sleep down from the blissful skies.
Here are cool mosses deep,
And through the moss the ivies creep,
And in the stream the long-leaved flowers weep,
And from the craggy ledge the poppy hangs in sleep.
Why are we weigh'd upon with heaviness,
And utterly consumed with sharp distress,
While all things else have rest from weariness'?"

The man took some time to re-evaluate the words. He continued with the letter. "When I first read it, I wanted to be the poppy! But perhaps we're not ever meant to feel rested. Maybe the fuel we need to make a difference is the same that keeps us toeing the line of madness? And without it, nobody would be thinking and that would get us nowhere!"

The man took a long, drawn-out breath. "For ages, I wished you were here to tell me what to do. But now I know. I know my purpose, my calling. You said that everyone is going through a tough time. Oscar Wilde, he said that 'the world is wide, and has many marvellous people in it', but there *are* also inherently bad people out there, Dad. I'm not talking about the ones taking orders; I'm talking about the ones giving them. After the Kaiser, there will be someone else and they must be stopped. I know that today I only turn fifteen, but one day I'll be turning forty and I'll be a man; a man able to make a difference. I know it's not down to age to make an impression on the world, but for what I want and for what I need to overcome, it will. I'm getting out these asylum walls, Dad. One day, when I'm better, I'll fly over them, I'll fly over those walls, and I'll be travelling east! I'll look down over our town and know that I've taken all I ever could from it and know where I'm going it will mean I can give it all back again, back to the people here who deserve to live their lives in peace. Because surviving and living is all we humans know how to do!"

The dying light crept its way down to the soles of his shoes and the man sucked the moisture from his upper lip back into his nostrils. He spotted the yellow down of a small songbird fall from the tree. There was a natter and the bird took flight. He folded the paper back into his pilot's jacket and collected his hat and goggles. "Right, that's me, Dad, see you again, from whence I return." He placed one hand on the ridge of the gravestone. "How strange, eh, Dad? How strange it is… to be human!"

There was a crackle as the wireless coughed.

"Four years ago, our nation and empire stood alone against an overwhelming enemy, with our backs to the wall. Tested as never before in our history, in God's providence we survived that test; the spirit of the people, resolute, dedicated, burned like a bright flame, lit surely from those unseen fires which nothing can quench. Now, once more, a supreme test has to be faced. This time, the challenge is not to fight to survive, but to fight to win the final victory for the good cause. Once again what is demanded from us all is something more than courage and endurance; we need a revival of spirit, a new, unconquerable resolve. After nearly five years of toil and suffering, we must renew that crusading impulse on which we entered the war and met its darkest hour'."

His gloved hand turned the switch. With the wireless off, the only sound was the purr and hum of his aircraft. With the wireless off, the lieutenant could be left alone with his thoughts.

Tonight, he was flying his favourite, the Bristol Beaufighter. Favourite because there was nothing between him and the world outside. He could leave his cockpit open, like a photo without its frame.

The lieutenant checked the gold watch laying against his wrist, brown strap battered by years of wear. He tapped it twice. The broken hands still reluctant to move from 11:40. He knew full well he was ascending too early for his mission, but this was a detour he needed to make. He had promised them that much. He had owed them that much.

With a firm clank, he encased himself inside the cockpit and made his final checks. He reached inside his breast pocket, removed the flattened shilling and studied it, George V glistening under the apricot tinge of the setting sun. The lieutenant pulled the coin towards his lips and closed his eyes.

"For keeps," he whispered.

Listening to the folding waves of the estuary, he

observed the uncoiling strip of runway, took a deep breath and gunned the plane. Gaining sufficient speed, he raised her up, departing the soft surface of the Earth, higher and higher until he was alone amongst the wispy clouds.

It was only when he flew above everything that he realised how every man was small. How big an impression a once small man could make on the world. The clusters of light below his aeroplane, the electricity a twinkling reminder of the greatness of a *once* small man. It wasn't an invention created with this view, nor from this height. It happened right down there between the narrowness, the claustrophobic busyness of everything else. He questioned how one could truly excel in this world, how one could possibly mark his name on the sky like his great predecessors. It was obvious to him when he was up at this great height, but he would sometime have to land and join the scurrying others.

The lieutenant always felt obliged to check in with his boys at the start of his shift. Those working the gun pits, the quick firing battery and experimental casemates. Those protecting the Homefront from enemies of the sea as much as he had a duty to its skies.

He dipped his aircraft over horseshoe barracks with its enchanting clock tower and parade ground. A game of cricket was in pursuit on the tangerine grass out in the square and officers trickled from the gunneries, brick powder magazines, cart and wagon sheds.

Gog's berth jutted out to the south of the estuary, its landing railway thronged with uniformed men carrying mounted guns and transporting freight towards barge pier. Dusk had a silent quality to it, and he could hear the mellow drum of the soldier's feet as they unloaded beside the armaments and stores. He gave one final swoop over the commander's houses, superintendent quarters, Garrison chapel and hospital.

"You're doing one mighty fine job boys," he saluted.

He slalomed his plane over mosaic habitats, saline lagoons and the salt marshes. Chiff-chaffs and blackcaps yawped beside the purr of his propellers.

Searching the nearby fields for an anchor, he dipped his wings lower. Between patches of forest, he spotted the renovated east wing of Thorndon Hall.

"Ah-huh." A small, cold droplet of rain fell across his cheek. He glanced up at the secreting nimbus clouds.

"Right, let's see now..." The lieutenant checked the coordinates from the great compass of the setting sun. "South-west!" He flipped his plane and chugged slowly over the humdrum town. The desolate row of barbers, butchers and bakers, eyelids closing against the delicate evening sky. Further along came the beat alleys, a serpent's tail of fisheries, florists and flop houses. He swooped like a giant bird over the clock of the town hall and the iridescent red brick of the Swan public house. He veered left, down the narrow parade of shoemakers and watch menders, chocolatiers, grocery shops and fire houses. Each of them no doubt displaying falsified signs reading 'Business as usual'. When, in reality, it was really anything but.

He spotted the old Cavern toy shop, library and sweetshop. Butterflies flapped their wings against his stomach, the ochre pillars outside the new Palace cinema and the bench they had sat on as children. He hovered over Woodlands Cemetery and called farewell to the graves of his family, but they weren't who he was here to see.

The quiet town dispersed. He circled the house on Myrtle Road. Soon, the streets gave way to golden wheat fields and deciduous woodlands. He saw the worming brook, the steam mill and the wooden viaduct. He saw himself as a child, a head of curly brown locks sticking through the struts. He saw the soldier doll hanging, the model of the Be2c twirling and on its banks, the ghost of Wilfred, Wilfred the boy, Wilfred the man. Nets of light casting against the steel beams. He followed them, tracks glinting the road of his youth, the road he was now taking. Suddenly, there was a gap in the coppice, and he saw its silhouette.

They were seated out the front, as they always were. Ants outside the gatehouse of some great museum. The asylum, with its impeding clock tower, shrinking them below the weight of the red and brown brick.

Officer Letchfield, adorning the uniform of a war gone by, a relic, a gallery exhibit, a hand trembling against its wooden rim. The lieutenant watched it move and imagined hearing the sound of it rattling, body and mind confined to that chair. Doctor Turner, with his white mossy beard, wireframe glasses and that thinking forehead seared with lines. Each one resembling a thought, a memory of everyone who had passed through those gates. The widest belonged to Jimmy Ford. Through squinted eyes, the doctor flattened four fingers, curled a thumb and slowly lifted a flat hand to his forehead. The lieutenant mirrored his salute.

He looked at Officer Letchfield; what of his mind?

Had it moved even a millimetre since that day? He thought about the shell that had got him there. He thought of himself, now, and the shell which had got him here. Neither of them had exploded; it wasn't the sounds that did it, it was the silences.

Of course, the officer didn't look up. He knew what it had all meant. He knew that Letchfield hadn't muttered a word since the day he passed through those gates. He knew that the officer was confined to that asylum in 1914, and never got out. Not to fight the war, not even to fight his own. But in all his youth, in all his madness, he had found a way to listen.

He thought of those since passed: of Alfred, of Doctor Campbell. He imagined the doctor was puzzled to his grave that he could not find a cure for Letchfield. It would only be a matter of time with Turner now at the helm. The dear doctor had fulfilled his wish; he was a psychologist.

He thought of those he considered might be still living: Oren, Lola, Fairlop, Slugs, Chat and Wilkie. He thought of Stephen, with his eyes wide and bulging, seeing everything with no choice on the matter. He thought of catatonic Martha with her damn arm raised for all eternity and her body no doubt buried that same way. He thought of Ethel and that damn clock stuck on 11:40. He thought of Allen, wise old Allen with his marine mumblings. One day he would tell their stories; one day he would write it all down.

He wondered what had become of them. If they ever found freedom. He looked down at dear Doctor Turner and thanked him for everything. He flipped his plane and barrel rolled. He could see that tremendous smile and those hairy hands clapping until they were sore. Every nameless patch of land is something to someone, just as the asylum was to him.

He departed. He left them, left them there exactly as they once were, exactly as they still were, preserved in that model village.

The lieutenant removed his glove and felt around the bullet hole which occupied his wing strut. Water had congregated inside. *Isn't it strange?* he thought. *How it can rain somewhere, and a single raindrop could witness a wedding or a killing or any other countless private moment? That same raindrop is absorbed by the earth, nature invisibly carries it back into the sky, borne by warm currents someplace far off, before transforming it back into a drop of water again… then what? Then rebegins the journey of the raindrop. If only that raindrop landed in someone's eye and they too could witness everything it had seen before? The story of our history, the story of our Earth. The great story of our world!*

Seeing a dead body, it changes a man. Especially if that man was only really a boy at the time. Seeing two, well… what difference did that make? It was who they were when they were alive, that's the difference. He was too damn young. Several years too damn young.

When your biggest fear as a child is losing those you love; when that happens, what then? You give yourself over entirely to another, knowing that one day, it's a dead certainty you will lose them too. But know that for every single day, every moment between this moment and then, you cherished them, you made the most of every single one of those moments. The words, the silences.

He saw her mouth first, always her mouth. It parted and popped in a rose-coloured pear drop. He watched her tongue as she licked the dusting of sugar, coating her fleshy pink lips. Her rounded cheeks and nose, that generous sprinkle of freckles. Then her eyes. Her eyes, blown out lanterns closed behind black shutters.

The wings of the plane tilted, and it joined the others forming triangles across the wide expanse of the sea. The planes dipped towards the surface, the calm, flat stillness like a mirror. Then all of a sudden, the glass, the surface shattered and out flew the majestic, rubbery wings of a thousand rays.

There was a crackle as the wireless coughed.

"After nearly five years of toil and suffering, we must

renew that crusading impulse on which we entered the war and met its darkest hour'."

A blue latex hand turned the switch.

"And who do we have here?" said the trainee doctor, pencil lead resting against his notepad. The hairy man reverently crouched in front of the patient.

"This here is the greatest man I ever had the pleasure of knowing."

"Is he—?"

The doctor nodded. "Hasn't uttered a word since 12th August 1917, the day before his birthday."

The trainee looked up from his notepad. "1917? Doctor Turner, what happened to him?"

The hairy man with the Adamic beard, pushed the wireframe glasses into his nose. "We couldn't tell you, even if we wanted to," said Doctor Turner. The trainee frowned, sensing he had placed an intrusion between the two men. He moved on into the rec room.

Doctor Turner leaned over his patient. "One in three don't explode," he whispered, squeezing at the white cloth which hung from his patient's legs. "Full circle."

Jimmy Ford stood beneath the great wheel.

Below the crosses of the Gotha, the fairground was silent. Masses of people lay strewn out over the floor with their hands cupped around their ears. Above the stone fountain, it opened.

Jimmy looked up, the mouth of the hatch; black, wide, screaming.

The shell tumbled out.

"I'm listening" he whispered. "I'm listening" he said. "I'm listening!" he shouted.

He saw the shell spiral. Inside its point, he saw the face of his dad, of Poppy, of Wilfred. He saw the face of his love, his sweetheart; he saw only her face now, the face of Grace Bergman.

The shrill became deafening. Jimmy glanced down at Grace. She lay on the floor the other side of the fountain, she was trembling, he was paralysed.

The shell continued its journey, resolute. She was facing the floor; she didn't see it. She'd covered her ears; she didn't hear it. He did, he saw it *all*.

It didn't explode into a million spasmodic pieces of flying debris. It didn't create a vacuum of unenduring heat. It didn't even disturb the water in the fountain between them. But it did *hit her*.

The point of the shell entered her lower back. Her spine was first to break, then her pelvis. Her ovaries crushed; eggs cracked. The yolk of life leaked out of her.

Turn her over, as they did minutes later, and you wouldn't have known it.

From the waist up, she was perfectly preserved, her face sprinkled with that delicate dusting of freckles, her nose slightly turned towards the sky. That calm powder blue sky. The hums of the planes silenced.

Her eyes were open, but the lanterns had blown. Grace Bergman, fifteen years old, below that great white wheel. Dead.

As for Jimmy, well…

"We couldn't tell you, even if we wanted to," said Doctor Turner. The trainee frowned, sensing he had placed an intrusion between the two men. He moved on into the rec room.

Doctor Turner leaned over his patient. "One in three don't explode," he whispered, squeezing at the white cloth which hung from his patient's legs. "Full circle."

He looked at the man with curls of golden-brown hair.

"What are you doing in *their* Jimmy?" he whispered, tears filling his kooky brown eyes. He patted Jimmy's shoulder and turned on his heels. "Inventing?" he mumbled, walking towards the rec room. "Writing? No...*flying!*"

With the wireless off, the only sound was the purr and hum of the aircrafts. There were hundreds of them in the sky, squawking like bloodthirsty pterodactyls heading east, heading south, heading to the shores of Normandy.

Jimmy Ford, seated in cotton white pyjamas sat in his wheelchair staring out of the lead-laced window. Plump, wet droplets exploded against the glass and meandered down the pane in front of him. Soon the entire window was mizzled with rain.

He stared dumbly through periwinkle blue eyes, pupils darting from one side of his skull to the other, in rhythm with the gold-plated watch. He didn't see the planes; he didn't hear the planes. He didn't even know they were there.

A sibyllic smile unfurled at the corners of his mouth which was soon joined by a single tear.

The salty tear wandered into the golden beard surrounding his mouth.

"I once was a soldier's son," came a whisper from still, cracked lips. "But now... now I am no one."

ACKNOWLEDGMENTS

Her sweet plump belly rises and falls in the bed beside me. I can feel her soft breathing against my cheek and the scent of milk lingering on her breath. She is Bettie-Rose, our beautiful two-year-old daughter. She is our whole world, she is life.

Beside her, my wife's little plump belly swells and mirrors her movements. We are expecting a second child. Our family.

Without those heroic souls, those brave great grandparents who made it through the Great War, to return home, to survive and conceive, my inimitable wife and I would have never met, our beautiful Bettie-Rose and her expectant brother or sister would not be forming right now in my wife's belly. We would have all been erased from existence inside a trench beneath an unidentifiable field in nowhere France. Erased from existence by a bullet or shell or bayonet blade.

Our family today, ceased to be.

Given the timing of this particular war, on both sides of our family's bloodlines, this would have been true. And it's true for many families and many wars if you travel back through time because everyone reading this has parents and grandparents who *did* survive.

So, I would like to take a moment to acknowledge all those courageous souls who lived, and died for all of our existence, today. Quite often, thank you just doesn't come close.

My wife Kat is an unfathomably kind and vivacious woman. Not only has she suffered my mind absences during the writing of this novel, she taught me everything I feel today. I love her with every sinew of my body.

For a period of time after we graduated from university, Kat worked in various roles in mental health. Her selflessness and empathy fascinated me from the moment we met, and she captivated me with the stories she regaled. Together we lived in Brentwood, in a small chapel on the grounds of an old asylum. The asylum which features in this very book. Outside our front door were their gravestones, the souls of the staff and patients who, for a time, really did live between the asylum walls.

Jimmy didn't, nor did any of the characters in this book for that matter, but madness is within us all and had it not been for the timing of our birth, I'm sure it could have been any one of us confined there. After all, madness often wasn't the criteria for institutionalisation in the first place.

My childhood in Essex is full of exceptionally happy memories. Today I am blessed with keeping the friends I made when I was four years old. Not much can penetrate such relationships. Much like Jimmy's childhood, our days were long and spent endlessly exploring the world outside.

But then, at eighteen, my dad died; sudden and undiagnosed heart disease. I was stuck somewhere between childhood and maturity when it happened, and that day— 3rd September 2005, was the day I became a man. I had my friends and family around me, and I had my childhood sweetheart beside me through the pain, the therapy and recovery. Being surrounded by love doesn't cure grief but it certainly soothes the scars on occasion.

If my dad hadn't of died, I probably wouldn't have written this book. I probably wouldn't have made half the decisions I've made in my life. But that's life and making the best of it, after any situation is all we can hope for.

I'm inspired by the people surrounding my life and so thankful to have lived during the same time as those still in it. So many of them deserve a mention.

Simon Smith, a friend since primary school and the most intelligent man I know, thank you for reading the early and later drafts of this novel and offering insight and opinion into pivotal moments in Jimmy's life. You are a teacher and I have no doubt those you teach will reap immeasurable rewards from you.

Janina Zachopoulos-Butler. Thanks to my brother Robin for falling for such a literate and well-read sister-in-law. This novel may well have been an extra 100 pages without your help.

I'm honoured and indebted to Nick Whybrow for the lovely illustrations he created which so masterfully bring the settings in this book to life.

To the honourable Nick Kindred for reading the mostly unreadable early drafts of this book when it was just jumbled up ideas inside my brain. You've always been there for me, the loyal avid listener.

I am humbled that the inspirational Neil Fendell agreed to create the cover artwork for this book. Your art style is weaved into the fabric of our hometown and seeing your design now in print just makes this all the more real.

To Paul Bates, my filmmaking mentor. Without you I would not have started Nirvana Studios or had the confidence to run a video production company. And there certainly wouldn't have been a book trailer!

Mum, you are the strongest human I know. After Dad died you played such a significant role in keeping us all grounded and ensuring that our lives continued. You taught me the philosophy and outlook I have on life today and I am grateful to the bottom of my soul for the happy experiences I had as a child.

Finally, thank you to the Book Guild for seeing something in this story and for allowing it to see the light of day.